Brides of
TEXAS

Brides of TEXAS

3-in-1 Historical Romance Collection

CATHY MARIE HAKE

BARBOUR BOOKS
An Imprint of Barbour Publishing, Inc.

To Love Mercy © 2006 by Cathy Marie Hake
To Walk Humbly © 2006 by Cathy Marie Hake
To Do Justice © 2006 by Cathy Marie Hake

ISBN 978-1-63409-669-0

Ebook Editions:
Adobe Digital Edition (.epub) 978-1-63409-824-3
Kindle and MobiPocket Edition (.prc) 978-1-63409-825-0

Scripture quotations are taken from the King James Version of the Bible.

This book is a work of fiction. Names, characters, places, and incidents are either products of the author's imagination or used fictitiously. Any similarity to actual people, organizations, and/or events is purely coincidental.

Published by Barbour Books, an imprint of Barbour Publishing, Inc., P.O. Box 719, Uhrichsville, Ohio 44683, www.barbourbooks.com

Our mission is to publish and distribute inspirational products offering exceptional value and biblical encouragement to the masses.

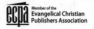 Member of the
Evangelical Christian
Publishers Association

Printed in the United States of America.

Dear Reader,

Have you ever read something that sticks in your mind? My freshman year in high school I set out to read the entire Bible. Not just any Bible would do. I chose the Bible my daddy gave me many years previously on the Sunday I accepted Jesus into my heart—a black leather, red-letter, King James Version. Having grown up in a God-fearing, churchgoing home, I knew most of the stories in the Bible. Or so I thought. Then I embarked on an incredible journey for myself.

I was seeking to find what God wanted of me. Books have been written on what God wants. Sermons and songs address the matter. But my journey was to discover on an intensely personal basis what God willed of and for me. Micah 6:8 jumped off the page. "He hath shewed thee, O man, what is good; and what doth the LORD require of thee, but to do justly, and to love mercy, and to walk humbly with thy God?"

Years—okay, decades—have passed, yet that verse still resonates with me. When I was asked to write this book, I prayed about it. In that year, I had three surgeries, a major car accident, and had to put my beloved dog to sleep. Through it all, I've clung to the knowledge that this verse isn't one-sided. God is the final arbiter of justice, even if I do not see the results here and now. He continually covers me with His tender mercies, and I never walk alone because He is with me.

I hope you enjoy reading about the Gregor brothers. Each received a gift and a piece of advice from their father, Micah. Their heavenly Father uses that to open their hearts to some very special Texas brides.

Love,
Cathy Marie

To Love
MERCY

Prologue

Y ou'll stay together?"

Robert Gregor curled his hand around his father's. "Aye, Da. You've my word on it."

"Dinna be grieving, boy-o. 'Twas my wish to see you to the New World. As for me, my destination's heaven. God and your mama will welcome me with open arms."

The ship rolled gently, and sorrow as deep as the Atlantic washed over Robert. It didn't come as a sudden shock but as a swell, carrying him from the security he'd known and leaving him adrift. *Not yet. Please not yet.* "We'll see land in another day."

"That you will." His father had a way of putting together words to intensify their meanings. He'd done it now, and Robert felt the tide of life shift in those moments.

"Rob?" Duncan looked down from the upper bunk. His black hair stood up boyishly, making him look only half his age.

"Go fetch Christopher." Robert knew his eldest brother would be pacing the deck. A restless man, Chris avoided situations where he'd bare his emotions or soul to others. Had it just been the four of them, he'd have stayed, but the ship teemed with hundreds of folks with nothing better to do than mind everyone else's business. Christopher left the crowded steerage compartment round about midnight, grief ravaging his features.

Lord Almighty, must You take Da yet? Robert knew the answer. As a doctor, he'd witnessed births and deaths aplenty. Powerless to do anything but give comfort, he smoothed back Da's thinning gray hair. "Save your breath, Da. The others'll be here soon, and they deserve to hear your love."

Minutes later, Christopher shouldered past the neighboring berths and knelt by the bunk. Duncan came to a halt behind him and rested a warm, calloused hand on his shoulder. Robert saw the tension in their jaws, the sheen of tears in their eyes. The Gregors were stoic with others, but among themselves, they always loved, laughed, and wept unabashedly—except for now. Time grew short, and Robert knew his brothers' hearts were breaking, as was his, yet they both stayed strong for Da's sake. A man ought to slip from this world and into God's arms with the peace of knowing those he left behind would fare well.

"I've been blessed to have ye, lads." Da drew in another breath. "Stay close to the Almighty so we'll meet again at heaven's gate."

Each of them gave that promise without reservation.

Da squeezed Rob's hand. "My da's watch—to Chris." He stared at his eldest and whispered, "Time is a gift, dinna waste it."

Christopher nodded solemnly.

"Bible—I'm wanting Duncan to hae it. He's a man of deep thoughts and quiet truths fit to soothe the soul."

"I'll treasure it, Da." Duncan bent closer. "I'll have a son and read to him as you read to us. He'll know the Word of God, and Da—I'll name him after you."

A smile chased across Da's features. *Aye, Da'd been right,* Robert observed. *Duncan just spoke words that gave comfort.*

Da then turned his head. "Robert—"

Rob leaned down and looked steadily into his father's eyes. "You already gave me my gift, Da. I know what you sacrificed for me." The compensation Da received for the arm he lost while working in the zinc mine had paid for Robert's medical schooling.

Da smiled. "Mama's ring. I kept it for ye, Son. Caring for bodies makes a doctor close off his heart so he doesn't have to feel the pain. Dinna do that. Take a chance at love."

Within the hour, it was all over. Rob wrapped Da; Christopher pushed everyone away and cradled his lifeless form up to the deck; Duncan carried the Bible. During the voyage, they'd assisted with other burials, but this was different. All three of them stood in a sorrowful knot as Chris prayed.

The *Anchoria's* captain made a motion as he somberly said, "Lord, we commend the body of Micah Gregor to You and commit his mortal body to the deep until the day of Your return."

It was over. Those who had come up to pay their respects murmured their condolences, then wandered off to leave the brothers some privacy.

Duncan opened the Bible. The ribbon marker was set in the book of Micah. He cleared his throat and read in an unsteady voice made thick with tears, " 'He hath shewed thee, O man, what is good; and what doth the Lord require of thee, but to do justly, and to love mercy, and to walk humbly with thy God?' "

Christopher nodded solemnly. "Da did those things."

Rob wrapped his arms about his brothers' shoulders. "Aye, and we will, too, in his honor."

Chapter 1

Ellis Island

The Gregor brothers stood shoulder to shoulder along the ship's rail as the *Anchoria* cut through the choppy waters. The copper Statue of Liberty towered over their vessel, but her long-awaited welcome felt empty since Da wasn't beside them to see the grand sight.

Duncan nudged Rob. "I'm thinking she has the biggest feet I've ever seen."

His joke lightened the tension. All three brothers chuckled. It made sense that Duncan would notice such a detail, him being a cobbler.

All about them, folks craned to see the sight. Mamas clutched their children close, and men stood a bit taller. Freedom. Opportunity. They'd scrimped, saved, sacrificed, and some nearly starved to come to America. Seeing Liberty did something—they'd gotten here...Didn't that mean other dreams and hopes could come true, too?

"Ellis Island," a sailor announced through a megaphone. "First-class passengers, please remain aboard. We will assist you with all your needs. Second class and steerage, gather your belongings and prepare to disembark."

"Remember what I told you," Robert murmured to his brothers. He shot a meaningful look at a woman coughing into her handkerchief. Americans didn't want diseased immigrants flooding their land. Processing newcomers through this facility allowed officials to turn back those they determined might be sickly. Robert had known that fact full well, but Da refused to listen. He'd insisted on making the voyage.

"We're hale as horses," Chris said as he withstood a hefty bump from someone on his other side. "I'm heartily sick of being crowded. I'm going below to get our gear."

"I'll come along." Duncan shifted sideways.

Robert didn't say a word. He'd given Da his promise that they'd stick together, and he'd meant it. From here on out, he'd be sure to keep what was left of his family intact. After an overcrowded, noisy voyage, the steerage compartment was eerily empty and silent. They walked down the companionway and wended past bunks to reach the berth they'd shared with so many others.

Chris and Duncan knelt and yanked Duncan's trunk from beneath the bunk. Filled with a cobbler's tools, the thing weighed a ton, but Duncan hefted it with relative ease.

Robert turned his hand over and felt under the bunk for a package he'd secured there when they'd first boarded.

"Is it there still?" Chris asked in an undertone.

"Aye." Rob untied the corners and carefully reclaimed his precious supply of medications and medical instruments. Theft below decks had proven to be a persistent problem, and he'd taken care to protect these things from sticky fingers and shifty souls. "I'll put this in my bag with the rest of the things now."

Two battered suitcases, a physician's bag, and a cobbler's trunk. The Gregor brothers carried all their worldly possessions off the ship and onto American soil. In short order, workers herded them through lines and into a large wooden building. Workers chalked numbers on the immigrants' baggage and gave them pasteboard tickets for each piece.

"I'll have that." A man tugged at Robert's valise.

"No." Robert held fast. "I'm a physician. 'Tis my bag."

"Why didn't you just say so?" The man shot him a disgruntled look and went on down the line to the next men.

Duncan folded his arms and looked about. "Aboard the ship, the noise all rolled back on us. Here, I can make out all of the different tongues. How are they ever going to be able to ask us all questions and understand our answers? 'Tis like the Tower of Babel in here."

"Chris." Robert elbowed him. Christopher had an uncanny ability to learn languages. "How many do you hear?"

"German. Dutch. French. Russian. Some of it sounds like Latin, so I'd venture that it's Spanish or Portuguese." He shrugged. "Probably both. Judging from clothing, there are Slavs aplenty, too."

Their group spent time in what looked remarkably like a livestock pen. Older folk slumped on wooden benches and toddlers fussed.

Women went one way; the men went the other. Robert watched in silence as each man underwent a cursory examination. Those with light sensitivity or red, runny eyes received marks on their coats. So did the ones whose coughs revealed consumption.

A father and son ahead of them were drawn off to the side; the son's eyes were diseased—would the father stay in America while his son was shipped back home?

Lord Almighty, what a horrendous situation. Da wouldn't have made it through this. You took him from us, and that was hard enough— but to have a stranger rip us apart would have been unbearable. I didn't realize at the time just how merciful You were being.

"Destination?" The tall man at the desk looked at Duncan for an answer.

"Texas," Christopher answered. He pulled Connant's letter from his vest pocket and carefully laid it on the desk. Connant had enclosed a note with that letter, warning them that New York teemed with immigrants. Officials would be glad to hear the brothers would leave the area.

"I can see you're all brothers." The man gave them a friendly smile. "Black Irish?"

"Scots," they said in unison.

"Brawny ones at that." The man scribbled something on a document. Robert wondered how someone in the midst of this madhouse managed to stay cheerful all day. Perhaps the news that they were headed clear off to Texas pleased him. *God, thank Ye for Connant's friendship and sound advice.*

"What trades do you boast?"

"Doctor, cobbler, and miner." Christopher jabbed his thumb at each of them in turn.

"Make yourselves useful, men. America needs men of peace and productivity." He stamped something and waved them onward.

"Now what?" Duncan frowned. "I'm not liking this business of them keeping our belongings somewhere."

A lanky man with a fringe of bright orange hair beckoned them. He'd gathered several others around him who all looked to be from the Isles. "Immigrant Society!" he called loudly.

"Connant wrote about them." Robert headed that way.

"There we are, then." The man smiled broadly. The lilt in his voice sounded wonderfully familiar. "America's a wondrous land, and I won't be sayin' otherwise, but I need to warn you that many an unscrupulous man waits across the harbor. They'll make promises and take what little ye've left, but 'tis little to no help you'll get back. The Immigrant Society will help, and 'tis honest. If you ken where ye be headed, we'll help transport you there at minimal cost and less fuss."

∞

"Minimal cost and less fuss turned out to be an honest assessment," Robert said later as he tucked his black leather bag beneath the train bench and took a seat.

Duncan chuckled. "It bewilders me, it does, how you recall every last word a body says. How long's the trip to Texas?"

"Three days." Christopher folded his arms across his chest and scanned the others filling the train car.

Robert watched the other passengers, too. Long ago, he'd learned he watched people just as avidly as Chris, but they saw entirely different things. Where from his clinical perspective he saw undertones in complexions, strained breathing, guarded moves, and grimaces from pain, Chris focused on eyes and hands because he'd learned to measure a man's ability to help or do harm. Together, they would evaluate their fellow travelers and exchange terse comments if something struck them as important.

Duncan, on the other hand, slouched in the seat so he'd be at eye level with a small boy. They'd struck up a conversation, and once the train set in motion, Duncan wrapped his arm about the lad's shoulder and nudged him to rest his head against Duncan's ribs. It wasn't but a few minutes ere the lad fell fast asleep, and the mama gave Duncan a look of sheer gratitude.

"Well?" Robert didn't even look at Chris when he asked.

"Left of the bald man in the green jacket—man's armed to the teeth. Behind us three rows are two Poles with more fight in their eyes than brains in their heads."

"That's all?" He slanted a glance at Chris and gave him a slow, easy grin.

"Aye." Chris pulled the brim of his hat down over his eyes, folded his arms, and stretched his long legs out before him. "I could whip all three of 'em without breaking a sweat, and you could wash the scratches on my knuckles afterward if you were of a mind to be helpful." His chin dipped to rest on his chest, he let out a throaty chuckle, and before long he slumbered.

Robert couldn't sleep. Then again, he'd learned to do with less sleep than most men needed. Relentlessly, the train chugged across the nation, belching clouds of black smoke and covering mile after mile of this huge, strange country. The rhythmic *clack-clack-clack* as they advanced didn't make him sleepy—it energized him.

Three days. Three days of stopping here and there. Of changing trains. Of going through big, stately cities that looked newer than anything Scotland boasted, past grand stretches where nothing but forests commanded the land, and past patchwork plots covered by verdant crops. The streets weren't exactly paved with gold, but from where he sat and what he saw, Robert knew America offered what every man craved most: an opportunity to make something of himself.

Back home, the zinc mine was played out. Christopher would have faced the humiliation of having no way to earn a living. Folks couldn't spend money on shoes when their bellies were empty, so Duncan had experienced a severe drop in demand for his skills. Even Robert found he'd been paid far less reliably by his patients. This would be a fresh start. They'd have a meager beginning, but that thought didn't trouble him, or his brothers, one bit. Strong, motivated men could forge a new life. Besides, they had one another, and they had God. In the end, those were what mattered most.

∽

Mercy Ellen Stein clipped the floss, turned over the dish towel, and smiled at the pattern. Violet-blue morning glories trumpeted across the corner, and she closed her eyes for a moment to imagine just how well they'd match the pale blue cabinets in Otto's house. Otto would be here for supper in less than an hour. Tonight they'd choose which Bible verses and hymns they wanted for the wedding. In preparation for that, Mercy had marked her favorite selections in the hymnal on the piano.

The family Bible always rested in the place of honor—a small oak table. Depending on the season, *Grossmuter* used to change the little tablecloths. Since her death last year, Mercy had followed the tradition. Fall's maple and sycamore leaves embroidered on ecru cotton gave way to holly and ivy linen at Christmas. During spring and summer, partly for fun and mostly because dust was so prevalent, a whole variety of scarves decorated with flowers and birds took turns each week. In honor of their wedding plans, Mercy had used the satin one with delicate orange blossoms and airy tatted lace edges.

The hope chest in her room held a plethora of such linens. She didn't need this dish towel at all, but she enjoyed needlework. The bodice of her wedding gown bore testament to that. She'd spent hour upon hour doing French cut lacework on the white cotton. They couldn't afford satin, but that didn't trouble her. Grossmuter had taught her to draw contentment from making ordinary things beautiful—and though it would be brazenly proud to speak the words aloud, Mercy believed her wedding gown to be the most beautiful thing she'd ever created.

Otto's mother came over yesterday to help her pin up the hem. She'd pronounced the dress exquisite. After Grossmuter died, Otto's mother had become Mercy's confidant and mentor. Helpful and kindhearted, Mrs. Kunstler would be a fine mother-in-law.

The back door banged and feet pattered on the new linoleum

floor. Jarred out of her musings, Mercy called out, "Walk in the house, Peter."

Her little brother swung around the corner and half shouted, "*Grossvater* said I can keep one of Freckle's puppies!"

Setting aside the almost-finished dish towel, Mercy laughed. "I suppose you've already decided which one."

"Come see!"

"Why don't we set the table first?"

"Mercy, I can't wait. Please come now."

She couldn't resist her eight-year-old brother's pleading brown eyes. "Okay. Let me check the roast first. The puppies aren't going anywhere."

Mercy glanced at the pan of green beans she'd cook in a little while, set potatoes on to boil, and peeked under the flour-dusted towel to be sure the dough was rising. The yeasty smell promised tasty rolls.

"You said you'd check the roast." Peter wriggled with impatience. "You're looking at everything else."

"You'll be glad later when you sit down to a good meal." She opened the door to the Sunshine stove and pulled out the gray roasting pan. Fragrant steam billowed as she lifted the lid. "Mmm." Quickly, she clanged the lid back down and pushed the pan back into the oven. No use letting out any moisture. Grossvater and Otto both loved gravy, so she'd want every last ounce of drippings she could get.

"Otto eats a lot," Peter said as she took his hand and started toward the barn. "That roast better be really big."

"Men who labor hard work up hearty appetites. Otto works hard, so he eats a lot. So does Grossvater. Someday, you'll do the same thing when you're doing a man's work around here."

Peter's lower lip poked out. "I work hard around here."

"Yes, you do." She resisted the urge to ruffle his wind-tousled brown curls. She hadn't meant to hurt his feelings. "Fast as you're growing, you'll soon be a man."

His face brightened. With that issue resolved, he seemed to concentrate on their destination. Peter tugged on her hand, silently urging her to walk faster.

Mercy wished she'd taken time to put on her shoes. Grossvater scolded her whenever she came out to the barn barefooted. It was just that with the oven's heat and spring sunshine, she'd peeled off her shoes and stockings in the house.

"If I guess which puppy you want," she teased Peter, "you have to gather eggs this week."

"Nuh-unh!" Peter yanked away and streaked ahead.

Caught up in his joy, Mercy laughed and ran after him. Early evening sun slanted into the barn, lending a golden glow to everything in sight. A horse whinnied, feet shuffled the straw-covered ground, and Freckle growled.

Mercy's eyes hadn't yet adjusted to the dim place, but she guessed what was happening. "Peter, be careful. Mamas don't take kindly to someone handling their babies."

A muffled sound made her stop and tilt her head. Something wasn't right. It was then that she saw Grossvater's legs and boots sticking out from a stall. She cried out in alarm.

"Shut up."

Mercy spun to the side. Cold horror washed over her. A stranger stood three feet away. Light glinted off the wicked-looking knife he held to Peter's throat.

Chapter 2

"What do you think?" Connant Gilchrist swung his arm in a grandiose gesture.

Robert took in the room with nothing short of delight. "It's perfect. And so modern!"

"Old Doc Neely's widow didn't know what to do with it. She sold the house and moved back to Boston to be with her daughter. The office—well, she told the mayor she reckoned the town folks bought most of this when they paid Doc for his services. The city council voted to pass it on to the next qualified physician."

"It sure pays to have friends in the right place at the right time," Chris said as he tested the examination table by pressing his palms downward on it.

Sturdy. Robert assessed the table with glee. He'd worked on many a patient who lay on a wobbly dining trestle. *Good height, too. I won't have to hunch over when I perform surgery.*

"You came in through the waiting room." Connant jerked a thumb toward a wide flight of stairs. "Two rooms up there—Doc Neely kept one as a sick room and used the other for himself on nights he needed to stay and keep watch on a patient."

"Stove there is big enough to cook on when you're not boiling instruments," Duncan said. "After being crammed in that ship, even a small bedchamber will feel roomy."

Connant nodded. "You can ask the bank for a loan or wait till you save up a bit, but the lot here's plenty big enough. You might want to be building a wee house and a shop for Duncan in the back."

"So the land is ours?" Robert gave his childhood friend a startled look.

"Aye, and why not? I put a stipulation in the contract, though." His grin looked smug as could be. "Says you have to stay here five years, else the land and all of the supplies go to the next doctor."

"That's more than fair."

Christopher's face darkened. "Is there a problem so no one wants to stay here?"

"Flash floods, scorching summers, and occasional tornadoes. Worst of all, the cook at the diner serves charcoal instead of food." Connant recited those flaws in a gratingly cheerful tone. "As my memory serves me, none of the lot of you ever did more in a kitchen than burn perfectly good food to cinders."

"True," Robert groaned. The best he could say about the food in the steerage compartment of the *Anchoria* was that it filled a stomach. Then again, the same could be said of anything the Gregor men cooked.

He walked over to the cabinet containing pharmaceuticals and noted a generous bottle of bicarbonate of soda. Good thing, that. More often than not, if they cooked for themselves, the Gregor men ended up needing bicarb to settle their bellies. He continued to scan the bottles and vials. All bore neatly printed labels and sat in alphabetical order. "Atropine. Belladonna. Calomel. Cascara sagrada. Chloroform," he read aloud. "I take it there's not a local apothecary since the supply here is so complete?"

"That's right. I have a key for the file cabinet. Doc kept his patient books locked in there."

"Good. Good." Privacy was important, and Robert planned to maintain it. Nonetheless, it would be wise for him to read the records so he'd be familiar with the cases he'd be taking on.

He turned toward the filing cabinet and made note of the fact that both drawers locked. *I'll move some of those bottles and vials into the second drawer.* In the years he attended school, he'd seen more than a few patients grow dependent on certain elixirs and compounds. At the earliest opportunity, he'd lock away most of the laudanum, cocaine muriate, and morphine sulfate.

Duncan looked down at his hands and made a face. "Half the soot from that train fell on me. We'd best wash up, even if the food at that diner turns out to be as black as the mess on our shirts."

Duncan and Christopher stripped off their shirts over at the washstand. "You're a filthy mess, boy-o," Duncan teased Chris.

"No more than you." Chris nudged him to the side. "But the admission galls me. Fill the pitcher again. I'm planning to scrub my head, and you can rinse it. I'll return the favor."

"I should go first. You've such a big head you'll use up all of the water!"

Robert let their good-natured horseplay fade as he continued to walk about the office, opening drawers and taking stock of what was on hand. *In my wildest dreams I never thought this is what I'd find. Everything I read said how backward the American West is, but this is the best medical setup I've ever seen. Holy Father, help me to use these things to Your glory.*

"Quit daydreaming and wash up. We're hungry," Chris called over to him.

Rob looked at his brothers. "I'm not daydreaming. I was standing here thinkin' on how proud Da would be to see such a grand arrangement."

"Aye, he would." Duncan nodded.

"True." Chris nodded curtly, then tacked on in a raspy tone,

"But he'd not want us to starve half to death whilst you gawked around. Let's go eat."

Duncan walked back to the waiting room where their trunks sat. "I'll get your clean shirt."

The cool water refreshed Robert. He scrubbed, enjoying the astringent scent of the soap. He moaned aloud at the simple pleasure of Connant pouring a pitcher of water over his head to wash out the dust, soot, and soap.

Dripping wet, shirtless, and with his suspenders hanging down, he wheeled around when someone burst through the door to the building.

"Sheriff!" A strapping man swayed in the doorway. "I killed him."

"Killed who?" Connant pushed the man into the nearest chair. "Who did you kill, Otto?"

"Don't know."

Robert assessed the man quickly. His eyes were wide with shock, his whole frame shook, and he'd been violently sick all over the front of himself. "Are you hurt?"

"No."

"Tell me what happened," Connant rapped out.

"They're hurt."

"Who?" Connant demanded.

"Mercy." Otto groaned, then leaned forward and retched.

Robert automatically held out the towel even though nothing came up. He turned toward the luggage to grab his bag.

Duncan had opened the trunk and gotten out shirts. He tossed one to Robert. Christopher's shirt hung open, but he'd moved on toward the next item of business. He was strapping on his gun.

"The Steins live about three miles out," Connant said as they all barreled through the door. He grabbed the reins to his own sorrel mare and yanked Robert up behind him. "That's Otto's horse," he told Christopher.

Christopher said nothing. He was swinging up into the saddle as Connant set off.

Robert leaned forward. "How many in the family?"

"Three. Old man and his two grandkids. Girl's engaged to Otto; the boy's a mere lad."

They dismounted and entered the house first. Something was burning in the stove, but the place lay empty. Chris and Duncan had gone toward the barn. "Here!" Chris bellowed.

Duncan exited the barn carrying a schoolboy. Blood dripped from a lump on the boy's head. Robert determined he was breathing well as Duncan rasped, "Old man's alive."

Once inside the barn, Robert paused by the body of a man. Connant had his pistol drawn and shoved Robert ahead. "It's not Stein."

"Back here," Christopher called. He squatted beside an old man and was slicing through his britches with a knife.

The lanky older man lay unconscious. Robert shouldered past Chris and knelt by the man's chest to quickly assess his condition. *Pale. Clammy. Shock. Breathing slow. Pulse thready.* An ugly bruise on his jaw proved he'd fought, but the real injury was impossible to miss. The pitchfork in his thigh hadn't hit an artery, but the extent of the damage couldn't be determined yet.

A young blond cradled the old man's head in her lap. She was tenderly smoothing his brow with her shaky hand, but the sight of her made Robert's stomach lurch. Her dress was torn, and hay clung to the back of her shoulders and hair. Her left eye was starting to swell shut, and other marks at her throat and wrists let him know she, too, had been hurt.

Robert knew he could patch the old man back together. The girl bore wounds no man could heal.

⌒

She knew the sheriff. The black-haired men were strangers. The first one—the one with the gun—scared her; the one who knelt closer touched Grossvater with a mixture of confidence and care. He looked her in the eye and spoke in a low tone, "I'll be able to fix him up. He'll be fine."

He sounded reassuring, but Mercy couldn't respond.

"My brother's going to take that out of his leg, and I'll hold a compress on it to keep it from bleeding. We'll be moving him into the house. Do ye ken what I'm telling you, lass?"

She swallowed and nodded.

Grossvater moaned a little when they did the deed, and she bit back a cry.

" 'Tis a good sign that he's feeling his leg, lass. I'm thinking the wound will make a mess of his bed. Is your dining table sturdy?"

She nodded and led them inside.

Another stranger in her kitchen looked much like the other two. He had Peter sitting in a chair and was dabbing at a knot on her brother's head. Peter jabbered about the puppies.

"This is Dr. Gregor, Mercy," the sheriff said as he gave the kind-voiced man's shoulder a quick pat. "He'll help your granddad."

She wrapped her arms about her ribs and stepped back.

"I could use some bandages. Do you have any?"

Mercy went to the cabinet where they kept the liniment, Epsom salt, and bandages. She set all of the bandages at the head of the table.

"There's a fine help." He pulled out a chair and patted the seat. "You sit here. If your grandda wakes, you'll be nearby. I'm wanting you to drink this for me, too." He set down a glass of water.

She slipped around the edge of the room and did as he directed, then watched in silence as he used the things from his black leather bag. Nothing he said seemed real. Most of it was muffled, but the tone and cadence lulled her.

Finally, he finished tending Grossvater. After he knotted the bandage in place, he took Grossvater's pulse again.

"Well?" one of the other men asked.

"I'm cautiously optimistic. Let's put him to bed."

The sheriff and the other man carried Grossvater to his bedroom, and the doctor took a look at the bump on Peter's head. "Nothing wrong there this won't cure." He drew a glass tube from his medical bag and pulled out a sour ball.

"Thanks!" Peter popped the candy into his mouth and regained his usual, cocky grin.

The doctor turned and held out his hand to Mercy. "Let's go see to things."

When she stood, her legs felt rubbery. Even so, she didn't take his hand. They walked across the kitchen, but to her surprise, he murmured, "They'll put your grandda in a nightshirt for you."

"Oh. Yes. Thank you."

He didn't touch her, yet his nearness made her sidestep. He pushed open the door to her room.

Mercy stared inside. *The tub. What is the tub doing in my room? And who put out my nightgown? It's not bedtime yet.*

"Miss Stein."

She jumped at the sound of her name.

"I'll stay out here and make sure no one bothers you. I thought you might want to bathe. Afterward, I'll see to your bruises and such."

Once in her room, Mercy locked the door. She didn't want to

undress with those men here, but she caught sight of herself in her mirror and choked back a sob. Her dress was in tatters and her hair hung in snarls. Those were just the outward things.

I can't stay like this. Grossvater and Peter need me. Her hands shook so badly, she could scarcely undress. Everything took great effort. It hurt to move. She stepped into the big galvanized tub, then knelt. All of the scrubbing in the world couldn't make her feel clean.

Chapter 3

The thin walls of the house didn't block out the sound of her weeping. Robert and Duncan exchanged a glance.

"Mercy's crying." The lad stopped eating the inside bits of the roast Duncan salvaged for him. "Does she need a hug?"

"She's upset that the bad man hurt you and your grandda." Duncan tapped the edge of the plate to divert the boy.

Peter wrinkled his nose. "You said Grossvater is going to be fine. I'll go tell Sis my head doesn't hurt too much."

Duncan put a restraining hand on the boy's arm. "Doctor will tell her. Hearing it from him will be more reassuring."

"Is she scared that bad man will come back?"

Connant and Chris were out in the barn at this very moment, loading the body onto a buckboard. Duncan shook his head. "I give you my word, lad—he'll never bother you again. Now you finish eating, then we'll chop up the crisp bits of that roast and go feed them to your dog. After whelping, a mama dog needs lots of food."

After they'd left with the body and while Duncan took Peter out to feed the dog, Mercy's door opened. Instead of putting on her nightwear, she'd donned a rust-colored calico dress. Avoiding looking at Robert or speaking, she sidled into the other bedroom.

Robert stood by the door and watched as she smoothed the quilt over the old man's chest, then combed back an errant lock of his white hair. Her hand shook.

Though she'd washed her hair, it was too thick to towel dry well.

Wisps that didn't make it into the simple bun started to coil around her wan face and nape, reinforcing a vulnerability that tore at him.

She didn't seem in a hurry to leave her grandda's side, and Robert struggled with that fact. If she drew comfort from seeing the old man was all right, that was good. She deserved solace whatever the source. Then again, he needed to examine her and hoped to have it finished before Peter came back into the house.

Hooking his thumbs into his suspenders so he'd appear friendly and casual, Rob said quietly, "He's resting well. With time and attention, he'll be up and about."

"Thank you."

She whispered the words so quietly, he almost didn't hear her. The hoarse quality to her whisper worried him. *Is she having trouble breathing? She has marks around her throat. If she screamed. . .* Robert shut down that line of thought immediately. It caused his ire to flare brighter, and she needed him to stay composed. He made the next overture. "Come out to the kitchen. I'll examine your eye."

She ducked her head and turned to the side, as if to hide the bruising, swollen eye.

"If we put a cool compress to it, you'll not look so bruised tomorrow." He paused. "Your little brother's out feeding the beasts in the barn."

She shuddered. "Peter—"

"We'll talk about him." Robert tilted his head toward the kitchen table. "Come."

'Twasn't an easy span of time, those next minutes. Mercy Stein left her grandfather's side only to hear about her brother's condition. Wary as could be, she tried to keep as much distance from Robert as possible.

Robert turned his back on her and took a dishcloth from the

rod by the pump. He dampened it, then methodically folded it into a compress. Each move he made was deliberate in an effort to keep from spooking the lass. As he drew close to her, she flinched.

"There, now. This will make a difference." He extended his hand and offered her the compress.

"I don't need it. Tell me about Peter."

The lass has grit. Robert laid the compress on the table easily within her reach and turned back to his bag. "Other than the bump on his noggin, he's right as rain."

The corner of her mouth twitched in acknowledgment.

After taking a few items from his bag and closing it, Robert approached her again. This time, he pulled out a chair and sat at an angle from her—close enough to touch, far enough that she wouldn't feel crowded. "This is witch hazel."

He opened his other hand. Cotton wadding tumbled free. "I'll dab this on your temple, throat, and wrists. It'll lessen the soreness."

She cringed back into her chair. "Don't need it."

"Miss Stein, did you hear Sheriff Gilchrist? You know I'm a doctor."

"I have witch hazel if I decide to use it."

"I'm here to help you," he said gently. He waited a beat, then stated, "Something happened in the stable."

Her breath caught.

"Women are delicate, easily hurt. It would be wise for me to—"

"Leave me alone!"

He stood and picked up the cotton wadding piece by piece, then took up the Thayer's witch hazel. "I'm going to take these into your chamber and bring out the tub. You want your privacy, and I'll honor that. Witch hazel is very safe and mild. A woman can use it anywhere she hurts. Do you understand me?"

He got no response and didn't wait beyond a heartbeat. His shoes made the only sound in the small wooden home as he went to her chamber. A tidy little place it was. An airy green-and-white quilt covered the iron bedstead, and matching cushions covered both a small chair and a dowry trunk.

A dowry trunk—no doubt filled with all sorts of useful linens she'd prettified as she dreamed of a happy future. Robert winced. The dreams could still come true, but she'd not go to her wedding with the joy of an innocent bride. Otto knew already. At least she'd be spared having to tell him.

Lily of the valley. He inhaled again. The scent from her soap lingered in her room. Robert lifted the tub and carried it through the kitchen to the back door. As he emptied the water into a flower bed, Duncan and little Peter came strolling back. Peter went on inside while Duncan stopped.

"I'll spend the night here. I want to be sure the old man's all right when he awakens. The lass isn't in any condition to do much, and if they needed help, the boy's too young to fetch it."

Duncan nodded. "Should I stay?"

"Nae. 'Tis already hard enough on the lass. The last thing she needs is folks hovering."

∞

Hours later, Robert moved from the old man's bedside and peered over the trundle to be sure Peter was sleeping well. Mr. Stein had awakened an hour ago. He answered questions appropriately and worried about Mercy and Peter before slipping back to sleep. In a day or two, he'd learn the truth. For now, he slept with the same innocence as his grandson, deaf to the sound of his grand-daughter's sobs.

Where's Otto? Connant said she and Otto were engaged to be married. If ever a woman needed comfort, now was the time. She deserved all of the solace and reassurance Otto could give.

Robert carried the kerosene lantern with him to the parlor. A photograph of a woman and the old man in his younger days standing in front of a different house was propped beside another photograph of a family of four. The third photograph was of the children with their grandparents. It didn't take much to deduce that Mercy and her little brother were orphaned and reared by their grandfather. *Puir lass hasna had an easy life.*

Even if Peter hadn't knelt and said a bedtime prayer, Robert would have known this was a believer's home. A well-thumbed hymnal, a much-loved Bible, and little colored picture cards from Sunday school bespoke that these people lived their faith. *And their faith was just put to an awful test.*

He didn't want to snoop. Casual observations were fine, but this parlor held too many personal touches. Robert went to the kitchen stove, where he stirred up the coals. Spending the night here was a prudent choice, but it wasn't a comfortable one.

He wanted to be sure Mr. Stein didn't brew a fever and hadn't lost his mental abilities. Between the punctures in the old man's leg and the bump on the back of his head, either of those complications could occur. So far, neither had materialized. Robert had confidence in his own professional skills, but medical science could only do so much. His faith in the Great Physician's healing knew no bounds, and he sought wisdom and assistance from the Lord for each case. In regard to Mr. Stein's welfare, his prayer was being answered.

Robert also stayed for Mercy's sake. He knew she didn't want him there, but folks often resented a physician's presence because it underscored problems they wanted to deny. She might seek care from him still; he'd discovered that in the dark of night, folks some-times could ask a doctor things they couldn't speak of in daylight.

He'd set a pot of coffee on to boil after he tucked the boy in for the night. Sickened by the violence these people had suffered, Rob hadn't bothered to eat. Grumbling in his stomach now made him lift the towel draped over a pan. The yeasty smell drifted up to him as he gazed at the dough that had risen and finally fallen flat. Fried in a dab of bacon grease, such dough still gave an empty belly satisfaction.

The scents of fried bread and coffee filled the house. Robert sat down at the table and ate by the light of that single lantern until a faint creak made him look up.

Still wearing her calico dress and clutching a shawl about her, Mercy slipped out of her own room and directly into the other bedchamber.

Robert walked to the doorway and whispered, "Peter's been sleeping like a bear. Your grandfather woke about an hour and a half ago. He knew where he was. He's able to move his leg and wiggle his toes—both excellent signs. I expect him to make a full recovery."

"I'll watch over them. You should go."

"I've no doubt you'd hover like a guardian angel if you had the chance, but 'tisn't necessary. I'm stuck here. I've no horse, and even if I did, I couldn't find my way back to town since I just arrived today. After I change the dressing on his leg in the morning, I'll leave."

She pulled the shawl more closely about her shoulders.

"You've yet to slumber, and you need your rest. I've powders in my bag that will help you fall asleep."

"No, thank you."

Robert grudgingly admitted to himself that Mercy shared a trait of his own—she knew her mind and stuck to her plans. Often, that perseverance paid off, but in this case, her stubbornness resulted in needless suffering. He decided it wasn't worth arguing with her. If anything, she needed to feel she'd regained control—however simple or slight it might be.

"Forgive me, Miss Stein. You're barefoot and likely catching a chill whilst I natter away the night. I'll go back to my coffee. If you'd like, I can pour you a cup."

"I'll retire." Though she stated her plan, she made no move to carry it out.

Robert turned and went back to the table. So that was the way of it. She'd refused to brush past him to leave the room. He couldn't fault her for being skittish; she had just cause to be wary—extremely wary. He'd have to earn her trust, and from this encounter, he reckoned it would take a good long while.

∞

Mercy woke and promised herself it was just a bad dream, but that false hope disappeared the minute she rolled out of bed and hurt all over. Deep purple-black ringed her left eye, and she turned away from the mirror as she pinned her braid into a bun.

The door to Grossvater's room stood open. A quick peek reassured her that he and Peter still slept soundly. Usually, Grossvater would be stirring, if not up by now. Knowing how he'd chafe at being kept in bed, Mercy hoped he'd sleep late.

She tiptoed past the doctor, too. He'd fallen asleep with his head resting on his folded arms at the dining table. The settee in the parlor was far too short for a man of his height to stretch out on. Just seeing him made her balk. She'd need to speak to him before Grossvater woke up. Would he honor her request to keep what happened from Grossvater?

Otto. Surely Otto wouldn't tell anyone. He'd shelter her from the humiliation of others knowing the full truth of what had happened. He'd responded to her screams and come—too late to stop the worst—but Otto knew what happened and killed that awful man. *I'm glad he's dead. Glad. He can't come back to hurt me again.*

Steeling herself, she stepped into the barn. Bile rose, and she swallowed it. Just off to her right was where *that man* died at Otto's hand. Another few steps and she was near the place where he'd held the knife to her sweet little brother's neck, then struck him in the head. Her legs shook so badly, she could hardly walk deeper into the barn. Over there, in that straw, he'd. . .

She stumbled and pressed the back of her hand to her mouth to keep from crying out. Evalina's lowing jarred her back to what she needed to do. *I can go on. I can. I'll do my chores and make it through the morning. Then I'll make it through the afternoon.*

Mercy rested her cheek against Evalina's warm side and listened to the *shhh-shhh-shhh* as the bucket filled with the rhythmic motions of her hands. The smell of milk, hay, and cow were so common. After promising herself that staying busy with tasks would keep her from remembering, Mercy discovered she'd been lying to herself.

How could life ever be ordinary again? Swollen as her left eye had become, she could see only a narrow strip out of it. The cuffs on her sleeves rubbed against the tender bruises on her wrists.

Shame and embarrassment kept her from accepting care from the new doctor. He'd tried to be helpful, but Mercy wanted to forget what happened. The aches in her body, heart, and soul wouldn't let her forget, though. The doctor said he'd leave this morning. She hoped he'd keep his word—in fact, that he'd sneak in, check on Grossvater's leg, and be gone by the time she got back to the house. She didn't want to face him—or anyone—today.

Pouring the milk into the separator strained her wrists. Everything she'd done this morning—combing her hair, washing her face, milking the cow—all of the simple pleasures of life had been tainted by painful reminders. Mercy felt a bolt of hatred. She'd never hated before, but she knew exactly what the emotion was. *I'm glad Otto killed him.* The thought went through her mind again. *Even hell is too good for a wicked man like that.*

A roar of pain echoed from the house.

Chapter 4

Mercy tossed aside the milk pail and ran for the house. She tore through the door and ran full tilt into Grossvater's bedroom, only to bump smack into a broad back. She shoved the doctor aside and stopped cold. The sheriff stood by the bedside, and anguish contorted Grossvater's dear face. She'd seen that look only once before—when Grossmuter died.

Grossvater turned his head and looked at her. Tears filled his eyes.

"What have you done?" she cried to the sheriff.

Hands curled around her shoulders from behind. She immediately struggled to free herself.

"Shh, lass."

"You told! You didn't have to tell him." Tears she couldn't hold back broke forth as her knees gave out. Strong hands gently tightened about her—not in binding restraint, but in comfort. The doctor kept her from collapsing.

"There'll be time to talk later," the deep baritone said from over her shoulder.

Mercy buried her face in her hands as the doctor turned her and led her from the room. He took her to the kitchen, leaned against the cupboard, and held her as she fell apart. "Why?" She finally looked up at him. "Why didn't you protect him? You could have spared him."

"Connant told him, Mercy." Slowly, he wiped tears from her cheeks.

"He had no business, no right—"

His blue eyes were somber and his face grim. "Peter was already awake. I sent him over to the neighboring farm with a request to borrow some honey. Your grandfather woke, and his first words were about the two of you."

"You didn't have to—"

"One look at your face and he would have known, Mercy. No man could mistake the truth."

She closed her eyes and bowed her head. *So everyone who ever looks at me again will know? Lord, how will I ever endure such shame?*

He clasped her to his chest and held her there. His heart beat steadily beneath her ear. Quietly he said, "I'm sure Connant wanted to spare you from having to tell him, Mercy. You're worried about protecting your grandfather; Connant was trying to make this easier on you."

She pushed away. "Easier? Easier! Nothing about this is easy. It is awful. It is evil."

"You're right. What happened was evil."

Sheriff Gilchrist's boots shuffled on the plank floor. He cleared his throat. "Mercy? Your grandfather wants you."

Mercy started to cross the floor, then paused. She didn't look at the sheriff or the doctor. Clutching her hands together, she murmured, "You men should go now. There is nothing for you to do here." Her voice caught, then she added, "Too much has already been said and done."

As she entered Grossvater's bedroom, she heard the screen door shut. *If only I could run over, slam the door, and lock out the world.*

"Mercy," Grossvater said from the bed. He'd wiggled his way up until he sat propped against the headboard. His face was ashen, his eyes haunted. It broke her heart when he silently stretched his arms wide to take her to his breast.

She wanted to fly across the room as she had when she was a small girl and lost her parents. He'd held her tight and provided a secure, loving life. Grossvater and Grossmuter did everything they could to fix her broken world. Grossvater couldn't fix this, though. She was a woman now, and she'd have to live with this tragedy. Mercy tried hard to control her tumultuous feelings as she walked toward him with measured steps. "How are you feeling? How is your head? Your leg?"

"I'll heal. But you, sweetheart—"

She sat on the edge of the bed and carefully leaned against him. His arms enfolded her. "Don't say anything, Grossvater. Please, don't."

He bowed his head and kissed her hair.

<hr>

Mercy stopped abruptly at the sight of the full egg basket by the chicken coop. *Who's been here?* Chills raced up her arms. Evalina lowed over in the pasture. *I left her in the barn!*

Mouth dry and heart pounding, Mercy started to back toward the house. *It can't be that man again. Otto killed him. Otto—he probably came over to help. That's it.* She let out a shaky breath. *Sturdy, reliable, devoted Otto. He still loves me!*

The grating sound of a shovel indicated someone was in the barn, mucking out the stable. Yes, Otto would have thought of the animals' welfare. The knot between her shoulders lessened, and she called out, "Otto?"

Footsteps sounded in the barn.

She tried to smile, but doing so pulled the skin. That tightness, teamed with the way she could only see a slice of anything from her left eye, registered. *He'll see my face. I shouldn't have called to him.* Mercy spun toward the side.

"Whoa!"

A scream ripped from her chest.

"I wasn't meaning to alarm you, lass." The doctor's hands hovered beside her arms, but he didn't make any contact.

Shuffling backward, Mercy called out, "Otto!"

"Rob?" A man stood in the barn's doorway.

It's not Otto. He hasn't come ever since—

"I startled Miss Stein, Chris. 'Tis all." The doctor looked at her. "I came by to check on your grandda."

Mercy made no reply. She led him to the house and stood by while he changed her grandfather's dressing. As he tied it into place, he said, "Mr. Stein, whilst you're recovering, you'll need a strong back and an extra pair of hands about the place. I've brothers—either Christopher or Duncan will ride out each morning to help."

"I could use the help, but I need to be up."

The doctor nodded. "That you do. Your muscles will weaken if left unused. My brother Duncan made you a walking stick. I'll allow you to use it 'round the house, but 'tis all. No taking the steps off the porch for another few days, else you'll suffer a terrible setback."

After Grossvater was up in a chair in the parlor, the doctor left. Mercy fussed around in the house all day. Though her hands stayed busy, her mind spiraled into a near panic. Four endless days had passed, but Otto hadn't yet come over. She took bread from the oven and searched for something—anything—else to do.

Heavy footsteps sounded on the veranda, then someone knocked. "I'll get it," Grossvater said.

Though she didn't know that he ought to be moving around much, Mercy allowed Grossvater to answer the door. She didn't want anyone to see her.

"Come, Mercy." For the first time since *it* happened, Grossvater sounded like his old self.

Mercy wiped her hands on the hem of her apron and went to him. As long as she kept her face turned, no one would have to see—

"Otto's here." Grossvater's words stunned her. Otto never knocked. Fully assured of his welcome, he always barged in.

"I killed a man." Anguish permeated Otto's stark words. Emotion contorted his features. "With my own hands, I killed him."

"You did." Mercy didn't move an inch. *Look at me. No, don't. But at least draw me into the shelter of your arms.*

"It was a bad thing." Otto's voice was nothing more than a ragged whisper.

Mercy couldn't hold back a strangled sound. The man she loved was trying to reassure her and chose his words so as not to shame her. The doubts and worries the past days fostered gave way to relief. She stepped forward, finally free to lean into Otto's consolation. Her arms barely started to close around him; her bruised cheek scarcely grazed the fabric of his shirt when he jerked away from her.

Mercy's head snapped back. "Ot—"

"I killed a man!" He stared at her. This wasn't the Otto she knew. His eyes weren't sparkling with laughter or lit with gentle love.

Her arms dropped woodenly to her sides.

Grossvater hobbled closer and managed to keep his balance while still wrapping an arm around her shoulders. "You did your best, Otto. You tried to protect those you love."

Leather creaked loudly in the awkward silence as Otto shifted from one boot to the other.

"With God's help, we will get beyond this," Grossvater said.

I don't know that I'll ever get beyond it.

Otto cleared his throat. "The wedding."

Not our wedding? The wedding? Mercy started to tremble anew.

"It's thoughtful of you, Otto, to give my granddaughter a little time."

In that moment, Mercy knew the truth. Otto's expression told her more than words could. The brutal truth hit her. "There will be no wedding."

"Mercy—" Grossvater began.

The dainty ring burned as she twisted it off her finger. "I no longer hold you to your promise."

Although Otto didn't reach for it, he didn't make an attempt to try to reassure her that their love could weather this catastrophe.

Tightening his hold on her, Grossvater growled, "There's no reason to be hasty—"

"I do not blame her," Otto said thickly. "I cannot live with myself, knowing I have killed a man."

"There's nothing wrong," Grossvater said, "with a man protecting those he loves."

Mercy trembled—unsure of what to do. *Can it be that Otto needs my love and acceptance now, more than ever, just as I need his?*

Otto looked at her. Never once had she seen him cry, but tears traced down his sunburned cheeks. "It was not about protection. He'd already done his worst. I sought vengeance." His hands came up and formed an ever-tightening circle. "I took a man's life. How am I to know God would not have redeemed him someday? All that was right and pure between us—what he did couldn't ruin that. What I did—that defiled everything."

Grossvater took the ring from her nerveless fingers and passed it to Otto.

⌒

"Excuse me." Robert pushed through a gaggle of women at the mercantile and frowned. "Stand back. 'Tis too close in here." If it weren't for the cracker barrel behind Mercy and Carmen Rodriguez propping her up, the lass would be flat out on the plank floor.

His inclination was to scoop her up, but Robert quelled that at once. Mercy spooked too easily. If she roused much, she'd likely fall apart as he carried her to his office. He knelt beside her and hoped she couldn't hear the suppositions the busybodies behind him whispered. When the community heard of Otto killing a man, Otto's mother sought to defend her son—but at Mercy's expense. As if the poor lass hadn't suffered enough, she'd been denied the ability to keep what had happened private.

Miss Rodriguez used her hankie to blot Mercy's brow. "If you help her over to my house, I can see to her. It's probably just. . . constriction."

Robert slid one hand behind Mercy's neck and unfastened the uppermost button on her high-collared shirtwaist. Taking her pulse necessitated unfastening the mother-of-pearl buttons on her cuff. Mercy's lids began to flutter, and he announced, "With that stove roaring, 'tis hotter than Lucifer's laundry pot in here. Miss Stein? Ah, there we are." He tilted her wan face toward his. "The heat's claimed you. Miss Rodriguez here is going to accompany us back to my office."

"I—I just need a moment." Mercy's words sounded every bit as faint as she looked.

"I agree." He nodded. "A short rest and a nice dipper of water will go a long way toward helping you."

Miss Rodriguez patted her. "I'll stay right beside you. The nice doctor is going to help you up now." She drew closer and whispered,

"Mercy, he's strong. He can carry you."

The very last vestige of color bled from Mercy's face.

"She'll lean on me. We all understand the necessity." Robert pulled Mercy to her feet and wound his arm around her slender waist.

Back in his office, Robert managed to get Mercy alone in the examination room. She promptly declared, "Truly, I've recovered. It was just the heat."

"I'm not so sure of that."

Primly buttoning her cuff, she said, "If it's not the heat, then it must be something I ate."

Robert pressed a glass of water into her hands in order to keep her seated on his examination table. He asked several questions, purposefully posing them in a rambling fashion so she wouldn't have a sense of what he needed to ascertain.

"This is unnecessary. It was simply the heat. Just as you said at the mercantile, all I needed was water and a short rest. I'm better." She looked ready to make a dash for freedom.

Sick to the depths of his soul, Robert rested his hand on her forearm. "No, you're not. Miss Stein, you're with child."

Chapter 5

Cold dread washed over her. For weeks now, she'd lived in terror of this possibility. Night and day, she'd begged God to spare her this. The last two weeks, her anxiety had mushroomed. Still, she didn't want to believe it could be so. "I truly must go." Mercy twisted to the side and slid off the table.

"Miss Stein—"

She shook off the doctor's hand. "Grossvater needs me." Desperate to get away, she opened the door out into his waiting room.

Carmen Rodriguez hopped to her feet. "Are you feeling better now? You've never swooned before."

"Then I suppose it was my turn. I really must get home."

"I'm due to pay a call on your grandda." Dr. Gregor picked up his black leather satchel. "I'll accompany you."

"Oh, that's so kind of you. I'd have worried myself sick if Mercy went home alone."

"Mercy!" Peter burst into the doctor's office.

"What are you doing out of school?"

"Teacher sent David to get more chalk from the mercantile. He told me—"

"Tales," Mercy said flatly. "We do not listen to tales, Peter. Now you march right on back to school."

The doctor waited until her little brother left, then he chuckled. "And to think I always thought growing up with *older* brothers was difficult!" As Carmen laughed, he smoothly took hold of Mercy's elbow. "Now that everything is settled, let's go see your grandda."

"He's fine. You saw him yourself at church just yesterday—and the two Sundays before that, as well."

"Aye, that I did. After six weeks of healing, the time's come to regain the strength in his limb."

"Can you do that?" Carmen pressed a hand to her bosom. "It's nothing short of miraculous how you didn't have to amputate. No one expected him to ever walk again."

"God gets credit for all miracles," the doctor said. "I take responsibility for the more ordinary—like teaching Mr. Stein some movements so his strength returns."

"And that Mercy rests," Carmen added. "Good-bye, then. Oh! Mercy, Leonard brought over a pound of coffee. He said that's what you came to town for."

Using that as an excuse to break away from the doctor's hold, Mercy reached out and accepted the bag. "I'll be sure to thank him when I go get my horse." She knew the doctor didn't own a horse, so Mercy figured she'd neatly managed to get rid of him entirely.

She wasn't that fortunate. Five minutes later, as they rode out of town, he'd finished telling her about how his brother Chris had bought the dappled mare for a pittance because it had been in such sorry shape. Clearly his medical skills extended toward beasts, too.

He cleared his throat. "My apologies for speaking so much, but I assumed you didn't want anyone asking questions, so I dominated the conversation."

Surprised by his insight, Mercy still grasped at the opening he'd provided. "Dr. Neely said he'd taken an oath to give patients privacy. Did you take that same vow?"

"Aye. The Hippocratic oath."

"Good. Then you are not going to tell anyone. . ." She couldn't bring herself to even say the words.

Dr. Gregor said nothing.

Terrified that a prompt agreement didn't spring from his lips, Mercy halted. So did he. Ever since *that day*, she'd hardly looked directly at anyone. Deeply shamed, she couldn't. But this was too important. "You took the oath. You must uphold it."

" 'Tisn't a secret that can be long kept."

"It can be kept until Grossvater is strong. Then I can go away." She tore her gaze away from him and stared off in the distance.

"Lass, your grandda willna be fully recovered for almost four more months. You'll not be able to hide the truth until autumn."

"Of course I can." *I have to.*

"I canna begin to imagine how difficult this is for you, but I'll be speaking plainly. Your brother will say something about you fainting. Even if you admonish Peter to remain silent, any one of a half dozen of the people who were in the mercantile will mention the episode to your grandda."

The reins slithered through her fingers. Everything was slipping through her fingers—her love, her reputation, and now even this.

The doctor leaned forward and collected a rein. Pressing it back into her hand, he murmured, "For your own sake as well as his, don't you think it would be best if we told him now?"

She gave no answer. They reached the farm shortly thereafter, and the doctor's brother sauntered in from the nearest field. Either or both of the doctor's brothers came each day. At first, they'd come into the house to ask Grossvater what needed to be done. As he'd improved, Grossvater made it a point to be out on the porch to meet them.

The doctor dismounted and helped her down. His brother strode over, and the two of them greeted each other as if they'd been separated for a year. The second Duncan turned her way, Mercy dipped her head.

"Your grandda is in the barn, Miss Stein. I brought over some of my tools, and he's repairing harnesses and the like."

"That was good of you. I'll go get lunch."

Duncan chuckled. "Only for yourself. We found the sandwiches you left and polished them off. Rob, while you're here, take a look at Freckle's runt."

"He's in the barn?"

"Aye." Duncan headed back out to the field.

The doctor looked at her. "Would you like to eat first?"

Rage swept through her. "First? The decision is mine to make."

"Yes, 'tis." He didn't pause for a second to frame his reply. "But Freckle isna about to let me near her wee little pup unless you're there."

He'd spoken the truth. Freckle didn't mind anyone playing with the other puppies, but she'd become unaccountably protective of the runt. Heaving a sigh, Mercy walked toward the barn. *It's only Monday. I'll have a few days as long as I make sure Peter says nothing.*

"*Schatze!* Did you have a nice trip to town?"

Mercy evaded the question. "Grossvater, look at you! I didn't know we had so many leather things."

A proud smile lit his face. "These are just the things that needed care. Most were still in working condition, but with a little attention, they'll last much longer."

The doctor set down his satchel. "That saddle is a thing of beauty."

"It was my son's." Grossvater gently buffed an edge. "Mercy's mama gave it to him the year they were married. Peter is about the age where he will treasure it."

"So you will give it to him for his birthday?" Mercy nodded. "He will be very pleased."

"If you're done riding for the day, I'll unsaddle your horse," the doctor offered.

"*Ja*, that is kind of you." Grossvater smiled. "And then I will ask you to help me hide this saddle."

Mercy added, "Peter's birthday is next month—on the fourth of July."

"There's a fine date." The doctor sauntered out to get her horse.

Independence Day. . .but I'll never be free again. In the doctor's absence, Mercy slipped away from Grossvater and leaned over Freckle's box. She scratched between the mutt's ears. The whole time the doctor unsaddled her horse, she lavished attention on Freckle and admired each pup. Finally, she lifted the runt. "I'll bring her right back."

"Duncan tells me the wee one isna feelin' so chipper."

Grossvater let out a deep sigh. "She crept out of the box today and followed Peter. While he was doing the milking, Evalina stepped on the runt's tail."

"Let's see." The doctor stepped closer. Mercy tried to hand him Dot, but he made a dismissive gesture. "I'll be better able to assess her tail if both hands are free."

His breath washed over her wrists, and Mercy longed to pull away. Deft and gentle, he examined the runt. The very last place he touched was its tail, and the pup whimpered.

"Ooch, now, there's a shame." The doctor crooked his forefinger and rubbed the runt between her ears, just as Mercy had done to Freckle. "Puir wee pup. Tail's broken."

"I feared that." Grossvater sounded grim. "Freckle's been licking it, but the skin's broken, and the runt'll get gangrene. We'll put it down before Peter gets home."

"He's blaming himself already," Mercy murmured.

"Now, that's premature." The doctor finally took Dot from her and cuddled the pup to the center of his broad chest.

Half an hour later, Mercy put Dot back with Freckle. "She doesn't have the part of her tail with the spot that we named her for."

"Stubby." The doctor's voice sounded vaguely humored.

Grossvater chortled. "Stubby! Ja, it is a good name."

Mercy straightened up.

"Mercy." Grossvater's voice suddenly sobered. "You do not laugh? *Was ist den loss?*"

What is the matter? Grossvater sometimes lapsed into German when he was emotional. He looked from her stricken expression to the doctor and back. Then he groaned and rubbed his hand down his face.

Everything in her wanted to scream a denial, to run. But no sound would come out of her mouth, and her feet wouldn't move.

The doctor pressed something into her hand. Mercy stared down at the handkerchief for a moment before she realized she was crying. Finally, she rasped, "I will go away."

"*Nein!*" Grossvater got to his feet and limped with the cane as fast as he could toward her.

"Are you wanting to be alone?" the doctor asked her softly as Grossvater approached.

Mercy nodded. A moment later, she and Grossvater wrapped their arms about one another. He stroked her back. "I won't let you go. You are not to blame, and neither is the child."

"But Grossvater—" She couldn't put into words all she felt.

"No sneaking off to hide." He held her tighter. "I have worried there might be a child. I have prayed. This child—we will love it, for it is yours."

The ball in her throat made it hard to speak at all, but she managed a strangled whisper. "I don't know if I can."

"We can." Grossvater's voice held great determination. "Ja, with God's help, we can do this."

Mercy clung to him. *With God's help? Why did He not help me so all of this didn't happen? Even if just the baby didn't happen? How am I to trust Him to help me now, when He's ignored my cries for so long?*

∽

"Dr. Gregor?"

Rob halted and looked across the street. "Aye?"

Carmen Rodriguez motioned toward him. He crossed the road and joined her on her veranda. "I've been wondering. . ." she half whispered. Color filled her cheeks. "Mr. Stein is doing whatever you showed him to do, and his recovery is remarkable. I was wondering. . ."

When her voice trailed off, Rob accepted the glass of sweet tea she extended toward him and sat in a wicker chair. He'd intentionally waited until he knew what she wanted. Ever since Mercy swooned in the mercantile almost a month before, folks tried to get him to speak about her. Some meant well; others were gossipmongers. Either way, he refused to discuss any private matters. Since Miss Rodriguez wished to broach a different topic, he'd listen. "You were wondering?"

"Could I do the movements? Would they help me?"

He made no pretense at ignorance. The lass had a noticeable limp. "You were quite young when you broke your limb, weren't you?"

She nodded. "Doc Neely wanted to amputate, but Papa wouldn't consent to it."

"When you showed interest upon hearing about the therapy, I made the assumption that you were hopeful something might benefit you, as well." Rob looked her in the eyes. He'd learned early in his career that patients inevitably coped better with bad news when given the dignity of a direct response. "I took the liberty of examining the medical journal Dr. Neely kept. The problem is that your bones knit together in puir alignment. Motion exercises address muscular problems, not skeletal. I'm sorry I canna make a difference for you."

"I suppose," she said in a tight voice, "I should be grateful for what I have."

"I'm sure the Almighty never tires of hearing our gratitude." He looked out at the garden she tended every afternoon. "What happened? Just yesterday your garden was brimming with blossoms, and most of them are gone now."

"Ada Meister's wedding is tomorrow." She clenched her hands in her lap. "You know what they say—the woman who marries in June is a bride all her life."

Rob hitched a shoulder. "To my way of thinking, 'tisn't when you marry—'tis whom. Even so, it was kind of you to share your flowers with Miss Meister."

"Thank you."

They exchanged a few more pleasantries, then Rob excused himself. As he started down the steps, Otto Kunstler passed him. They exchanged nothing more than a polite nod, but Rob overheard him.

"Hello, Miss Rodriguez. Is your sister home?"

The rest of the afternoon passed with an assortment of cases that demanded the doctor's attention. His last patients were from two towns over. Suspecting that they, like Carmen Rodriguez, were hoping for a miracle, Rob took additional time with the Heims. In the end, all he could do was tell them the sad truth.

"I'm sorry, Mr. and Mrs. Heim, but you'll not be having any children."

Mrs. Heim sobbed quietly, and her husband held her close. He looked just as shattered. "Are you sure?"

"Aye." Rob explained the details as gently as he could.

Chester Heim heaved a sigh. "We were told the same by the doctor in Austin. We hoped he was wrong. Lena and I—we talked about it. If there is no hope for us to have a child of our own, we would consider adopting."

"If anything comes up, I'll keep you in mind."

Wearily washing his hands, Rob let out a long sigh. *Mercy is carrying a babe that was forced upon her; the Heims desperately want a child and cannot have one. It's not for me to question Your ways, Father, but I have to admit I dinna understand them. Common sense says the solution to everyone's problem is clear, yet that's man's planning and not Your wisdom. Unless, or until, You give me a clear sense that You want me to approach Mercy about relinquishing her babe, I'll wait in silence.*

∽

"Kunstler!" Grossvater's voice sounded loudly through the open barn door.

Mercy swiftly set Stubby down next to Freckle and headed toward the other exit. Ever since Otto broke their engagement, the only time she'd seen him was at church. Never once had he offered to come help with the chores or crops when Grossvater was unable to work. Not once had his mother thought to bring by food. When gossips whispered about the babe Mercy carried, it hurt. But buried in that hurt was the hope that Mrs. Kunstler would come and speak privately with her, to let her know what to expect, to console her and promise to help with the birth. Those hopes were in vain. Mercy tugged on the barn's back door.

It was stuck.

Chapter 6

Otto would come inside and walk the length of the barn so he could inspect the reaper. For a moment, Mercy considered scrambling up into the hayloft. *No. This is my home.*

She sat back down beside Freckle's box and filled her skirts with puppies. A minute later, Grossvater and Otto came inside.

Otto caught sight of her and averted his gaze. Still, he kept coming. He stood above her and cleared his throat. "Miss Stein, those are fine hounds there."

Miss Stein? This man who was supposed to have been her husband now greeted her as if she were practically a stranger. Mercy looked down at the wiggly little bundles of fur and nodded. "Ja, they are fine, indeed."

To her relief, Grossvater leaned against the wall of the stall. "Even the runt is growing to good size."

"Everyone knows Freckle's pups all become good hunting dogs." Otto hunkered down and reached for a solid brown male. "Since the day you promised me a puppy, I've looked forward to claiming one."

Mercy sucked in a pained gasp as memories washed over her. *He used seeking a puppy as an excuse to come over, and he asked me to marry him that afternoon.* Unable to quell the emotions, she blurted out, "More than one promise was made that day."

Otto's head shot up. Finally, he looked at her. "So is that what you want? For the sake of a promise you would marry a man who cannot bear to look at you? Who, every time he sees you, remembers how he slew a man? You would want me to rear the child of the man I killed?"

"What I want?" Her voice shook. "Do you think I want any of what has happened? To bear the pain, the shame, and to carry a child? No! I don't want any of that. I wanted a man who would love me regardless of what life brought and who would stand beside me in the bad times. You were right to break your promise to wed me, because you are not that kind of man."

"Mercy," Grossvater said softly.

Her eyes swam with tears. "I do not know whether my grandfather is calling my name or reminding me to treat you with mercy."

"This has been very. . .difficult for both of us," Otto said.

One by one, she placed the puppies back in the box. "In three weeks, the pups will be weaned. We will reserve that one for you." She went into the house, opened the bottom drawer of her wardrobe, and pulled out a white bundle. Until now, she'd dared to hope that Otto would overcome his upset and realize his love for her was stronger than what had happened. He wouldn't.

Slowly, she unfolded the beautiful gown she was to have worn. All of it wouldn't fit in the stove at once, so she cut it. Piece by piece, she burned it. As the last threads burned, Mercy retied her apron strings. Her waist hadn't changed a bit. In time, it would expand, but she didn't know when—and she couldn't ask anyone. Never had she felt so alone.

∽

"I thought to ask your opinion of this drawing." Rob laid the floor plan out on her dining table. "It's a house plan."

Drying her hands on a dish towel, Mercy said, "I've seen many plans in *American Woman's Home* and in *Ladies' Home Journal.*"

"On the train from New York, everyone shared their books and magazines. *Scientific American* captured my attention. It featured some of George Barber's homes."

Mercy merely nodded.

"My brothers both think I'm daft for mailing away for this, but it seemed to me that since Barber is already well known for his plans, it only makes sense to lean on his experience."

"Then why do you ask me what I think?"

"Because you're a woman. Three bachelors are liable to overlook something important when it comes to the practicalities of running a household. When Chris or Duncan marries, it would be a shame to find out we'd forgotten or been ignorant about an essential."

"What makes you think Mr. Barber has not given thought to such matters?"

"He," Rob paused and gave her a rascal's smile, "is a man, too."

Mercy approached the table hesitantly. Robert didn't move an inch. Ever since the first time he'd seen her, she'd been jumpy—and understandably so. But over the last few months, he'd made a subtle attempt to show her understanding and make her feel safe.

Manufacturing excuses to be around her was fairly easy. He was passing by the Stein spread while making house calls, he needed to confer with whichever brother happened to be out in the field that day, the Stein mailbox at the mercantile was full. . . In the church-yard, he'd make sure to compliment her on a dessert she'd sent home with one of his brothers or praise her for having accompanied the choir on the piano. Delivering the babe would be difficult enough—hopefully, he could get her accustomed to his presence so she wouldn't be overwhelmed when the time came.

"You have two plans," she said.

"I can see why you'd think so since they both have doors and a veranda. The one to the left is the downstairs. The one to the right is the upstairs. The upstairs veranda can be enclosed later to form another bedchamber."

"I see." She leaned a little closer. "This is the kitchen?"

"Aye." He glanced at how her kitchen was arranged. "I imagine it would be set up similar to yours."

"No." She shook her head. "Grossmuter and I often regretted not having a mudroom. Everything gets tracked in." She pointed toward a room. "What is this here?"

"Duncan's shop. We don't need a separate dining room—the kitchen will suffice. He can do his—" Rob watched as she shook her head. "What's wrong?"

"Do not mistake me. Being a cobbler is an honorable profession, but the leather—much of it together in the same place smells bad. Between the smell and the hammer pounding on it, it would not be pleasant in the house."

"Good point." He tapped a pencil on the edge of the blueprint. "A workshop just a stone's throw from the house would work. That would free up space for your house to have a mudroom. You could divide that space and make it useful. The pantry you show here, beneath the stairs—it will not work well because you and your brothers are all tall. What if you have a mudroom, washroom, and pantry here?"

"An indoor washroom?" Robert chortled. "That's very progressive. I like it! Is this a good spot to place the stove?"

She made a few more suggestions, then went over to the stove and stirred a pot. "When will you build the house?"

"Within the next month or so. I'll telegraph a company in Knoxville, Tennessee. They'll mill and cut the lumber, then send it by the railroad."

She dropped the spoon. "You are mail ordering a house?"

"Aye, that I am. It will save considerable time and labor here, and the cost of the kit is actually quite thrifty by comparison."

"A kit."

Amused at how she echoed the word, Rob chuckled. "Indeed. The notion takes a little getting used to." He slipped a different page to the top of the stack. "This is the exterior view. When I order it, I'll tell them not to send all the spindles and such."

"Gingerbread." She returned to the table and said, "Grossmuter called all of the lacy scrollwork and wooden fancies gingerbread."

"Now there's a grand description." He shrugged. "But I couldn't care less about how it looks on the outside. 'Tis the inside that counts."

"This is too much, but a little would give charm to the house." Mercy tapped the fanlike piece spanning from the peak of the roof to the eaves on either side. "Can you keep some of it?"

"What do you recommend?" Rob felt a spark of hope. For the first time since the tragedy, Mercy seemed to be coming out of her shell. He'd hoped the sketches might be a good tool for drawing her into a conversation. With a few leading questions, he enticed her into discussing the plan in infinite detail.

After awhile, she went back to the stove. "In a month, the wheat harvest should be done, and the corn harvest won't quite be ready. That was good planning. The farmers will be able to help you."

"Speaking of help. . ." Rob scribbled a note to himself in the corner of the page before rolling it up. "I'd like to hire you to cook for the men who come work."

She shook her head. "Not one penny have you or your brothers accepted for the care or the help you have given."

"And you've not accepted a single penny for all the delicious meals you've sent to us." He crooked a brow. "Have you ever eaten at the diner?"

"Once."

"And only once." He nodded. "That says it all. Indeed, my brothers and I all agree—our cooking is no better than the diner's. We've come out far ahead on the bargain. And since we're on the subject of food, I'm trying to find a way to invite myself to lunch. Whatever you're cooking smells delicious."

"Ham and beans. And you are always welcome at our table."

"That's so wonderful to hear!" As Mrs. Kunstler scurried in from the wide open door where she had obviously been eavesdropping, Robert noted that Mercy startled at her interruption. Mrs. Kunstler looked from Mercy to Rob and back again before continuing, "Things work out, don't they? And now my Otto won't be worried about hurting your feelings as he courts Ismelda."

Color rushed to Mercy's face, then bled away just as rapidly. She shook her head.

Rob took the spoon from her, set it down, and pushed her into a chair. Keeping a hand on Mercy's shoulder, he looked at Otto's mother. "Mrs. Kunstler, you misconstrued matters."

"What was I supposed to think?" Her gaze kept darting from Mercy to him. "You're alone, together, in the house. Decency—"

"I'm sure you didn't mean to question Miss Stein's reputation or impugn my integrity." He stared at her.

"I—um—it, well, of course I didn't." A nervous smile twitched across the woman's face.

Rob directed his attention toward Mercy. "I'll get you some water."

"Oh, I'll do that." Mrs. Kunstler pumped water and hastily shoved the glass into his hand. "I didn't mean to upset her."

"Drink." He pressed the glass to Mercy's mouth. Beneath the hand he kept on her shoulder, he could feel how she shook. Mercy reached up and took the glass from him. For a fleeting second, Rob considered asking if Mercy wished for him to leave. Just as quickly, he dismissed the notion. Distraught as she was, she might still swoon.

He curled his hand around hers and lifted the glass to her mouth again. At the same time, something odd occurred to him. In the three months he'd been in America, he'd been astonished by the Texans' hospitality. Not only did women always offer refreshments and extend an offer for a meal, but they went so far as to take a gift or food whenever they went calling on someone else.

But Otto's mother came empty-handed.

"Mrs. Kunstler, since Miss Stein isn't feeling her best, I'm sure you'll understand—"

"I—we are still neighbors." The woman started wringing her hands. Rob took in how fine beads of perspiration dotted her face and she couldn't maintain eye contact. For her, the situation had to be uncomfortable, but he didn't consider that even a fraction as important as Mercy's heartbreak.

"We are still neighbors," Mercy said in a bleak tone. "Your son was here yesterday. He still plans to borrow Grossvater's reaper and claims one of Freckle's pups. But me?" Her voice caught. "He said he cannot bear to look at me."

"He scarcely sleeps, remembering how he killed that man."

Mercy took another sip of the water. " 'It is not good that the man should be alone; I will make him an help meet for him.' That is the verse from Genesis you recited to me the day Otto asked me to marry him." Mercy set the glass on the table with exacting care. "God does not change, but man does. Otto still needs a helpmate, yet he no longer wants me." Her head came up and she squared her shoulders. "Was there any other reason you came today?"

Mrs. Kunstler slumped against the table. "We thought it best for you to know before you saw them together. Please, Mercy, be kind to them."

"You speak to me about kindness?" Mercy shook her head. "You are the one who went about town telling everyone how that awful man shamed me."

"I didn't want anyone to think badly of my Otto if you were with child! I did it for you, too."

Ruthlessly wiping away her tears, Mercy whispered in a raw tone, "Do not tell me this. You did not do it on my behalf. This is the first time since it happened that you have come here. You did not seek to help or comfort me. Today you have not come to ease my burden. What you ask is for me to make things easier on your son. It wasn't necessary." Mercy rose. "He is the man I was to have married, and the love I held for him would keep me from wounding him in any way."

Aching silence filled the house. Robert cupped Mercy's elbow. "Go lie down, lass. You need to rest."

"I need to churn butter." She sidled toward the stove, moved the pot off the heat, and then wiped her hands on her apron. "You will both go now."

He and Mrs. Kunstler went outside. Stopping by her mare, Robert glowered at Otto's mother. "Am I to understand that you've not sought her out to give her a woman's advice?"

"The situation is strained. I'm not the right woman to—"

"No," he agreed abruptly. "No, you're not."

"You don't see—"

"I see all too clearly. I'll help you onto your horse. You don't belong here." Once Mrs. Kunstler left, Rob stared back at the house. *Three months. It's been three months. All this time, I thought she was being comforted and counseled by a woman who could show sensitivity. What kind of doctor am I? I've failed a seventeen-year-old lass who's been facing this all on her own. No more.*

Chapter 7

H er palms were moist. Mercy traded the house plans from one hand to the other so she could slip her hands on the edge of her apron to dry them. Duncan arrived this morning, declaring the doctor needed the plans. Of course, he did that immediately after promising Peter that they'd go fishing once the weeding was done.

Though early in the day, the June heat had begun to build. The door to the doctor's office was open. Mercy stood at the threshold and decided she ought to knock—after all, the doctor didn't just work here; he and his brothers lived here, as well.

"Hey, Rob!" Christopher Gregor appeared in the hall and shouted up the staircase as he yanked Mercy inside. "The plans are here!"

Of all the brothers, Christopher was the one who never ceased to startle her. His actions were invariably swift and often unexpected. Mercy barely kept from screaming.

Chris grinned at her, completely unaware of how he'd practically sent her into a panic. "Rob said you think we ought to keep some of the embellishments on the house. You'd better be ready for a fight, because I'm holding out to eliminate every last one."

"It's your house." She managed to scoot away from him.

"That's what I'm telling them. I'll do most of the construction. I used to do a lot of the mine construction back home."

"Oh."

"Good morning, Miss Stein." The doctor descended the stairs.

"I gave your brother the plans." She started to turn toward the door to make a quick escape.

"Actually, while you're here, I'd appreciate some help."

"No fair askin' the lass. It's your own fault." Chris folded his arms across his chest and growled at Mercy, "He slept through breakfast."

"I didn't mean anything about food," the doctor snapped.

Chris leaned toward her. "Pay no heed to his surly attitude. He gets that way often enough. One night with a few paltry interruptions and he gets cranky."

"So you need some breakfast?"

"No, I dinna need you minding my belly." The doctor scowled at his brother. "Go make yourself useful."

"Nae. 'Tis too much fun staying here for the moment."

"This is a touchy subject," the doctor began.

The whole matter seemed far too dubious. Mercy murmured, "Then perhaps you ought to have someone else assist you."

"I seriously doubt anyone else could help." The doctor heaved a sigh. "Come out to the back."

"You go on ahead. I'm not fool enough to chance it," Christopher announced.

"Coward," the doc muttered.

Mercy tagged along and tried to ignore the smell of scorched oatmeal as she passed by the stove. She had no idea what she was getting roped into, but the brotherly banter struck her as amusing. Once she reached the back steps, she gave the doctor a confused look.

Features strained, he whispered, "So you dinna know what to do, then, either?"

She blinked. "About what?"

The doctor cringed at the normal volume she'd spoken in and whispered even more softly, "That." He pointed to a huge pasteboard box.

Mercy leaned forward, looked inside, and started to giggle.

"Now then"—the doctor's brows puckered—" 'tisna all that funny."

"Just yesterday, you told me you were going to get a house kit. I didn't think you meant this kind." She went down on her knees by the box where a cat was nursing a litter of kittens—but in contrast to all the other marmalade-colored babies, one was black and white.

Doc leaned down and clamped his hands on her upper arms as she reached for the baby skunk. He murmured, "I wasna askin' you to get rid of the beast—just for some advice. I read about them, and I dinna think it's wise for you to be so close."

"He's a spotted skunk. If he's ready to do mischief, he'll stand on his hands." She didn't pick up the kit. Instead, she rubbed each of the tiny kittens in the litter. "They're all about the same age and size—about six weeks."

"So how do we reunite him with his mother? And how do we get rid of them all?"

Mercy sat back on her heels. "Spotted skunks don't stay any one place for long. They roam. The mother could be anywhere—in a rotten log or an abandoned burrow. She probably came to the house because you've set food out for the cat."

"So she could return tonight and reclaim her kit?"

"It is possible but not probable. When mothers and their babies are set apart, they don't come back together again." She turned to look at the doctor. "What you read told you how stinky a skunk is, but they are shy creatures. They only protect themselves if they feel threatened."

"Why do you think three grown men are whispering and tip-toeing around?"

Mercy smothered a smile. "He isn't old enough to be completely weaned." She paused a moment and decided to tease him. "Spotty. You should name him Spotty."

"There's no need to name something when it's not staying."

"Hey, Rob," Christopher's subtle-as-an-ox whisper drifted out to them. "I've never been happier that you're the doctor."

"Why?"

"I just read something." Chris stuck his head out the door. "You can operate and take out the stink glands. Yep. You're the doc." Just as quickly, Chris disappeared again.

"There's no need to be hasty," the doctor said.

Mercy grimaced. "Actually, after four weeks, they start to practice spraying. By six or eight weeks—"

"We're not keeping it around that long!"

"If the mother took him out at night, he's about six weeks."

Looking thoroughly disgruntled, the doctor announced, "His mother will come get him tonight."

Suddenly the humor of the situation evaporated. Mercy averted her gaze. "Just because you want something does not make it happen."

Dr. Gregor sat on the wooden plank veranda beside her. " 'Tis a harsh truth you just spoke."

Mercy tried to rise, but he stopped her. "Dinna run, lass. You needn't speak a word a-tall. I plan to do a bit of talking." For good measure, he scooped a kitten from the box and tucked it into her hands.

"I have chores to do at home."

"A woman's work is ne'er done. Or so my ma always said, God

rest her soul." The corners of his bright blue eyes crinkled. "I canna be certain whether she's finally resting in heaven, or if she's still bustling about with a broom, trying to make the streets of gold gleam brighter."

The image coaxed a twitch of a smile from her.

"I oughtn't cast stones. My brothers taunt me about my tidy ways."

"Your patients would develop infections if you were slovenly."

He inclined his head as an acknowledgment. "Aye. But I also remind them cleanliness is next to godliness." He glanced over his shoulder, then whispered, "Betwixt thee and me, 'tisna always the case. Times when my soul's been the most troubled, I've tried to busy my hands so as to keep from thinking or praying."

Her breath caught.

"My da—he passed on to Jesus just a day before we reached America."

"I—I'm sorry."

"I still grieve for him, but 'tis only my selfishness that causes me to. He was ailing for a long while, and now he's whole once again and in heaven. A mining accident took his arm several years back—'twas the guilt money they settled on him that paid for my medical training. He claimed God took a bad situation and used it for good."

Anger flashed through her. *He'd better not tell me it's all for the good that I'm with child and Otto has abandoned me.*

Unaware of her reaction, the doctor kept talking. "But 'twasna until his last hour that Da pointed out something that was right before me for years. I cared for Da—leastways, for the needs of his ailing body. But Duncan—he's a man with a knack for wrapping quiet comfort like a blanket about others whose hearts and souls are aching. Chris—well, he manages to scowl others into behaving so peace is maintained."

Mercy concentrated on tracing the soft stripes in the kitten's fur. The doctor was right: the Gregor men were vastly different in their strengths and personalities.

"None of us is good at everything. We have strengths and weaknesses. God created us that way so we'd rely on Him and on our brothers and sisters." He reached over, gently stroked the kitten, and said in a somber tone, "You're a fine woman, Mercy Stein. Aye, you are—but you're going to have to lean on God and others to help you through all that lies ahead."

She started to tremble. "I must leave now."

He took the kitten and gently put it with its littermates. "I'll walk you out."

It would be rude to refuse his assistance rising from the veranda. Once she was up, Mercy snatched back her hand. Her plan was to dash down the steps and go around to the front, but the doctor stopped her.

"We obviously have a mama skunk close-by. Go back through to the front." As she started through the doorway, he added, "Is there anything I should put out to entice that mother to come get the kit?"

Relief flooded her. She could salvage her pride by leaving on a better note. "What did you have out last night?"

Chris must have overheard her, because he started to chortle.

Mercy gave the doctor a questioning look.

His neck and ears went red. "Leftovers."

"Dinna believe him." Chris served his brother a wallop on the back that would have felled a smaller man. "Rob tried to bake beans. I've chewed on softer bullets."

It's my fault. I was rattled yesterday and didn't send food home with them. She stared at the far wall and said, "Eggs. Skunks like eggs."

"How many?"

"I'd suppose you have only one female and her litter of kits."

Doc chuckled. "One's more than enough. I meant, how many eggs should I put out? Half a dozen?"

"One or two."

He looked uncertain. "Fried?"

"Raw." She hastily added, "Still in the shell."

Christopher seemed to find the whole exchange vastly amusing. Until today, he'd always been so stern. Discovering it was nothing more than bluster made her bold. Mercy walked toward freedom and called back over her shoulder, "Christopher Gregor, you owe me for helping you out. It's going to cost you."

"Is that so?"

"Ja." She turned to the doctor. "I count on you to make sure he pays this debt."

"You just name it," Doc said.

"I can hardly wait." Christopher looked too smug.

She gave the doctor's brother the same look she used on Peter when he misbehaved. "Gingerbread."

"Uh. . .I'm not any better at cooking than my brothers."

The doctor tried to smother his laughter with a cough.

Mercy cast him a quick glance, then mused, "But you are good at building things?"

"That's a fact." All of a sudden, Christopher's face contorted. "Not my house!"

"Our house," the doctor corrected. "Miss Stein, what will satisfy the debt?"

"I'm a fair woman." She ignored Chris's rude snort and continued. "The fan-styled inset at the apex of the eaves. And if the mother returns and takes away the kit, whichever is cheaper: a spindled veranda or scalloped clapboards for part of the building."

"If the skunk is gone, you'll have both, and we'll be coming out better on the bargain."

"You're demented." Chris shook his head. "Any sane person would want a skunk as far away as possible, and you're trying to get it to come up on the porch!"

"You suggested I bring a skunk into my office and perform surgery on it!"

Mercy left, surprised she was still smiling at the Gregor brothers' antics. But she'd ridden no more than five feet before it happened again. Women gave her pitying glances and turned away. The tiny bit of happiness she'd had withered, and misery swamped her.

Chapter 8

"No gingerbread. Not a stick." Chris stomped into the surgery and half bellowed, "Did you hear me?"

"Half of Texas heard you." Rob calmly placed a bottle of arnica on the shelf and shut the door to his pharmaceutical cabinet. "I take it we still have the skunk?"

"No, we dinna. *You* now have two!" Chris glowered at him. "I'm working at the farm today. You and Duncan can find a way to rid us of those beasts."

Rob stood chest-to-chest with his brother and glared at him. "You're not going."

"And why not?"

"You'll bellow at the lass. She canna take it. I'll send off the telegram to order the house, and you can start the foundation."

"I can't yet. Connant insists we have a cellar to hide in when there's a storm. He hounded me until I relented and said I'd dig it." Chris looked exasperated. "I'm too busy to worry about cowering from a gust of wind."

"Last day of last month, Bell and Falls counties lost ten men to tornadoes. Connant has yet to steer us wrong about America."

"Exaggeration. It has to be. These Texans pride themselves in telling tall tales. Connant's always had a talent for stretching the thinnest thread of truth into a yarn. He's warmed up to the Texan tradition. Every time he mentions a tornado, it gets more powerful. He started with telling me about the hail that's the size of a fist. Then he had flying cows. At last telling, brick houses were torn to bits."

"You gave your word; you'll dig the shelter."

Rolling up his sleeves, Chris muttered, "Hot as it's getting, I'll probably be striking Lucifer with the shovel—and most likely within the first few inches."

"Now look who's spouting Texas-sized tales!" Rob folded a paper up and tucked it into the pocket of his vest. Miserably hot as the summer had proven to be, he felt a spurt of thanks that the men didn't feel it necessary to wear a coat and hat.

"It's a crying shame Connant wasn't stretching the truth when he told us it gets hotter than the hinges to Hades in the summer."

"Speaking of the devil's domain. . ." Rob stared at his eldest brother. "I've waited for you to tell the truth about those trips to Thurber."

Chris shrugged. "I haven't lied."

"You've not been forthcoming with the real reason you went, either." Rob knew Chris had spent time in the mines. "Did you think I wouldn't recognize the cough?"

Chris didn't look in the least bit unsettled or repentant. "Don't fault me for doing my trade."

"We're relying on your talents with construction. It's time to build the house. You're getting irritated about me getting called out in the wee small hours, and Duncan's snoring is driving me to distraction."

"Duncan's busy with all manner of leatherwork, and your practice is booming."

Rob knew he had to tread lightly. Chris was a proud man. "Aye. I canna deny either of those statements. But we'd have to pay dearly for anyone else to do the construction. We're relying on your skill."

"I haven't done a scrap of work on it yet."

Rob nodded. "And glad I am that you haven't. You were where you were most needed. The Steins would be in sorry shape had you not worked their land."

The tension in Chris's jaw eased only slightly.

"It's not just the farming you do that's vital. You've seen how skittish Mercy is." He saw Chris's eyes flare. "Having a strong man there lends her a sense of safety."

Chris grunted.

Rob knew he'd succeeded in making his point. With Chris, it was better to back off so he felt he'd made the decision. "You're so big and ugly, there isna man nor dog that'd tangle with you."

"I'd tell you to look in the mirror, but you'd break it." Chris stared out the window. "I'm not done in Thurber. I'm going back for two more days."

Rob glowered.

"It's lignite. They're opening shafts four and five, and some idiot set up shoring in them that's got exposed nails. You use your knowledge to save lives. This time, I'm using mine. One spark and the whole thing would burn for months."

"Which is why I don't want you down there at all." The railroad desperately needed the soft coal, but Rob didn't want his brother to continue mining. Mining ruined a man's lungs, if it didn't claim life or limb first. "You're done with that trade."

"In case you didn't notice, I didn't ask what you thought."

"We pledged Da we'd stay together."

"I'm still in Texas!"

"Not good enough," Rob shot back.

Chris banged his fist against the back of a chair. "I'm not about to concede to your whims. Not after you decided our house needs to have more frills than an Easter bonnet."

"Sore over that, are you?"

"No." The corner of Chris's mouth kicked up. "Any gingerbread's going to go on Duncan's workshop, and I'll pound you into the ground if you warn him."

"You haven't succeeded in distracting me. I still expect you to put mining behind you after these last two days of consulting."

"You haven't distracted me, either. Duncan gets any of the silly frills."

Rob nodded. "We have a deal."

"You've wasted half the morning. I have a stupid basement to dig in the heat of the day now that you're done clucking like a hen."

Rob grabbed his medical satchel and a slip of paper. He'd already composed the order for the house—including all of the "standard" features, which included a plethora of the frills Chris was grousing about. In addition to the house, Rob had estimated enough boards to construct the partitions in the downstairs to create the washroom and Duncan's workshop. He grinned to himself. Chris agreed to the bargain that Duncan got all of the gingerbread—but Chris didn't consider one important fact: Duncan could put the gingerbread wherever he wanted to.

∞

"Grossvater is in the cornfield." Mercy pinned Peter's shirt to the clothesline.

Doc didn't stride off. Instead, he announced, "I sent for the house and extra lumber to construct Duncan's workshop."

"The men will all want to help, but this kit—will it come with instructions?"

"Aye, and each piece is numbered. 'Twill require two cars on the train to hold all of the material."

Mercy kept hanging up clothes. "Two! That much to make a house?"

"It surprised me, too." Rob reached over and held the hem of the dress she'd taken from the basket.

"You'll get wet." She tried to tug it away.

"I'm sweltering, lass. That's not a threat; 'tis a promise." After she pinned the calico dress to the line, he pinched the cloth on either side of the waist. "You'll be needing new frocks soon."

Mercy pretended she hadn't seen nor heard him.

"You've not asked, and I'm—"

"I'm not asking anything." She snapped a dishcloth in the air, then savagely pinned it up.

"Between Christmas and New Year's." His words came out in a patient tone. "I just thought you might want to know."

Heat soared from her bodice to her forehead. Rattled, she tried to jam the wrong end of a clothespin onto the line.

"If it's too hard for you to discuss, I could write down a few things for you."

"Let me be!" Once she cried out the words, Mercy felt guilty. "I don't want to be rude. Just please leave me alone."

"I respect you immensely, Miss Stein, and I'll respect your wishes." He didn't even pause but changed the topic. "Your grandda is healing better than I anticipated, but I'd best not find him working too hard. If he is, I'll scold him like he's six instead of sixty."

"Duncan's with him."

"Good, good." He nodded. "Duncan's grown quite fond of your grandda and Peter. They didn't get a single nibble whilst fishing yester noon because the three of them kept trading jokes and made too much noise."

"Fish don't have ears."

"Ah, but they do." The doctor pulled a pair of britches from the basket and held it to the line so she could hang it. "They have an ear stone and little hairs inside at the back of the head. They sense vibration—much like you feel the vibration of a tuning fork or a bell."

"Hmm."

"Just because we canna see something doesna mean 'tisn't there."

Everyone knows that. Why would he say such an odd thing?

"Though I canna see the Almighty, I still know He's with me because of how He resonates in my heart."

I used to feel that way. Now I don't. God hasn't listened to me or talked to my heart for months now. She glanced at the doctor, and he gave her a quizzical look. Embarrassed at her thoughts, she stammered, "It is odd, you speaking of fish and God in the same discussion."

His eyes twinkled. "Ooch! Now, lass, many a man will tell you 'tis no place like sittin' by a stream with a pole in your hand to let your heart go still. 'Be still, and know that I am God.' Aye, I'm thinkin' that verse applies to the hours when I fish."

Eager to veer away from discussing spiritual matters, she pretended to play with a clothespin. "So then, go talk to Grossvater in the cornfield. Maybe he could take you fishing sometime."

"That I will."

As the doctor walked off, Mercy hung the last of the laundry and went to the garden. She picked some vegetables and took them inside. The doctor had said he stayed busy when his heart ached. Mercy envied him. *No matter how hard I work, nothing fills up the emptiness inside me—nothing but that evil man's child.*

Chapter 9

"No being surly," Rob warned Chris as they rode to the Stein farm.

"Of course he willna be surly." Duncan thumbed back his hat. " 'Tis Peter's birthday, and Chris wouldna think to spoil it with a dark mood."

"I'm not surly." Chris shifted the box on his lap. "I'm impatient."

Duncan looked at Rob. "Peter's growin' a year older today, and I'm thinking Chris is going backward in age."

"You chose more fireworks than I did." Chris gave Duncan a mock scowl. "But if you think they're just a schoolboy's toy, I'm sure Mercy would let you stay in the kitchen and wash dishes while the rest of us enjoy the lights—don't you think, Rob?"

"We'll not light a single one till everyone can enjoy them."

Chris smirked. "Duncan, you're my witness. Rob just volunteered to do dishes."

"Aye, that he did!"

Rob chuckled. "Since when did I mind getting my hands wet? Washing dishes is a far sight easier than sterilizing my instruments."

Duncan moaned.

"Keep talking about that." Chris grinned at Rob. "Duncan goes green whene'er he even hears about blood and gore. It means there'll be more food for us."

As they approached the farmhouse, Peter ran out to greet them. "We get to have a picnic! Grossvater said we could!"

As they hitched their horses, Peter hopped from one foot to the other. "You got three horses now?"

"Aye, we do." Chris gave his gelding an affectionate pat.

"Was yours sick, too?"

"Nae. Just bad-tempered. His owner didn't know how to treat him."

"There's not a beast alive Chris couldn't charm," Duncan boasted.

Mercy came out onto the veranda. "Except a skunk."

Rob chortled. "Aye, and that's the truth. Chris, will you be telling the lass, or do I?"

Mercy's eyes widened. "The skunk didn't—"

"No," Chris snapped. He heaved a sigh. "You were right. The skunk was in that log. While she went to our porch for the eggs, I chopped up the log so she'd move on."

"And she took every last one of her kits with her," Duncan added.

Rob gave Mercy a slow smile. "So mayhap you ought to be reminding Chris what gingerbread is to go on the new house."

"I'll remind him later." Mercy pushed a golden strand of hair behind her ear. "I wouldn't want to spoil his appetite."

"Mercy made a cake for me. Wanna come see?"

"Later, Peter." Mercy made a shooing motion. "Go take the blanket and spread it out. Don't lay it by the redbud tree. There's an anthill there."

"And after I do, I getta choose a watermelon."

"Now, I think I'm going to have to set this box down and help you with that chore. We'll find the biggest watermelon in the garden."

Peter went up on tiptoe. "What's in the box?"

"A surprise." Chris set the box down on the veranda. "It'll be the last thing we do today."

Peter shuffled backward. "It's not a switch is it?"

"What," Rob asked, "would make you think of a thing like that?"

"Johann's father says that when he's been naughty."

"I see." Rob heard the gritty undertone in Chris's voice.

"Mr. Honig is a firm man, but fair." In spite of the heat, Mercy wrapped her arms around herself. "It's a case of his bark being worse than his bite."

"That's good to know." Chris straightened up.

"I think you'd better worry about my bite." Rob grinned. "I'm smelling fried chicken. While the others go spread out the picnic blanket and choose a melon, I'll come help with the food."

"That kind of help will leave the rest of us hungry," Duncan predicted.

"He wouldn't do that to us." Peter looked up at him. "Would you, Doctor?"

"Never. I'd be sure to save out three pieces—one for you, another for your sister, and the last one for your grandda."

"Does the gizzard count as a piece? It's awful small."

"Seeing as it's your birthday, I'd save that one for you as a treat."

"Okay, but I like the leg."

"Hey!" Chris looked at Duncan and half bellowed in outrage, "They're plotting to leave us out."

Duncan crooked his finger at Peter. A moment later, he whispered something in the boy's ear that sent him into a fit of giggles.

"The both of you are up to no good."

"And what else would you expect of us?" Duncan settled his arm around Peter.

Five minutes later, Rob held a tray with dishes on it. A substantial thump sounded from one of the bedrooms, and an immediate *shhh!* followed.

"What—" Mercy wheeled around toward that room.

"Else do we need to take out?" Rob cut in as he stepped in front of her. He tilted his head toward the direction of more rustling and winked. "That chicken platter is heavy. Do you want to take it out now"—he shook his head from side to side—"or get it on the next trip?" He nodded.

Mercy took the cue. "Perhaps the next trip. Right now, I could take the potato salad out."

"Aye. That's a fair plan. So off we go. How many watermelons are in your garden?"

"I haven't counted." Mercy stepped out of the house.

Rob followed and immediately set down the tray and held a finger up to his lips. He shut the door and stomped twice in place, then lightened his footfall to imitate the sound of them walking away. He winked at Mercy.

She carefully set down the bowl she carried and gave him a baffled look.

He held up one hand and crooked one finger at a time to count down five seconds. "Ah-ha!" Rob shouted as he threw open the door.

Peter screamed, and Duncan caught the platter of chicken before it fell. They traded a guilty look.

"What's wrong?" Chris demanded as he hastened up the steps.

"What's wrong?" Duncan groused. "I'll tell you what's wrong. You didn't cause sufficient diversion!"

Mercy's eyes popped wide open. "Christopher, you were a part of this, too?"

"It's your fault," Chris retorted.

Pressing her hand to her bosom and sounding completely bewildered, Mercy said, "I am to blame?"

"Aye, 'tis a fact." Chris nodded.

Rob smiled at her. "You're a grand cook, and we're desperately hungry men."

Mercy laughed. "You are all little boys having your fun. Now, everyone, carry something and we will have supper."

Duncan held fast to the chicken platter and headed out the door. The look on his face dared anyone to reach for a bite. Mercy slipped to the side and picked up the bowl she'd set down, while Chris rumbled to Rob, "She thinks 'twas all a game."

Duncan let out a bark of laughter.

Rob couldn't. He was too focused on Mercy to pay much attention to his brothers. For the first time since he'd met her, Mercy had laughed.

Throughout supper, Rob hoped to hear her laugh again. Chris and Duncan were in rare form, teasing one another and pulling Peter or Mr. Stein into the middle of nonsensical debates. Mercy smiled a time or two, but that was it.

After they'd demolished the supper and decimated the cake, Chris surveyed the scattered collection of plates. "Well, Rob, I'm thinking you willna hae to work too hard, washing the dishes. We practically licked them clean for you already."

"Speak for yourself," Duncan said in an affronted tone. "You might hae eaten like a ravening beast, but I didna stoop to that level. Neither did Rob. We sopped up the last morsels wi' Mercy's fine bread."

"That, we did." Rob grinned. "It was efficient and mannerly. Mercy, you'll have to excuse Chris. He's never been one to act civilized."

The banter continued as they carried everything back to the house. Even as Rob washed the dishes, Duncan dried them, and Mercy put them away, lighthearted teasing kept on.

"Now?" Peter pled. "Now can I see what's in the box?"

"Sure." Duncan swung Peter upside down and carried him in that position out onto the porch. " 'Twill be dark enough to play with these in just a little while."

"I can't open the box when I'm hanging like this."

"Rob," Chris asked, "did you hear that? Peter's seven now, and he's still a weakling. Do you have a tonic to help?"

"Eww!" Peter squirmed. "Tonics taste awful. I don't want any!"

Duncan flipped him right side up and set him down. "I dinna blame you. Rob's potions taste e'en worse than his cooking—and that's saying a lot."

Peter knelt by the box and pried off the lid. "Grossvater! Look! A giant paper candle!"

"It's called a Roman candle." Duncan sat beside Peter. "It's a firework. They're beautiful but dangerous."

Peter accidentally bumped the box. "Mercy! There are two of those Roman paper candle fireworks."

"Gently lift those off and look deeper in the box," Rob instructed.

Peter eagerly complied. Three more layers yielded an assortment of fireworks. "Can we set them all on fire now?"

"It would be safest to have a few buckets of water on hand first," Rob said. "Don't you think so, Mercy?"

"Ja, that would be wise."

After Peter fetched the water, Rob insisted that three buckets of sand were also smart. "If something accidentally goes up in flame, we need to be ready."

Mercy gave Rob a puzzled look as Peter dashed off after one last bucket. "Do you not want him to set off the fireworks?"

"Oh, we will. I was delaying a bit because when it's darkest, the lights shine more brightly."

They all enjoyed the showers of light. As the last one burst into a wondrous display, Rob looked at Mercy. He'd hoped to see joy shining in her eyes. Instead, the sadness he saw there made his breath freeze in his lungs. Just as quickly, he tamped down his emotions. Pity would cripple her. The prudent thing to do was to treat her just as if she weren't tormented by the violence that begot the bairn she carried. *If I'm to be able to treat her medically, I must not allow compassion to weaken me. She has friends and family—there are a strong handful of those, but she'll have but one doctor—me. They can fret o'er her emotions. Me—'tis her health and that of the babe with which I must concern myself. I'll guard my professional demeanor and keep enough distance that I not lose my objectivity.*

∞

Mercy filled a bucket with cool water and grabbed a pair of dish towels. She walked out into the field.

"Danke." Grossvater dipped the first towel into the water and handed it to Duncan, then wet the other. The men continued to discuss plans for threshing as they cooled down—first with the damp cloths, then by taking huge gulps straight from the edge of the pail.

"Lunch will be ready in an hour." She headed back toward the house. Duncan and Christopher Gregor had participated in the reaping of the fields, and the wheat had dried. Men in the county pulled together to do the next step—moving from one farm to the next with the big steam threshing machine. Women helped one another feed all those hungry men—at least they always had. This year was different.

Grossvater owned the only reaper in the county, and everyone had borrowed it. Years ago, all of the farmers went together and bought a thresher. Each farm used it in turn, in the same pattern as the reaping went. The Stein farm would be the first to have all the men come for threshing.

But Mercy knew the women wouldn't all come with big vats of food and fill the day with happy chatter. They barely spoke to her at all, and only when it was unavoidable. Carmen and her sister felt the same way the doctor and his brothers did—that she bore no blame for the child. Asking Carmen and Ismelda to come help cook had been embarrassing, but Mercy had done so to avoid the shame of not being able to feed the men.

She dreaded threshing day. Three days later, as soon as the men began to arrive, Mercy knew her fears had been well founded.

Chapter 10

My mother—she is not feeling so good today. She sent this." Otto pushed a large bowl into Ismelda's hands.

"She's sick?" Ismelda made a sympathetic sound. "Is there anything I can do to help?"

Mercy tore herself away from the scene just outside her kitchen door. It all hurt so much—for Otto to be courting another girl so soon, for his mother to have suddenly turned cold and silent, and for the women to all shun her as they did.

Over the next half hour, man after man arrived. A few ventured toward the kitchen with a dish or loaf of bread. Weak excuses accompanied those offerings.

Working feverishly, the three women did all they could. Carmen had come over for the past two days to help make things in advance. Even then, as the men all washed up at the huge tubs of water and Mercy scrambled to put the last dishes on the tables, she worried there wouldn't be enough to satisfy them.

Texas held many different cultures, but until recently the German community had stayed pretty much to itself. Foods the men expected were on the table—ham, roast beef, fried chicken, mashed potatoes and gravy, cucumber salad, coleslaw, pickles, pickled beets, watermelon pickles, green tomato relish—but also now, there were dishes they'd not known. The exotic dishes Carmen and Ismelda made seemed so out of place—yet Mercy pretended the spread was the same as it had traditionally been.

Grossvater raised his hand in the air, and the men went quiet. "I want to thank all my friends and neighbors for their help. Let's say grace and eat!"

Well-worn straw hats came off.

The food flew off the tables just as quickly. Between filling cups and putting out more food, Mercy had an excuse to dash around and not speak.

In times past, the men spoke little as they ate—mostly just, "Pass me the gravy," and, "Good chicken, Miss Stein." This meal, as if to make up for the lack of women calling things to one another, the men tried to fill the silence with hearty jokes or conversation. The awkwardness didn't keep them from decimating apple pie, raisin pie, blue plum *kuchen* and cakes. The custard with caramel on it that Carmen called flan seemed to please the men.

When the men went back to work, Carmen surveyed the tables. "I've never seen men pounce on food like that!"

"They liked your ta-mals."

Carmen laughed. "Tamales. I didn't make them very spicy. If I want, I can season them so your tongue begs for deliverance."

"I like sweet foods and tangy things—not so much the hot ones." Mercy stacked the empty pie tins. "I hope a little of your flan is left. The men praised it lavishly."

"A few grunts are lavish praise?" Ismelda shook her head. "Such a strange custom."

"Be sure I am very thankful for all your hard work." After the dishes were all washed, dried, and put away, Mercy pressed a small cloth bag into Carmen's hand. "Molasses cookies."

"Oh, you know how I love them!"

Ismelda gave her a hug. "Thank you, Mercy, for letting everyone know that we're still friends. I know you truly wish Otto and me every happiness."

"I do." Mercy stared down at the grimy hem of her apron. "You saw today—the other women didn't come. I will not blame you if—"

"Nonsense!" Carmen gave her a stormy look. "You're my friend. Nothing will change that."

"Exactly." Ismelda grinned. "Now will you write down the recipe for that cucumber salad?"

Mercy obligingly did so. By late afternoon, the chugging of the M. Rumley steam thresher stopped. Not long after, all the men left. Those whose wives sent food came to the back veranda to fetch the dishes, and Mercy had all of the dishes lined up there for them—each with a small bag of molasses cookies to show her thanks.

There were enough leftovers for her to feed Grossvater and Peter supper. Mercy didn't have much of an appetite. She went to bed and curled up, feeling horribly alone. Always in the past, threshing was a day of joy—thankfulness to God for a good harvest mingled with the merry visiting of neighbors. *But God let that man hurt me, and the women who are my sisters in Christ have turned their backs on me.*

Sleep wouldn't come.

The sky was still violet. Soon, the rooster would be crowing the sun up. Mercy lay in bed and stared at her bedside table. A thin layer of dust covered her Bible. She hadn't read the Word for weeks now. Setting aside quiet time for devotions was too hard. The minute she ceased doing chores she started drowning in a sea of feelings.

Deciding what to make for breakfast, she shoved off the sheet. It was far too hot to use blankets. Suddenly, she froze. Lying still, she closed her eyes and tried to steady her breathing. A few minutes later, it happened again—an infinitesimal fluttering low in her tummy. Light as butterfly wings, the sensation came and left again.

The baby?

Mercy slid her hand down the soft-from-a-hundred-washings cotton nightgown. Resting her palm where she'd experienced the sensation, she waited. And waited. And waited.

Is that you?

⌒

"Hello, Dr. Gregor! Welcome! You're just in time—the men are coming in for lunch."

Rob didn't dismount immediately. "I was concerned about you, Mrs. Kunstler. My brothers said Otto mentioned you were feeling puirly."

"I'm hale as a horse. I don't know where—" She halted abruptly as color rushed to her cheeks.

Crossing his hands on the saddle's pommel, he looked across the table. "Mrs. Grun, I'm glad to see the terrible sprain you had yesterday has healed so swiftly. You're walking without any difficulty. Mrs. Voran, Mrs. Stucky—I'm gratified to see your children are bounding around so easily. I was made to understand they were ailing yesterday, as well."

Mrs. Kunstler bustled past him and waved the men over. "Come. Yes, come now. Dinner is ready. There is plenty!"

Chris yelled, "Rob, what are you doing here?"

Rob shrugged. "A whole lot of nothing, much to my surprise. Just yesterday, you said many of the women or children were sick. I'm delighted to report everyone's in the very pink of health."

Rob joined the men at the washstands, then ate with them. As he rose, he said, "What a grand meal this was. I've never seen men eat half as much. You women—all of you women—worked hard to keep sufficient food on the table."

"We all help one another," Jakob Lintz said.

"Ahh. So that's it." Rob nodded his head sagely. "None of the ladies went to help at the Stein's threshing yesterday. I'm supposing 'twas because none of us Gregors thought to pledge that one or two of us would work the threshing on the Stein's behalf." He let out a big sigh. "I'm relieved. Aye, I surely am. I should have known better than to worry as I did."

"Worry?" someone asked.

"Aye. I'm ashamed to confess I worried mayhap something else was behind puir wee Mercy working her fingers to the bone. Now I see 'twasna a case of anyone reviling the lass. Glad I am of it, too. She's but an innocent lamb, hurt in the verra worst way by a godless beast of a man. She and the babe—I'm glad to know you'll all be thinkin' kindly of them and extending Christian charity toward them through the coming months and years."

"I'm sure you're right, Rob." Duncan stood and scanned the young women who stood around the edge of the yard, their hands full of empty pie plates. "I'm betting not a man here hasna given thought to the fact that it could have been his daughter or granddaughter who fell victim to such a tragedy. Connant told us this community was strong in the Lord. 'Twas our fault—the Gregors should have pledged to you all that we'd represent the Steins. From now on, you can count on us."

"Aye, that you can." Chris slapped a straw hat on his head. "Now I'm getting back to work ere I yield to the temptation to take a nap after all that food."

Rob rode over to the Steins'. Mercy was in the garden wielding a hoe. Rob dismounted and chuckled. "I canna help wonderin' whether you're merely killin' that weed or if you're trying to send it clear down to the devil himself this verra minute!"

"I'd gladly send him and all his brothers."

"This is a lovely garden patch. You must have quite a fondness for sweet corn."

"We all do." Mercy surveyed the long rows of corn. Suddenly her eyes went wide and her hand went to her middle.

"The babe's bootin' you, eh?" Rob made a casual gesture. "The timing is right. The next three months, you'll not be feeling so sleepy. The last three, you'll be worn out and have your back achin' fiercely, but that's all to be expected."

"Oh."

She's not cutting me off. I dinna dare push too far, but the lass needs help. Lord, give me the wisdom and words she needs.

" 'The barest of flutters.' " He smiled. "That's how the first mother-to-be I doctored many years back described it. Later, she declared that same babe was stompin' in hobnailed boots inside her." Hitching his shoulder, Rob admitted, " 'Twas her eleventh babe. My hands caught him—a fat, squalling boy—but that woman took a mind to tell me half of what I needed to know wasna in my medical texts."

"She told you this? Your patient?"

"Aye, and right she was." Rob casually patted his chest pocket. "Now there's a pity. After each visit I paid her, I wrote notes to myself. Ever see that small red book I carry? I could quote page upon page, but still I carry it with me on the days I'm to see a woman who's in a motherly way."

"Why?"

"That book serves as a reminder that 'tisna always the mind that teaches us the important things—ofttimes, 'tis the heart."

Mercy started hoeing again with a vengeance. "You're supposing everyone has a heart. You're wrong, Doctor. Write that down in your book, too."

Chapter 11

As soon as the bitter words left her mouth, Mercy regretted them. They were honest—but too stark. Concentrating on a small dirt clod, she beat it into oblivion as she muttered, "I should not have said that."

"And why not? There's nothing wrong with speaking the truth as you see it."

"I'm not a child. You do not need to humor me."

"I'm not humoring you. As a matter of fact, I think you have plenty of call to question if anyone has a heart. You've suffered greatly because of what others have done."

She stared at the soil. "It was not others about whom I spoke. It is myself."

"Without a doubt, Miss Stein, you have a heart of gold. You love your brother and grandda. You even pet baby skunks."

"It does not say much for my character that I care for the young, the old, and the helpless. These days, those are all I do care for."

"Your heart has been wounded as surely as any other injury you have suffered. To my way of thinking, there's nothing wrong with you guarding yourself. You need time."

"Time will not help." Mercy stared at the earth. If anything, time would only make matters worse. People already shunned her. How much worse would it become when her belly grew huge? And how would they treat her after she had the babe?

How will they treat the baby? The thought made her breath

catch. Until this morning, she'd resented the life she carried. All she'd been able to link it to was the horrific act. Only now things seemed different. That life was so very small, so helpless. *The gentle-as-raindrop patter I felt inside—how could I have thought I would hate such a thing?*

"Time doesn't cure everything." The doctor let out a rueful chuckle. "If it did, I'd be out of business. What I've found is, as weeks and months go by, we gain wisdom and are better able to make decisions."

"I have no decisions to make." Mercy's head shot up, and she stared at him. "These days, all I do is live with the way things are because of what others have done or thought or believed."

"I'd be a fool of a man if I said what others think and believe doesna matter. Instead, though, why not give some consideration to what it is that you think and believe?"

Embarrassed that she'd been blurting out thoughts she ought to have kept private, Mercy decided to sidestep his probing question. "What I think is that I have chores to do. All the talk in the world won't get them done."

"These cabbages here look ripe and ready. How many are you wantin' me to pick?"

"I didn't mean for you to set your hand to my work!"

The doctor squatted down and absently brushed a little dirt from the side of the nearest head of cabbage. "I wasna born with a scalpel in my hand. Some of my most cherished memories are of helpin' Ma in our garden." He smiled at Mercy. "I confess, I often took a can along, just in case a worm turned up. Fish and vegetables make a fine meal."

"Why did you come here today?"

"I had a couple of reasons." He reached toward her. "Knife."

"How do you know I have a knife with me?" Ever since *that day*, she'd carried a knife in her apron pocket.

"Any practical woman would when her garden brimmed like this." He accepted the knife, cut a cabbage, and hefted the head a few times. "Round and heavy and the color's good." He tilted his head to the side. "I've said the selfsame thing about a few of the babes I've delivered."

I knew not to trust him. She turned away as she said in a flat tone, "You came to talk to me of the child of my shame."

"Stop right there." He straightened up and stepped in front of her. "Whatever else you think, Mercy Stein, know this: I have not, and I never will think of you as being shamed. Shame implies you did something that makes you guilty. You did nothing wrong."

"If I did nothing wrong, then why is God punishing me?" She slapped her hand over her mouth and stepped backward, away from him. Something hit her ankle, and she started to fall.

"Careful." The doctor's fingers clamped around her wrist and drew her upright. His strength amazed her. Until now, he'd always been restrained and gentle. His brothers came and did physical labor, so the fact that he was every bit as tall and broad as they hadn't registered. "The hoe was behind you, lass."

"You're strong." It came out as an accusation.

"That fact needn't trouble you. I've taken an oath to heal, not to harm."

Mercy stared at him. *How did he know I'm afraid?* Just as quickly, she resented the fact that he knew of her vulnerability. "You talk too boldly."

"I'm a plainspoken man. Hiding behind fancy words never suited me. Cutting to the heart of a matter is best. I admire how you've been doing that today. The things you've said thus far—you've shown rare courage for admitting what others would gloss o'er."

Courage? Mercy shook her head. "How can you tell me not to be troubled by your strength in one minute, only to suggest I'm brave in the next?"

"Because until you're honest enough to confess your doubts and fears, you canna get beyond them. God created us with physical bodies, but just as surely He filled us with feelings and placed a soul within us. 'Tisna just your body that is changing. Your feelings and faith are, too. You've come to the point where you recognize that fact."

Mercy watched him nod his head as if he'd just solved the problems instead of starkly laying them out. Loneliness swamped her. No one could possibly understand—

"I'll not insult you by spouting platitudes and saying I know how deep your sorrows flow." The doctor gave her wrist a tiny squeeze, then loosened his hold and slid his hand down until his fingers laced with hers. "I came today to promise to help you through the weeks and months—aye, and e'en the years ahead. As your doctor, I'll inform you what to expect.

"If you'd like, I'll loan you my little red book. I took care not to write the woman's name in it, and she gave me leave to put down whate'er I wished. You needn't worry that we'd be prying into her privacy. Think on it and let me know if you'd like that. Since you dinna hae a mother or grandma here to instruct you from a woman's perspective, it might be nice."

Mercy couldn't unknot all of the feelings coiling inside her. His offer was everything she needed but not what she wanted. Why couldn't one of the ladies from church pay a visit and privately teach her such intimate things? But the women all kept their distance and withheld their counsel—yet the doctor didn't because he felt she and this babe were blameless.

"You asked why God is punishing you. Terrible things happen, but they are not always His doing."

"But He lets them happen."

"There's no denying that." He paused. "Hae you e'er noticed that for all the trials that beset Job, God ne'er took His hand off the man? Just as surely as I stand here and hold your hand in mine, He is with you and has not loosened His grip."

One by one, Mercy uncurled her fingers. She dragged her hand free from the doctor's hold. "Job's friends still stayed by his side."

The doctor snorted. "Some friends. Even Job's wife told him to 'Curse God, and die.' That kind of help is worse than none a-tall. Job held fast to his faith, and that's why the story has such a grand ending."

"There's not a good ending for my story. There can't be."

"I disagree. To say that, you give up your faith in God's love and goodness."

Mercy closed her eyes. Pain washed over her. The loneliness she felt wasn't just for friends. In the maelstrom life had become, she'd lost her faith, too.

"Earlier, you asked why God's punishing you. In the midst of all this, dinna be shy of asking those hard questions."

"It makes no difference," she said in a tone that sounded as heavy as her heart felt. "There are no answers."

"I've noticed something. Christians who grow up as believers most often come to a crisis at some point in life. 'Tis then all they were told is stripped away. All they have left is a skeleton of faith. Just as your grandda has had to work to build up his wounded muscles, you have to build up your strength of faith so you can continue on your walk with the Lord. 'Tis by asking the questions, praying, and reading the Word that you will succeed."

I can't get past asking the questions. Praying and reading the Bible—I can't. As soon as she told herself that, something inside shot back, *Can't, or won't?*

∞

"Here is your book." Mercy's voice was barely audible as she palmed the tiny leather book to Robert.

He casually tucked it into his pocket and surveyed the huge assortment of crates and dishes in the back of her buckboard. "You brought enough food to feed an army for a year."

"Everyone is talking about your house kit. I expect a whole army of men to come help. They would come anyway, but their curiosity will have them arrive early and leave late."

"Hot as it's been, it makes sense that we start early." Rob hefted the closest crate. "Do you have any particular order to this?"

"That one can be stored back—it is for late in the day. This one," she said as she started to lift another, "I will need—"

"Put that down." Rob's throat ached with restraint. It took every shred of self-control not to roar the order at her.

"It is not heavy. I—"

He shifted the crate he held to one side and jerked the other from her. "Go open the screen door."

She scampered ahead. Once inside, Rob set down the crates and turned on her. "You canna be lifting things like this."

"I'm not weak. I put them all in the wagon myself."

"Miss Stein, it has nothing to do with strength. Your delicate condition—" The color flooding her cheeks left him feeling crass and mean. He'd made his point, so he changed tactics. "Three men live here. We're strong of muscle but feeble in the kitchen. Stay here and direct us as to where you want each crate to go."

"Cabbage and carrots in this one," Duncan announced as he carried in a bushel basket.

"Go ahead and put those wherever you want," Chris said as he entered on Duncan's heels. "I've got strudel here. I'm taking it upstairs. If either of you says a word about it, you won't get a bite."

Mercy shook her finger. "Christopher Gregor, you behave yourself."

"I am. I offered to share this with my brothers."

"You will share it with all of your brothers in Christ tomorrow morning."

"If any is left, I will." Chris sounded downright reasonable.

Mercy smiled. "You cannot always have whatever you grab for."

Chris scowled at Rob. "She's teasing, right?"

Mercy's head dipped. "I am not that kind of woman."

"Hey—I didn't mean—"

Rob swiped the strudel and set it on the cramped "kitchen" table. "Chris, you're thinkin' with your belly instead of your brain. Mercy, you'd think the man's never eaten a single morsel."

"Your logic is flawed," Chris snapped back. "It's because I've eaten Mercy's strudel that I'm claiming it. She should be flattered by that fine praise."

"Mercy, Chris is too dense to apologize properly." Rob tapped the toe of his boot a few times. "But now that Chris has given it consideration, he's wanting to let you choose another piece of gingerbread for the house."

"I am not!"

Duncan slapped Chris on the back. "We should have known you'd be in a generous mood, Chris. Mercy, he wants you to choose two."

Mercy's head was still bowed. Rob glared at Chris to make

him watch his words, then pasted on a smile. Tilting Mercy's face upward, Rob asked, "So what do you think?"

"I think you Scotsmen are crazy."

"Not as crazy as my house is going to look," Chris muttered.

"*Our* house." Duncan shoved Chris toward the door.

"I'm going to have the last word," Chris growled. "Just you wait and see."

Rob stepped closer to Mercy. Her eyes widened and the pulse at her throat pounded far too fast. *I've got to teach her she's safe with me.* "I have to tell you something secret."

Chapter 12

"You do?"

He nodded and crooked his finger. She hesitated for a moment, then leaned the tiniest bit closer. Rob cupped his hand and leaned toward her ear. "Chris and I have an agreement."

Her brows puckered.

"He decided to give all of the gingerbread to Duncan, and I agreed—other than all of the pieces he owes you."

"Duncan does not know this?" Mercy started to pull away.

Rob closed the space and whispered, "Duncan doesna know yet. . . but the jest is on Chris. He wasna mindful of his words when we came to the pact. Duncan gets all the gingerbread—but Chris didna think to say where Duncan had to put it."

Mercy's lips parted in surprise.

"Whatever this is," Chris declared as he returned with two large pans, "it smells good."

"It is not for you." Mercy scooted past Rob and swiped a pan from Chris.

Chris let go, but he got a fierce look on his face and held fast to the second one. "Why not?"

A smile lifted Mercy's lips. "Because you do not like gingerbread."

∽

"I've never seen such a mess," Mercy said that noon.

"Ooch, 'tis true." Rob wiped his brow. "But 'tis an organized mess. Since Chris has gotten everyone working on a specific portion of the kit, the chaos has ceased."

Mercy heaved a sigh. "You are a man of science, Robert. An intelligent man. How can you stand in the midst of this madness and hold out any hope that such confusion will build your house?"

"I have faith."

Mercy gave him a dubious look.

Rob motioned toward the lot. "The frame is almost done, and the external walls are coming along. Suddenly, everything will fit together. Wait and see."

"Two days. It has been two days, and still, it has so far to go. Do you know that these same men who are helping you all get together and put up an entire barn in just one day?"

"By tomorrow, the bulk of the work will be done. The rest, Chris wants to do on his own. He's gotten excited by the challenge."

"Excited? Is that what you call it when he complained about the bay window? Or is excited when he stubbed the toe of his boots against the scalloped shingles for the bottom half of the front wall?"

"Nae, lass. Those moments were just mild irritations. Excited was when he bellowed because you'd bested in that bargain you struck." Rob chortled softly. "I dinna think Chris will e'er eat strudel again without thinking on how he agreed to put that onion top on the turret instead of the plain cone design he planned on."

Mercy grimaced. "In truth, Rob, I thought that was all a joke. I did not think your brother took me seriously."

"It served him right. His greed got the better of him."

"Are you saying that because he ate that whole strudel all by himself?"

The doctor's mouth kicked up into a rakish smile. "I'm not going to answer. Just you wait, though—after tomorrow, the house will be well on the way. And better still, after that, Chris will be so busy with constructing the rest, he'll not be restless and underfoot all the time."

"Perhaps I should make more bargains with him. Was there any special piece of the gingerbread you liked?"

"Let's see. You have the fan at the apex of the eaves, the onion top on the turret, and the bay window. . .and there's the fish scale clapboards in the middle third of the front. . .and the spindled veranda."

"Don't forget the pretty scrolled gingerbread in the upper corners of the windows."

"I couldn't forget that." The doctor's grin grew wider still. "That was when Chris started moaning that the place was going to wind up looking more like a wedding cake than a house."

"I think you are enjoying this," Mercy accused.

"And I think, Mercy Ellen Stein, that you are a very smart young woman." The doctor walked off, calling, "Chris, Mercy and I were just talking. . ."

Chris let out a groan that sounded over all the hammering.

∽

"What a pretty new apron!" Carmen greeted from her veranda.

"Thank you." Good manners demanded Mercy acknowledge the compliment, even though she'd hoped no one would notice her apron. Instead of the bibbed, tie-in-the-back aprons she'd always worn, this one reminded her of a pretzel. The front hung from neck to hem, but the back pieces swooped up to the opposite shoulders. Instead of accentuating a slender waist, this one was meant to hide a tummy that now bulged outward.

"Everything's ready." Carmen hobbled down the walkway. "Duncan Gregor brought over canning jars last night."

"Good." Relief flooded Mercy. She didn't want to have to walk down the street and into the mercantile. Ever since the week of threshing, people had changed. The women didn't avoid or shun her anymore—but they took pains to avoid the topic of childbearing, babies, and child-rearing. That left awkward silences and tense moments whenever Mercy was around.

Her hand slid into her apron pocket. The doctor's little red book was there. Every couple of weeks, he'd slip it to her. She'd pore over the pages at night in her room. Each time she returned the book, Mercy felt as if she'd lost a friend. Every time the doctor left it in her keeping, solace blanketed her.

"What are you daydreaming about?"

"Oh!" Mercy jumped. A thought flashed through her mind. "I cannot remember if I took the iron off the stove."

"In this heat, you shouldn't be ironing anything other than Sunday-best clothes." Carmen linked arms with her and started dragging her across the street.

"This is the wrong way," Mercy said in a wry tone.

"I suppose I'd better warn you, we have more to do than we'd planned on."

"Why is that?"

"The doctor's been paid for several accounts in the past week."

"I see."

Carmen giggled. "Mercy, you're too nice. Ismelda's been moaning all morning about it."

"She decided she liked the pickles we made last time with the cucumbers."

"But this time, it's—well, you just have to see this for yourself." Carmen led her around the side of the doctor's office to the yard between it and the fancy new house as she whispered, "I didn't want to miss this."

Mercy took a look and started to shake.

∞

It would be rude to laugh. Truly, it would. Mercy covered her mouth and pretended to muffle a cough while she marshaled her self-control.

Duncan stopped poking at the armadillo and rapped on it with his knuckles. " 'Tis like a knight's armor."

"There's got to be a chink in it. Every defense has a weakness," Chris declared as he rolled the creature over.

The doctor came out of the house with every cutting tool ever invented. "Good morning, Mercy! Have you seen them?"

Mercy bit her lip and nodded.

The doctor laid out an ax, a cleaver, four knives, a saw, a scalpel, and a pair of pruning shears. " 'Tis a most curious beast. The exoskeleton is osseous—reminiscent of a turtle or a crab, but—"

"Rob," Chris half growled, "hot as 'tis, the beasts are going to cook in their shells if you muse all the morning long about their scientific merits."

"I doubt the hide's usable." Duncan drummed his fingers on the odd-looking beast.

"My grandmother had a purse made from one," Carmen said. "She used it to carry all of her healing herbs."

"Very interesting." Duncan stared at the armadillo more critically. "So how was the shell cut?"

While Carmen and he spoke, Mercy sidled closer to the doctor. She slid her hand into her pocket and fingered the little book, took a deep breath, and passed it to him. Subtle as could be, he tucked it in his pocket.

"I saw Cletus." The sheriff sauntered up. "He said he paid you four armadillos. Any of them a hairy screamer?"

"Hairy screamer?" Mercy echoed.

The doctor turned his attention on the sheriff. "Are there different varieties?"

"Don't be so gullible, Rob." Chris elbowed him. "Connant's grinning like a fool. This creature is so odd, God wouldn't have created more than one type. Even Mercy thought 'hairy screamer' was absurd."

"Chris, you're such a skeptic," the sheriff said. His grin didn't fade in the least. He nodded toward the armadillo on the battered wooden table. "Those are good eating. Taste a lot like—"

"Chicken?" Chris inserted in a disbelieving tone. "Have you noticed how everything is supposed to taste like chicken? Snake, for example."

The sheriff ignored him. "Pork. Armadillo tastes like a nice, juicy pork roast. Funny things, though. They can swim."

"Texas tall tale," Chris muttered.

"Texas tales are an important tradition," Mercy said. "You are supposed to admire them."

"That's right," the sheriff nodded. "But armadillos' talents don't stop at swimming. They can jump hip high when they need to."

The doctor chortled softly. "Aye, Connant. I'm supposing though they've wee, stubby legs and claws made perfect for burrowing, they'd far rather jump o'er fences than skitter below."

"This one's got the best-looking hide. Let's butcher one of the others first." Duncan dropped it down beside the other three.

With a shriek, one of the others jumped astonishingly high and plopped loudly onto the table.

Instantly, the doctor whisked Mercy behind his back. Duncan shouted, and Carmen screamed. Mercy couldn't see around the doctor's broad shoulders, and he kept her against his spine in an unyielding hold. "Check the others," he ordered someone.

The sheriff's whooping laugh stopped just long enough to

declare, "You wouldn't have believed me if I said they sometimes play dead."

"Cletus said they were dead," Duncan said.

"Well, that one is surely dead now," Chris asserted.

The doctor's hold eased. In a lithe move, he turned around and held Mercy by her shoulders. "Are you all right, lass?"

She nodded.

" 'Twas a shock. Let's sit you down."

"I'm okay."

Carmen let out a nervous giggle. "I told you we had to be here, Mercy."

The sight on the table made Mercy's brows rise.

Dr. Gregor pivoted to block her view and tugged on her arm. "Come, now. 'Tisna good for you to see such things."

Mercy looked into his steady eyes. "I think Christopher has been taking lessons from me—from when I kill chickens. But I just use the ax and behead a chicken. Your brother—he used the ax and a knife and—"

"If," the doctor interrupted as he tried to divert her from what his brother had done, "your fried armadillo tastes half as good as your fried chicken, 'twill be fine eating, indeed."

"Oh no." Carmen shook her head. "Roasted, barbecued, or in a casserole. That's how they're cooked."

"I told you they don't taste like chicken," the sheriff groused.

"When you have them butchered, we'll cook them." Carmen looked at the creature. "After all, we don't want to open the oven and have one hop out of the roasting pan."

"Are you sure?" The doctor searched Mercy's face.

She nodded solemnly. "Yes. He'd track the drippings across the floor so we couldn't make gravy."

Chapter 13

"When other helpers fail and comforts flee, Help of the helpless, O abide with me."

Robert followed the soft alto notes of the plaintive hymn and found Mercy in the field. She wore a cloth bag over her left shoulder and was stooping to pick beans. The fullness of that gathering sack couldn't hide the distinctly maternal shape of her form.

"Hello." Rob plucked several beans and slid them into the gathering sack. For the first time, Mercy didn't reflexively flinch or scoot away to avoid any proximity. He hummed a few bars of the hymn, then picked a few more beans. Without looking at her he said, "The hymn you're singing—'twas a scant week or so after my ma's death that I heard it for the first time."

"I'm sorry. Did I make you sad?"

"Does the hymn make you sad?" he countered.

Her brows puckered. "It is not our way to speak of our feelings."

"Yet you asked me about my feelings." He held up a hand to keep her from apologizing. "It didn't offend me, Mercy. It touched me, knowing my reaction mattered to you. You've a tender heart. Knowing that as I do, canna you see how I'd care for your feelings just as you'd care for mine?"

"Sunday, the pastor—he said we must live by faith, not by feelings."

"Dinna ye think the God who gave us those feelings knows us

well enough to understand them? And that He walks beside us e'en in the valleys when the shadows are the darkest?"

She shrugged and continued to pick beans.

"The passage in Ecclesiastes comes to my mind. Recall how it speaks of the different seasons in life? On how there's a time to weep and a time to laugh, a time to mourn and a time to dance? 'Tisna that we're not to have the feelings. We're to hold fast to God regardless of the moods of our hearts."

Her hands slowed. In a barely audible voice, she whispered, "I'm reading my Bible again."

Again. The lass stopped for a time. The revelation didn't surprise him, but Rob ached for her. "God will honor your diligence. Aye, that He will. Are ye havin' a rough time talking to Him?"

Mercy's eyes grew huge, and tears filled them.

Not waiting so she'd feel pressed to give him an answer, Rob took the gathering bag from her shoulder and slid it onto his own. "Mercy, we're meant to bear one another's burdens. Just as surely as I can hold this bag, I can hold you up to the Lord. Indeed, I have been all along. I was remiss in not telling you that afore now."

Her tears spilled over.

Why didna I think to say anything long ago?

"It's so hard—praying. I don't have the words to say."

"You were talking to the Lord when I arrived. Your soul was reaching toward Him in song because your heart was too muddled to put everything into words."

"Do you think so?" Anguish tainted her thready voice.

"Aye, that I do. He hears our thoughts. He knows the desires of our hearts. Even when we're so burdened all we can manage is to groan or cry, He understands. God is faithful. He abides with you, Mercy Stein."

On the ride out to the farm, Rob had thought about presenting the possibility of Mercy relinquishing the babe and having the Heims adopt it. Each evening, he'd prayed over that issue, but God hadn't directed him to say anything yet. Rob looked at her and knew the truth: the lass couldn't make a wise decision until her heart was spiritually settled. Until then, it would be cruel to say a word.

A thought occurred to him. "Do you remember Peter's birthday?"

"The fireworks." She cleared her throat. "You Gregors brought fireworks. They were beautiful."

"Do you recall us discussing how there was only a half moon and few stars?"

She nodded.

"A good thing, that—the darker the sky, the brighter the fireworks glow. 'Tisna that the fireworks wouldn't go off just as well on a full moon's eve, but the contrast wouldna be the same. So, too, in our journey with God—on fair days, the sunlight is all we need to get by, but in the dark of night, if we seek His light, 'tis a thing of rare beauty. You might want to think on that."

Mercy nodded slowly. They worked in silence for a short time, then she cleared her throat. "Did your brothers tell you? Something is getting into the last of the melons and our pumpkins."

He chuckled. "Aye, and you ought to hear my brothers discussing how best to trap an armadillo. They took an immediate liking to that meat."

"They are hoping in vain, because Grossvater showed the tracks to Peter. He said the pest is either a raccoon or a possum. They have front prints that are much alike, but a possum's rear print is funny—it is because they have something like a thumb back there to help climb trees."

"So is it a raccoon or a possum?"

Mercy paused a moment. "I don't recall!"

"Is either of them edible?"

She wrinkled her nose. "I have heard they are, but I have never prepared them, either."

"I dinna dare ask Connant. He'd take advantage of my ignorance and weave a tale for the ages. After that crazy armadillo jumped and screamed, I'm liable to believe just about anything he'd concoct about these wild animals in America."

"You didn't have any of these animals in Scotland?"

"Skunks, armadillos, and opossums are all American creatures."

"Was it hard to give up all you'd known and come so far from home?"

" 'Twas equal parts anticipation and fear. Losing Da on the way near broke my heart—but my brothers. . ." He tucked more beans in the sack. "We're here together. That's what counts."

"And so now you make a new home."

Rob winked at her. "And we built one, too. Chris is proud of that house. Dinna e'er take exception to his grumbling. He takes a secret pride in finding ways to complain just so we can admire it aloud all over again. Remember those scalloped shingles for part of the clapboarding? Just last night, he stood in the yard and complained that our house has more scales than a fish."

Finally, a smile chased across her face and brightened her eyes. "You must tell him something. He isn't a Scotsman any longer. By telling such a tall tale, he proved he is now a Texan. That means it is not just a house; now it is a home, for this is where you will all stay. Texans never want to leave."

"So you're stuck with us forever." As soon as he spoke the thought, Rob practically dropped the harvesting bag. *I almost said "me" instead of "us." How can it be?* Just as quickly, the answer struck him with blinding clarity. *Da was right. He warned me I'd close off my feelings so I wouldna feel my patients' pain. All along, I've struggled with keeping my distance from Mercy. More and more, what she needed and wanted mattered to me. The reason—'tis plain as can be. Over these months I've lost my heart to the lass, and I didna even know it.*

Reluctantly, Mercy shut the hymnal and got up from the piano stool. Ever since the doctor pointed out how she'd been using music to talk to God, she'd found great solace in singing, playing, or even humming. Then, too, the psalms of David suddenly took on a whole new meaning. He'd been sorely troubled often in his life, yet he'd used his psalms and played his harp to tell God how he felt.

The spicy scent of pumpkin permeated the house. Pumpkins with stems would store well for a long while, but those without stems tended to spoil. She'd baked three pies and six loaves of pumpkin bread and had roasted pumpkin seeds. Tomorrow she and Carmen would make pumpkin marmalade and can puree.

Puree. Mercy stared out the window. *When do babies start eating food like that?*

Peter burst through the door.

Mercy automatically called out, "Wipe your feet!" Stubby scampered past her. She heaved a sigh and swept up the pup. "Peter, you know the rule. You must train—" Her voice died out as Grossvater shouldered past Peter to ease something through the door. He took a few steps into the house, then set the oak piece on the floor. A light push set the cradle into a gentle rock.

"There!" Grossvater nodded approvingly. "It is still as good as it was when I made it to hold your own papa."

Mercy started to shake as the runners rocked a rhythm of impending doom.

Grossvater wound his arm around her. "The day I finished this and gave it to your grandmother, we put it by our bed. Each morning, we stood beside it and prayed for a healthy child and that we would be good parents. I will stand beside you, Mercy. We will pray those same things."

I don't know if I can be a good mother. And Grossvater—he is old. He will not be here all of the years it will take to rear this babe. Panic started to envelop her. Her heart hammered loud in her ears. *Gott in Himmel, how will I ever—*

"We can do this together," Grossvater crooned.

Mercy bowed her head. She didn't want to admit her doubts or confess her worries. Regardless of his assurance, the fears exploded.

"Mr. Stein," a voice came from the doorway. "Have you—"

The beat got louder and drowned out the man's words. Boots stepped between her and the cradle—the doctor's boots. Instinctively, Mercy reached for him as everything started to swirl around her.

Chapter 14

"There now, lass." Rob blotted Mercy's colorless face. He wasn't sure whether he was trying to comfort her or reassure himself. On a medical level, she was fine—but that didn't take into account her feelings. *In the midst of her panic, she reached out to me. That counts for something.*

Another mewling sound came from her as her eyes fluttered again. This time they stayed open. Rob fought the urge to scoop her into his arms and murmur all was well. Instead, he leaned over her bed and said in a stern tone, "You canna be wearin' that whalebone cage any longer."

As she gasped, Mercy's hand fumbled beneath the bedsheet.

"I cut it off. An absolute wonder 'tis that you've not been swooning thrice a day whilst being constricted so severely." The whole time he chided her, he tenderly petted back tiny wisps of hair that coiled around her face.

"You cut it?" Her whisper held a squeak of outrage.

"The laces, I did." He scowled. "Though if you dinna give me your word that you'll leave it off, I'll consider cutting some other part to render it unusable."

Color filled her cheeks as she turned her face away.

Determined to be matter-of-fact so she'd get over her embarrassment, he stated, "You needn't fret o'er this discussion. 'Tis common sense, a woman not trussing herself up whilst she's with child—especially in her last months."

Mercy refused to look back at him. Rob placed his hand on her tummy, and she went as rigid as her stays had been. "The babe—'tis growing fast now and needs to be free to tumble." As if on cue, the mound beneath his palm squirmed. "In this next month, the freedom you give the babe is vital—'twill allow him to settle his head downward. Trussed in the corset, your body canna yield sufficient room. I'm tryin' to spare you a breech birthing."

Still, she said nothing. Until now, Mercy hadn't ever allowed him to examine her. Other than peppering their private conversations with medical information and providing her with the little red book, Rob hadn't been in a position of asserting himself. *May as well seize this opportunity.* He slid one hand over hers and dragged it downward. "Feel this? 'Tis round and hard—the babe's head. Down here, 'tis round, too—but soft. 'Tis his backside."

At least she wasn't jerking away.

"When he's kicking and pushing, which side do ye feel it on most?"

A few seconds passed, then she feathered her fingers to the left.

"Ah, so that's the way he's facin'." Rob chuckled. "And kickin'! He's got some strength."

Mercy pushed away his hands. "I have work to see to."

"As do I. I'm on my way out to pay a call on the Stuckys."

"Someone is sick?" Finally, Mercy looked at him.

"Not exactly." Rob hitched his shoulder. "Their stallion's got more spirit than sense. He kicked out of his stall. I put stitches in him late last week, and the time's come to remove them."

"They don't have a goat or a mule." Mercy held the sheet clear up to her nose. "One would help."

"How would a goat help me remove sutures?"

"A goat or a mule in a stable makes the horses calm down.

You could borrow Sadie."

"Sadie has a knack for chewing my clothes. I'll have you come along."

Mercy's eyes grew huge. "Are you calling me a goat?"

Rob stared at her. "Of course not. How did you—oh." He gave her an apologetic grin. "I can see how that must have sounded. I meant that if I had you along, you'd make Sadie behave while Sadie made the stallion mind his manners. Somewhere in the midst of that, I lost both my mind and my manners."

"It was a simple mistake is all."

He turned toward her wardrobe. "I presume your blue-and-white frock is in here." Ignoring her splutters, he opened the door and carried on in a conversational tone, "I'm not one to pay much mind to what a woman wears, but this one you've stitched for yourself caught my attention."

"Because it's the size of a revival tent," she muttered.

"Nae, not a-tall. My ma—she had a plate she dearly prized. Delft, she called it. This frock, it puts me in mind of that plate. Just seein' you in it makes my day improve."

She blinked in surprise.

"I'll drape it here and wait for you out in the parlor."

"I need to stay and see to supper. Peter can go with you."

Rob didn't argue with her. He left her room, pulled the door shut, and walked over toward the kitchen where Mr. Stein and Peter stood.

"My granddaughter—"

"Is fine." He grinned at Peter. "When your sister grew faint, I'm sure she accidentally put Stubby in the cradle. Best you take him back out to the barn ere she sees him in there."

Peter snickered and dashed to freedom with the puppy.

Rob cast a glance at the bedroom door. "Mercy's needing some fresh air. I aim to have her accompany me to the Stu—" Rob halted when Mr. Stein shook his head.

"This is not done." Mr. Stein's voice came out in the barest of whispers. "You do not know our ways. For a young man and woman to spend time together, alone—"

"I've been in Texas a little over half a year." Rob stared into the old man's eyes. In that moment, everything felt so right. "I'm fully aware of the implications. I came here today to declare my intent."

Mr. Stein shook his head. "I made a mistake once before. Without praying about it, I told Otto he could have my grand-daughter as his wife."

"I've not spoken rashly." Robert tapped his chest. "In my heart and soul, I ken Mercy's the one for me."

"Robert Gregor, you're as fine a man as God's made, but that doesn't change my stance. I'll not lean on my own understanding and let her suffer heartbreak as the result again. Until I'm certain that it is God's will for her to be yours, you are not to court her. This isn't about what men think or want. It's about waiting on the Lord and seeking His wisdom."

"Fair enough," Rob said. "Until I spoke with the Almighty o'er this, I kept silent. God doesna change. He'll be givin' you the same assurance He gave me."

Sadness radiated from Mr. Stein's craggy features. "Only a great work of God will give my Mercy any peace."

Hearing Mercy's soft footfall, Rob pointed at the pie and raised his voice ever so slightly. "Give her two pieces. I'm supposing she was so busy baking, she forgot to eat at midday."

Her door opened and she emerged.

"Mercy, when you brought lunch out to the field, you did not eat." Her grandfather shook his finger at her. "You must eat for two."

"If I eat any more, I'll grow bigger than Evalina!"

"You're hardly in danger of being even half the size of your milk cow." Rob rubbed his jaw thoughtfully. "If you give me your word that you'll not skip meals and will have either a glass of Evalina's fine milk or a slice of cheese between those meals, we'll not fuss at you about what you eat."

"You need not fuss. When I'm working in the kitchen, I take tastes."

"Mercy Stein!" Rob managed to sound scandalized. "You baked today. Are you telling us you licked the bowls?"

A fetching blush tinted her cheeks. "And what do you know about licking bowls, Dr. Gregor?"

"Not nearly enough. 'Tis the drawback of having big brothers." He gave her a woebegone look. "From now on, I'm going to have to plan a house call on the days you bake. Aye, I am."

∞

"Is he gone?" Carmen peeked around the door.

"Who?" Mercy pretended not to know what she meant.

"The doctor." Carmen came in and clomped toward the table. "Duncan mentioned his little brother was coming by here today."

"It is hard to think of the doctor as being anyone's little brother." Mercy finished icing the cake. She fought the urge to look at the bowl over on the counter. The doctor had swiped his finger all along the inside of the bowl and licked the batter off his finger as the cake baked in the oven. Once or twice a week he came by. Though he never stayed long, his visits invariably left Mercy feeling. . .better.

Carmen leaned against the counter, but she didn't take off her shawl. "All three of those Gregor men could masquerade as giants."

"Ja, this is true." Mercy looked at her friend. "But something is bothering you. Why don't we have some coffee and cake and talk about it?"

Carmen's features twisted. "You might not want me to stay."

"Nonsense." Mercy put down the butter knife and poured two cups of coffee.

"I don't know what to say or do." Carmen flopped onto a chair. Her dark eyes filled with tears. "I love my sister. You know I do."

"Of course." Mercy sat beside her.

Carmen snatched her hand and held it tight. "Her good news is our bad news. Mercy, Otto asked her to marry him."

The news left Mercy feeling strangely old and empty. "You must tell Ismelda I wish her to be happy."

"But doesn't it break your heart for Otto—" Carmen pressed her fingers to her mouth. "I'm sorry. That was rude of me."

"You didn't mean to hurt my feelings, and you have not." Mercy stared through the open doorway to her room and spied the cradle. "Things have changed. Otto is a different man, and I am a different woman. The dreams of my girlhood are long gone."

Carmen's hold on her hand tightened. "It's a good match, but I'm jealous. Isn't that awful of me? Mercy, no man has ever expressed any interest in me. I'm the older sister. By custom, I'm supposed to marry first—but I'm going to be a crippled old spinster, and Ismelda will have a husband and children."

Mercy twisted and pulled Carmen's head down onto her shoulder. Holding her, she whispered, "It is hard when dreams die."

"What do I do now?"

Mercy finally straightened up and rubbed her back. "All around us, we see girls marry and have babies. We both assumed that would be God's plan for us, too. Now, instead of telling God what we think, we have to ask Him what He wants."

"I'm in trouble, then." Carmen sniffled and tried to smile. "I'm far better at talking than at listening."

"Me, too. I've started to sing hymns and recite Bible verses. I read one a few days ago. It was where David is talking to Solomon. 'For the Lord searcheth all hearts, and understandeth all the imaginations of the thoughts: if thou seek him, he will be found of thee.' So see? God knew our dreams. But it is our job to seek Him instead of what we imagined for ourselves."

Carmen looked at her for a long while. "You're right, Mercy. You have changed. Months ago you were a girl with stars in your eyes. Now you are a woman."

"Life changes us all. I'm trying to change in the ways God wants me to. I have to—not just for myself, but for my baby."

Carmen didn't end up staying long. After she left, Mercy added seasonings to the split peas and a ham bone in the simmering soup pot. Finished with other chores, she sat in the rocking chair in the parlor and darned Peter's socks. Once those were repaired, she stared into her sewing bag. A small ball of yarn and several crochet hooks rested there. Slowly, she took out the yarn and selected a hook.

The first thing her mother taught her to crochet had been a cap for her doll. As Mercy started the hook into motion, she began to sing the hymn her mother had sung that day. *Weißt du, wie viel Sternlein stehen. . .Do you know how many stars. . .*

⌒⌒

"Dr. Gregor!"

Rob kneed his mount toward the fence. "Mr. Stein."

"I have something to ask."

Rob kicked out of the stirrups and dismounted. "Aye?"

"This baby my granddaughter carries—what do you think?"

"I think he's going to be healthy enough to bellow down your

121

house." Rob grinned. "Which is why he should grow up in mine."

The old man's weathered face broke into a smile. "So you would allow Mercy to keep this child?"

" 'Tis borne of the woman I love. That alone will cause me to love him." Rob tipped back his hat. "If Mercy wishes to keep the babe, 'twill be ours."

"*If* she wishes to keep it?" The old man looked scandalized.

"Aye." Robert didn't back down. "You and I love Mercy and will love her child. But Mercy—she was forced. In the end, she must decide whether she can love the babe entirely or if it would be best to give him to a childless couple. It is a choice only she can make."

"Have you said something to her?"

"Not yet." Rob squinted toward the house. "I know of a couple, but that doesn't mean they are meant to have this baby. I've held my silence and waited for Mercy and God to show me what's right."

"But a woman who could give away her own flesh and blood—"

"Is a woman who is honest with herself and willing to give that baby a better life than she herself could give the child, holding the feelings she may have. I love Mercy. That love willna change regardless of whate'er decision she might make."

Mr. Stein let out a long sigh. "I was so busy praying about whether you were right for her, I never thought to pray about if I was giving her the right guidance myself."

"Grossvater!" Peter shouted from the porch. "Supper!"

Mr. Stein slapped Rob on the back. "Come. Stay for supper."

They stopped at the pump and washed up before entering the house. "I hope you don't mind—" Rob began.

Mercy turned from the stove. "I've said you are always welcome. Peter saw you, so we have a place waiting—see?"

"What have you done?" Mr. Stein's voice was rich with emotion.

Rob had been so intent on Mercy, he'd not noticed anything else. He looked over his shoulder at Mr. Stein.

Mercy breezed past them and into the parlor. "I've been busy." A shy smile flirted at the corners of her mouth as she started to tuck little bits into her sewing box. "It's probably well past time that I started making my baby some clothes."

Never before had he heard her say, "*My* baby." It was always, "The baby." It wasn't just what she said, but how she said it, too. Rob knew then and there that God was going to bless him with a wife and child at the same time.

Chapter 15

"S o I learned an important lesson," Ismelda said as she clipped a thread. She gave Mercy a wry look. "It doesn't matter how long he's lived in Texas, a German farmer still doesn't know what he's asking for when he says spicy food is okay."

"I've tasted your chili. I know better." Mercy finished hemming the baby gown.

"We made mild tamales for lunch. You don't need to worry." Carmen patted her hand.

"I do love your tamales." Mercy smiled. "That, and your sweet corn casserole. For Thanksgiving, you might want to make that."

"Otto won't need to wash away the taste with a whole pitcher of milk," Carmen teased. "Ismelda, stop snitching my scissors!"

They continued to chatter and sew. As lunchtime neared, Mrs. Kunstler arrived, and she brought along a gentleman. "Isn't it lucky you are in town today, Mercy? I've been wanting to introduce you to Chester Heim. He's my cousin's cousin."

Mercy stammered what she hoped would pass for a polite greeting as she tried to subtly cover her large tummy with a length of cloth. A woman with a mere month to go before having a child only associated with family and very close friends. It was embarrassing enough for Otto's mother to have introduced her to this stranger— surely she wasn't trying to play matchmaker!

Carmen gave Mercy a confused look.

"Ismelda, why don't I help you set the table?" Mrs. Kunstler bustled away.

Mr. Heim mopped his brow. "Miss Stein, I've been eager to meet you. Please understand how much this means to me."

"I'm sorry. I don't—"

He sat beside her on the settee and grabbed her hand. "Time is short."

Mercy snatched her hand away. "Mr. Heim, excuse me."

"The baby, I want it," he blurted out.

Carmen bolted out of her chair. "Mr. Heim, you need to leave."

"My wife and I—we'll take it!" Mr. Heim clamped his hand around Mercy's arm. "It's for the best. I know you'll agree."

Mercy stared at him in horror. In a matter of seconds, Mrs. Kunstler was standing beside him, testifying to his character. At the same time, he was pleading on behalf of his wife. Carmen had fled, and Ismelda stood in mute horror.

"You can rid yourself of your shame this way," Mrs. Kunstler declared.

"You won't be encumbered," Mr. Heim asserted. "Someday, maybe another man will come along. You wouldn't have to confess—"

"That's enough!" The doctor's bellow silenced the room. He strode right up to Mercy. "Mr. Heim, you are to leave now."

"No." Mr. Heim puffed out his chest. "You knew about this, but you didn't help us. I'm taking matters into my own hands." He turned back to Mercy. "Don't you see? This way you won't be completely ruined."

"Mercy was never ruined." The doctor's voice came out in a rumble that would make thunder sound like a mere whimper. He knelt beside her. "I'll let no man slur her."

"I didn't mean it to sound badly," Heim stammered. "You're alone, Miss Stein. My wife and I—we want children."

"Miss Stein is not alone. She has family who love her." The

doctor slid his hand over hers. "Aye, and there's a man who loves her, too."

Mercy tore her gaze from Mr. Heim and gawked at the doctor.

" 'Tisna like I'd planned, but I dinna regret making my declaration." He squeezed her hand.

"He's the one, Doctor." Carmen limped back through the front door, her features strained. "He needs to leave."

"Everyone needs to calm down," Mrs. Kunstler said.

Mr. Heim tugged on Mercy's sleeve. "Listen to me. My wife and I would give your baby a good home. If the doctor will take you, the two of you could have your own children."

"If I'll take her?" Rob's voice resonated with outrage. "I'd be blessed if she'd take me!" He stared into Mercy's eyes. "Your value is far above rubies, Mercy. Whate'er decisions you make, they need to be based on what you know and feel deep down in your soul. Dinna allow anyone to discount how special you are, for you are a daughter of the King of kings." He rose and helped her to her feet.

The minute she stood, self-consciousness flooded her. Mercy knew just how huge she looked.

The doctor tilted her face up to his. "You're every bit as beautiful as you are innocent."

He had her halfway across the street before Mercy could speak. "Are you taking me home?"

"In a manner of speaking." He took her into the beautiful home that they'd built and seated her on the veranda. "Wait here for a moment." He left and reappeared in a matter of seconds. Kneeling beside her once again, he pulled a thin gold band from his pocket. "My Da's last gift to me was Ma's ring and a piece of advice. He knew caring for bodies makes a doctor close off his heart so he doesn't have to feel the pain. He warned me not to do so but instead to take a chance at love."

Mercy stared at the ring. *So he's willing to take a chance and marry me out of pity.*

"Clear down to my soul, I love ye, lass. 'Tis been hard, waiting to tell you. I pledged to your grandda I'd not court you without his leave. It's felt like an eternity, but I finally gained his permission yesternoon. I'm askin' you to be my wife—and for no other reason than the love God gave me for you cannot be denied."

Slowly, he tucked the ring in her palm and curled her fingers around it. "You hold my heart in your hand. 'Tis a matter all on its own. I canna expect that you dinna have questions or concerns, so I'll not mince words.

"The child you carry—I'll honor your decision whate'er you choose to do. Just as I love you, I'll cherish this wee one and rear him as my verra own. But if you sense you canna love him without reservation, I'll understand if you wish to allow others to take him into their hearts and home."

She swallowed. "So you're not trying to salvage my honor so the baby is not a—" She couldn't bring herself to say the vile word.

"Blessing. *Each* child is a blessing." He looked at her steadily. "You've two separate decisions to make, Mercy. On one, I've told you I'll support whate'er you decide. On the other, though. . ." He lifted her closed hand and kissed it. "I'm going to do everything in my power to sway you into consenting to be my bride. I'll love you with every breath I ever take, Mercy. Marry me."

Her hand stayed in his, but she turned it over. "A woman in my condition does not think of finding a man who can love her. I once said I wanted a man who would love me regardless of what life brought and who would stand beside me in the bad times."

"I'm that man." The truth sparkled in his eyes.

"But there is another part. That man—I should love him with all that is within me." She opened her fingers, and the ring fell into his palm. "I care for you—and today, I find I care for you in a way I did not realize. It does not seem possible."

"With God, all things are possible. This love is from Him, Mercy."

The last reservation she held crumbled. "I do love you, Robert."

"Duncan! Go fetch Mr. Stein. Chris, grab the parson. We're getting married!"

Mercy yanked on his sleeve. "Robert! I cannot get married. Not like this."

He cupped her face in his hands. "The day I showed you the plans for the house, I told you I couldn't care less about how it looked on the outside. 'Twas the inside that counted. Well, I meant that then, and at the same time, I'm taking those words back this verra minute. You're beautiful, and you're wearing the delft frock I fancy. You couldna be more perfect than you are at this moment. I'm not goin' to give you a chance to change your mind. Nae, I'm not."

"There's no need to rush."

"Ooch, lass, I've been longing to profess my love for you. Now that I have, I dinna want to cross that threshold unless I'm carrying you across it. I'm a reasonable man. I'll give ye a whole hour."

"An hour!"

He nodded. "Carmen can help ye wi' some of her posies. She and her sister can fuss wi' your glorious hair and make themselves pretty so they'll stand alongside you. Aye, since I'll be havin' Duncan and Chris stand wi' me, it's fitting your two friends are there. Your grandda and brother—they're the only others who really matter, aren't they?"

Mercy thought for a moment, then admitted slowly, "Yes."

"Good! Then 'tis set." He gave her an enthusiastic kiss.

One slim hour later, Carmen finished brushing Mercy's hair and topped it with a flower wreath she'd hastily made. "You're beautiful!"

"Here. We made this for you." Ismelda pressed a bouquet into her hands.

Mercy's lips moved, but no sound came out.

"Ready?" Grossvater asked.

"Yes," Carmen answered. She and Ismelda rushed to the front pew.

Autumn sunlight poured through the church windows. Mercy wondered how that could be because she felt so cold. Robert wasn't waiting at the altar for her, and fear welled up. Unaware of her feelings, Grossvater walked her down the aisle. He got her to the front of the church, then patted her hand.

It wasn't until then that Robert's brothers entered. Chris came first, and then Duncan. By then, Mercy wasn't cold at all. She couldn't be—not after the shocking sight of the men wearing red, green, and white tartans that bared their knees!

"They're wearing *skirts*!" Peter blurted out.

"Kilts," Chris corrected him.

"Highlanders wear their kilts for important occasions," Mercy declared. She was marrying into Robert's family, and a wife owed her husband loyalty and allegiance. Not only was Robert marrying her, but his brothers were showing their acceptance of the union by wearing their odd garb. Her chin lifted. "I'm honored."

Chris and Duncan had already been standing straight and tall, but at her words, their backs nearly snapped from pride.

Robert approached her. He, too, wore his tartan. Having gotten over the original shock of seeing the men in their kilts,

Mercy decided then and there that no man had ever looked half so handsome as her groom did in his kilt. His voice was as warm and steady as his hands when he held her close and proclaimed his vows.

Mercy repeated her vows, and each of the promises she made came straight from her heart.

"What God hath joined together, let no one put asunder," the pastor said at the end. "You may kiss your bride."

"We Gregors have a special tradition." Robert smiled as he pulled a length of cloth from the leather tie at his waist. The cloth matched his kilt.

Draping the cloth over her shoulder, he quoted:

"As fair art thou, my bonnie lass,
So deep in luve am I,
And I will luve thee still, my dear,
Till a' the seas gang dry.
Till a' the seas gang dry, my dear,
And the rocks melt wi' the sun!
And I will luve thee still, my dear
While the sands o' life shall run."

He drew her close, and his kiss promised all the love she could ever dream for.

To Walk
HUMBLY

Chapter 1

Y ou've got to come now!" Duncan Gregor shouted hoarsely as he burst through the door.

Carmen Rodriguez's gasp of surprise turned into a groan as the flan she'd been tipping out of the pan slithered and slopped into an unsightly mess on the plate. "You're early. I thought we were having supper at six."

"Nae, lass. 'Tisna that a-tall!" Duncan slumped against the door-frame, his chest heaving and his blue eyes huge. "Mercy—the babe!"

"Why didn't you just say so?" Carmen ripped off her apron and put on a fresh one as she hobbled toward the door. "What does Robert say?"

"Rob's not at home! He's out somewhere."

Well, that accounts for why he's flustered. Carmen gave Duncan a reassuring smile. She fought the urge to smooth the wayward lock of inky hair back from his forehead. "I'll stay with Mercy while you go fetch him."

"We canna recall where he went." The man sounded as though he'd been forced to gargle vinegar before making that confession. His gaze swept the house. "Where's your sister? We need all the help we can get."

"Ismelda is at Otto's, helping his mother. She'll be back by six for supper."

"Why can't everyone stay put? Especially Rob. A man who's about to become a father has no business gallivanting off."

"He's a doctor," Carmen pointed out.

"Exactly." Duncan glowered at her. "And just who else is supposed to be helping Mercy through her travail?"

He'd left the door wide open when he barged in, so Carmen stepped out onto the veranda. Cool days like this always made her left leg ache. She'd broken it as a child, and the bones hadn't healed correctly. *It's nothing—especially in comparison to Mercy's travail.*

Duncan cupped Carmen's elbow. "I'm worried about her."

"I'm sure she'll be fine." She reached to shut the door.

Duncan muttered, "This is takin' too long." He shut the door, swept her into his brawny arms, and carried her across the street to the clinic. Once inside, he roared, "Where'd you put her, Chris?"

Silence met them.

Carmen tried to wiggle so he'd put her down. Bad enough her crippled leg kept her from being able to dash around in an emergency—but for him to cart her any farther rated as complete humiliation. "They're probably still at home."

Duncan's face went colorless. "Oh no." He kept possession of her, plowing out the back door and across the yard to the house he shared with his brothers and new sister-in-law. "I'm counting on you."

"I'd do my best, but I've never helped at a birth."

"And you shouldn't have to." Under other circumstances, his scandalized reaction would have amused her, but Carmen couldn't make fun of Duncan. The poor man looked downright sick. "I'm countin' on you to talk sense into Mercy. Tell her she has to wait awhile to have the babe. And be sure to make her promise to go to the clinic. 'Tis safer there."

"Safer?"

"Aye." Dark head bobbing emphatically, Duncan declared, "Rob's got enough medical equipment and drugs there to cure every man, woman, child, and beast in three counties. Whate'er Mercy needs, he'll have it on hand." He kicked open the front door and strode in. "Chris! What's takin' you so long? You were to have Mercy at the—"

"She's refusing to budge." Christopher Gregor looked thoroughly disgruntled.

"Hi, Carmen." Mercy sat in the rocking chair and patted her tummy. "It looks as if we're going to have a New Year's Eve baby."

"Not if I can help it." Chris glowered at her. "You could cooperate and wait a day or so."

"At least go to the clinic," Duncan tacked on as he let go of Carmen's legs and slipped her to the floor. The man looked terrified, yet he instinctively handled her with consideration and didn't turn loose until he was certain she'd become stable on her feet. "Don't you think that's a grand notion, Carmen?"

"I—"

Mercy curled her hands around the chair's arms and rocked faster. Carmen wasn't sure who moaned—but it wasn't Mercy. About a minute later, Mercy relaxed. "I'm having this baby here, Duncan, and you're not going to change my mind."

"We'll see to things." Upon making that declaration, Duncan nodded to Chris. The brothers bracketed the rocking chair and hefted it.

Mercy let out a surprised yelp.

"What are you men doing?" Carmen stared at the odd scene.

"She wants to be in the rocking chair. We're humoring the lass." Chris spoke as if she'd turned into a half-wit.

Duncan jerked his jaw in the direction of the door. "Run on ahead to the clinic, Carmen. Aren't you supposed to be boiling water or something?"

"The reservoir on the stove is full." Mercy tapped Duncan and

Chris on their shoulders. "And unless you put me down, the roast in the oven is going to burn."

"Don't care about the roast. I'm more worried about the wee little bun in your oven." Duncan ignored her insistent tapping and started to walk. Ostensibly not to be dissuaded from his convictions, Chris followed suit.

"If you men carry me to the clinic, I'm just going to walk right back here."

"The pangs are addling her mind," Duncan muttered.

"No, they're not." Mercy wheedled, "It's still early. Robert's books say labor is likely to last twelve hours, if not twice that long. You can't expect me to spend my first New Year's Eve as a married woman anywhere other than in my husband's wonderful home."

Carmen secretly admired Mercy's wiles. She'd obviously come to understand she couldn't fight both of her brothers-in-law, so she'd divided them by appealing to Christopher's pride at having built the house. Chris stopped walking, and Carmen suspected as anxious as Duncan had grown, he'd carry Mercy in circles all night if someone didn't intervene.

"I'm relieved to see you men are trying to protect Mercy from any eventuality." Carmen smiled at Duncan. "It's going to grow nippy tonight. Just in case Mercy relents and decides to have the baby in the clinic, you'd better go light a fire in the stove there so she won't catch a chill."

"Put water on to boil, too," Chris demanded.

"I'll stay right here with her." Carmen motioned to set down the rocker.

∞

Two hours later, Duncan stared at Carmen and ground out, "Cookie cutters?"

"Of course." Mercy concentrated on cracking eggs into an earthenware bowl. "When everyone comes to visit the baby, we need to show them hospitality. You don't want to shame me by making me face them without cookies."

"Plenty of cookies don't require cookie cutters." Chris scowled as he motioned behind his back to make Duncan put away the ironing board. Until Mercy took a mind to bake cookies, she'd ironed every shirt in the house twice.

"But those are everyday cookies." Mercy dumped two cups of sugar into the mixture. "Guests should receive special cookies."

"Anyone paying a visit to a house with a new baby ought to be bringing the cookies." Duncan paced from one end of the kitchen to the other. During his third transit, he tucked away the ironing board. "Aye, no doubt about it; they should be bringing the cookies. I distinctly recall Ma taking food when she went to a home where there'd been sickness or death."

"I'm neither sick nor dying." Mercy looked suitably appalled at his comment.

Chris mopped his brow. "But you're going to be the death of us, trying to have this babe with no help at hand."

"Don't you insult my dear friend that way." Mercy waved a wooden spoon in Carmen's direction. "She'll help me. Won't you, Carmen?"

Though her apprehension far outweighed her confidence, Carmen nodded. After all, her friend needed her, and loyalty demanded she be a staunch ally.

Duncan pulled Carmen from the kitchen. "Some kind of help you are! You were supposed to get her to the clinic, not to the oven!"

"I had a choice to make—either I make you happy or I comfort my friend who happens to be in labor." Carmen stabbed her finger into the center of his broad chest. "I didn't think I'd have to listen to a grown man whine—especially when a woman under his roof is in labor and has yet to let out a single cry."

"I dinna whine!" He looked thoroughly affronted. "I'm reminding you of what's important. Cookies willna matter a whit if she or the babe dinna get through the ordeal."

"You need to have more faith," she whispered. "Now go on over to my house. Ismelda just used the cookie cutters yesterday. They're in the orange box to the left of the sink."

"This is it, woman. I'll not be humoring any more of these ridiculous requests."

Carmen pretended she didn't hear him. Truthfully, for the last couple of hours, Carmen had concocted a variety of tasks for Chris and Duncan to accomplish. It kept them from hovering, at least part of the time.

Duncan shook his finger at her. "Dinna feign innocence. You ken full well what I mean."

"You could cooperate. Staying busy has kept Mercy from panicking about the fact that Robert's not here."

"He'd best better hie on home." Duncan's brows knit. "Chris sent Connant after him over an hour ago."

"We have to stay calm. You go get the cookie cutters. I'll set the table." Carmen returned to the kitchen. Mercy urgently motioned to her, and Carmen headed her way. With every step, she promised God she'd do any number of good deeds as long as she didn't have to deliver this baby on her own.

Mercy pulled Carmen close. "I've done it now."

Chapter 2

Carmen clamped her lips together to hold back a moan.

"I wasn't paying attention. I didn't just add sugar to the cookies. I added a whole cupful to the mashed potatoes!"

Disbelief forced Carmen to laugh. She tightened her apron strings. "I'll add a few eggs to make them hold together, then fry slabs."

"Like potato pan–caaa—" Mercy curled forward and lost the last part of the word. When the pain ended, she fretted, "I wanted this supper to be perfect."

"You've talked the men into wearing their kilts, Chris brought in a log that could burn for a month, and the pewter candlesticks are at least a half inch shorter after you set Duncan to polishing them. It'll be a supper they remember for a long time."

Mercy let out a doleful sigh. "I was talking about the food."

"The roast is big enough to feed everyone for three days." Carmen cast a quick look at the door. "Duncan and Chris are so worried that I don't think they'll taste a single bite they wolf down tonight, anyway."

"It's taking Robert a long time."

"You yourself said it'll be hours yet." Carmen hoped with every fiber of her being that her words were true.

"*Ja.* You work on the potatoes. I'll start rolling out the cookie dough—oh, and put the apple cider on the back burner. I want to mull some spices in it and serve it with dessert."

"I think," Carmen glanced about furtively before continuing, "we ought to have Chris and Duncan take the cookies over to the clinic to bake."

"They'll burn half of them." Mercy grinned.

"Fine. We'll have to mix up another batch. That'll keep them occupied a little longer. I'll hurry and start boiling rice. It'll go with the roast and gravy."

Chris and Duncan fought over who got to go bake the cookies. It was then Carmen fully appreciated just how terrified they were that they might have to help with the delivery. She sent both. They'd return to the house only long enough for Mercy to plop the next round of cookies on the sheets, then run off to the clinic oven again.

"That's the last of them," Mercy announced as she handed her brothers-in-law the cookie-laden sheets. "Chris, you and Duncan, when you've baked them, change into your kilts, and we'll have supper on the table when you come back." She waited until they were gone, then pled, "Can you haul me out of this chair? I'm not moving so good."

"Sure." Carmen helped her up.

Mercy stood, curled forward, and moaned with the next pang. When it was over, she straightened and said, "The table looks beautiful. I wish my husband were here to see it."

"I'm sure he'll get here soon, Mercy." *He'd better. I'm starting to get as nervous as Duncan. Well, I'm not going to let Mercy see that. If she can stay calm, so will I.* "The only thing left is for me to make the gravy."

"I can do that. Will you get some honey from the pantry?"

"Sure."

The door opened, and Ismelda came in. Holding the plate with the destroyed flan, she gave Carmen an uncertain look.

"Oh, flan!" Mercy sounded truly thrilled over the mess. "I love your flan."

Ismelda asked, "*¿Olvidó de traer este?*"

"Yes," Carmen answered her sister in English, "I forgot to bring that. I was excited because Mercy's in labor."

"How wonderful!"

"Tell that to Duncan and Chris." Mercy's wry smile slid into a grimace.

By the time they sat down to supper, Carmen tried not to fault Chris and Duncan for seating Mercy, then hastening to the chairs farthest from her for themselves. After all, they were gentlemanly enough to pause long enough to seat Ismelda and her on either side of Mercy. Folding his hands, Duncan said, "I'll ask the blessing."

Carmen bowed her head. Duncan's prayers never ceased to touch her. He spoke to the Lord in a way she'd never heard a man pray—with a rich blend of reverence, respect, humility, and love. Tonight's prayer ought to be particularly special.

"Lord, the food looks good, but the only blessing I'm asking tonight is for You to help our Mercy through and for the babe to be all right. Amen."

" 'Men," Chris chimed in.

While Carmen blinked in astonishment over the prayer, Chris picked up the carving knife and proceeded to hack a picture-perfect roast into an assortment of chunks spanning every possible shape and size. Carmen consoled herself that the irregular hunks would hide how lumpy the gravy was. And the gravy would add moisture to the rice, because it turned out a tad dry. Those paltry facts were lost on the men, who inhaled the food with blinding speed.

Mercy barely picked at her plate.

"What's wrong?" Chris squinted at her.

"Nothing." Her lips thinned, and she went silent.

"Nothing?" Chris threw back his head and groaned. "If Rob

doesna walk through the door in the next five minutes, I'm goin' to skin him alive."

"You will not." Mercy let out a small sigh and pushed away her plate. "I'm just being choosy tonight. I wanted to save room for dessert."

"Me, too!" Carmen hopped up. As she and Ismelda cleared the table, Carmen seriously questioned her own sanity. Mercy had accidentally thickened the apple cider instead of the beef broth and drippings to make "gravy." In order to salvage the situation, Ismelda turned the broth to gravy and Carmen "fixed" the cider.

"What's for dessert, Mercy?" Chris sounded hopeful. "You said you had something special planned."

"I'll bet you've never had this before," Ismelda murmured.

"That's right. It's a new recipe." Carmen slapped the fried, sweetened mashed potato slabs onto plates, added diced apples, spooned blobs of flan atop them, and then topped the whole affair off with a mulled, spicy apple "glaze."

Mercy attacked hers with gusto.

Chris gave his serving a dubious look. "What is it?"

"Happenstance," Carmen blurted out as she picked up her fork.

"Probably another Texas dish," Duncan said. "There's not been one yet I haven't liked."

Duncan's fork practically created sparks on the plate, he ate so fast. Chris matched him bite for bite.

Carmen exchanged a look with her sister. "Ismelda, why don't we share mine? I made a plate for Robert, but if Connant comes back with him, we wouldn't want him to go without."

"Connant could have Rob's, and Rob could go hungry," Chris growled. "'Twould serve him right for leaving his kin in a time of great need."

Duncan nodded as he pushed to his feet. "Food was good. Filling. You ladies worked hard cooking it, so Chris and I'll do the cleanup."

"Yeah." Chris rose. "And since nothing's keeping you here, Mercy, Carmen and Ismelda can take you over and settle you in the clinic now."

"I can't go to the clinic!"

Chris scowled at Mercy. "And suppose you give me a good reason why not?"

"She's not in her nightdress," Ismelda replied.

"You can jolly well change once you're there." By now, Duncan and Chris bracketed Mercy like a pair of menacing gargoyles.

Suspecting they were about to pick up Mercy's chair once again, Carmen tapped her fork on the edge of her dessert plate. "Once Ismelda and I finish our. . .uhh. . .happenstance, we'll be happy to help Mercy change. Won't we, Sister?"

Ismelda looked at the dish, and Carmen had the sinking feeling her sister was going to either use this as an excuse to get out of eating the mess or offer to help Mercy and allow Carmen to eat it all by herself. Alarmed at either possibility, Carmen gave her little sister a behave-yourself look.

"You take a bite, then I'll take one."

Relief flooded her. Carmen assessed the dessert and decided the safest thing to do would be to isolate and eat each item independently. She speared an apple and popped the slice into her mouth.

It seemed Ismelda came to the same conclusion. She took a miniscule dab of flan.

"You'll be here until the Second Coming, eating that slowly." Chris drummed his fingers on the back of Mercy's chair.

"My friends are ladies, not field hands." Mercy's voice went up in volume, then petered out on the last word.

"Another one? She's having another one." Distress tainted Duncan's voice. "I'm not liking this one bit."

"What aren't you liking?" a voice asked from the door. "And why are the lamps on over in my clinic?"

∞

Duncan bellowed at his brother, " 'Tis far past time you showed up!"

Robert set down his medical satchel. "I'm sorry I'm late for supper. It couldna be helped."

"You should have had your sorry hide home hours ago," Chris grated.

Maddeningly casual, Rob crossed the room, pressed a kiss on Mercy's temple, and said, "Aida and Stuart had a wee little boy tonight. Mother and child are right as rain."

"What were you doing there?" Chris bristled. "You were supposed to be at the Stuckys'. I sent Connant there to fetch you."

"I said I was going to Stu Key's." Rob hadn't straightened up. He stayed down close to Mercy and said softly, "I take it you're planning to make me a father tonight?"

She bit her lip and nodded.

"Now then, that's a fine piece of news. And 'tis plain to see you're faring well. Since the day we knew you to be with child, I've prayed 'twould go easy on you. God is faithful."

Duncan stared at his brother. Clearly, he didn't understand just how serious this was—either that or he was demented. "Mercy's been having pangs for hours now," Duncan intoned, trying to get Rob to comprehend the gravity of the situation.

Rob crooked a brow. "Have you, now?"

"Only since noon." Mercy's smile faltered, then disappeared entirely.

"Noon!" Chris roared. "And you didn't tell us then?"

Rob wheeled around and stood nose to nose with his oldest brother. "Dinna raise your voice at my wife!"

" 'Tis you I'll yell at. She needed you, and you were off with another woman!"

"Stop this!" Mercy's eyes filled with tears.

"Now look what the both of you did." Duncan swiped the napkin from Mercy's lap and blotted her face. "Upsettin' a wee mother-to-be. Shame on ye."

Carmen rose. "I'm sure you gentlemen will excuse us."

Now that Rob was home, Duncan's nerves settled. Asking Carmen to come had been a move of desperation. It wasn't right to ask an unmarried woman to play midwife. Carmen hadn't confessed to being worried, but Duncan knew she'd calmed tremendously since Rob arrived. He could tell because her accent grew thicker when she was upset. Suddenly, her tongue's rich-sounding roll when she pronounced *r*'s and the softening of the *t* sounds weren't as strong.

"You can't go!" Chris went right back to yelling.

Clearly not intimidated, Carmen glared at Chris. "I wouldn't dream of leaving her tonight. The only place I'm going is upstairs to help Mercy change into her nightdress."

"That's a fine plan." Rob's voice took on his everything's-under-control flavor. He wound Mercy's arm about his neck and scooped her out of her seat.

She turned her face into his neck and started to cry.

"There, now. There you are. Aye, lass. You needn't worry a bit now." Rob kept a steady stream of reassurances as he carried her up to their bedchamber. Even after they were out of sight, Mercy's weeping drifted down the stairs.

"I'm thinkin' you're right. Mercy might want a woman's help,"

Duncan said quietly to Carmen.

Carmen nodded. Compassion shimmered in her deep brown eyes. He admired the woman. Others in the community hadn't known how to react to Mercy since her child was conceived by an act of violence. They'd kept their distance; Carmen hadn't wavered in the least. She'd been a stalwart friend.

He decided to repay her kindness. "Whilst you're up there with her, I'll dump out your happenstance. No use in all of us sufferin' indigestion."

Carmen's eyes grew huge.

"Did you think we didna see Mercy put sugar in the mashed potatoes?"

Ismelda squeaked, "Why didn't you stop her?"

"I couldna bear to rattle the lass." He pulled out Carmen's chair. Duncan fought the urge to carry her up the stairs. He'd already dented her pride by carrying her across the street earlier in the day. She did her best to get around and ignore the pitying glances folks gave her. Indeed, she managed life quite nicely. But if he offered her assistance, she'd likely take it the wrong way.

Carmen mounted the stairs methodically. Soon after she disappeared from sight, Rob appeared. Rubbing his hands together, he announced, "I'm hungry as a draft horse."

"Eat dessert first," Chris advised as he shoved some of the disastrous dish at Rob.

Duncan swiped the plate right out of Rob's hand. "We canna have him gettin' sick. He's got to deliver the babe."

"Mercy's never made anything that didn't taste grand." Rob reached for the happenstance again.

Ismelda giggled. "But Mercy's never been in labor before."

"How far along is she?" Chris dumped chunks of meat onto a

plate. "How much longer?"

"I can't say for certain."

"You're usually able to give a fair estimate," Duncan said.

"Aye." Rob shot a look at Ismelda, who'd taken the dessert plates to the back door to rid them of the monstrous concoction. Rob's voice dropped to a confidential whisper, "But those women have been long married." He paused a moment to choose his words carefully. "And they dinna suffer crippling modesty."

Duncan grimaced. He rested his hand on Rob's shoulder and gave him a powerful squeeze as a sign of his support. *Rob told Mercy he'd been praying for her to have an easy delivery. I never gave much thought to how hard this will be for her—and for him, too. Lord, You hae the power to calm them and ease things. Please grant them that.*

"You're in your kilts." Rob accepted the plate of roast and rice from Chris.

"At your wife's request." Chris grinned. "We may well be in Texas, but she's showing promise. With time, she'll understand the honor of marrying a Highlander."

Rob ate quickly and cast a look at the stairs.

"You need to get her o'er to the clinic," Duncan urged.

"She's wanting to hae the bairn in our own bed."

"Make her see reason." Chris started pacing. He practically mowed over Ismelda. "It's 1892. Modern women should avail themselves of the best medicine has to offer. Your clinic is the finest there is."

"I promised my old-fashioned bride a solid half hour of privacy so she could wash up, change, and have Carmen help her with her hair. After that, we'll see how she is."

"Half an hour?" Duncan shook his head in disbelief.

"She's rattled. Carmen has a knack for making Mercy feel

better. Just you wait. I'd estimate that right about now, my wee wife's calming down."

"I will not!" Mercy shouted from upstairs.

Rob winced.

"No, no, no, no." Mercy's voice went from a shout to a strangled moan.

"That doesna sound like a woman who's finding her serenity. Go help her, man!" Chris shoved at him, and he raced upstairs.

Less than a minute later, Mercy's voice held a shrill edge. "You promised thirty minutes!"

Rob came back downstairs, grinning like a fool. "Things are progressing well."

"If that's 'well,' you'd best stuff cotton in your ears once you hae her at the clinic. The lass is liable to scream you deaf once she's in the thick of it."

"Bein' a mite temperamental is a fine sign. It indicates a woman's toward the end."

"Toward the end of her rope, I'd say," Chris muttered.

Someone knocked once while opening the front door. Connant stuck his head into the house. "I'm relieved to see Rob's horse. I've ridden all over and couldn't find him. How's Mercy?"

They all looked toward the ceiling. As if she'd heard Connant's question, her stricken voice echoed down the stairs. "No one needs to know!"

Connant's eyes widened. "I'll go now."

"She didna hear you. She's talking with Carmen." Rob motioned him in. "Come. Eat."

The sheriff looked appalled at the notion. "I've got things to do."

"Is that so?" Rob asked. His tone sounded entirely too entertained.

"I'll help." Chris rushed toward the door, to freedom.

"No. No. Everything's under control. Happy New Year." The sheriff shut the door with obvious alacrity. Chris looked like a man about to be stuffed into a cannibal's pot.

Half an hour later, Carmen descended the stairs. "Mercy's asking to go to the washroom."

Rob shot to his feet.

"Before you go up there," Carmen's voice carried a vaguely amused flavor, "I've been ordered to warn you men that if you try to take her to the clinic, she'll avenge herself."

Chris snorted. "Mercy wouldn't swat a fly. Her threat's all bluster."

Rob scowled over his shoulder. "Don't vex my wife, Chris." He went up the stairs and came back down with Mercy in his arms. She was bundled in a heavy flannel nightgown. Instead of wearing her hair up in its usual style, Mercy now had a single, fat braid swinging back and forth with each step Rob took.

From the way Mercy clung to Rob, buried her face against his chest, and moaned, she was embarrassed for them to see her in such a state. Duncan figured the least he could do was be casual about it. As they went past him toward the washroom, Duncan proclaimed, "The lass is whiter than her bedgown, Rob. Talk sense into her."

Ismelda shoved a soapy dish into the rinse water. "Shhh."

"Here you are," Rob said as he turned sideways to carry his wife through the doorway to their modern washroom. Duncan silently gave his brother credit for sounding so calm and remembering to turn so he didn't knock Mercy's head or feet against the doorframe.

"Out!" Mercy's voice took on a shrill edge. "Out this minute, Robert."

Rob stepped out of the washroom, shut the door, and finally had the good sense to look concerned.

Chris kicked the chair Duncan leaned against. "Don't just stand there. 'Tis cold out. Rob'll be wanting to wrap Mercy in a blanket whilst he totes her to the clinic."

"I hhhheee–aaarrd thaaaaat!" Mercy shouted.

"Now, Mercy," Rob wheedled.

Silence hung in the air. Rob shifted his weight from one foot to the other a few times, wiped his hands down his thighs, and cleared his throat. "Mercy?"

"Leeeeve meee aaa–looonne!"

Duncan decided it was a good thing Rob told them Mercy might be getting a wee bit testy. She seemed to be embracing the role with zeal.

A mere breath later, Mercy's voice changed to a bewildered, "Rob?"

"Aye, my sweet?"

She sounded so uncertain, so lost. "I don't know what to do."

A tiny wail rent the air. Rob yanked the washroom door straight off the hinges. Duncan collapsed into the chair. Having a baby was far more taxing than he'd expected.

Chapter 3

"How's little Elspeth today?" Carmen called across the street to Duncan. He sat in the open doorway of his cobbler's workshop, stitching something.

"Fat and sassy." He grinned at her. "That garden of yours surely takes a lot of attention."

Carmen caressed a narcissus. "I hope these and the fern-leaf lavender bloom for the wedding."

Duncan nodded. "Those pinkish-red things behind you are a sight."

"The azaleas? I love them, but they're not easy to put in a wedding arrangement. Same with my crocus. Ismelda didn't want to wait until March when the whole countryside will be abloom."

"That tree Mercy calls a redbud is blossoming. Could you use a few branches?"

His offer pleased her. "Thank you. I'll keep that in mind."

He nodded and went back to work. All day long, every day, he'd sit out on the porch attached to his workshop. An eye-popping array of spindles, fans, turnings, and trim should have made the outside of his shop look tacky or garish; instead, it seemed whimsical. Folks would walk down the street, drop in and chat with Duncan, then meander off.

"What are you doing?" Ismelda asked from the corner of their yard.

"Checking on the flowers." Carmen turned around. "I need to

water some of them a little more."

"Otto's mother offered to come help me pin up the hem of my gown, but I told her you would." Ismelda clasped Carmen's hand as she went up the four steps to their veranda. "I wanted to talk with you about something."

"Sure."

"You won't move into the Kunstlers' with me?"

"No, I won't." Carmen shot her sister a stern look. "You and Otto need to be husband and wife. I'd be underfoot and in the way."

"His mother is there."

"I know." Carmen stopped. "You and she get along well, and I know in my heart that it'll be a happy arrangement. But Mrs. Kunstler and I wouldn't be happy under the same roof. Besides, I love our home here."

"But I was wondering about something else."

Carmen waited for her sister to speak. Try as she might, she couldn't quite get past the hurt of everyone else finding mates and having babies. Her own sister didn't even hold out hope that some man might come along and develop affectionate feelings for Carmen. The reality that she was trying to make arrangements for Carmen's spinster years stung.

"Mr. Stein and Peter—they're faring decently, but with Mercy in town now, I think he'd be delighted to have a housekeeper. Why don't you talk with him about it? We'd be neighbors!"

Carmen merely shook her head.

"You already take a dish over there once or twice a week."

"If that is a reason for me to become someone's housekeeper, half of our neighbors would already employ me."

"But maybe it's time for you to get something in return for all the good deeds you do."

"I don't want anything, Ismelda. I'm content. I have a home and friends. Papa left us enough money that I needn't worry about finances." Carmen shook her head. "I'd be lying if I told you I would think about it. Go put on your gown. I'll wash my hands so I don't smudge it."

The heavy white satin felt smooth and cool in Carmen's hands as she pinned the hem. She forced a laugh. "I was just picturing Otto standing at the altar waiting for you."

"What's so funny about that?"

"I imagined him in one of the Gregors' kilts."

Merry laughter bubbled out of Ismelda. "Never. After church on Sunday, Otto told me if I have any plans to make him wear odd costumes, I'd better forget them."

"They're not odd costumes. The Gregors are proud of their heritage. I thought they looked. . .unified at church on Sunday." The pastor had called Mercy and Rob to the altar on Sunday to present Elspeth to the congregation and say a blessing over her. Duncan and Chris stood on either side of them. All of the Gregor men wore kilts, and the length of tartan Rob had draped over Mercy's shoulder for their wedding now served as the infant's blanket. "And I also think it was very touching how Duncan mentioned they'd named Elspeth after their own mother."

"It was." Ismelda sighed romantically. "I told Otto I'm wearing Mama's bridal mantilla as my something old. In a year or two, maybe I could drape it over our baby, too. Don't you think that would be a lovely tradition?"

"Mmm." Though tears filled her eyes, Carmen smiled up at her sister. *She's so sure I'll never be a bride.*

Ismelda pressed her hand to her bosom. "Oh, do I look so

beautiful that you're in tears?"

"*Muy hermosa.* Very beautiful."

"You're such a wonderful sister to make me feel lovely in my gown."

"Never once forget how beautiful I think you are—inside as well as out."

"Are you done pinning me up?"

Grateful to break eye contact, Carmen reached for the pincushion. She pulled out another pin. "Just one more. Here."

"Now that we've finished my gown, we need to decide on yours. I don't care if the gringos here think red is for a loose woman. You look beautiful in red, and—"

"Be practical, Ismelda. I'd never be able to wear it again. If I put work into making a dress, I ought to get some use out of it."

Her sister made wavelike motions. "What about layers and layers of yellow and orange?"

"Since when did we wear layered skirts? Mama always dressed us in designs featured in *Godey's.*"

Ismelda shrugged. "You were talking about heritage. I thought it might be fun to have some of our heritage in my wedding."

"You could carry our Spanish Bible."

Eyes alight, Ismelda proclaimed, "You can! I'll hold a sheaf of flowers from our garden, just as I always dreamed, and you can carry Papa's Bible. In fact"—Ismelda clapped her hands—"you could read a verse from it."

"That doesn't seem right. Otto doesn't know any Spanish. A groom ought to understand the whole ceremony."

Ismelda wrinkled her nose. "I guess you're right. I know she doesn't mean to be rude, but his mother often speaks German to him in front of me. I'm so determined to understand them I'm having Otto teach me new words all of the time!"

"Chris Gregor rattles off German like he's one of them, and he's getting good at Spanish, too."

"I'm glad." Ismelda blushed. "He can translate for the doctor now. Duncan—he hasn't learned much Spanish or German, but everyone understands him, and he understands whatever someone else is trying to say."

Carmen started to unbutton her sister's gown. "That stream of people wandering past his shop and visiting with him—it's that way every day, all day long."

"Really? I hadn't noticed." Ismelda let out a trill of laughter. "I love Otto so much that I don't seem to notice anything else at all."

Carmen gave no reply. Duncan Gregor was a nice man. A good man—godly and gentle and kind. People couldn't help responding to his warm and humble personality. *He'll never be lonely, but I will.* That thought hit her hard. *What does he do that I don't?*

"You look so sad!"

Summoning a smile she was far from feeling, Carmen knew she didn't dare confess her fears. She wanted her sister to bask in the joy of her marriage, not to fret over things that couldn't be helped. She softened the truth. "I was thinking how empty the house will be. I'm going to miss you."

"So you're reconsidering my suggestion about becoming the Steins' housekeeper?"

"No." Carmen didn't have a hard time looking appalled at the notion. "I'm going to have to find ways to keep busy once you're not here to pester me."

"You can come visit me whenever you want." Ismelda carefully stepped free from her gown. "We still haven't decided about what you'll wear for the wedding."

"Leonard mentioned he's gotten a shipment of bombazine in at the mercantile."

"Bombazine is for widows and chaperones. You said you want to be practical—well, then we'll have your gown be a bright color in a lightweight silk or a challis. That way, you'll be able to look festive all through the spring and summer."

"Come spring and summer, I'm going to want lightweight cotton so I can stay cool while helping you with the extra chores that come from being a farmer's wife."

"Then we'll have to be sure to get material for two dresses for you." Ismelda grinned. "In addition to the fabric for the dress you'll wear for the wedding."

Accustomed to her little sister's stunts, Carmen laughed and nodded. "Yes, *querido*. One for me and one for you." *And maybe a few more yards of cotton, besides. I could make Mercy's little Elspeth a couple of gowns, and with old Mrs. Lintz becoming bedridden, I'm sure she'd appreciate a crisp nightdress and soft pillowslips. And Mr. Rundsdorf— it must be so hard for him to find shirts to fit his twisted frame. I'm going to devote myself to the people who need love and might not get it otherwise.*

Relieved to have come up with a solution to battling the impending sense of loneliness, Carmen went to fetch her reticule.

⁂

"Rob took Mercy and the baby home." Duncan offered Carmen his arm.

"It was nice of them to come to the wedding." She slid her hand into the crook of his elbow and walked toward the buggy with him. When she glanced up, her deep brown eyes carried a wealth of emotion. "I know Mercy loves Rob with all her heart, but it was especially nice of her to treat Ismelda so kindly. Some people were still talking about how just a year ago Otto was going to marry Mercy."

"It's time everyone let go of the past and embrace the future. It's plain to see Rob and Mercy love each other. As for Ismelda and Otto—he was a broken man, and her love did wonders for him. Both men are blessed."

As Carmen allowed him to lift her into the buggy, Duncan noted her new dress. He waited a moment while she gathered up the extra material from her fancy gown. "Your frock's comely. It puts me of a mind of the heather from back home."

"Thank you."

The buggy swayed as he swung up beside her. For all the fabric in their skirts, it was easy to forget how tiny most of the women were. Carmen was of average height but fine boned. He saw how she tried to drag her left foot out of the way.

"You must be exhausted."

She bristled. "What makes you say that?"

He flicked the reins. "I'm thinkin' on how you've babied the garden so there were flowers aplenty and that you've stitched yourself a pretty frock. You cooked and cooked and cooked. And ooch, those Mexican wedding cookies—you baked hundreds of them. I'm not exaggerating, either, because I ate a good half dozen all on my own. Then you saw to any number of trifling details to make the wedding all your sister e'er dreamed of. Just reciting the list of what you've done leaves me weary."

The tension drained from her shoulders. "I'm afraid now that the wedding is over, I'll be bored to distraction."

"You?" Duncan chuckled. "I dinna think the word *leisure* is in your vocabulary. Rob tells me you've been cheering up old Mrs. Lintz, and I ken you've helped o'er at the Rayburns'."

"Mrs. Rayburn's splint should come off next week."

"Aye, but a woman with a broken arm and a passel of children is a sorry sight."

"They're dear children—well behaved and affectionate."

"I've not been 'round them enough to agree or disagree." Duncan grinned. "You're a fine woman, and I'm sure they love you on your own merit. That bein' said, e'en the naughtiest of bairns would toe the mark just to have a taste of your *bunuelos* and *empan*-things."

"*Empanadas.*" She smiled. "I'll be sure you have some the next time I make a batch."

"I confess, I would hae never thought the Germans and the Mexicans to hold much in common, but the cinnamon-sugar desserts and the polka sort of music are startlingly similar. In the end, 'tis fun to see how much alike we all are."

She nodded. "I suppose it all boils down to a simple truth—we really all are the same. Young or old, blond or black-haired, we want to belong, to love, and to be loved."

Chapter 4

"Duncan, did you think I wouldn't notice?"

Duncan ignored Christopher's bellow and assisted Mr. Rundsdorf up the single step leading to his workshop's porch. "I've been waiting for you."

"I can come back later if this is a bad time."

"Your timing couldn't be better." Duncan grinned. "Chris swears he canna stand all the frills that came wi' the house kit. Just to keep him on his toes, I've been tacking up a piece in or on the house every now and again."

Mr. Rundsdorf's gaze roamed the workshop. "Your brother's far ahead of you in the race."

"He likes to think so."

Chris stalked over. "Take it away by noon, Duncan, or I won't be responsible for what happens next."

"You gave me all the gingerbread. 'Tis mine to do with as I please."

"Bad enough we have enough scales to cover ten dragons on the outside of my house. Worse yet, you tacked a bunch of those stupid curlicue things together and hung them in the washroom."

"I made a shelf for Mercy," Duncan explained to Mr. Rundsdorf, who nodded in appreciation.

"But my bed?" Chris practically thundered the words.

"What did he do to your bed?" Mr. Rundsdorf asked.

Chris suddenly went ruddy.

"Dinna leave the man wondering." Duncan nudged his brother. "Tell him."

"He, uh. . .tacked something onto a post," Chris muttered darkly.

"What was it?" Mr. Rundsdorf leaned forward.

Chris gave Duncan a murderous look. Duncan shrugged. "Dinna give me that scowl. You're the one who decided to bellow. The least you could do is answer the gentleman's question."

"I don't feel like it." Chris rested his fists on his hips.

"Then I will." Duncan turned to the old man.

"He stuck a birdhouse on my bedpost!" Chris sounded livid. "Seeing it first thing in the morning was enough to ruin my whole day."

Duncan happened to glance across the street. Carmen stood in her garden. She held her hand clapped over her mouth, and he knew she'd heard every last word booming out of Chris. "I tell you what, Chris. I'll let you take down the birdhouse on two conditions: Carmen has to approve of it and you hang it over at her house."

"Done." Chris stalked off.

Duncan made a sweeping gesture. "Come on inside, Mr. Rundsdorf. I've got the brace all ready for you." A moment later, he threaded a strap through the device he'd created after conferring with Rob on the design. "The sheepskin ought to keep it from rubbin' you. If you feel a wider pad would help, dinna hesitate to tell me."

Mr. Rundsdorf wiggled his twisted torso within its new confines. He let out an appreciative sigh. "I can tell already this is going to work."

No brace in the world would ever begin to correct the man's deformity. Duncan didn't pretend otherwise. "Rob said the support might bring you some comfort."

"Unh-huh." Rundsdorf buckled the last strap into place. "Stamina, too—not that I expect this contraption to turn me into a schoolboy. But if I can stay up for two or three hours at a time, it'll be twice what I can do now."

Duncan picked up the misshapen shirt and held it for Mr. Rundsdorf to slide into.

"I'm twisted as mesquite."

"I'd never seen mesquite until I came to America. 'Tis a rare beautiful shrub."

A rueful bark of a laugh left the man.

Duncan went on to defend it. "Mesquite's got character. I've admired many a piece of furniture or bowl made from the wood. If that's not enough, the wood burns slow, and the flavor its smoke lends to Texas barbecue—" Duncan waggled his brows.

"I never thought of it that way."

"God made mesquite, just as He made pines and oak. He took pleasure in His creation and said it was good. If He took pleasure in that, how much more must He love a son who strives to live to serve Him?"

Rundsdorf stopped buttoning his shirt and gawked at him. A slow smile spread across his pain-etched face.

"I'm planning on having to fiddle wi' the brace so we can get a perfect fit. Dinna be shy about telling me what feels odd or where it puts too much pressure."

"It's perfect as it is."

"Aye, and I've heard the selfsame thing from plenty of folks when first they tied on a pair of shoes. 'Tisna just the fit when a body is at rest that matters. Pressure and rubbing are bound to happen—and that's when you discover the difference between bliss and a blister."

Fastening the last of his buttons, Mr. Rundsdorf cleared his throat. "You didn't say how much this cost."

The man needed to keep his pride, so Duncan gave him the answer he'd already made up. He swept his arm to encompass his workshop. "I used nothing but scraps and wee bits and pieces. They cost me next to nothing."

"But your time—"

"Has some value. I grant you that. But I wanted to help a brother in Christ, so here's what I've decided. More than a few men have said you've a talent with wood. In your spare time, using nothing but scraps, why don't you make something for my shop?"

"What do you need?"

Duncan let out a shout of a laugh. "That all depends on who you're listenin' to. Chris thinks I need ambition. Rob says I suffer from the affliction of clutter and wouldna recognize order if it bit me. My sister-in-law is the most dangerous of all. She's of the opinion that I need a wife." Duncan chuckled along with his customer. "Me? I'm content just as I am."

Rundsdorf looked pensive. "It must be nice to feel that kind of peace."

"The apostle Paul wrote of it—e'en whilst in jail. 'Tisna the circumstances a man finds himself in that matter. God is present with us and loves us. All we have to do is open our hearts to him."

"Like Sunday's hymn, 'Just as I Am.'"

"Aye. And I canna help believing that since He takes us just as we are, then the grace He bestows ought to flow through us—not only to others but to ourselves. As for me, I've found when my heart's in tune with Him, He can fix my flaws." Duncan let out a diffident chuckle. "I've faults aplenty, so I keep the Almighty busy. But I'm content to serve God to the best of my ability."

"I'm thankful you do." Rundsdorf smoothed his hand over the front of his shirt. His fingers bumped up and down as they passed over portions of the brace. "Maybe that contentment is contagious."

∽

Later that afternoon, Duncan worked out on the porch. He looked up and bolted to his feet. In a matter of seconds, he'd crossed the street and yanked a bucket from Carmen's hand. "What are ye doin', woman?"

She turned three shades of red.

Duncan reconsidered his question. He'd allowed her no privacy. "I meant to ask, 'Why are you hauling water up these stairs and into your house?'"

"My pump broke."

"And you didna ask for help?"

"I'll ask Otto after church tomorrow. I'm sure he'll be willing to come look at it next week."

"Nonsense." Duncan stomped up the last steps and plowed into her house. "Did the pump just suddenly stop working, did it sprout a leak, or what happened?"

Carmen stayed in the doorway. "The handle's been getting stiff, and suddenly the works just stopped."

Duncan nodded and thumped the water onto her stove. He paused a second to appreciate her kitchen. Mercy kept their kitchen neat as a pin. The white cupboards and gingham curtains looked cheerful. In contrast, Carmen's kitchen was an explosion of color and scents. Chili peppers hung in exotic-looking spills from lengths of twine. Garlic did, too. The hutch held a cheerful display of red, yellow, green, and blue dishes that matched the same hues as the brightly striped cloth running down the center of the table. The place felt as vibrant as its owner.

"Thank you for carrying the water."

Duncan cast a glance at the red pump. "I'll take a look and see what's wrong with your pump."

"That's not necessary."

Duncan leveled a stare at her and slowly crooked a brow. "Why is it you can run all over the county, feeding and helping everyone else, but you shy away from accepting any help in return?"

"It's not that way."

"Oh? And how does this differ?"

"To begin with, it's not proper!"

Duncan made an exasperated sound. "I'm going to grab some of my tools. While I'm gone, gather up your sewing or some such thing. Whilst I'm here repairing the pump, you can sit out on the veranda." From the way she winced, Duncan gathered he'd spoken with more force than diplomacy. He softened his tone into a teasing lilt. "That way, you can admire your new birdhouse."

As he worked on the pump, Duncan's mood darkened. Carmen sat out on the veranda sewing a shirt for some little boy. The next-door neighbor called over and suggested that Carmen might think about taking supper to a certain family since the mother was ailing. Yet another woman appeared and dropped off her baby and a cranky toddler so she could go to the mercantile. She'd no more than retrieved her children before another woman dropped off three.

Duncan cleaned up his mess, washed his hands, and dumped his tools back into a box. It wouldn't be right to speak to Carmen about it in front of anyone. The next time he caught her alone, he was going to say something. Just because she had a big heart and a willing spirit didn't mean she ought to work herself into an early grave by doing favors for everyone in Texas. *I'm going to tell the lass she's a blessing to all who know her, but she canna let people take advantage of her.*

⚭

"I made empanadas." Carmen stood by Duncan's shop and extended a basket of the sweets to him.

He wiped his hands on a rag, then leaned over and took one. "One of these days, when Elspeth isna wakenin' Mercy every other hour, you'll hae to show Mercy how to make these." He took a bite and closed his eyes with a hum of appreciation.

"You don't need to wait until then to have more. Any time you'd like empanadas, just ask me." Carmen set the basket on a nearby table.

Duncan's eyes popped open. "I'd ne'er do such a thing!"

Stinging from his tone, Carmen stepped back. Her foot landed poorly, and she struggled to keep her balance. Duncan wrapped his hand about her upper arm, stabilizing her. The way he shook his head made her heart plummet. The one thing she couldn't bear was for people to pity her.

"What kind of man would I be, making demands of you? You're a friend and neighbor, not a servant."

"It's because we're friends and neighbors." She pulled away from his touch. "You fixed my pump and gave me a birdhouse. You fixed my roof last week, too. I'm returning a favor because you said you like empanadas."

Duncan held the other half of the treat up between them. "Dinna mistake me, Carmen. This is a fine mouthful, but on occasion when I come o'er and help out, 'tis without expectation of getting anything in return."

"I know." She wasn't willing to leave the topic. "Just as when I bring your family something, I'm not hoping to talk you into doing a chore for me."

"Fair enough." He finished the other bite. Like a small boy who didn't want to miss the last little taste, Duncan licked the cinnamon sugar from his lips. He was such a man of contrasts—so mature and wise at one moment, only to be delightfully childlike the next instant. Though huge and strong, he exhibited a gentleness that evoked a sense of trust. *He's such a fine man. Handsome, too. The next wedding will probably be his. Any woman would be delighted to have such a husband.*

"I've been meanin' to talk with you about something."

"Would you mind too much if we discussed it later? I need to be over at the Rayburns' in an hour or so."

" 'Twill only take a moment." He nodded toward a chair. Once she sat down, he folded his arms across his chest. "A man could get dizzy watching you going to and fro all day."

No man would ever watch me, so that's a ridiculous statement.

"You canna continue to allow others to take advantage of your kind heart. There's not another woman around who's constantly dashing off to lend a hand. You're going to be worn to a frazzle."

"I like helping others."

"And well they know it. Still, dinna feel that every single time someone mentions a need, you're the one meant to meet it."

Carmen couldn't fathom what he was talking about.

Duncan stepped closer. "They're taking advantage of you, getting you to mind their bairns, bringing them meals, doing all manner of chores. . . . If you have a hard time telling them no, then we'll work on that. But—"

"No one's making me do anything. I offer them my help, Duncan."

"Let me be sure I'm hearing you right." He tilted his head to the side, and his brows formed an ominous black V. "You got yourself into this fix, and you keep on volunteering?"

"Fix?" Carmen tried not to laugh. He looked so serious that it warmed her heart. "Duncan, I'm happy to be busy. There's nothing wrong with me helping our neighbors and church family."

"I'm going to disagree wi' you there." His voice held reservation. "Dinna be so wrapped up in actions that you fail to do as the Bible instructs—to be still and know that He is God."

"Of course I know He is God." Carmen rose. "And I know who my brothers and sisters are, because Christ is our Savior. It all fits together. By serving them, I serve Him."

The grooves along the sides of his mouth deepened. Shaking his head, Duncan said, "You've the cart before the horse. 'Tis by serving God that we serve others. When our hearts are in accord with Him, our cups run over and shower blessings on the lives of others. You canna rain showers of blessings forever on your own strength and merit. Your own cup will go dry."

His words left her feeling unsettled. Carmen resented that. *Instead of wallowing in self-pity because I'm crippled and alone, I'm filling my days by helping others. He just doesn't understand.*

"Think on it," he urged.

"Only if you hurry and eat another of those. I think you need to sweeten your disposition today." She forced a laugh and hobbled out of his shop and back to her empty house.

Chapter 5

"Things are wrong." Duncan did his best not to glower at Carmen.

"What's wrong?" She finished tying a ribbon around the bottom of a little lassie's plait. "Go ask Nestor to give you a cookie."

"Miss Carmen, are you telling me to get a cookie?" The lassie shot a jealous look up at Duncan. "Or are you telling him to?"

"I dinna have an appetite for cookies today." Duncan served Carmen a telling look.

The little lass tugged on Carmen's sleeve. "Do I getta have his cookie, then?"

"You and Nestor may share it, *chica.*"

Duncan fought the urge to shoo all of the children back to their homes. His talk with Carmen had made a difference—but the wrong one. If anything, she'd taken on even more responsibilities. The woman looked tired. From clear across the road, he'd noticed how her steps dragged. As a result, he'd closed his shop and come over so she wouldn't have to mind the rowdy bunch of children who filled her yard all by herself.

Her flower garden wasn't the wonderland it used to be. Her walkway wasn't swept, either. Little things—none of them alone said much, but put together, they nearly shouted something was wrong. He'd stay here until every last child left, but then Duncan planned to nudge Carmen into seeing the truth.

"So you mentioned something is wrong?" She gave him an expectant look.

"Aye." She'd prodded him into the discussion before he'd anticipated, but Duncan decided he might as well get things out in the open. He fisted his hands and rested them on his hips. "Speakin' as your friend, I'm reminding you that Christ was happier with Mary for sitting at His feet than He was with Martha for dashing about."

"Miss Rodriguez!" The little girl ran back over with her lower lip poking out and quivering. "Nestor says he already gave away all the cookies."

"*Pobrecita.*" Rich with compassion, the word rolled off Carmen's tongue. She gave the child a hug and murmured, "Next time you come, I'll make sure you get two."

"I get two po-citras?"

Shaking her head, Carmen explained, "*Pobrecita* is a special word in Spanish that means I was feeling sorry for you and I care."

"Oh." The child's eyes brightened with greed. "But I still get two cookies the next time!" She ran off shouting, "Nestor!"

"It actually means 'poor little girl,' but it isn't in regards to money—it's just a sympathy word." Carmen absently brushed a smear of something from her skirt.

At times when he'd seen her with Ismelda, Duncan had overheard Carmen speak in Spanish. "Chris is the one who'd have figured that out. I dinna have a talent with words."

"I disagree. It's true, Chris learns languages so he can communicate." Her hands started together and separated outward. "Your gift is in choosing the right words to comfort." Her hands reversed the action, but she ended by pressing her hands to her bosom.

He'd never thought of it that way. It was a fine compliment, but Duncan refused to be distracted. "My words to you today won't bring you comfort. I'm aiming to urge you to take stock and make changes."

"I don't want to change."

Stubborn woman. He heaved a long, drawn-out sigh for her benefit. "Busy hands dinna mean a full heart."

She smoothed her skirts. " 'Faith without works is dead.' "

"Aye, and you'd best be glad you've held that faith when you work yourself to death."

Carmen's eyes flashed with ire.

He studied her beautiful golden brown skin. The dark circles beneath her big brown eyes alarmed him. Duncan gentled his voice to coax her into reason. "E'en the Lord God Himself took the seventh day to rest."

"And by keeping these little ones, I'm giving their parents a time of rest." Carmen lifted a crabby tyke who'd toddled over and now clung to her skirts.

One quick whiff let Duncan know Carmen was going to be doing those parents a bigger favor still.

She laughed. "You've turned an interesting shade. With Elspeth—"

"My niece has enough sense to wait until her mother or father is around to do that."

"Mercy said all of you Gregor men change diapers."

"We do." He nodded briskly.

"Then—"

"Elspeth behaves herself for Chris and me."

The speed with which he made that assertion sent Carmen into giggles. Her laughter floated out to him as she tended the baby inside.

Duncan sat on the steps. Kids were a joy. Why, the three

scrambling to sit on his knees and hang around his neck were all full of sunshine and laughter. But their parents were wrong to take advantage of Carmen. Ever since her sister got married, everyone seemed to think the woman didn't have a thing to do.

"Piggyback!" Nestor pled.

"Sure, and why not?" Duncan was giving the second child a turn about the yard when Carmen came back out with the babe. She sat in a wicker chair and popped a bottle into the toddler's mouth.

By the time he'd given all the children two rides, their parents came to collect them. As they walked away, Carmen turned to him. "You'll make a good father someday."

"I'm looking forward to it. E'en promised Da I'd name my first-born son after him, but that day's a long while off. Carmen, I was serious when I said 'tisna right, you doing so much."

"I'm enjoying myself."

"You're wearin' yourself to a frazzle. You dinna e'en hae time enough to tend to your flowers any longer. The garden's a sad shadow of itself."

"But the children have more room to play."

He yanked the diaper she'd slung over her shoulder as a drool cloth. "They can do that at their own homes."

Carmen yanked the cloth from him. "Yes, they can. But I like them to come to my house just the same. Our town is friendly. I enjoy spending time with—"

"The old and the sick and the lonely?"

"They are my friends and neighbors." Her eyes flashed.

"That doesn't mean you have to be responsible for other people's children, too. Not a day goes by that you aren't minding someone else's bairns."

The passion he'd seen in her eyes just seconds ago dimmed.

The spirit in her voice did, too. "I'll never have children of my own. Why do you want to deny me the few hours I can enjoy someone else's?"

Before he could answer, she turned and fled up the steps. Her awkward steps made it difficult, and he could have easily caught up, but Duncan stayed behind. He tried to meet her gaze as she turned to shut her door, but she kept her head bowed. That was bad enough, but her shoulders—the way they lifted and fell wasn't due to exertion.

I made her cry.

Duncan lumbered up to her door and knocked. He didn't know what he was going to say, but he couldn't set a woman into tears and just walk away. When she didn't answer, he stood there and knocked again—harder and longer.

The door opened a mere crack—just enough for him to catch sight of a tear-streaked cheek.

Suddenly, he knew exactly what to say. He felt badly and wanted her to know he cared. "Pobrecita—"

"I'm not a child, and I don't want your pity." The door clicked shut.

"I'm a cobbler," he said at a pitch he knew would reach her. "I'm good at making shoes, but I'm e'en better at stickin' my feet in my mouth." She didn't respond. After another minute or two, Duncan went back to his shop.

Needing to wear off his frustration, he yanked out a case of metal stamps and a hammer, then started whacking the stamps with notable force to impress a design on a strip of leather. An intricately tooled design emerged.

It's not half as complicated as that woman. I vowed to Da that I'd hae a son, but I didna think through all that meant. I'm going to look long and hard to find a placid woman. Someone fiery like Carmen would be the death of me.

∞

"She'd be here with you for about four months. Preferably five, if you don't mind her staying a month to recover."

Carmen set down her coffee. "Even six months is fine."

"If you have any reservations at all, it's okay." The doctor didn't so much as blink. "I've not mentioned this to a soul, so no one need e'er know if you feel 'tisna right for you."

"You didn't even mention it to Mercy?"

Dr. Gregor shook his head. "Nae. My wife honors the way a man of my profession must hold confidences. If you agree to boarding the young woman, you should know part of the usual arrangement is that she's to help about the house with normal chores. She's also to attend church."

Folding her hands in her lap, Carmen sought a polite way to ask how she was supposed to coax a soiled dove to worship. "Is she accustomed to attending church?"

"Not as of late. But when she asked for assistance, she specified she wanted her baby to go to a good Christian home. It's my hope that during her months here, she might turn her heart toward the Lord."

"That would be wonderful. How soon can I expect her?"

"Her current situation is undesirable. The sooner, the better."

Carmen nodded. "I just finished my spring cleaning. Ismelda's old bedroom is ready. I could take her today if necessary."

"She's a full day away by train."

"Tomorrow, then." Carmen bit her lip. "Shall I say my cousin is coming?"

Dr. Gregor stood and leaned against the veranda railing.

"Carmen, I didna seek you out because of your Mexican heritage. This lass—Jenny—I've been told she's Swedish. I asked you because when Mercy discovered she was with child, your support for her never wavered. You looked past the sad circumstances and poured out Christian love and charity. If Jenny is to turn her heart toward the Lord, I'm thinkin' you and the Gregors are goin' to hae to drench her in His love."

"I'll expect Jenny tomorrow."

∞

"No!" Duncan thumped down his coffee mug, and everything on the supper table jumped from the impact. He glowered at Rob as he got to his feet. "Meet me in my workshop." Without waiting for a response, he stomped out of the house.

Rob sauntered into the shop a few minutes later. "You canna bellow like a wounded bull whene'er you take a mind to, Duncan. You woke Elspeth again."

"Dinna try to distract me. It willna work." Duncan glowered at his little brother.

Rob simply stood in the center of the shop and said nothing.

"It willna work, I'm tellin' you!"

"It must have. You've forgotten why you dragged me out here."

"Are ye daft? Maybe you're goin' deaf. I told you, it willna work. You canna expect Carmen to give shelter to that woman."

"I met with Carmen yesterday, and we settled all of the details. She made Jenny feel right at home today."

"Aye, Jenny felt fine, but what of Carmen? I'm askin'—what of her?"

"What of her?"

"We've been here for a year now. I've ne'er once seen a single gentleman pay a call upon that fine lass. She's married off her kid sister and put on a good face, but she's hurting deep inside. I didna see the truth till a few days ago. She's brokenhearted o'er the fact that she'll ne'er marry and hae bairns of her own—and what did you go do?" Duncan stabbed an awl through the center of a choice piece of leather. "You go and rub her face in it, that's what you've done."

"I gave her every opportunity to refuse. Instead, she expressed an enthusiasm that convinced me this was the right thing to do."

"And how was she to refuse? Carmen's heart is bigger than Texas. Once she learns of someone else's needs, she puts them ahead of herself." He shook his head. " 'Tis a rare day I disagree wi' you, but that day's come. I've been trying to make the woman stop playing a dangerous game."

"What game is that?"

Duncan fought the temptation to tell Rob to mind his own business. But if speaking confidentially to him would spare Carmen heartache in the end, it was worth it. "The lass is forever doing something for someone—baking treats, taking a casserole somewhere, minding another woman's children. . . ."

"And she's happy as a lark."

"Nae, Rob. She isna. Just look into her eyes and see the sadness there. That wee little limp of hers has her convinced she's not worthy of love, so she's trying to fill up the aching hole by working to earn appreciation. God doesn't care about the deeds one does—He cares about the soul. I've been tryin' to get her to see that."

"Have you, now?"

"And you went and ruined it all with this scheme of yours. I canna support this."

"It's too late to change things now."

"No, 'tisna. Move that mother-to-be into one of the bedrooms in the clinic. She can join us Gregors for meals and e'en help out your wife." Duncan nodded. "Aye, that's the solution."

"It's a foolish plan. Once people figure out that Jenny's unwed and carrying a child, her reputation will be in tatters. Leaving her alone in the clinic is a sure invitation for disaster."

Duncan glowered at his brother. "So you've asked Carmen to protect Jenny? What man asks that of a woman?"

"There's a world of difference between sheltering and protecting."

Duncan let out a loud, derisive snort. "Only in your feeble mind."

"As I said, it's too late to change things now. We'll have to make the best of it."

"Wipe that smile off your face, Rob, before I do something rash."

Rob sauntered over, picked up a shoe, and pretended to be fascinated by it. "Just when," he asked slowly, "did you appoint yourself Carmen's guardian?"

Chapter 6

Someone has to look out for her. The woman doesna give a moment's consideration to her own needs."

"Hmm." Rob set the shoe down with exacting care. "And how is it you've paid attention to whether men have called on her?"

"Her house is directly across the street," Duncan snapped. "Take a look—her garden and porch are the view from where I work. I've not been skulking or spying on her."

Rob went over to the window and clasped his hands behind his back. He nodded sagely as he examined the view for himself. "Duncan?"

"Now what?"

"I like Carmen."

"You've an odd way of showing it, putting her in this painful predicament."

"Much as I like Carmen, Mercy loves her even more."

Duncan let out a low growl of frustration.

Rob turned around and grinned. "We'll be happy to have her as our sister-in-law."

Duncan gaped at his brother.

Rob held up a hand to forestall any response. "Dinna deny it. You've feelings for the lass. Your reaction tonight shows those feelings run deep."

"Friendship doesna mean I'm marching down the aisle."

"Good thing, that. We dinna have any more of our plaid. I'm

thinkin' by the time 'tis ordered and arrived, you'll be wanting a length to drape o'er your bride's shoulder."

The image of Carmen dressed in a bridal gown with the Gregor tartan gathered over her shoulder hit Duncan so hard, he dropped down onto his bench.

Rob grinned like a drunken jester. "You love her."

"I'm a rough man. Why would a fine lass like her hae anything to do wi' me?"

"Remember that song the sailor was singing when we were waiting for the train?"

"About America? What does that hae to do with this?"

"You're in America now. This is the land of the free and the home of the brave." Rob snickered. "Only if you're brave, you'll no longer be free—you'll be married to a fiery little woman."

Duncan shot his brother a dark look. "You're far too amused by this."

"Aye, that I am. But what you just did is telling."

"What did I do?"

"Actually, it's more what you didna do."

Duncan got up and started pacing. "You're driving me daft. Will you make up your mind whether it's something I did or didna do?"

"What you didna do was deny what I said. You love her. If your heart weren't involved, you'd have challenged me."

Duncan folded his arms across his chest. In that moment, everything fell into place. His brother spoke the truth, and Duncan couldn't deny it. He didn't even want to. "I've made up my mind. Aye, I have."

"About what?"

"I'm going to court the woman. She's not had a swain, and I'm going to ease her into this slow and sweet. When we're old and gray, she'll look back and feel every last tender hope she e'er held in her heart was fulfilled."

"Women are romantics. If you plan to fulfill every last tender hope, you'll be old and gray and still not be married to her yet."

"You'd best watch what you say. I'm still sore at you for sticking that young girl into Carmen's care."

"You ought to be thanking me. Now that Carmen's not alone, you can go over there without raising any questions of propriety."

"The only thing I'll thank you to do is keep this conversation confidential." He stared out the window. "There's every chance Carmen might not love me back."

☞

" 'Tis a bonny day to go fishing," Duncan announced as he crossed the road with a shovel in his big hands.

Only a few days had passed since Carmen had blurted out the shameful fact that no man would have her and she had to resort to borrowing children. That alone left her wanting to crawl off somewhere. But Duncan had listened to that appallingly personal confession and rumbled "pobrecita" at her as if she needed his pity. Carmen decided she didn't want to crawl off somewhere after all; she'd rather bake a special batch of empanadas for him and dust them with cayenne and chili instead of cinnamon. She wouldn't, but just the thought brought a tiny measure of glee.

"Aye, I'm going fishing."

She pretended not to hear him and stooped down to pick a weed.

The hulking Scotsman kept coming.

Carmen fought the urge to tell him to stop wasting time and go fishing. *This is all his fault. I don't have a hard time minding my manners with anyone else. Duncan—he's polite and kind to everyone else.*

Why can't he just leave me alone and keep his opinions to himself? The man's an insensitive brute and needs to mind his own business instead of prying into mine. If he says anything—

Boots stopped half a yard from her. Ordinary brown boots. Carmen hadn't figured out yet why Duncan's boots were so basic and plain. A cobbler could wear the finest and fanciest, yet he didn't. She looked up to tell him so.

"I'm going fishing," he said again as he reached down to assist her up.

Carmen accepted his help, then snatched her hand back and wondered why she'd let him assist her. Scrambling to find something to say, she blurted out, "Most men take a pole fishing, not a spade."

He chortled softly, and the fine lines crinkling from the corners of his eyes reminded her that he laughed often. " 'Tis the truth. I've some method to my madness, though. This time last year, you were planting flowers. Why dinna I turn the soil for you and swipe a few worms whilst I'm at it?"

Astonishment and relief flooded her. He was acting as if they'd never had that horribly awkward and embarrassing exchange. "That would be nice. Thank you." *And I'm going to bake you some empanadas with cinnamon, not cayenne and chili.* "Duncan, I have a friend staying with me for a while."

"Rob told me." His voice took on an undertone that she couldn't interpret.

Carmen called, "Jenny?"

Jenny stepped out of the house. "Ja?"

"Come meet our neighbor." She waited until Jenny reached her side. "Jenny Sigrids, may I present you to Duncan Gregor. Duncan, my friend Jenny."

" 'Tis a pleasure to meet any friend of Carmen's. Nice to meet you, Mi—"

Realizing the fact that Jenny was unwed would cause for awkward moments, Carmen interrupted. "Oh dear, I should have mentioned that with three Gregor men across the street, it makes for a lot of confusion if we use formal address. Duncan, I hope you don't mind if Jenny follows my example and calls you by your Christian name."

"Not a-tall."

"And Jenny, it's only fair that you reciprocate. There." Carmen smiled broadly. "Duncan, since you're turning the soil, maybe Jenny and I can go to the mercantile and choose flower seeds today."

"You already have a beautiful garden," Jenny said.

"Actually, it's a pitiful mess right now. Isn't it, Duncan?"

"Shameful as 'tis to confess, I did tell you that just a few days back. Last year, the blossoms in your yard rivaled all of God's flower-strewn fields about us."

"Oh my." Jenny sighed. "I never had a garden. It will be so fun to grow something."

"You know," Duncan said, stretching, "if you'd like, we could go on a walk. I'll take a wheelbarrow, and we could transplant some of the wildflowers so you can enjoy them until your seeds sprout and blossom."

"What about the worms?" Jenny asked.

"I'm sure we'll happen across a few." Duncan's glance skimmed down their gowns. "You're both wearin' lovely frocks. Best you go change into ones that willna be spoiled by layers of dust."

"Though it sounds like a delightful notion, I'm afraid Jenny and I need to do something else today."

"Perhaps later in the week." Duncan didn't ask—he told. When had he become so bossy?

"Oh, that would be so much fun," Jenny said.

Carmen couldn't dash Jenny's enthusiasm. Though Jenny was tall and large boned, she still seemed startlingly childlike in some circumstances. So far, she and Jenny had politely limited their conversations to impersonal things. Carmen wasn't sure how old her guest was. For now, she would indulge the girl. "We'll be able to go in a few days. The timing would be better. By buying seeds first, we can transplant the wildflowers to places in the garden where they'll have the best effect."

"Best effect?" Jenny wrinkled her nose. "I thought they were just supposed to look pretty."

"Me, too." Duncan grinned at Jenny.

He's impossibly handsome. He's charming her, just as he charms everyone else. He turned his steady blue gaze back onto Carmen. "Why dinna ye tell us just what kind of effect you are talkin' about?"

"What I meant was, we don't want to plant whistly blue behind paintbrush or bluebonnets. They're tall and would block out the flowers that are low to the ground."

He nodded. "That makes sense. Good thinking. Back home, Rob always kept an herbal garden so he'd have medicinals on hand. Each plant belonged in a specific location, but I dinna ken whether 'twas so he could tell them apart or because one might taint another if they grew too close."

"He didn't put in an herb garden here." Carmen frowned. "Why not?"

Duncan compressed his lips for a moment and then grimaced. "Chris dug straight through it when he put in the basement. He thought the herbs were weeds. Best you not mention it to either of them unless you're set to witness a shouting match."

"You Gregors don't fight," Carmen said.

"They don't?" Jenny sounded completely flummoxed. "Men always fight."

"Now I suppose that depends on the men." Duncan shrugged. "I've known many a man to lose his temper, but of all the men I've known, I admired my da the most. I canna recall a single time when he lost his self-control."

"He must have been quite a man," Jenny said softly.

"Humility, meekness, self-control—those are all traits a man of God strives for." Carmen looked at Duncan. "Your father must have been a godly man."

"The finest, and I thank you for sayin' so."

"Jenny, why don't we wash up and go to the mercantile?"

"All right." Jenny shoved her hands into the pocket of her apron. "I hope the fish are biting once you go fishing, Duncan."

"Now there's a grand thought."

Carmen didn't mention how she'd noticed Jenny's hands remained fisted deep in the apron pockets. Was she truly excited to go on the walk, or was she just afraid to have to be out and meet people here in town?

They went inside, and Carmen went to the washstand. "It never fails to amaze me how filthy my hands become after just a few minutes in the garden."

Jenny didn't respond.

As she dried her hands on a scarlet towel embroidered with big, sunny yellow flowers, Carmen turned to her. "I like to sew. Do you?"

"For my grandmother, I used to sew all of the time. She was a dressmaker."

Carmen smiled. "Wonderful. My friend Mercy—she's the

doctor's wife—she recently had a baby. I remember her making special dresses during the time she was—" Carmen caught herself just before she said, "in the family way." Jenny wasn't going to keep the baby, so mentioning family would be cruel. Instead, Carmen simply said, "—increasing. I'm sure you're going to need some roomier clothes, too. Maybe we could drop in on Mercy and ask her for advice before we buy fabric."

"My other dress is bigger." Jenny paused a second, then blurted out, "I don't have much money. I had to run away from the saloon. Bart thought I was going to the doctor to get rid of the baby, so all I have is what he gave me to pay the doctor."

"Jenny!"

Jenny hung her head. "I'm sorry. A nice lady like you shouldn't rub elbows with—"

Carmen stopped her by wrapping Jenny in her arms. "I'm so proud of you. You're a brave girl. You did the right thing."

Jenny drew away and looked nonplussed.

"It must have been hard for you to get help and keep everything a secret."

Jenny bit her lip and nodded.

"But here you are. And we have those three big, strong Gregor men across the street to protect you if that awful Bart finds out where you are."

"Why would they want to protect me?" Just as quickly as she asked it, Jenny answered the question. "Because of the baby."

"No. If you'd run away from a bad situation and weren't with child, they'd still defend you. They're noble men." Carmen squeezed Jenny's hand. "Mercy and I both enjoy sewing and doing embroidery. Won't it be pleasant to sit together in a shady spot and stitch together?"

A stiff shrug tattled on Jenny's reservations.

"Tacky as it might be for me to discuss money, you ought to know that on occasion someone chooses to be a secret benefactor to a woman in your situation. I know that's true in your case. You'll have an account at the mercantile, so it shouldn't be a problem for you to purchase fabric and other necessities."

"Someone would do that for me? A stranger? They didn't know what kind of woman I am."

"What that person knows is that you are a woman who is willing to give her child the wonderful gift of a family who will cherish him or her in ways you know you cannot."

"Don't you think whoever that is would want me to spend the money to make blankets and clothes and diapers for the baby?"

"Absolutely not!" Carmen released Jenny's hand. "The couple who receives the baby will take care of those details. Why don't you freshen up while I jot down a few things?"

While Jenny took a turn at the washstand, Carmen sat at the ornately carved oak secretary her mother once treasured. She didn't have much time, so she dipped the pen in the inkwell and quickly wrote:

CONFIDENTIAL.
Dear Leonard,
*   Set up an account for Jenny. Twenty-five dollars. No one—*
especially Jenny—is to know I'm funding this. Thank you.

She hastily signed only her initials and glanced over at Jenny.

"I'm in no hurry. If you'd like to tame your hair, feel free."

"Oh. Okay."

Carmen took another sheet of paper and hastily started writing down anything she might vaguely need from the mercantile.

"That list must be getting long," Jenny said as she patted one last strand of hair into place.

"I've been doing a lot of baking. One peek into my pantry and you'll think we're in danger of starving." Carmen blotted the list and folded it to hide the note.

Chapter 7

D uncan yawned and stretched. He'd gone to bed late and
gotten up early so he'd have today's work done by breakfast. That freed him to take Carmen for a nice stroll.
Women liked to walk and have a man pick flowers for them. Surely
this would be a time she'd remember fondly. It would be a fine start
of their courtship.

The thought of taking a picnic lunch along crossed his mind,
but Duncan decided he'd use that as another outing. Aye, he'd plan
a string of pleasant activities and idyllic afternoons, and he'd make
a point to go over to her house more often to handle some minor
repairs and do general upkeep.

Small gardening hand tools jostled merrily in the wheelbarrow
as he wheeled it across the street. Duncan mentally traced the route
they'd take again. He'd wandered the nearby fields to plot out a lei-
surely walk that wouldn't tax Carmen. Though she didn't complain,
he knew her leg pained her—and she loathed having anyone notice
that ridiculously paltry limp of hers. But because she'd be mortified
to be unable to exert herself, Duncan circumvented the difficulty by
planning everything in advance.

"Good morning!" Carmen stepped from her house. The morning sun glossed her raven-black hair and made Duncan wish he
could yank out the pins and run his hands through her tresses to
see how long they were.

"Yeah. Good morning." Jenny stepped out of the house, too.

"Aye, 'tis. And it just got better, what with a pair of pretty ladies to go on a walk wi' me."

They sauntered down the street. Pride squared Duncan's shoulders. With Carmen by his side, he felt ten feet tall. The moment they reached a fork in the road, he started to veer south.

"Have you ever seen such a sight?" Jenny stared in rapture at the field that went north.

"I don't know what it is about flowers." Carmen smiled. "I always think the one I'm looking at is the most beautiful ever."

Jenny shaded her eyes with one hand and pointed into the distance. "Could we get some of those little blue ones?"

"What a wonderful idea. I'm always charmed by wind-blown."

Duncan tilted his head to the side. "Aren't all wildflowers windblown?"

"Most are," Carmen allowed. "But that particular flower's name is wind-blown. Jenny, I'll show you more of them. It's amazing, but wind-blown comes in a huge array of colors. If you keep watch, you soon see them in everything from a pale blue to a bright pink."

To Duncan's consternation, the women headed north toward the wind-blown. He wanted to snatch Carmen back to his side. He told himself it was simply because he wanted her to take the easier route he'd planned. He promptly called himself a liar. He didn't want her away from his side—and that was the truth of the matter.

"You mentioned whistly blue the other day," he said to Carmen. "I've found several stretches of it, but I'd rather hae them be among the beauty we gather after we gain a collection of taller varieties."

Carmen smiled. "That's good planning."

"I was wondering"—Jenny scanned the field—"can we fill the wheelbarrow today and put the flowers in the garden tomorrow?"

" 'Tis up to you, Carmen."

Carmen shook her head. "It's too dry and warm today to do that. We'd run the risk of losing them. It would be a shame to pluck up a flower, only to make it so it won't survive."

Jenny made a wry face.

"You're unhappy with my decision?" Carmen gave Jenny a surprised look.

"The only thing I've ever seen dry out in a wheelbarrow is a man. At the saloon, they'd dump a drunk into the wheelbarrow and push it over by the ditch."

Carmen's eyes widened.

"Oh, they did that so when he woke up and puked, no one would have to clean up the mess."

"They treated a man like that?" Carmen's voice sounded both sad and outraged.

Jenny shrugged. "A real man can hold his liquor."

"A real man doesna need liquor a-tall," Duncan said. "But any man who's weak enough to drink to that kind of excess still deserves better than to be treated like refuse."

Jenny's mouth twisted wryly. "Neither of you have ever had to mop up after a drunken fool."

"I far prefer having flowers in your wheelbarrow, Duncan."

Duncan flashed Carmen a smile. She'd bent the conversation away from Jenny's unfortunate past and back to something pleasant. Admiration for her diplomacy filled him. He nodded. "Flowers and ladies on a beautiful day are definitely to my taste." He managed to steer them all back toward the route he'd chosen.

At one point, an almost two-foot-wide crack in the ground broke the path. Duncan knew it was there, and he'd intentionally led them toward the rift. It provided an excuse for him to cup Carmen's waist and lift her.

"You ladies wait a moment whilst I get the wheelbarrow over there. If the edges here take a mind to crumble, I'd rather it not be under your feet." Proud of that excuse, Duncan made short work of hefting the flower-filled wheelbarrow over to the other side. Straddling the divide, he reached for Jenny first. That way, Carmen wouldn't feel as if he was making allowances for the insignificant problem she strove so hard to deny.

"You're so strong!" Jenny cooed at him as he swung the big-boned lass over the divide.

"Compared to the things he hauled when they built their house, you weigh nothing at all." Carmen smiled as she vouched so casually for his strength.

Her praise meant a lot to him, but the fact that she'd been watching him gave Duncan a glimmer of hope. Maybe the attraction was mutual after all. "I'm ready for you now, Carmen." *And not just to lift you across this.* He slowly cupped her waist and made sure he had a secure hold.

Unlike Jenny, who'd rested her hands on his shoulders, Carmen carefully rested her hands on his upper arms. The shyness in her beautiful brown eyes beguiled him. She was normally confident and saucy, so he'd not seen this side of her. *Give me time, lass. I'll show you just how lovely you are and that you can entrust yourself to me entirely.*

"Is something wrong?" Embarrassment colored her whisper.

"Not a bit." Duncan grinned. "I was appreciating your perfume. It's a tad spicy—like you."

"I like it," Jenny said.

"Aye, as do I." Duncan lifted Carmen. He would be content to stay there the whole day, holding her and inhaling her scent. Instead, he set her down by Jenny and waited a second to be sure she was steady before releasing his hold.

By the time Duncan returned to his workshop that afternoon, he couldn't stop grinning like a fool. Aye, he'd set his heart on that black-haired, brown-eyed woman, and courting her was going to be pure delight.

∽

"Holes?" Carmen glanced at her windows in consternation. "I didn't notice any."

"Aye, a close look at the screens will tell you I'm right." Duncan clomped across her veranda and pointed at a few spots. "They're wee small holes yet, but that's when we need to catch the problem. If they get any larger, you'll be plagued with flies in the house."

"Thank you for pointing that out. I think I have a scrap of screening material somewhere."

"A scrap willna do."

Carmen gave him a patient look. "I can sew little patches if the holes are tiny."

"That brings to mind the verse about not putting new wine in old wineskins."

Carmen noticed Jenny's perplexed expression and made a mental note to explain the biblical verse to her later. "Wineskins are different. A more accurate analogy would be resoling a pair of boots." Pleased that she'd countered his assertion with something Duncan would relate to so well, Carmen gave him a smile.

Duncan's brows rose. "I'd not recommend resoling boots that dinna have enough life left in them to make it worthwhile."

"How old are your screens?" Jenny poked her finger at the screen door. It went straight through and left a jagged little tear. "Oh, I'm sorry!"

"There you have it." Duncan nodded. "They're all wanting replacement."

Otto was busy on the farm. Carmen knew he couldn't afford the time to accomplish the job. "I'll decide which ones are the worst and ask Otto to do one a week."

"Ooch, lass. And why would you be doing that when I'm willin' to get the job done now?"

"You're a busy man, Duncan."

"Not too busy to help out a neighbor. I'll do your screen door first, here on your porch, so you'll still be able to catch a breeze for the rest of the day. Elsewise, your house will be miserable as the inside of an oven."

"You've already done so much, Duncan. You turned the soil for our garden and helped us get the flowers."

"Dinna forget that I helped myself to some worms to bait my hook and caught several fish. Aye, and I had the joy of your fine company for a stroll the day we gathered flowers."

"You shared the fish," Jenny pointed out.

"Aye, but then you ladies shared your flower seeds with Mercy. She wept for joy when she discovered you'd started a garden for her."

"Elspeth keeps her so busy, we knew Mercy wouldn't have an opportunity to plant flowers." Carmen turned to Jenny. "Isn't that so, Jenny?"

Jenny nodded. "Carmen and I had fun planning where to put each flower."

"And you turned the soil so the ground would be ready, Duncan. You were every bit as much involved in the project."

"I just finished making that saddle for Mr. Stucky. This is a good time for me to take on doing your screens. I dinna like to start a new pair of shoes or a saddle when I'll have to skip working the next day."

"Oh." Jenny's voice went flat. "Tomorrow is Sunday."

"So there you have it." Duncan folded his arms across his chest as if he'd won an important debate.

"What do I have?" Jenny glowered at him.

"You hae the reason why you ladies ought to accompany me to the mercantile. We'll get the screening so I can fix Carmen's windows by sunset."

"It's been three days since we went to the mercantile, Jenny," Carmen remarked. "Those things you ordered are probably in by now."

Jenny wilted into a wicker chair. "Could you pick them up for me? I'm hot and tired."

"Sure we could." Duncan spoke before Carmen could insist Jenny come along.

On their walk to the mercantile, Carmen tried to think of a way to broach the delicate topic. Several different phrases occurred to her, but she dismissed them.

"You're quiet as can be."

She sighed. "It's Jenny."

Duncan stopped. "If things are strained, I'll hae Rob find a different place for her."

"No, no. She's not been here a full week yet. Settling in will take time."

"You're dillydallying around. Why dinna ye just say what needs to be said?"

Heat tingled in her cheeks. "It's not that easy."

Duncan tilted her face to his and spoke in a low, soothing tone. "We're friends, Carmen Rodriguez. We're trying to help a lass who's got a dark past and a difficult future. You're a cultured woman. I ken there are matters not normally discussed between a lady and a man, but this isna a normal situation. Troubling yourself over finding the proper words is silly. I'll not think less of you for doing what's necessary to help Jenny. Deep down, she's a sweet lass, and I'm wanting to help her, too. Speak to me from your heart."

His earnest words helped. Carmen blurted out, "Jenny doesn't want to go to church. She didn't even want to go to the mercantile the other day. Once people understand what she is, she's sure they'll shun her."

"Mmmm." Duncan stretched out the sound. "I see."

"Remember how long it took for everyone to face Mercy once her tragedy happened?"

"Aye. 'Twas a harsh time for her. Once we stood firm on her side, folks came around. We'll do the same for Jenny."

"There's a difference between their cases. Mercy was innocent."

"True." Duncan let out a long sigh. "Times like today, when I mentioned the wineskins, she's baffled. From what I gather, she's not a believer. We canna expect her to hae walked the straight and narrow path when she wasna shod with the preparation of the gospel of peace nor protected with the shield of faith."

"Ephesians six," Carmen murmured. He did that—slipped biblical references into his conversation. Often, it was so seamless, anyone who wasn't steeped in the scriptures would miss it.

"Exactly. 'Tis wrong to judge others. No one makes it to the Lord by good deeds or based on the opinions of others. 'Tis grace through the blood of Christ Jesus that redeems us. I'm thinkin' 'twill be our example of grace and love that will woo Jenny to the Lord. If others judge her, they'll be accountable to Him."

"So there will be the Gregors and me."

"To start with." Duncan began to walk again. "But just as surely as God can do a work in Jenny's heart, He can supply compassion to others so they can show it to her."

"As long as we're talking, Duncan, I may as well confess another worry to you."

"You can always share your worries with me."

She gave him an appreciative look. Duncan wasn't a glib man. He spoke directly and from the heart. That invitation wasn't just a platitude. He'd meant what he said. "Remember when Otto's mother dragged that awful man into my house so he could beg Mercy for her baby? It didn't occur to me until yesterday that once Mrs. Kunstler comes to church tomorrow and finds out about Jenny staying with me, she'll bring that man back again."

"We've discussed that at home. Mercy received a letter from Chester Heim that same week. He apologized and sought forgiveness. He and his wife are so verra eager to hae a bairn to call their own. In thinkin' back, Mercy said he'd implored her to gie them the babe, but 'twas actually Mrs. Kunstler who'd spoken the harshest words."

"Since Ismelda married Otto, Mrs. Kunstler is family, and she is my elder. Part of me says I owe her respect, no matter what. On the other hand, I feel if she dares to say anything, I'll lose my temper. So what do I do?"

"Just as you came to fetch Rob last time, you can always run to us for help. Neither Rob nor Mercy thinks Chester Heim will trouble Jenny. Though 'tis true Mrs. Kunstler is kin to you since Ismelda wed her son, I'm not mincing words. I think it best if ever she comes to pay a call that you instruct Jenny to come help Mercy."

"Thank you. I'll do that."

They'd arrived at the mercantile. Before he opened the door, Duncan gazed at her intently. "Dinna forget, Carmen, I intend to be your partner."

Partner. Such an odd word. It suggested both a union of minds and a distance of hearts. All at once, Carmen felt supported and yet very, very alone.

Chapter 8

"Och, Carmen, you're looking grand today."

A blush filled her cheeks. "Thank you. Wait till you see Jenny. She's wearing her new dress."

Duncan nodded and winked. Carmen made for a good partner in this project. By mentioning Jenny's gown, he'd have something to praise her over so she wouldn't fret as much while they walked to church. The church bell began to toll. "Best we get started."

Once Jenny stepped onto the veranda, he mused, "I'm not a man who knows much about posies, other than to say they're charming wee things. But your gown—'tis the same shade as those bachelor buttons in the garden."

"Leave it to a man to know the name of a flower named bachelor." Carmen laughed as she shut the door.

Duncan escorted the women down the street. Jenny held tightly to his arm, giving away the fragile state of her nerves. "Elspeth kept Rob and Mercy up half the night. They're going to sit in the back pew. I hope you dinna mind sitting with me today."

"We'd be happy to. Wouldn't we, Jenny?"

"Yes."

Duncan ignored how she sounded as if she'd rather have Rob pull all her teeth than attend worship. "Mercy directed me to invite you both to lunch."

"You just said she was up half the night." Carmen frowned. "Maybe some other Sunday."

Duncan intentionally waited until the church bell rang so Jenny wouldn't get mobbed by everyone and feel overwhelmed. Even then, as they reached the church door, Carmen found it necessary to introduce Jenny to a few people.

As they sat in the sanctuary, Duncan stared at the cross behind the pulpit. *Lord, 'tis good to be in Your house again. Teach me what Ye would hae me know, and if it be Your will, begin to prepare Carmen's heart so she'll become my bride. Most of all, Lord, open Jenny's soul to Your salvation. Blind her to any unkindness, and grant others a special love for her so she can see the difference Ye make. Amen.*

The sermon was about the woman at the well. The pastor kept echoing Christ's admonition, "Go, and sin no more." He applied the concept to the sins, great and small, that are so common to man. Duncan considered the sermon outstanding.

It wasn't until he escorted Carmen and Jenny back to the Rodriquez house that Jenny finally spoke. "I don't want to go back. Ever. I know it's part of the arrangement, but can't we change it?"

"What was so bad?" Carmen sat beside her.

"He told that story just because I was there. Why didn't he just point his finger at me and tell them all I'm a—"

"Sinner, just like the rest of us?" Duncan cut in strategically. "I venture to say everyone is probably sitting at home thinkin' the parson's been spying on them. Impatience. Gluttony. Greed. Gossip."

Some of the tension in Jenny's shoulders eased. "He did say those things, too."

"The Bible says we've all sinned and fallen short of God's glory." Duncan met Jenny's troubled gaze and confessed, "I can only speak for myself, but I cringe and squirm inside when those dark things are brought to light, because I know I have room to improve."

"Me, too." Carmen took Jenny's hand in hers. "I'm guilty of vanity."

Duncan didn't breathe a word, but he thought Carmen had plenty to be proud of. No other woman on earth was half as pretty. Her eyes were aglow with intelligence, and her skin matched the shade of sun-warmed honey. The lively chatter and laughter bubbling from her lips lifted a man's spirits, and, despite her limp, the woman carried herself like a queen.

"You're not vain," Jenny objected.

"Oh, but I am. I'm crippled and I limp. If I used a cane, I'd be more stable, but I won't because I'm vain. Proud, too."

"What the parson said was the most important thing, Jenny." Duncan looked at her. "Jesus Christ didna stand there and condemn that woman. He forgave her and told her to start anew. What's done is done. He instructed her to change her ways and do better."

Jenny didn't look the least bit convinced. "I went to church. I don't want to think about any of that stuff until I have to go again next week."

"But you will go." Carmen's voice rang with authority.

"Aye. And I'd be honored to escort the both of you."

"Duncan!" Mercy's alarmed voice wavered in the air.

Duncan bolted out of his shop and toward the house. "Aye?"

Mercy held Elspeth over her shoulder and shouted, "The sky's gone green!"

He halted. "So it is. An ugly—"

"Hurry and fetch Carmen and Jenny. This is tornado weather!"

He needed no further urging. Duncan raced across the street. Without bothering to knock, he burst right in. "Come along now."

Carmen held Jenny's wrist and was dragging her into the hall. Jenny cried out, "I thought tornadoes didn't strike here!"

"I've seen a few," Carmen said. "The safest place—"

"Isna here. You're coming home with me. We've a large basement. I'll keep you safe."

Carmen turned loose of Jenny, and Duncan felt a spurt of relief. She was being practical and cooperative. At least she was until she turned into a room.

"Woman!" he bellowed.

Carmen ignored him, so he chased after her. A man had no business being in a woman's bedchamber, but Duncan figured survival rated above etiquette. He'd never seen a tornado, but from what he'd heard, no one tangled with one and came out the victor. Knowing Carmen was in danger sent him blustering into her room. She eluded him by ducking under his arm and called, "Jenny! Go with Duncan. I'll be right behind you!"

"This is absurd. We're leavin' this verra minute."

"Give me a second." The daft woman swept back the magnificent star-patterned quilt covering her bed and crawled onto the mattress. "Grab that quilt—just in case."

Duncan didn't know precisely what she meant, but that didn't matter, anyway. He grabbed for her. "Woman!"

She half stood on her bed and grabbed a beautiful mahogany and gold crucifix from the wall. "This was Mama's."

When Carmen gasped as he cinched his arm about her waist and yanked her down, he declared, "I'm takin' no chances."

"Stop blustering and help me gather the quilt for protection."

The woman was daft as a drunken duck if she thought a quilt was a match for a wind that could knock over a barn. Realizing he'd waste more time arguing with her than in snatching it up, he kept hold of Carmen and grabbed the quilt.

Jenny waddled out of the other room. Duncan had no idea what she'd managed to stuff in the pillowcase she held.

Carmen smacked him on the chest. "Put me down. You can carry Jenny's bag."

"I willna!" He shouted at Jenny, "Drop that and come on!"

Jenny shook her head.

Duncan wanted to drop the quilt, grab the lass, and haul them both across the street. He couldn't, though. A woman in Jenny's condition oughtn't be squashed about the middle. He dropped the quilt anyway and grabbed her wrist. "I'll come back for that junk."

In the blink of an eye, Jenny shoved her bag into Carmen's hands, jerked free from Duncan, and slapped him. She scooted back and wrapped her arms around her ribs. "Don't grab me. Don't ever grab me."

He hadn't let go of Carmen yet. She wiggled away and ran to Jenny's side. "It's okay. He's not mad at you."

"We're wasting dear time here." Duncan swept Carmen into his arms again. "Let's go!"

"You go ahead." Jenny's words were hard to hear over the wind.

"You run ahead of us, lass." Duncan jerked his chin toward the door. "I'll no' leave you behind."

He finally got them to his house, and Mercy called from the basement, "Come on down here!"

Duncan didn't want Carmen to have to limp down the steep stairs. "Jenny, scamper on down. There you go." He followed right behind her with Carmen held close to his chest.

"I'm so glad you're here." Mercy set Elspeth in a crate she'd lined with a blanket and then hugged the women.

Duncan headed back up the stairs. "Stay," Carmen called to him.

"I'll be back."

"Hail starts to fall right before a twister." Worry vibrated in her voice.

"I'm sorry." Jenny's voice sounded shaky.

Duncan turned around. "You've nothing to be sorry about. When I return, I'll give you my apology. You stay put." Duncan turned to his sister-in-law. "Mercy, what about Elspeth? What do you need for her?"

"I already have blankets and diapers here. Please stay."

He didn't reply. After carefully closing the door to the basement, Duncan ran to the clinic. "Rob!"

Nothing but the sound of wind met him. Satisfied that his brother wasn't there, Duncan scanned the street. Not a soul stirred, so he went back to the women.

"What do you need down there?"

Carmen shouted, "You!"

His heart soared.

∽

"Ismelda!" Carmen embraced her sister. "I'm so relieved that you're okay."

"I'm fine. So is Mercy's grandfather. The twister was small. It left a zigzagging path about a mile from us."

"So no one got hurt?"

"We're all fine." Ismelda grabbed Carmen's hand and cast a quick look over at Jenny. Since Jenny didn't speak any Spanish, Ismelda said very quickly, "I think it's wonderful how you've taken this girl in. My mother-in-law is very upset, though. She feels you've tainted yourself by association. Otto and I talked it over. We want you and Jenny to be sure to sit by us in church tomorrow."

"Of course we will," Carmen replied in English. "After church, you and Otto ought to come here for Sunday supper. I'm teaching Jenny how to make tortillas. For a *gringa*, she does a good job."

Jenny let out a small laugh. "When I was small, my grandmother would give me the scraps from pie dough. When I pat the tortilla between my hands to flatten it, it feels just like when I played with that dough."

"We'll make lots of them and bake enchiladas. Why don't we have the Gregors over for supper, too?"

"There's not enough room at the table for that many of us." Jenny hitched a shoulder as if it didn't matter to her one bit as she said, "I'll just eat in my room."

"*No. Absolutamente. ¡Absurdo!*" Ismelda and Carmen said in unison.

Ismelda giggled. "Mama used to say that."

"And she'd say that here and now, too." Carmen shook her finger at Jenny. "There's always room at my table for you."

After Ismelda left, Carmen and Jenny sat together and made tortillas. Carmen hesitated, but her curiosity wouldn't let her remain silent. "You've mentioned your grandmother. Since she was a dressmaker, why didn't you go into that profession?"

"I didn't have a choice." Jenny slapped down a tortilla and began another. "I was thirteen when she died. No one would hire me— no one but Bart."

"You were just a baby!" Carmen stared at her in shock.

"It was a long time ago." She shrugged. "But I want better for my baby than what I had. My mother—she wasn't married. She died when I was a small girl, and all I had was Grandma. This baby—the doctor promised it will go to a husband and wife. There will be grandparents and cousins, too."

"Your baby is fortunate, Jenny. Not just because of the family it will go to. It's blessed because you've thought matters through and are giving it to a better home than you can provide."

"I can't keep it, you know. After I have the baby, I thought I'd take the train west. Now that I'm sixteen, maybe someone who doesn't know about my past will hire me. But I won't be able to work if I keep the baby with me, so I couldn't even keep a roof over our heads."

Aghast, Carmen echoed, "You're sixteen?"

"Unh-huh. I don't know if this is going to be enough tortillas. Those Gregor men eat a lot."

"Why don't I go over and make sure they can come for supper? You ought to lie down and rest awhile, anyway. Dr. Gregor said you should nap more."

Carmen stumbled into Mercy's parlor and finally gave vent to her outrage. "Mercy?"

"Yes?" Mercy remained in the rocking chair. The Gregor tartan draped over her shoulder, hiding Elspeth as she suckled.

"Jenny's only sixteen! I thought she was much older."

Duncan appeared beside Carmen. He pressed his handkerchief into her hand. "Hard living ages a body. 'Tis plain to see that's the case with Jenny."

She should have been surprised or even embarrassed, but Carmen didn't feel either emotion when she realized she was weeping. She let Duncan pull her close, and she soaked his shirt with her tears. "It's so dreadful. We have to help her. She can't go back to a life like that."

"Sure and enough, you're right. We'll come up with a plan, won't we, Mercy?"

"Of course we will."

"Now dry up." Duncan tilted her face to his and brushed away the last of her tears with astonishing tenderness.

How can a man be so big and strong, and yet so gentle?

He reached down and took her hand. "I'll walk you home. I have a little something to give to you and Jenny."

"Actually, I came over to invite you all for Sunday supper tomorrow—enchiladas."

Duncan's eyes lit up. "Those are the rolled up tortillas with stuff in them and sauce atop?"

Mercy laughed. "Carmen, he'll eat an entire pan of them all by himself. What can I bring?"

Carmen thought for a moment. "Do you mind giving me a little cheese?"

"Duncan," Mercy asked, "could you go fetch a wheel?"

He went down into the basement.

Drawing the baby out from beneath the tartan, Mercy chided softly, "Since when didn't I have enough cheese to share?"

"But it's such a chore to make it."

"Going to Grossvater's farm twice a week is a joy for me. The things I do while I'm there—they're no burden. I'd have no room here to make cheese. It's my excuse to go, because Grossvater worries that I should be here all of the time."

"Here we are." Duncan reappeared with a twelve-inch wheel of cheese. "I need to stop by my workshop for a moment."

After saying good-bye, Carmen accompanied Duncan to his workshop. He snatched something off his table. "Okay."

Jenny hadn't gone to take a nap, after all. She'd been making more tortillas and was just now washing her hands. "I couldn't seem to stop."

Duncan set the cheese on the table and stepped closer to her. "I made you something." After she dried her hands, he placed a green leather book in her hands.

Jenny ran her fingertips over the vine pattern he'd tooled into the center of the leather to form a heart. "This is so pretty."

"I thought that maybe you'd like to write letters to the bairn.

That way, when he grows up, he'll hae some of your thoughts and hopes to let him know you loved him. I asked Rob, and he said 'twas okay."

Clutching it to her bosom, Jenny didn't say anything. She just nodded.

Duncan then turned to Carmen. "And this, 'tis for you, Carmen. Mercy tells me you keep a journal, but 'tis spring already. I thought you might like to hae plain pages so you could sketch or keep a record of your garden since it's always brought you such great joy."

He'd stained her book's cover the shade of a pomegranate. An odd interlocking circle design filled the center. She traced it with her finger.

"That's a Celtic endless knot called the Four Seasons. It represents not only time, but friendship."

Her fingertip kept going round and round. "It is endless. How clever. Thank you, Duncan."

That night, Carmen lay in bed and stared at the book. *Friendship*. Duncan extended friendship to everyone. The man could charm a rabbit into a stewpot. But the book he made for Jenny had a heart on it. Was he falling in love with her? He'd been coming over much of the time—and that started after Jenny's arrival.

Rob married Mercy and they're raising her baby. I can see Duncan marrying Jenny and loving her baby, too.

Tears filled her eyes and slid onto her pillow. *Lord, I don't understand. I try to live according to Your will. Your Word says man looks on the outward appearance and You look upon the heart. I'm so tired of my twisted leg scaring men off. Why can't You send me a man who sees me through Your eyes?*

Chapter 9

"Well, what do you think?" Duncan stepped back and grinned at Carmen.

She looked at the windows. "It sort of reminds me of that design you made on my book."

"Aye, it does." Duncan stepped forward and dabbed paint on one last little wooden curlicue. Once he'd put up new screens, he'd used that as an excuse to sand and paint all of the windowsills—and now he'd tacked on some of the gingerbread left over from the Gregor house kit. "As long as I'm painting, I'll do the veranda, too."

"You don't have to, Duncan."

"I know I dinna, Carmen. I'm happy to, though. I brought o'er a few odds and ends. Let's decide what pieces of that wooden lace will look best where."

"Jenny!" Carmen beckoned. "Come here."

The lass knelt over by a row of flowers. Getting up had to be difficult, so Duncan strode over and assisted her. She always looked stunned when he extended common courtesies to her. *Puir wee lassie doesna count herself worth anything. If only she could see that the King of kings longs to have her as His daughter!*

"I'll go get some sweet tea and bunuelos," Carmen murmured as soon as they approached.

"Better still, I'll go fetch them." Duncan grinned. "Whilst I do, why dinna ye both lay out a blanket, and we'll hae a picnic. 'Twill be easier to move about those bits of wood if we're already on the ground."

"Those are pointy; these are round." Jenny pushed away a few pieces. "Since Duncan put swirly ones for the windows, I think the roundish pieces would look best."

"Thank you," Carmen said as Duncan handed her a glass of sweet tea. "Jenny's leaning toward using these pieces."

Duncan took a gulp out of his own glass. "You dinna hae to limit yourself. You can hae e'ery last piece there. There's still more in a crate at the back of my shop."

Carmen smothered a laugh.

"What's so funny?" Jenny's brows knit.

"Suppose," Duncan said as he sat between the women, "you tell us what's amused you."

Carmen gave him a sly look. "Am I to assume you're keeping a supply on hand so you can nettle Chris?"

"Trials build character." Duncan smirked. "I'm doing my best to see that Chris's character is fully developed."

"Chris isn't fond of architectural embellishments," Carmen explained to Jenny.

"That doesn't make sense." Jenny craned her neck to look across the street. "He built the house and workshop, and they've got all sorts of fancy details."

"Much to Chris's dismay, the kit we ordered came with a plethora of frills." Duncan reached across the blanket and flipped a piece of gingerbread.

"Depending on his mood, Chris has called the place everything from an Easter bonnet to a wedding cake," Carmen said.

Jenny laughed.

"Dinna be forgettin' him sayin' the place has enough scales to cover a legion of dragons."

"Oh. The last time I heard, it was only two dragons."

"Chris was just a tad surly that day. When he's vexed, it's a legion." Duncan grinned. "He'll be none too happy tonight, once he sees what I've done."

"What?" Carmen and Jenny asked together.

"I took two of these and one of these and tacked them together just above his washstand."

"A gingerbread heart? Oh, Duncan!" Carmen dissolved into giggles. "Chris is going to have a conniption."

"Oh, that's only half of it. I hung his razor strop from it—with the help of a wee porcelain knob that has roses on it."

"What will he do to you?"

The worry in Jenny's eyes and voice halted Duncan's mirth. "He's my brother. He'd not harm me. Oh, he'll bellow and bluster, but in the end he knows 'tis his own fault. He didna want a single piece of it on the house, so he made a pact with Rob that I'd end up with it all. Rob's a clever one, though. He forged the promise without Chris specifying what I could or couldna do with all those pretties."

"So he tried to trick you and it backfired." Jenny wrinkled her nose. "You mean to tell me the times I hear him roaring at someone, he's not punching or throwing things, too?"

"I told ye before, lass. We dinna fight. Rob's patched too many foolish men together to think violence solves anything. I enjoy horseplay, but when tempers flare, I know full well a soft answer turneth away wrath. Chris, he believes law and justice are the routes to peace among men. Connant Gilchrist keeps trying to convince him to become a deputy."

"I like this *corazon*." Carmen touched the example he'd made of the heart.

"Cor-a-zone?" Duncan looked into Carmen's bright eyes and

willed her to see how he wanted to please her. "Does that mean heart?"

"Yes."

"I thought 'twould be pretty to hang this corazon to the side of your front door."

She smiled at him. "I'd love that."

Ahhh, lass, but if only you'd love me, too.

⁤⁤

"I've never understood the whole notion of getting a certificate that stands for money when the value of it isn't stable." Carmen cranked the agitator on the washing machine. "First, the stock market did that crash thing in May. Now the paper says many of those certificates are worthless and there's talk of a depression."

"I'd never trust someone else with my money." Jenny's brow puckered. "You can't trust anyone but yourself."

"I trust a few people." Carmen stopped cranking and lifted the lid. Judging the garments done, she drained the metal drumlike machine. "The only One who won't ever fail me is Jesus, though."

"Then why bother?" Jenny helped her pull out the soggy clothes and dropped them into a galvanized bucket with a *splat*. "If you don't depend on anyone, then you won't get hurt."

Carmen looked at Jenny. "There's pain in loneliness, too."

"How would you know?" Jenny shook her head. "You have a sister who adores you. You and Mercy do everything together—from cooking to canning to sewing. Duncan and his brothers are around all the time, and children drop by almost every day. Just talking about it makes me tired."

"I do manage to stay busy. Family and community are important to me. Very important." Carmen summoned a smile. "But you forgot to mention someone who matters a lot to me."

"Who?"

"You, Jenny. We've been doing practically everything together for months now." Carmen lifted one handle of the bucket.

Jenny automatically lifted the other. With Jenny's waddle, Carmen didn't have to push herself to hurry as they walked to the clothesline.

"After I have the baby, I'll be leaving. We both know it. I'm not going to let myself miss you. You shouldn't miss me, either."

"Of course I'll miss you. I've grown so very fond of you. Haven't you noticed?"

Jenny turned away and started to hang up clothes. The action didn't fool Carmen. Jenny guarded her emotions with a desperation that nearly broke Carmen's heart. Bravado was all she had. Nonetheless, Carmen wanted Jenny to know the truth. "From the first day you came, Jenny, I felt a special spark. Our time together has been wonderful for me. I hope you feel the same way. Even if you can't allow yourself to feel anything for me, I want you to know how I've come to love you."

"You're fond of everyone. I'm not like that. Some folks are just plain nice, but most only care about themselves. You were sheltered, so you've been spared learning just how ugly men can be. Women, too."

Carmen thought for a moment and admitted slowly, "I don't know how I would have turned out if I'd been reared differently or been through other circumstances."

"If you'd lived like I have," Jenny said in a jaded tone, "you wouldn't be so trusting and caring. You'd have to look out for yourself."

"I'm an independent woman, Jenny. I do look after myself." Carmen detected Jenny was seeking information in a roundabout fashion. "There's something I do know, deep down in my heart. Jesus will never fail me."

"I bet a lot of people who have those worthless stock certificates wonder why Jesus failed them." Jenny finished pinning up a petticoat.

"God isn't like a genie in a children's fable. He doesn't jump at our commands and give us all we wish for."

"Then what is He good for?"

"He forgives our sins and never forsakes us. No matter what we have to endure, He is faithful to carry us through. Joys or sorrows, God remains with us."

"I think it would be nicer if He was a genie who did give me whatever I wanted."

"What do you want?" Carmen waited for a response.

Silence crackled between them as they finished hanging out the laundry. Jenny finally said, "I want this to all be over."

Carmen didn't say anything.

Jenny, ostensibly watching water drip from a petticoat to make tiny little plops that turned the earth into a polka-dotted mud patch, finally said, "What I don't want is to feel the baby kick all the time. It just reminds me over and over that I don't even know who the father is and that I won't know who his new father will be. I don't want to go through the labor. I don't want to go back to living in a saloon just so I'll have food to eat."

The sadness in Jenny's voice and eyes made Carmen want to weep. "We have to have faith, Jenny. There will be good that comes from this, and Doc Gregor will make certain the man and wife who rear that baby will do a fine job of it. As for you—we'll make certain you never have to go back to that way of life. I promise you won't."

Duncan carefully placed Carmen's gift in a hatbox and smiled to himself. *She's going to be so surprised.* The ornate leather strap he'd created out of frustration went with the purse perfectly. The lid to the box didn't want to go on. Why, when he could create even the tiniest baby shoes, did his fingers suddenly fumble at this simple task?

So far, his plan seemed to be going well. Carmen appreciated his gifts and praised the work he'd been doing around her home. And she often brought treats she'd baked to his shop. A woman didn't cook for a man unless she held feelings for him.

"Duncan?" Mercy walked into the shop. "What a beautiful hatbox!"

"Aye. Think Carmen will like it?" He ran a rough hand over the elegantly striped pasteboard, then rubbed his thumb along the red velvet ribbon running along the top's edge.

"Crimson is her favorite color."

"So I guessed. All the bright shades she wears—they make her match her beautiful garden."

Mercy smiled. "You certainly helped her have a spectacular garden this year."

"Jenny helped, too."

"Chris mentioned Grossvater wanted to spend a day with you, tending to his harnesses and such. Last year it kept him busy as he healed."

"I'll be happy to go out to the farm."

"That's so kind of you."

"Your grandda—he's surely taken Jenny under his wing. I'm sure 'tis his example that has many of the old men growing tender toward her."

"Grossvater has a big heart."

Duncan drew a deep breath. "Mercy, I aim to broach a topic wi' you. 'Tis less than polite."

"Did I do something wrong?"

"Nae. Carmen's limp. I'm thinking I could fashion shoes for her that would even out her gait."

" 'Gait' makes her sound like a horse."

Duncan filed away that little detail. Insignificant things like that mattered a lot to women. "When you pin up her hems, what's the difference in length from one side to the other?"

His sister-in-law's brows rose.

"I warned ye, 'twas a touchy subject. I need your help, Mercy. I canna proceed without knowing, and I'd not shame my Carmen by posing such a delicate matter to her."

"I'm a little surprised—but more at the thought of no one thinking to solve the matter this way than in the topic itself."

"I didna mean to shock you."

"You mean to help my friend. Of course I'm willing to assist you. The left side of her hems. . ." Mercy held her thumb and forefinger apart. "About an inch. Maybe a tiny bit more. But the measurement won't help you any. You need to trace her foot, and she'd never allow you to."

"I ken, 'tis true, so I cheated. She left footprints in the mud after watering the flowers she planted for you. I measured those and drew a pattern."

"You're very ingenious."

"Whilst you're here, I want to ask something. I ken you're busy as can be, but whene'er you bake, could you see fit to make wee little cookies for me?"

She nodded. "You'll have to tell me just how small."

"About the size of a quarter would be grand. I'd like to offer them to my customers."

Bless her, Mercy simply nodded.

Duncan reached for the mesquite bowl Mr. Rundsdorf had made for him. "I'll keep them in this."

"Ohhh! Duncan, that's breathtaking!"

"I think so, too. I'm supposing when folks see it, they'll be going to him, seeking something else he's made." He put down the bowl and stroked the hatbox. "I'll be back after awhile. I'm taking this to Carmen."

"It would be nicer if you gave it to her when you're alone. Why don't you go over and bring Jenny back? I've been talking to her so she'll know what to anticipate."

Appalled, Duncan blurted out, "You're not going to hae her birth her bairn in the washroom!"

Despite her blush, Mercy assured him, "Of course not."

"Chris and I still think you kept your vow," he muttered.

"What vow?"

"If anyone breathed a word about you delivering your babe at the clinic, you'd avenge yourself." When she had the nerve to laugh, Duncan swallowed sickly. "Twitter all you want, Mercy Ellen Gregor, but you left a dreadful, bloody mess for us to clean up."

Mercy shook her finger at him. "You have no right to complain. After all, I did what you asked. I waited until Rob got home to have Elspeth."

"Good thing, that. With your next babe—"

Mercy's eyes grew huge. "How did you know?"

Delight speared through him. " 'Twas hope speaking. So you're carrying another wee bairn?"

"Rob and I are keeping it a secret for now."

"I'll not breathe a word." He patted her arm. " 'Tis kind of you not to celebrate your glad tidings when you know Jenny's going to give away her babe."

"Go ahead and send her on over to me."

Duncan didn't have to be told twice. He hastened across the street. No one answered the door, but the smell of lye soap reminded him it was Carmen's laundry day. Duncan went around behind the house and heard weeping. "Carmen?"

"Car–men's—not—heeeeere."

Duncan pushed between two sodden towels on the clothesline and stopped dead in his tracks when he discovered Jenny huddled on the bench by the flowers, sobbing. Cold dread washed over him.

Chapter 10

"Y̵ou're not having the bairn—not now!"

Jenny shook her head.

"Good!" Relief added zeal to his voice. A moment later, Duncan frowned. "Are ye hurtin'? Do I need to fetch Rob?"

She shook her head.

Duncan stepped closer. "You're weeping. Why?"

"Carmen said Jesus would never fail her."

"Aye, and she's right. Our Lord Jesus Christ will ne'er forsake us."

"I don't have anyone like that. Everyone dies or they just use me and walk away."

"Puir wee lassie." He drew closer. "I canna imagine how sad and lonely it must be, you tryin' to face life on your verra own. You dinna hae to, though."

"No one will have me."

The sadness in her tone tore at him. "Jesus would welcome you with open arms."

"I'm not dying."

"Glad I am of that. He's more than eager to have you as His daughter."

Tears spattered her bodice as she shook her head. "Not me. I'm just a cheap wh—"

"You," Duncan cut in, "Jenny Sigrids, were bought by the blood of Christ. Never consider yourself cheap, because the price was paid in full—and 'twas the Son of God who paid the ransom for your eternal soul."

"Ransom? Like with a kidnapping?"

"Aye, only in this case, 'twas the devil who stole your soul. All you need to do is believe that God loves you so much, He sent His beloved Son to pay the price that would redeem your soul."

"You don't know what I've done."

Duncan shrugged. "What you've done in the past is of no importance. Remember how the preacher has mentioned stories in the Bible of women who lived in sin?"

"Like me," she murmured.

"Aye. Jesus forgave them. He gave them a new chance at life by telling them to go and sin no more."

"But other people knew what those women were. Everyone knows what I've been."

"Aye." Duncan nodded. "And Christ told them they could cast stones at the woman only if they'd ne'er sinned themselves. You see, sin separates each of us from God. 'Tisna our own goodness or the deeds we do that redeem us—'tis because Christ paid the cost. I'm heartily thankful He did, and I took Him at His word. I accepted salvation and let Him wash my soul free from the past. Carmen and Mercy and my brothers—they all did likewise."

He let that sink in for a moment and then quietly asked, "Would you like to ask Him for forgiveness and a fresh start?"

"What do I give Him back?"

"Your thankful and obedient heart."

Wrapping her arms around herself, she sighed. "It can't work that way. It's too simple."

"Carmen cares for you like a sister. Even when she didna know you, she opened her arms and heart and home to you. If she could do that, think how much more God can and will do."

"I don't know if I can get up if I kneel down."

Duncan glanced at her middle and silently agreed. "It won't matter. God is delighted to have you just as you are."

"Like that church song last Sunday?"

"Aye. 'Just as I Am.'"

"At church, folks have to get down on their knees."

She wasn't being quarrelsome. Duncan saw the sincerity in her eyes. She wanted to do this correctly. It mattered to her. "Since we'll be praying together, why don't you sit there, and I'll kneel."

∽

Carmen heard the low hum of conversation and limped around the clothesline. The breath froze in her lungs. Jenny sat on the garden bench, and Duncan knelt at her side.

I knew it. I knew he had tender feelings for her. Rob married Mercy and—

"Carmen!" Joy brightened Jenny's voice.

Duncan rose. "Carmen, we have the most wonderful news."

"Do you?" Her voice sounded strained.

Jenny beckoned her over. "Duncan just asked me if—" her voice broke.

"Jenny's decided to ask Christ into her heart."

"Jenny!" Carmen hurried over. Every step made her repent for the jealousy she'd felt.

"You can help me pray, too. I want to do it right."

"Nothing would make me happier than to share this moment with you."

Duncan motioned to her. "Why don't you sit next to Jenny?"

Carmen sat down and embraced Jenny.

"I don't know what to do," Jenny confessed. "Am I supposed to fold my hands, or are we supposed to hold hands together?"

"Either way is fine," Duncan said. "What would you like?"

Jenny thought about it for a minute. "I think I'll fold my hands. I'm afraid if I hold your hands, I might crush them."

Duncan knelt again. He reached out and held on to the wrought iron arms of the bench, and the action gave a special sense of intimacy to the moment.

Jenny bowed her head and whispered, "What do I say?"

"Prayer is talking to God." Carmen exchanged a look with Duncan, then asked, "Would you like to have one of us say a prayer, and you repeat the words?"

"That's a good idea. I'm afraid I'll forget something important."

"All right, then." Duncan bowed his head. "Lord Jesus, I'm sorry for my sins."

"Lord Jesus," Jenny repeated, "I'm sorry for all my terrible sins. I've done a lot of bad things."

Duncan patiently waited. "You died on the cross so I could be forgiven."

Jenny echoed the sentence.

"So I'm asking You to forgive me and come live in my heart. Amen."

"God, I'm asking You to please forgive me. Since You're washing all the bad out of my heart, there's a lot of room in my heart for You to come live there now. Amen." Jenny looked up. "I feel so. . .right. Deep down inside, I feel. . .good."

Carmen squeezed her tightly. "I'm so happy for you."

"I'm happy for us all." The corners of Duncan's eyes crinkled. "You know, Jenny, now you're our sister in Christ."

Jenny smiled, but just as quickly, her smile faltered. "At least till I leave after I have the baby."

"Nae, lass. E'en if we're parted here on earth, we'll all be together in heaven."

"Absolutely! And after you go, we'll write to one another." Carmen emphasized her assertion with a passionate nod. "I'm going to insist on it. How will I ever come to visit you if I don't know where you are?"

Jenny's eyes grew huge. "You'd come visit me?"

"Yes. I'm inviting myself. I know it's rude, but you're my sister, so you'll ignore my bad manners."

As he stood, Duncan chuckled. "Carmen's a strong-willed woman, Jenny. Once she determines something, there's no dissuading her. She'll be sure to visit you. Why don't the two of you go see Mercy? Jenny can give her the grand news."

∽

Mercy cried for joy.

Though Duncan hadn't accompanied them to the house, he entered a short time later. Carmen's breath caught as she recognized the item in his left hand. She'd looked at it a few times over at Leonard's mercantile. "Jenny, lass, this is for you." He handed her the beautiful cherry wood presentation box.

"For me?" Jenny opened the box. "A Bible! My very own Bible?"

"Aye. Read and reflect on the truths. 'Tis how we walk close to God."

He hadn't dashed out and snapped up the cheapest Bible in the store; he'd parted with money at a time when the nation's finances were strained. The gesture bespoke a deep affection. Until now, the biblical command not to be unequally yoked kept him from courting Jenny. Now that she'd accepted Christ, there wasn't anything that would preclude him from making her his wife. *He's not wasting any time at all. I suspected he was sweet on her. This proves it.*

Duncan turned and lowered a hatbox onto the table in front of Carmen. "And this is for you, Carmen."

"Ohhh." She looked at him. "Why?"

He stared back at her. "Because."

Tracing her finger over the velvet ribbon, she whispered, "It's gorgeous. Elegant."

"Open it up."

"There's something inside?"

He chuckled at her surprise. "Aye, there is."

Slowly, she opened the lid and looked inside. The sight before her left her speechless.

"What is it?" Mercy stood on tiptoe and peered inside.

"A purse made from an armadillo—just like Mercy's grand-mother had." Pride rang in Duncan's tone.

"Hers is the only other one I've ever seen," Carmen said faintly. It was all she could concoct. The thing was hideous.

"You didna say exactly how your grandma's was fashioned, so I did the best I could."

Carmen gingerly lifted the leather strap. "Oh, look at this strap. Have you ever seen such intricate tooling?"

Duncan's chest puffed out. "I'm glad you like it."

Mercy reached over and tentatively touched the odd, half-curled hide. "Carmen, something this rare should be used for very special occasions."

Grateful for the way Mercy just gave her an excuse for not hav-ing to carry the monstrosity with her all the time, Carmen nodded.

"Grandma only used hers when she paid calls on sick friends. She kept healing herbs and powders in it."

"You go see sick folks all the time." Jenny reached over and fid-dled with the creature's funny ear.

Carmen found the urge to shiver. "I've always loved traditions. Perhaps this is a way for me to keep the tradition."

"I've noticed how you treasure your traditions." Duncan folded his arms across his chest. "No matter where we go or what we become, 'tis always important to remember and honor the past."

"Like when you wear your kilt," Carmen said. From the way he beamed, Carmen knew she'd managed to say the right thing and diverted his attention from the revolting purse. *But one of these days, he'll ask me where it is.*

∞

"Where is she?" Duncan took the seat next to Carmen as some of the parishioners met at the parsonage to discuss church projects.

Carmen froze for a moment. He hadn't asked about the armadillo purse yet, but he was looking at her hem—possibly to see if she'd carried it with her here. She looked at him. "I beg your pardon?"

"Did Jenny come along with you?"

Of course he'd ask about her. Just look at the twinkle in his bachelor button–blue eyes. Well, he won't be a bachelor much longer. Carmen shoved aside her musings and answered. "No, she's spending the afternoon with Mercy."

Mrs. Kunstler sat on Carmen's other side. "Mercy—she is a good wife for the doctor. Ismelda told me Mercy helped the doctor when he saw her."

Carmen stared at Mrs. Kunstler and strove not to let her shock and hurt show. "Ismelda?"

"I told her to tell you. Well, now you know." Mrs. Kunstler twitched an embarrassed smile. "She's trying to spare your feelings since you're older and—"

"You'll be a wonderful aunt," Duncan said. "Children flock to you. Ismelda probably wanted to get you alone to share her good news. She's got a kind heart and wouldn't want to flaunt her joy in front of Jenny, knowing the lass is going to give up her babe."

Carmen summoned a smile and nodded.

"Maybe so." Mrs. Kunstler shrugged. "But Jenny—she got herself into this fix."

Carmen set aside her own hurt and rushed to defend Jenny. "She's confessed her sins, and God's forgiven her."

"Aye, and we've all fallen short of the mark in some way or another." Duncan bobbed his head. "Forgiveness is ours for the asking—and I admire Jenny for knowing her babe would be better off with a stable married couple. She's suffering from the consequences of her past, and yet she's giving someone else a gift beyond words."

"I've told the doctor it's only right that my cousin's cousin should get the baby." Mrs. Kunstler rubbed her hands together. "Since Carmen is housing the girl and Ismelda is my daughter-in-law, we've kept this within the family."

"No." Carmen shook her head. *How could she condemn Jenny and then still claim the baby?*

Duncan patted her hand. "You're in the right of it, Carmen. The adoptions are secret. Only the doctor knows who gives or receives which babe."

"Well, he should give this one to Chester," Mrs. Kunstler grumbled. "Especially after he kept Mercy's baby for himself."

"My brother," Duncan said in a low, slow tone that dared anyone to challenge him, "cherishes Mercy. We all do, just as we adore Elspeth. You canna be suggesting he acted out of anything but love when he wed her."

"No one would ever say such a thing," the pastor said.

Carmen shot the pastor a startled look. She'd been so intent, she'd forgotten where they were.

"Let's begin," the pastor said as he motioned to a handful of people to come take seats. They all complied, and he opened the meeting with a prayer. After that, he smiled. "It's good to see so many of you here. God must be pleased to see so many of His children eager to serve Him with their talents. I've started a list of the needs within our congregation and community. Let's pour out God's love upon our church family and neighbors."

The first needs the parson brought up seemed so urgent, Carmen quickly volunteered.

When the parson said the church ought to be painted, Duncan signed up for that task.

Knowing she couldn't do that kind of work, Carmen thought ahead. In a few weeks, Jenny would have the baby. In less than two months, she would recover and leave. With loneliness looming, Carmen determined to stay busy. She even mentioned a few families who needed help.

At one point, Duncan scowled at her.

She frowned right back. He was a strong, healthy man. He didn't have a wife and children or a widowed mother to support. Surely he could commit to more than just helping paint the church.

Unless he wants the church to look fresh in time for him to marry Jenny. When Mrs. Kunstler spoke badly of her, he rushed to her defense. A man with a new wife and a baby wouldn't have much time for projects. Is that why he doesn't jump in to do more?

Chapter 11

As the meeting broke up, Mrs. Kunstler tugged on Carmen's sleeve. "When Ismelda tells you about her baby, you act surprised."

"Why would I lie?"

"It's not lying. You *were* surprised. She deserves to have the delight of seeing that."

"Then you should have held what you knew in confidence." Carmen shook out her skirts. "When I see Ismelda, she'll know how thrilled I am for her and Otto."

Duncan offered, "I'll walk you home, Carmen."

Thankful for the excuse to leave, Carmen nodded. "I'm ready to go." Carmen didn't say anything until they were out of earshot from anyone. "I keep reminding myself that she is a good mother-in-law to Ismelda. That's all that matters."

" 'Tisna all that matters, but I grant you, I'm glad for Ismelda's sake 'tis the case."

"Jenny's baby—"

"Dinna fret o'er the bairn. I can say with every confidence the arrangements will be good."

Carmen twitched a wry smile. *He might as well just announce that he's going to claim Jenny and the baby as his own.*

"I'm fit to be tied o'er something else, though." He stopped.

"What?" Carmen halted, too.

"Reading to old Mrs. Lintz. Organizing a meal for after the

Warner funeral. Helping sew the quilt for the bazaar. Playing the piano every other week at church. Polishing all the wood inside the church. . ." He continued as if reciting a litany.

"There's nothing wrong with my helping out."

Duncan looked as if he'd sucked on a lemon.

Carmen started walking again. *He has no right to dictate how I spend my time.*

Duncan strode alongside her and bellowed out a prolonged sigh for her benefit.

"Maybe you're reacting this way because you're convinced that you're not doing enough." She shot him a look. "Painting the church is a good start, but there were other things you could have offered to do, too."

"I dinna run off and sign up for every last thing. What I'm to do is go where the Lord calls me. In the future, when He leads me toward other projects, I can put my hand to them then. But until He calls me, I'll wait."

His words nettled her. Her skirts swirled about her as she halted. "Are you saying I don't?"

"Come along." He grabbed her elbow and took a step.

Carmen jerked away. "I can walk just fine. Don't treat me like I'm a cripple."

His eyes narrowed. "I'd help any woman o'er these jagged roots. Ne'er once have I treated you like a cripple. Heed me well, Carmen Rodriguez, a special pair of shoes could even out your walk, but 'tisna the insignificant difference in your stroll that hinders ye. No, 'tisna a-tall. 'Tis your heart."

"There's nothing wrong with my heart."

"Ooch, lass, there is. Let's go to your veranda where we can discuss this privately."

"No one is eavesdropping here. Say what you have to say."

Duncan glanced up and down the street. His brow furrowed, but he gave her a curt nod. "You've a sickness in your heart of hearts, and 'tis twisting your spirit. I've spoken wi' you on other occasions, but ye've not listened. God doesna need you to do the work of a dozen and find an early grave just to enter the kingdom of heaven. Nae, He doesna, for Christ paid the price."

"I know that!"

"Do you?" He stared at her solemnly. "Then all these works you take on—what is the purpose?"

"To help others."

He wagged his head from side to side and let out a profound sigh. "You're a bonny lass, Carmen Rodriguez. Aye, you are—not only on the outside, but in your heart, as well."

She stared at him. No man had ever complimented her, yet this wasn't exactly a compliment.

"Anyone who needs you to do labor on their behalf ought to be thankful for all you do. Nevertheless, their caring for you ought ne'er be based on what chore you accomplished but on the fact that you're a fine woman."

Though tempted to respond, Carmen held her tongue.

Duncan seemed more than intent on speaking his piece. "You dinna hae to earn your way into the hearts of others by exhausting yourself. And if you dinna think that's what you're doing, then you need to wonder why 'tis so important for you to fill every last waking hour with rushing about. 'Tis in stillness that we calm our hearts and commune with the Almighty."

"You heard the sermon last Sunday, about the gifts God gives and expects us to exercise. The gift of helps—that's mine. I'm being a faithful follower to go forth and help others."

"I agree 'tis your gift."

"Then there's no problem."

He gave her a long, intent look. "Your gift is not to be a burden that strains your every waking moment. I'm concerned."

"Over nothing." When he'd looked at her, he'd ended at her hem—and it all came back to the same thing. He considered her feeble.

"Carmen, you've gotten so caught up in staying busy on the account of others that you've forgotten to listen for the Lord to direct your efforts."

"I don't need thunder to shake the heavens to direct me where the needs are. God gave me eyes to see them and ears to hear the pastor and others mention how someone requires help."

"Those people can be His messengers—but had you considered that others present are meant to assume some of those responsibilities?"

"The Lord loves a cheerful giver."

"Aye, He does. But I dinna recall e'er reading in His Word that He loves a frantic giver."

"Frantic!"

Duncan nodded. "Pray, Carmen. You're so caught up in deeds that you're losing sight of the One to whom you're devoted."

Carmen reared back. "Did it ever occur to you that some of us wouldn't have to do so much if others of you would step up and do your share?" She didn't wait for his reaction. Carmen lifted her skirt and hastened over the tangled roots as fast as her crooked leg would allow.

∞

Duncan reached over and buffed the toe of a boot. He used buttery soft kidskin and created a pair that would yield ultimate comfort.

Though he'd never once heard Carmen complain, Duncan knew her feet and legs had to bother her after she exerted herself. An elastic gusset would make it quicker for Carmen to pull on the boots, but Duncan opted to make the ankle-top boots lace up. They'd give more support.

At first glance, someone might think one boot was propped up on a small block, but it wasn't. Fashionable women's footwear featured heels that narrowed down to a three-quarter-inch circle. Both heels on this custom-made pair measured an inch in diameter, but he'd added a full inch in height to the sole and heel on the left and subtracted half an inch from the heel on the right. The net result was a pair of shoes that would compensate for the difference Carmen's twisted limb caused. Aye, she'd be able to walk more smoothly and even leave a footprint that wouldn't tattle on the compensations.

Kept busier still by the things she'd volunteered to do, Carmen didn't seem to be home much. Duncan wasn't fooled, though. He'd hurt her feelings. Since he couldn't catch her to give an apology, these boots and a note would speak for him.

Three crumpled, ink-blotted tries later, Duncan scuffed his own boots on the floor of his workshop. He'd not been this ill at ease with a pen in his hand since he'd been a schoolboy and had been forced to write a treatise on peregrine falcons.

He dipped into the inkwell again.

I did not mean to hurt your feelings. If you felt I was taunting you, I apologize. I'm a rough man, a mere cobbler. Though I spoke what was on my heart, my words were stark. I humbly ask your forgiveness.

He didn't scribe her name at the beginning nor his at the end. The boots themselves made it clear he was addressing her. Satisfied with this note, Duncan crossed the street, set the shoes by Carmen's door, and tucked the folded note between them.

⚮

"You didn't come to church yesterday." Carmen took the egg basket from Ismelda. She'd intentionally waited until today because she hoped her sister would come to her. She hadn't.

Ismelda let out a nervous little laugh. "I wasn't feeling well. In fact, I'm not feeling good at all in the mornings anymore."

"You should have told me. Didn't you think I'd be delighted that you and Otto are going to be blessed with a baby?"

"Otto and I—we decided not to tell anybody because Mercy and Rob just shared their good news. Especially after what Mercy went through the last time, I thought it would be nice for her to have everyone get excited for her."

"That's sweet of you, but I'm not just anybody. I'm your sister!"

Ismelda wound her arm around Carmen's waist. "And you're going to be my baby's aunt. You don't know how happy that makes me. I promised Otto that I wouldn't tell a soul, though. You wouldn't want me to break a promise I made to my husband. Since I missed church yesterday, I'm sure people must suspect the truth."

Carmen nodded. Telling Ismelda that her mother-in-law had said something would spoil her joy. "I knew this day would come. I've already bought some fabric, but I hid it away in my bureau."

"It would be too hard for Jenny." Ismelda smiled softly. "You know, when you first took her in, I wondered if it was such a smart thing. But the moment I met her, I knew God had a reason for sending Jenny here. Otto and I—we've been praying for her. Knowing she's accepted Jesus is so exciting. Now we're praying that maybe God will put a man in her life, just as He did for Mercy."

"Maybe so." *He probably has—it's Duncan Gregor.*

"Stay for the day. We could make tortillas. Otto's mother can't make them right. She keeps thinking they should be rolled out like pie dough."

"You'll have to teach my niece how to make tortillas."

Ismelda laughed and rested her head on Carmen's shoulder. "We'll come visit you all the time, and you can teach her that yourself. Yours are always perfect circles. Mine are as lopsided as those eggs you're carrying."

∞

After spending the day with her sister, Carmen headed home. She'd rented a buggy from the livery and driven it back without any trouble. From the day she'd fallen off a horse and broken her leg, she'd never again ridden. Ismelda told Jorge at the livery about how horses made Carmen nervous. He always made sure she didn't have to be near the horses, so as soon as she reached the livery, he hopped into the buggy and drove her home.

"Look!" Jenny greeted her at the door and gestured toward the settee. "I must have been napping when Duncan dropped by."

Carmen stared at the floor and clapped a hand over her mouth to muffle her scream.

Chapter 12

I knew you'd be thrilled." Jenny pushed her toward the boots waiting on the settee. "Try them on. Aren't they beautiful? The leather is so soft and supple."

Pulling away, Carmen mumbled something that she knew didn't make sense and raced for her bedroom. She shut the door, threw herself across the bed, and slammed her fist into her pillow. Mortification and rage left her shaking. Duncan told her special shoes would correct her step—and now, he was proving his point.

Tap, tap, tap. Jenny slowly opened the door a mere crack. "Carmen? You don't have to be embarrassed. Ever since my grandma died, nobody loved me—but you have. Don't you think I love you enough to be glad that you can wear such clever shoes so it's easier for you to walk?"

"I—" She couldn't find words.

"It's just Duncan. He probably put the shoes there so neither of you would have to say anything about it. Most men blurt out whatever they want. Believe me, I know. Duncan's not like that. He cares. Come try them on."

"Maybe later." Once she mouthed those words, Carmen knew the truth. She'd never put them on.

∞

"I'm coming. I'm coming." Duncan trudged toward the door.

Chris stood at the head of the stairs, holster in hand. He'd been helping Connant keep law and order whenever necessary. Anyone banging on the door at this time of night either wanted the doctor or the law.

"What do you—" Duncan started at the sight of Carmen. She wore a sapphire blue robe, and her hair billowed out in a dark cloud past her waist.

So that's what her hair looks like down—wavy and shiny and longer than—

"Jenny," she said.

Duncan jolted and hollered, "Rob! Jenny's needing your help." He stepped out of the house only to realize he was barefoot. So, too, was Carmen. "I'll take you home and then carry Jenny back to the clinic."

She nodded and spun to take flight.

"Wait!"

Carmen shook her head. "I can't leave her alone!"

"Fine, then." Duncan swept her into his arms. When she stiffened, he rasped, "She willna protest me carryin' her if she sees me totin' you in the door."

When they reached her front door, Duncan dipped and ordered, "Turn the knob, lass."

Carmen complied. She barely allowed him to cross the threshold before she struggled free of his hold and hobbled to Jenny's side. "How are you?"

Jenny sat huddled in a tight ball and moaned.

Duncan fought the urge to moan, too. Instead, he cleared his throat. "Well, so this is the day. Or night. Well, I'm supposin' it'll be daytime when—" He shut up. Any medical issue turned him into a blithering idiot.

Carmen patted Jenny's arm. "Duncan came to carry you to the clinic. Dr. Gregor will meet us there."

"Okay."

Less than reassured by Jenny's tiny voice, Duncan slid one hand behind her back.

"Wait, now." Rob came in.

Duncan wondered how his brother managed this feat. In a matter of a few minutes, he could wake from a sound sleep, dress, comb his hair, grab his satchel, and calmly face whatever emergency God plopped in his lap.

"Jenny, let's just check you here in your bedroom. You'll be much more comfortable there." Rob motioned to Duncan.

Duncan carried her to the bedroom and darted back out as soon as humanly possible.

Carmen and Rob spent five minutes with Jenny, and then Rob came back out. He slapped Duncan on the shoulder. "It'll be a long while yet. Carmen will come get us when the pains are four minutes apart or so."

"She should be at the clinic!"

"Nae, Duncan. She's got hours of laboring ahead of her. Come on home. I'm going to have to ask you to fill in for me tomorrow."

"Fill in?"

"I'll tell you when we get home."

Duncan wouldn't budge. "Carmen? I'm going home only long enough to change into my jeans. I aim to stay on your veranda—"

The bedroom door opened, and she hissed, "You will not. Go home, Duncan Gregor. Go home this instant!"

He scowled at her. She didn't seem intimidated in the least. Come to think of it, the sassy woman had a habit of ignoring his scowls. He'd have to work on that flaw of hers. With Jenny laboring, this wasn't the right time, though. He announced, "If you need help, you just shout. I'll be here in an instant."

Walking back across the rutted road, Duncan muttered, "You do surgery in the clinic. You stitch up wounds and set broken bones. Just what do you have against bringing a bairn into the world there when you've every modern medical convenience at your fingertips?"

"Bairns have a way of entering the world without a lot of fanfare. Mothers labor best where they're comfortable."

"You're daft, Rob."

Rob had the nerve to chuckle.

A minute later, Duncan repeated, "You're daft! Daft, I tell you. I am not gallivanting off to fetch a bairn and take him to the Heims. Not when Jenny's baby's about to arrive right here!"

"Do you need my help, Rob?" Mercy called out.

"Not for a long while yet, my love. Catch a wee bit more sleep if you can."

Rob turned back to Duncan. His face hardened. "You'll do no good here. You canna stand to be with anyone who's sick or bleeding."

"Chris will do it."

"Stubborn, hardheaded Scot," Rob growled.

"Aye, Chris is those things, but he'll help you." Duncan nodded. "If he's hesitant, tell him I'll not pester him with a single piece of gingerbread for a whole week."

"E'er again," Chris demanded at the breakfast table. "If I fetch this babe and take it to the Heims, Duncan canna e'er again bedevil me with those benighted wooden frills."

"A week is as good as you'll get from me," Duncan snarled. He'd not gone back to sleep, and his nerves were on edge.

"A year," Chris barked back.

"You're fetching a baby, not a wife. And you're giving it away this afternoon, anyway." Duncan gave him a sour look. "One month.

'Tis the best you'll get out of me, and there's not a reason in the world why you shouldn't have gone in the first place."

"What," Mercy said in a frosty tone as she thumped the coffeepot onto the table, "is wrong with having a wife?"

"Nothing." Duncan gave her an affronted look. " 'Tis the wooing and getting one that's so aggravating."

"Just when did you make any effort to—" Chris snickered. "Jenny or Carmen?"

"Carmen, you dolt!"

Chris hooted. "All this time she's been thinking you were sweeping her walk, and you were tryin' to sweep her off her feet!"

"You've no room to tease him, Chris. You're the eldest, and you've yet to court a lass." Rob spooned a bite of egg into Elspeth.

"I'm in no hurry." Chris cracked his knuckles.

"Yes, you are." Mercy laughed. "You have to be on the eight o'clock train for Austin."

Chris wolfed down his breakfast and accepted a slip of paper from Rob. As he rose from the table, he groused, "I've spent my life watching out for my baby brothers. How'd I get saddled with another bairn?"

"I thought you didn't mind watching Elspeth every now and then," Mercy said quietly.

"Of course I dinna! She's not a bairn. She's a beauty!" Chris bent down, planted a kiss atop Elspeth's downy head and strode out.

Mercy waited until he was long gone and then dissolved into giggles.

"What's so funny?" Rob asked.

She looked at both of them. "Mrs. Kunstler is going to find out that Chris took that little baby boy to her cousin. The woman has her flaws, but she sure tries hard to take care of those she loves. Your brother is going to be her hero."

Rob choked on his coffee.

"I dinna care how great a doctor you are, Rob. There's no cure for the agonies our brother will suffer once that woman takes a shine to him."

∞

"By this evening, there's going to be a foot-deep rut in the road going from my house to yours."

Carmen smiled at Mercy's comment as she watched Rob cross the street and go back to the clinic.

"Duncan's been here twice as often as your husband." Jenny pressed both hands to her lower back and winced as she rubbed.

Carmen brushed aside Jenny's hands and massaged her. "He cares about you. We all do."

As if to prove that point, Duncan thumped on the door and barged in. "Traditions are important."

"What prompted that announcement?" Carmen gave him an exasperated look.

"Fetch your healer's bag. I'll hae Rob put the essentials in it. Then you can carry them o'er to the clinic." Once she gave him the monstrosity, he left.

"Well, that hideous thing did serve a purpose." Mercy smiled. "It kept him busy."

"He's going to have a conniption when he finds out you've decided to have the baby here, Jenny." Carmen rubbed her back again. "When he finally figures it out, we'll tell him how glad we are to have whatever he stuffs in that purse."

Carmen exchanged a look with Mercy. They'd made plans for this day months ago. Keeping Jenny distracted would help a little.

"Jenny, has Carmen ever told you how she kept the men

occupied when I was having Elspeth?"

"Noooo." Jenny's answer got swallowed up in another moan.

Carmen began telling Jenny of Mercy's memorable labor.

Not five minutes later, Duncan tramped back in with Elspeth over one shoulder and the bag over the other. "She's growing a mite cranky."

Carmen grinned to herself. *What baby wouldn't when faced with the terrifying sight of that armadillo?*

As Mercy took her daughter, Duncan decided, "I'll wait on the veranda. Once you're done, I'll take the wee little lassie home."

"Go use my bedroom," Carmen murmured to Mercy. Since Jenny wouldn't keep her baby, Mercy thoughtfully left her own babe at home when she came to help with the birth. After Mercy nursed and calmed Elspeth, Duncan carried his niece home.

"I spent a good part of my labor in the rocking chair." Mercy nudged Jenny to sit down. "Try it."

"Mercy tried to cook while she was in labor." Carmen shuddered. "She tried to turn apple cider into gravy."

"And I added a cup of sugar to the mashed potatoes." Mercy laughed. "But Carmen's the one who put it all together with apples and flan as dessert. Happenstance, she called it. You've never tasted anything half as good."

"Good?" Carmen looked at her in disbelief.

Mercy headed for the kitchen. "I distinctly remember enjoying it. Maybe we could make some today."

"Only if you're planning to stuff that dead armadillo with it," Carmen muttered.

Gunshots drowned out Jenny's weak laughter.

Chapter 13

He's dead." Rob remained on his knees in the middle of the street as he turned to the next man.

"It's Connant," Duncan said in utter disbelief.

"Connant's dead," Rob rasped as he shoved at Duncan's shoulder. "Give me your bandanna."

His brother's command made no sense, but Duncan complied. He stared at their lifeless friend. A trio of other men lay bleeding in the street.

Mercy demanded, "Rob, what do you need me to do?"

"I'm putting a tourniquet on Rundsdorf's leg. Stay with him while I check the others. Duncan." Rob jostled him. "Duncan! Get some men to help you carry him to the clinic."

Duncan ignored the order and lifted Mr. Rundsdorf by himself. Mercy scrambled alongside of him as he hastened to the clinic. Once he laid Mr. Rundsdorf on the examination table, he gawked as Mercy took a pair of shears to the hem of the man's britches. "I'll do that."

"No, you won't." Mercy barely spared him a strained glance. "You're already green. Get out of here before I have two of you to take care of."

Others spilled into the clinic. "Doc said Kondrad's to go upstairs," the preacher said.

"Duncan," Mercy said sharply, "you know where the gutta-percha sheets are. Throw one on each of the beds up there."

240

He dashed upstairs and threw the rubbery, waterproof sheets on the beds. Jorge grunted in pain as they laid him down. Duncan couldn't understand a single word of the rapid-fire Spanish pouring out of the man's wife. *Is there anyone who could help? Chris is gone delivering that baby. Carmen—Carmen! She couldn't possibly come translate. She has her hands full.*

Duncan stood out of the way as they carried the third man up the stairs and put him to bed. He herded everyone back down the stairs and loudly announced Rob's standard rule in times of trouble. "One family member can stay with each man. The rest of you, go on home."

Rob promptly shouted, "Eliza Wagner, Harriet Brun, and Gertrude Besselmen, you stay. Each of you keep watch on one of the wounded. You know what to look for. The rest of you, go. Pray."

The parson managed to get the rest to leave. Duncan strode over to Mr. Rundsdorf. "I'd take it as a favor if you wouldn't get in the habit of collecting bullets."

"He didn't collect it," Rob declared. "It went straight through. Mercy, get the ether."

Duncan's nose twitched. The smell of ether invariably left him woozy and often made him puke.

"Duncan, go see to Elspeth."

Glad for the reprieve, he left. In the midst of the excitement, he'd run to Carmen's to protect the women. Once he made sure they were fine, he and Mercy left Elspeth in Carmen's care so they could go help. It hadn't been that long ago, but he'd forgotten Elspeth was at Carmen's. Right on the heels of that realization, Duncan recalled Jenny being in labor. He decided he'd grab Elspeth and leave. It was a sound plan.

"Thank God, you're here!" Carmen yanked Duncan inside and leaned against the door. She didn't want to chance having him rush back out. The disturbance across the street following the gunshots told her the doctor and Mercy would both be busy for a long time.

"I just came to grab El—"

"You can't leave!" She kept her voice as quiet as she could, but it cracked with terror. "I don't know what to do!"

"Neither do I." Duncan gave her an appalled look. "You're a woman. You're supposed to be able to tend to such matters."

Jenny let out a long, guttural moan from the other room.

Duncan reached past Carmen for the doorknob. "I'll go get some help."

Carmen didn't budge. "Mercy and Rob are saving lives. They're not coming."

"I'll grab someone else!" He wiped the sweat from his brow on his sleeve.

"Who? Eliza Wagner?" From the way he swallowed hard, Carmen knew Doc had Eliza helping him. Frantically searching for any other possible prospect, Carmen asked, "What about Gertrude Besselmen or Harriet Brun?"

Even as he shook his head, he swiped across his brow again. "Think of someone else."

"All of those women are busy?" The words came out in a strangled gasp.

"Three got shot, and Connant's dead." As she gasped, Duncan tried for the doorknob again.

Carmen slapped his hand away. "You're not going anywhere, Duncan Gregor. So help me, if you try to walk out this door, your brother's going to have another patient."

Rushing over to the table, Duncan practically tripped over his own feet. He grabbed the armadillo bag. "Here. Whate'er you need, 'tis in here."

Carmen shoved the bag back at him. "Your brother packed it. You know more about medical things than I do."

He shoved the bag at her. "Go tell Jenny she'll have to wait."

"I'm not telling her that!" She forced the bag back into his keeping. After all, she'd never liked the stupid bag to begin with, and now it wasn't just ugly, it was frightening.

"I know! I'll prop up the foot of the bed. That way, the bairn will be sliding toward her head. 'Twill buy us some time."

I can't come up with a better solution. "Do you think it'll work?"

"It has to." Putting an end to their demented game of hot potato, he shoved the armadillo bag into her keeping. "I'll get something to do the propping."

"Carmen!" Jenny sounded panicky.

"I'm coming!" Carmen gave Duncan a piercing look.

"We're coming," he said.

He'd given his word. Satisfied that he'd not leave, Carmen rushed to Jenny.

"Hurts," Jenny cried out as she writhed on the bed. "Hurts. Hurts-hurts-hurts-hurts-hurts-hurts-hurts-hurts."

"Pobrecita." Carmen grabbed a damp cloth and blotted Jenny's face. "It'll be over soon."

Duncan came in with an armload of thick books. He looked just as scared as Jenny. Just as quickly, his features altered into determination. "We're here. Aye, we are."

"Duncan!" Jenny reached for him.

Carmen blinked back tears as Duncan dropped the books. He strode to the bed and smoothed back Jenny's hair. He didn't say a word, but everything about him radiated loving strength.

Jenny grabbed his hand. "Can't do this!" Her face twisted, and for the very first time since the day she'd arrived, Jenny began to cry.

"Ooch, lass, 'tis hard. But Carmen and I—we'll pull you through."

Carmen nodded. Frantic as she felt inside, she knew Jenny needed them to be calm. For the past half hour, her prayer had narrowed down to a desperate, "*Dios, ayudame.* God, help me. Dios, ayudame. Dios, ayudame." He'd sent help in the form of a cobbler who didn't know anything more than she did—but God was faithful.

"Hurts." Jenny arched her back and began the heartrending chant again. "Hurts-hurts-hurts-hurts-hurts. . ."

Once the contraction ended, Duncan squatted at the foot of the bed and started to gather up the books. Carmen went to help, and he muttered, "Lord, give me stones for my slingshot." He glanced at Carmen. "I'd rather face Goliath than this."

"Propping up the foot of the bed won't work," Carmen whispered. "The pains—they're starting to come hard and fast, just as they did for Mercy toward the very end."

Duncan bolted to his feet.

Jenny let out a cry. This time she clutched Carmen's arm with bruising force.

Duncan pried her free and let Jenny crush his hand. When the pain was over, he murmured something nonsensical and pushed Carmen back to Jenny's side. He picked up the books, but instead of raising the bed with them, he set them aside.

He moved them so I wouldn't trip.

The last one he lifted made his brows rise and the corners of his mouth lift. As he flipped through the pages, he nodded with great satisfaction. "Instructions!"

Whether hours or minutes passed, Carmen couldn't say. Time seemed to stretch out for an eternity during a pain and then speed up in between. Then Jenny started to strain down.

Duncan pointed toward the bag. "You'll be needing that soon, Carmen." He cupped her face between his hands. "You can do this. Aye, you can. Not only do I have faith in God, but I believe in you, too."

Warmth poured through Carmen. "I'm so glad you're here." She was. Even if he knew nothing more than she did, Carmen knew for certain nothing disastrous would happen. God and Duncan wouldn't allow it.

"What-is-happening?" Jenny panted.

"Time's short," Duncan explained. "I've the instructions. I'll read them to Carmen, and she can tend to matters." He picked up the book and headed toward the door.

"Don't go!" Carmen wasn't sure whether she'd cried the words or if Jenny had.

" 'Tisna proper, my being here."

Jenny made a funny sound. "More than a hundred men have—"

"Nae, Jenny. You're a new woman in Christ. Your past is forgiven and forgotten."

Carmen fought the urge to weep at the poignancy and mercy of his words. There wasn't time to indulge in those feelings now. She pointed to a chair. "Pull that up by her shoulders, Duncan. I'll need you to help with the baby."

Jenny started to strain down again. "Something's"—she gasped and strained—"wrong." She panted and strained again. "I'm all wet!"

Duncan yanked the chair up by the bed and turned so he'd be facing the headboard. He flipped open the book and riffled through the pages as Carmen whipped back the sheet.

"Here." Duncan cleared his throat. "The bag most often ruptures when birth is imminent."

Jenny let out a low groan as she strained again.

Carmen dumped the contents of the armadillo bag onto the bed. The scissors and strips of gauze looked daunting. "Tell me what to do."

Duncan pored over the book. "Hooves will appear first, with the muzzle between the forelegs."

Thunderstruck, Carmen still knew she couldn't yell at him. Besides, the baby was partway out. "What about the cord?"

Duncan turned the page. "If necessary, the mother will bi—" His voice died out.

Chapter 14

C armen and Jenny exhibited grace under this ordeal, and he was blithering. Duncan cleared his throat. He couldn't let them down. He scanned farther down the page to give Carmen useful instructions. "We're to dry the newborn off immediately. Blankets or straw. Um, blankets." He slammed the book shut. "You have blankets, right?"

"Oh. Oh!" Jenny strained until she turned purple.

"Almost there. Almost." Awe colored Carmen's voice. A small gurgling noise was followed by a cry. "It's a girl, Jenny. A perfect little girl." A minute later, Carmen handed him a blanket-wrapped bundle. "Go dry her off and diaper her."

Duncan took his cue from Carmen and left the bedroom. "Ooch, you wee little lassie. Dinna cry." He gently jostled her and began to sing. "Jesus loves me, this I know. . ."

Duncan calmed the babe only to have Elspeth start squalling. Since Mercy allowed her food from the table, Duncan poked through Carmen's cupboard and located molasses cookies. He ate one and gave another to Elspeth to gum.

Boiling water filled the reservoir and three kettles on the stove. Carmen slipped out of the bedroom and took a kettle back with her.

Determined to help as best he could, Duncan decided he'd bathe the baby. On occasion, he'd helped with Elspeth's bath, so he pumped water into a dishpan and added enough boiling water to make it a comfortable temperature.

Mercy rushed through the door. "How—" She stopped cold.

"A lass, and a hefty one at that." Duncan pulled back the blanket so his sister-in-law could inspect the babe.

Mercy swept up Elspeth in one arm and trailed her finger across the new baby's forehead. "She's beautiful. How's Jenny?"

"Carmen's seeing to her. I thought to tub this wee one."

"No. Remember when Elspeth was newborn? Just sponge her."

"How're all the men doing?"

"They'll all pull through. I'll go help with Jenny."

Duncan methodically set out the water, soap, a towel, and a diaper on Carmen's table. He'd just started to wash the babe when Carmen joined him.

"Mercy's bathing Jenny and taking care of things. How's the baby?"

"See for yourself."

Carmen kept her gaze on the baby. Tears filled her big brown eyes. "Mercy didn't say anything, but I know something bad happened."

Duncan kept one hand on the newborn as he slid his other arm around Carmen. "The bank was robbed. Three men were injured, and Connant Gilchrist was killed."

The sound of pain curled in her throat.

Duncan nestled her closer as if to shelter her from that dreadful truth. Jenny's baby gurgled, and he decided to redirect Carmen's attention. "We ken Connant's with the Almighty this verra moment. The Lord took home His boy and gave us a wee little lass at the same time. I'm thinkin' we'd best tend to her."

Carmen was more of a hindrance than a help. She kept touching and smearing soap bubbles on spots he'd already rinsed. "She's perfect. Look at her. Isn't she beautiful?"

"Absolutely."

"Her grip is strong. How's her other hand?" Carmen chuckled.

"It's fine, too. Oh, Duncan, isn't she just perfect?"

"She's getting noisy."

"That means her lungs and heart are healthy. It's a good sign. Oh, look at her pretty little feet!"

Duncan listened as Carmen exclaimed over and over about the baby. Once he finished the bath, Carmen diapered the little one and swaddled her in a blanket. "It's a shame to cover her up. She's so. . ."

"Perfect?"

"Yes!" Carmen glowed.

"I'd have ye tell me, would this lassie be any less worthy of love if she weren't perfect?"

Carmen reared back and blinked. "How could you ask such a thing?"

"Because you keep assuring yourself that she's hale and bonny." Duncan led her over to the settee. He made sure she and the babe were comfortable, then dared to sit on the settee, too. It was a bold move. A man didn't sit alongside a woman on her settee unless he had honorable and lifelong intentions.

"Don't be ridiculous, Duncan. Anyone would love this girl. Just anyone."

"You've my most hearty agreement. She's as sweet a miracle as I've e'er seen."

"Yes. A miracle. And sweet. Perfect." Carmen cooed softly to the baby in Spanish.

Lord, I've asked You for an opportunity to say something to Carmen. "Love doesna consider whether someone is perfect—either in body or in behavior. We're all flawed in our own ways. Love overlooks imperfections and doesna demand that someone strive to earn a place in the heart. At least, love that is worth having."

"God loves like that. Men don't."

He fought the desire to declare his love. He wanted an armful of flowers and carefully thought-out words. "Some men do. Just as God is able to love us even though we're cracked vessels, we can love one another—ofttimes not in spite of those imperfections, but because of them. Think on that." *Please, think on it.*

∽

Jenny's room lay empty. She'd left, but just to the Stein farm. Mercy's grandfather asked if she'd be willing to become his house-keeper. It was a happy arrangement.

Since Rob and Mercy needed to mind the wounded, Duncan was the one who went away carrying Jenny's babe and the dark green leather book she'd filled with her loving thoughts for the child. He'd left with tears in his eyes and returned the same way. Though he'd not reveal where he'd gone or who received the baby, Duncan repeatedly reassured Jenny and Carmen that the baby's mother and father were wonderful, loving Christian parents.

But the house was so very quiet. Carmen walked through it and felt so empty. The boots Duncan made for her peeped out from beneath her bed. She'd been so angry and humiliated about them, she'd shoved them out of sight. Pride kept her from saying anything to Duncan.

It's not in Duncan's character to taunt someone. He sat me down and said imperfections didn't halt love. Once he even called my limp insignificant.

She sank to the floor and drew out the boots. *I'd rather have my shoes look clumsy if it meant I wasn't so awkward.* She took off her boots. The new right boot fit wonderfully. The leather felt so soft and comfortable. But she stared at the left one. Duncan raised the sole like a platform and even angled it in such a way that it would conform to the twisted shape of her foot. The heel was stacked twice as high as the right one, too. It was ugly.

Until she put it on.

It fits perfectly. How could he have known how to do that?

For the first time in years, Carmen stood and didn't wince at the pain of putting weight on her left leg. She tried a few steps. Then another...and a few more...until the new boots carried her to Duncan's workshop.

A magnificent saddle rested over a frame. He stood behind it, buffing the leather until it gleamed. Every time she saw him working, Carmen noticed how his features bore the stamps of contentment and concentration. Today was no different. He happened to look up. "Hello, Carmen."

"You're busy." The last thing she wanted to do was leave, but it wasn't right for her to take him away from his labors.

"If e'er I'm too busy to spend time with a friend, then I'm too busy." He set down the cloth he'd been using and motioned toward a bench.

Would he notice how evenly she walked? Carmen slowly crossed the plank floor and sat down.

"Mercy baked cookies last night." Duncan carried over the beautiful mesquite bowl he treasured. Mr. Rundsdorf had made a similar one for her when she'd sewn shirts for him.

After Carmen accepted a cookie, she raised it to her mouth and lowered it without taking a bite. "My house feels so empty."

" 'Tis just you there now."

She stared down at the cookie and confessed, "I'm lonely, Duncan."

"So am I."

Her head jerked up. "You? How could you ever be lonely? You have a wonderful family, and everyone adores you."

He tapped the center of his chest. "In here, I'm lonely. Though 'tis true I've a fine family and many a friend, I'm in sore want of the woman I love."

Carmen set aside the cookie. "Jenny."

Duncan gawked at her. "Jenny? That wee lassie? She's a sweet friend, but I feel no more than brotherly love for her." Shaking his head, he drew closer. "There's but one woman in the world for me."

"You're strong and kind and good, Duncan. Handsome, too." As soon as she'd said that, Carmen felt mortified that she'd let slip that she considered him so masculine and handsome. For some odd reason, she kept babbling, though. "Any woman would be happy to have you. Your lonely days are numbered."

He cocked a brow. "Are they?"

"I'm sure they are." Carmen blinked back tears. He deserved a fine wife. She wanted that for him. Truly, she did. But once again, the lonely life stretching out ahead made her ache to the depths of her soul. "I'll be happy to help with the wedding."

"That's a fine offer, but you'll be too busy."

Carmen shook her head. "No, I won't. I'm not volunteering for everything anymore. You were right—I was trying to earn love and a place for myself in our community. Now I'm waiting on the Lord and asking Him to direct me instead of charging ahead and reminding Him the work of my hands was dedicated to Him."

Duncan's rough hand slid over hers. "You're not the only one who's done that. It nearly shook me out of my boots when I realized I was playing that same foolish game—only 'twasna with the Almighty. 'Twas with the woman I love. I tried to win her heart by making myself indispensable."

"She should have been flattered. I know I would have been."

Duncan's mouth tilted upward. "Nae, Carmen, you weren't."

"You're wrong, Duncan. Words can't begin to say how thankful I am for your friendship and all the time you've spent helping Jenny and me. Just think of that day when we took that walk and filled your wheelbarrow with wildflowers. And what about the picnics? I could go on for hours reciting things we've done and times we've agreed to pray about something. Don't you think for one minute that I don't appreciate you—and not just for the things you've done—"

The way he trailed a finger down her cheek silenced her.

"Carmen"—he stared into her eyes—" 'tis you I love."

His words hovered in the air. Carmen couldn't tear her gaze from him. Heat shot through her. "But I'm a cripple." As soon as she finished her mortifying confession, she rushed to add on, "But I'm wearing those beautiful boots you made for me. I barely limp at all in them. Did you notice?"

"Nae. And why should I? 'Tis an insignificant thing, and if all that matters to a man is how his woman walks or dresses or cooks, then he's a pathetic wretch. You're beautiful from the top of your raven black hair to the tip of your turned-in toes, Carmen Rodriguez. Most of all, you're beautiful on the inside."

Duncan rose and pulled her to her feet. "You've some thinking to do. I'll walk you home, and after you've thought on it and prayed o'er it, you can tell me whether you'll allow me to court you."

"You've given me a garden full of flowers. You've laughed at my jokes, complimented my cooking, and walked me to church. You made that pretty journal for me."

The side of his mouth pulled. "The design on it—"

"The interlocking rings that form the four seasons and friendship?"

"Aye. Well, tradition also says the design stands for a love that has no beginning or end."

"You've had feelings for me since then?"

"E'en before then."

And I was jealous because I thought he wanted Jenny. How could I have been jealous if I didn't love him and want him to love me in return? "What more is a man supposed to do to pay a woman court?"

Duncan brushed his thumb back and forth on her wrist. "He has to win her heart."

"You have, Duncan. I love you, too."

Then and there, he got down on one knee. Holding her hand as if she were a princess, he looked up at her. "I want to do this right."

"Oh, Duncan!"

"Quiero compartir todavia de mi vida contigo, mi amorada."

Tears filled her eyes. *"I want to share all the days of my life with you, my beloved one."* He'd gone through the trouble of learning how to say something romantic to her in Spanish.

"¿Me se casará usted? ¿Será usted mi esposa?"

"Oh yes! I'll marry you. I'd love to be your wife. *Te amo, Duncan.* I love you."

⚭

Mama's lace mantilla flowed gently around Carmen as she knelt at the altar beside Duncan. The golden band Duncan had just slipped on her finger gleamed in the candlelight. He kept her right hand in his while the pastor read the thirteenth chapter of First Corinthians from Duncan's father's Bible. The pastor then asked God's blessing on their marriage. After the prayer, Carmen joyfully accepted Duncan's assistance to rise. He wasn't helping her because of her leg; she knew his actions stemmed from affection. She smiled up at him.

"Duncan Gregor," the pastor said, "you may greet your bride."

Just as Rob had done with Mercy, Duncan freed a length of Gregor tartan from his waist and began to gently drape it over her shoulder. She remembered the Gregor tradition was for the groom to recite the romantic Burns poem. Duncan's tender smile told her he would mean every word of it.

"Como la feria usted es, mi chica bonita," he began.

Her lips parted in amazement. Spanish. He was reciting the love poem in Spanish!

"Tan profundamente son yo;
Y adoraré usted de todos modos, mi querida,
Hasta que todos los mares vayan secos."

After those precious words, Duncan drew her close and gave Carmen her very first kiss. It was worth the wait.

To Do

JUSTICE

Chapter 1

I'll be leaving in the morning." Chris Gregor waited until supper ended to make his announcement. No use spoiling a good meal with the inevitable conflict that would ensue.

Rob gave him a piercing look. "You gave me your word you wouldn't set foot in the Thurber mines again."

"And I won't."

Mercy patted Rob's arm. "Your brother wouldn't go back on his word. He's a Gregor. Will I need to pack a meal for you, Chris?"

"You rest." Carmen gazed pointedly at Mercy's pregnant tummy and started to rise. "I'll do it."

"No, but I thank you for the thought." Chris looked at his family. He'd always watched out for his younger brothers, but they were both married men now. Duncan had just moved in across the street after marrying Carmen, and Mercy was expecting her second child. No one needed him here.

But he had a job to do.

Duncan chuckled softly. "I'm thinking Chris is going to try to sneak away ere Mrs. Kunstler comes to pay a call again. He's fearing for his reputation."

Everyone laughed; Chris glowered.

"Come now, Chris." Rob plucked little Elspeth from her high chair. "No use in you being sour o'er a joke. We all think it endearing, how the woman keeps droppin' by with a treat to thank you. After all, you did deliver that strapping baby boy out to her cousin and his wife."

"Aye, and I rue the day."

Again his family laughed, but their laughter died out when he didn't join in. He gritted his teeth. "I should have been here that day." Until now, he'd never spoken the thought aloud.

The only things filling the air were Elspeth's babbling and the lingering aromas of pork chops and coffee. Chris stared at the center of the table and repeated himself. "I should have been here."

"You couldn't have saved Connant." Rob handed Elspeth off to his wife. "They shot him straight through the heart."

"If I had been in town instead of playing stork, Connant would have acted differently. He had no one he could count on to back him up or cover him."

"Other men responded." Mercy's voice sounded soft and low.

Her tone might have been for Elspeth's comfort, but Chris suspected she'd used that voice to soothe him. It didn't work. Matters were far past words; the time had come for action. Instead of getting mired down in suppositions and conversation, he said what he needed to. "I'm becoming a Texas Ranger."

"No." Rob glared at him. "I barely managed to pry bullets out of the other men and keep them alive. I dinna need another patient—I need my brother!"

Jaw hard, Chris said, "My mind's made up."

"You're out of your mind!" Rob snapped.

Duncan shook his head. "Vengeance belongs to the Lord, Chris. Dinna take it into your own hands."

"Justice. That's what I'm seeking. An eye"—he pounded his fist on the tabletop—"for an eye." He repeated the action.

"We need a sheriff here," Carmen said quietly.

Shifting Elspeth to her shoulder, Mercy started to sway from one side to the other. "Having you here with us is a blessing, Christopher. I feel safe knowing you're close-by."

"No one is safe—not with Whelan and his gang out there."

"So once Whelan is captured, you'll be done with this nonsense?"

"Nae, Rob. I willna. Not too long ago, Dalton and his gang terrorized Kansas. Evil men exist. 'Tis an unchanging fact. Get rid of Whelan and his followers, and the devil will make pacts wi' other men."

"My wife is right." Duncan slid his hand over Carmen's. "We do need a sheriff here. You've the heart of a warrior, Chris. But there's every bit as much valor in protecting our friends and neighbors as there is in chasing after the devil's brigade."

Chris stood. "I made my decision."

"We promised Da we'd all stay together." Rob stared at him. "You gave your word."

"Aye, and I'm not breaking it. I'll still be in Texas. Be assured, I'll come 'round often enough for you to grow heartily sick of me. I swore an oath today to serve as a Texas Ranger. As Mercy said, Gregors keep their word."

Duncan's features remained taut. "I'll not pretend to like your decision, but I'll honor it. You hae my support."

Carmen nestled into Duncan's side. "And our prayers."

Chris dipped his head in acknowledgment. He'd already thought this through and knew Duncan would respect his decision. Rob might well take a few years to get around to accepting it. Nevertheless, Chris looked to him.

Rob's heated glare could have sterilized his medical instruments.

Tension crackled between them, but Chris stood his ground. *Lord, I dinna want to leave at odds with my brother. Soothing words are his talent, not mine. Even so, I'd take it as a favor if You'd give me something to say.*

Rob shook his head. "If I wouldn't have to patch you up afterward, I'd be tempted to beat you to a bloody pulp."

"I'd be bloodied, all right." Chris paused a second. "But the blood would all be yours. You'd break your fingers and lose all the skin on your knuckles after the second blow."

"You arrogant—"

"Confident, not arrogant." Chris folded his arms across his chest.

"You're brothers." Mercy's voice held both censure for their scrapping and a plea for them to make peace.

Carmen laughed. "The Gregor men bellow and bluster, but they'd never come to blows. Duncan even told Jenny so. Isn't that right, Duncan?"

" 'Tis true. I did. Fretting's not good for the bairn, Mercy. Dinna let this upset you."

Chris faulted himself for having broached the topic in front of his sisters-in-law. Gentle women oughtn't be caught between warring men. Rob slid his arm around his wife's shoulders and drew her into the shelter of his side. *'Tis wondrous how he loves Mercy.* As soon as that thought flashed through his mind, Chris knew God had given him the way to make peace with his brother.

"Think back on the day Da passed on. Are you remembering how we read from his Bible on the *Anchoria's* deck?"

Duncan and Rob both nodded.

"Micah 6:8. 'He hath shewed thee, O man, what is good; and what doth the Lord require of thee, but to do justly, and to love mercy, and to walk humbly with thy God?' We made a pact that day to live that verse because God mandated it and because 'twould be a tribute to Da. Rob, 'tis undeniable that you love Mercy." Chris turned to Duncan. "And you—you and Carmen walk in step with the Lord and serve Him in the kind and gentle ways. Justice is left. Aye, 'tis, and I'm to fulfill that mandate. As a ranger, I'll do justice."

"You could do justice as the town's sheriff." Rob's molars might crack if he gritted his teeth any tighter.

"Mollifying you 'tisna what I'm called to do."

Resignation stamped Rob's features. "You're going, no matter what I say."

"Aye. You hae your calling. I hae mine. I'm doing what I must."

"Then God go wi' you."

The tension knotting Chris's neck melted away. "Aye, I'm counting on Him being with me. But I'm also relying on Him to stay here and keep His hand on the lot of you."

∽

Color streaked the dawn sky as Kathryn "Wren" Regent left her shack and headed for Hepplewhite's Emporium. The clopping of horse hooves caused her to halt at the boardwalk and shove her glasses up a bit. An enormous, dust-covered man rode into town. He squinted at the buildings lining the street, then nickered softly to urge his mount onward.

Two men followed after the large man. He'd shackled their hands behind their backs, tied rope around their waists, and half dragged them toward the jailhouse.

A bounty hunter, Wren decided. Judging from what she'd overheard her brother say, bounty hunters weren't any more law-abiding than the criminals they chased. It wasn't her business, though. She ducked her head and hastened to Hepplewhite's Emporium.

Every morning she drew a steadying breath before unlocking the door. Hepplewhite could have posed as an ogre in a child's book. Uglier on the inside than he was on the outside, he filled her days with misery and strife. *But what I have is better than anything*

I've ever had before. She shoved the key into the lock and gave it a savage turn.

Wren hurriedly went to work preparing breakfast. She soon set a plate of biscuits and gravy and a slab of ham in front of Hepplewhite. She always ate as she cooked so she wouldn't have to join him for meals. While he slurped his coffee and belched over the plate, she set out the spittoons she'd polished the night before, dusted shelves, and cleaned the glass display cases. Washing the breakfast dishes stripped the ammonia smell from her hands, but that was part of the routine she'd created. Now she could handle yards of fabric without spoiling them.

Her shop took up the back corner of the emporium. Though Hepplewhite owned the bolts of cloth, spools of thread, lace, ribbon, and buttons, Kathryn owned the sewing machine. The Singer was her pride and joy. With it, she provided for herself.

The morning passed quickly. A bachelor brought in a shirt that needed a new button. Another brought socks that needed darning. Old Widow Marsby toddled in to get her new petticoats, which Wren discreetly slipped into an empty sugar sack.

Around those little tasks, she put the finishing touches on Ella Mae Tolliver's dress. Made of gold, water-stained taffeta, the gown was a nightmare to work on. The fabric wanted to fray, so Wren painstakingly candled the edge of each piece to fuse the threads. If that weren't enough, Mrs. Tolliver ordered that thin black braiding be stitched onto the skirts in an ornate pattern. That detailed embellishment took days of work, but *Godey's Lady's Book* could easily feature the resulting garment. Mrs. Tolliver would be in tomorrow, so Wren sewed jet buttons down the back of the garment.

The bell over the mercantile door clanged, and Mrs. Tolliver trundled in. Kathryn swiftly took one last stitch, knotted the thread, and snipped it. "Mrs. Tolliver." She stood. "I didn't expect to see you until tomorrow."

"You were wrong. I distinctly recall telling you at church Sunday that I'd come on Thursday."

"Today's Wednesday," Hepplewhite announced. He and Mrs. Tolliver were cousins, and they shared the exact same ugly disposition. Both were tall, blocky, and had mean-looking dark eyes and a permanent sneer. Once they started quibbling, Kathryn turned away and shook out the gown.

"Well, don't keep me waiting all day." Mrs. Tolliver snatched the dress from Kathryn's hands. "It's taken you long enough to get this done."

Defending herself wouldn't do any good. Kathryn knew the minute she so much as opened her mouth, Mr. Hepplewhite would suddenly remember Ella Mae was his kin. The last thing Kathryn wanted was to trigger his temper. Instead, she motioned toward the screen.

Mrs. Tolliver swept past her and declared, "It's taken you so long to finish this dress, the price should be discounted."

Wren didn't reply. The contract for the dress rested in the top drawer of the treadle machine's stand. The cost and date were clearly stipulated, and she refused to budge. She couldn't afford to. Mr. Hepplewhite made her pay for every spool of thread and inch of fabric out of her own pocket whenever she started a project. He also took 30 percent of the price she charged her patrons.

The emporium's bell jangled once again, but this time the bounty hunter filled the entire doorway. He scanned the store as he stepped inside. Kathryn's heart jumped as he started toward her.

"Hey, Wren!" Mr. Hepplewhite leaned on the pickle barrel. "Git movin' and make my dinner!"

After several muttered comments and a lot of bumping around, Mrs. Tolliver emerged from behind the screen, yanking at the cuff of her gown. "You can wait, you old goat. Wren has to alter this at once. It's abysmal. I'd be ashamed to be seen in it at all!"

"She ain't gonna stay on to do her stitchin' iff'n she don't make me grub quick-like. 'Sides, Ella Mae, you can't much expect her to fit you into anything less than a tent. You ain't lost anything you put on 'tween babies."

The bounty hunter came to a stop about five feet away. For being such a big man, he walked with the lithe grace of a cougar. He took off his hat and waited patiently. Since she'd seen him earlier, he'd managed to dust off and wash up. Now his hair was wet, so she couldn't determine whether it was black or a deep sable. Silvery blue-gray eyes gave him an air of aloofness.

Mrs. Tolliver continued to splutter and cluck over her gown.

The stranger jutted his chin toward her. "Ma'am, I think that's a fine gown. I was in Chicago just a week ago, and none of the fancy society matrons wore anything that would put yours to shame."

Ella Mae stopped midtirade and gave him a withering glare. "Mind your own business."

"As a matter of fact, I came in to do business with the young lady. Her reputation—"

My reputation! Wren's mouth went dry.

"Wren!" Hepplewhite bellowed.

The stranger shot her a bolstering smile and continued on as if he hadn't been interrupted, "—is well known. I need to get a shirt."

In the background, the ringing sound of metal dropping on a hardwood floor failed to drown out a nasty stream of oaths. "Wren! You ain't even seen to the spittoons yet!"

"I did. The Clancy boys came by for eggs—remember?"

Hepplewhite snorted. "Gal, you gotta git me my food! My ribs are rattling!"

Mrs. Tolliver struggled with the waist on her dress. "You were intentionally mean-spirited when you made this. You tried your hardest to make me look fat!"

"Wren! I'm gonna starve!"

Wren took a deep breath. "Mrs. Tolliver, if you give me another day, I'll work on your gown. Sir," she paused and shot a wary look at the bounty hunter, "I have to cook. If you'll but wait, I'll gladly give you my portion."

His face darkened. "If you'll forgive me, ma'am, you look like a stiff wind could take you clear to the coast. I'd far rather see you eat whatever you're fixing. Go on and see to things. I can look around."

"Thank you, sir. Mrs. Tolliver, do you need help with your buttons?"

"I'm not a lackwit! I can take care of myself!"

Mr. Hepplewhite slouched over. "Gal, I done tole you, you gotta work to keep yer space. Yer long overdue for dinner, and I full well 'spect pie after supper tonight. And see to them spittoons again."

Wren's shoulders sank with weariness.

"What are you a-standin' there fer? Go cook!"

"Yes, Mr. Hepplewhite."

The storekeeper grabbed her arm and glowered. "I want somethin' good. None of them chicken an' dumplin's or chicken stew."

"Other than the ham for breakfast, you've allowed me only one chicken to feed us for the week, Mr. Hepplewhite."

"Don't get snippy with me!" He let go, reared back, and smacked her across the face.

Chapter 2

Chris didn't believe his eyes. He reacted out of sheer reflex and caught the poor girl as she flew toward him. After he set her to the side, he automatically spun back around. "That's more than enough!"

"Shuddup. Ain't none of your affair." The storekeeper sneered at the lass and took a menacing step toward her.

Chris stepped between them and growled, "Don't."

"This here is my place."

"Owning a place doesna give you license to harm anyone." Chris slowly closed his hands into fists. Hepplewhite might be big, but none of it was muscle. His eyes narrowed and the veins in his neck bulged—both telltale signs of a building temper.

"Get outta here," Hepplewhite sneered.

Chris didn't budge an inch, but when the storekeeper threw the first punch, Chris didn't hesitate to defend himself. A left to Hepplewhite's middle and a right uppercut to his jaw dropped the man like a ton of bricks.

"Miss Wren, are you all right?" Chris turned back in time to see her try to readjust her spectacles, only to find they were mangled from Mr. Hepplewhite's smack. Tears filled her eyes, making them look like the flowers Carmen called lobelias. If her tears weren't enough, a big red handprint, complete with rapidly growing welts, painted her cheek.

"Oh no!" she whimpered.

"You're white as a sun-bleached bone. Let's sit you down. I'll go get a wet rag to press to your face. Come on, sit here in this chair before you swoon." He gently cupped her elbow and led her to a battered cane chair. The poor woman's knees gave out on her, and he caught her in the nick of time. Easing her onto the seat, Chris couldn't help but note how thin she was.

The whole while, Ella Mae Tolliver screeched at an ear-splitting level. Chris gave her a nasty look and snapped, "Hush up and get out your smelling salts."

"I'm not about to aid that...that...*trollop*. I'm not going to help a murderer, either!"

"He's not dead. Dump water over him, and he'll come to."

The door burst open, and the sheriff entered with his pistol drawn. "What's going on in here?"

"That man," Ella Mae screamed as she pointed at Chris, "tried to kill my cousin!"

Having turned two prisoners over to the sheriff this morning, Chris reported, "He struck Miss Wren, continued to pose a threat, then took a swing at me. Self-defense."

"Now what did you do, Wren?" the sheriff asked in an exasperated tone as he holstered his weapon.

"She did nothing at all," Chris asserted.

The sheriff glanced at the tiny woman's face and grimaced. "He got you pretty good this time."

"*This time?*" Chris roared as his blood went from a heavy simmer clean into a rolling boil. The poor wisp of a woman didn't deserve even one smack—how could any man ever raise a hand to a woman? And from the sound of it, this wasn't anything new.

Miss Wren deserved her unusual name. Plainly dressed in a mud-brown day gown and wearing her ordinary brown hair scraped back in a schoolmarm bun, she seemed as dull and dreary as a common wren. Even the bright yellow tape measure she wore looped over her neck seemed to fade and droop.

Dark moons hovered beneath her eyes, and she bit her lower lip—most likely to keep from crying. Chris felt an odd need to shelter the little wren from the storm. He scowled at the sheriff. "This woman deserves protection."

Wren's lids lowered in shame, and she leaned away from the sheriff's touch. Once his hand dropped, she dipped her head. Chris watched how badly her hands shook as she tried to fix her mangled eyeglasses. Something deep inside him twisted. He paced across the worn plank floor, snatched a red bandanna from a display stack, shoved a dipper to the side of a tin water bucket, and dunked the cloth inside. After wringing it out, he hunkered down by Wren and gently reached up to press its cool dampness to the fire in her cheek.

She threw up her arm in an instinctively defensive move and flinched.

Chris wrapped his hand around her stick-thin wrist and slowly lowered it back into her lap as he made a soft sound of reassurance. Folding the bandanna so another cool surface was available, he ordered in a tone milder than a spring breeze, "Miss Wren, you'd best go on and hold this to your face. It has to be paining you a fair bit."

Once she took the cloth, Chris rose and glowered at the sheriff. "The man flat out assaulted her."

"Oh, he had cause!" The old battle-ax pointed at Wren. "She only got what she deserved—could've gotten more and had no cause to whine. My cousin took her in out of the goodness of his heart. He lets her work here and even feeds the girl. She got fresh mouthed."

The sheriff scratched his shoulder. "It strains a man's imagination thinkin' Wren could muster even a few fresh words."

Hepplewhite started to rouse. He groaned and rolled onto his side before struggling to his feet. Rubbing his jaw, he cursed vividly. "He done went an' busted me in the chops. Go stick him in the jailhouse!"

"Can't. You struck Wren, and then you threw the first punch at him."

Mr. Hepplewhite turned on Wren. "I put up with more'n enough, gal. Git out. Now."

Wren's mouth twisted as she cried out.

"Git, I say!"

The sheriff sighed. "Wren, he owns the place. Go on and gather up everything that belongs to you."

"She ain't takin' a thang! I git a third of everything she sews, seein' as it's my place, but she ain't paid this week."

"You owe her for cooking and cleaning," Chris gritted. "Call it even."

"I don't owe her a cent."

"That wasn't the agreement you made with her," the sheriff growled. "We all thought you gave her a wage for her extra work."

"Thangs change."

"That does it," Chris said. "Miss Wren, do you have any kin?"

"Only a stepbrother. I haven't seen him in years."

"Fine." Chris gently flipped over the compress and set it back in place. "Let's send him a telegram."

Hopelessness tainted her voice. "I don't know where he is."

Poor woman. He looked to the sheriff. "Where else can she go?"

Ella Mae simpered, "No decent folk are going to take her in."

Mr. Hepplewhite held his jaw and snorted. "Told ya. Folks have dirty minds. All of 'em think you an' me—"

"Say one more word—" Chris snarled. He didn't need to finish his threat. Hepplewhite shut up, but the damage was done.

The blood drained from Wren's face, making her horrified expression all the more stark.

Chris glanced at the sheriff, his eyes asking an unvoiced question.

"Ain't much I can do. Hepplewhite's been drinkin' like a trout, an' he's been tellin' tales."

"Don't even think to ask me to take her in. I've got children. No scarlet woman is going to taint my home!"

The sheriff heaved a sigh. "Now, Ella Mae, you just heard your cousin. He's just been spreadin' lies—"

"She's opened herself to lurid speculation. I won't have men riding out to my place because they figure they'll have a turn with her." Mrs. Tolliver disappeared behind the screen and reappeared a few minutes later. She tossed the golden dress onto the floor. "I don't want this, after all."

As the sharp-tongued woman sailed out the door, Wren bowed her head.

"Miss Wren," Chris said as he tilted her face up to his, "go on and get packed. I'm taking you out of here."

Flinching again from his touch, she wailed, "You lost me my job!"

"No, Songbird. I freed you from slavery."

She eased away from him as she rose unsteadily.

Chris looked her over slowly, taking in her mussed hair, trembling lips, and shy, deep blue eyes. He saw how her shoulders squared with pride, just as he noted her breaths came far too fast and choppy to indicate she felt sure of herself or her situation. She held her clasped hands right at the base of her ribs, and her knuckles were white.

Chris clenched and unclenched his fists as he realized this defenseless woman had the tiniest waist he'd ever seen. Her drab dress hid her assets, and he began to wonder if she hadn't planned the effect.

"Old Pickersly's wagon." The sheriff shifted from one boot to the other. "It ought to last long enough to get you to a new place. Don't know what to suggest about an animal to pull it."

Chris tamped down a moan. The last thing he needed was to be saddled with a helpless female. Then again, he couldn't turn his back on her. *Mercy could probably use some help. I'm on my way home anyway.*

He locked eyes with the sheriff. "Miss Wren will come with me. I'll find her a good placement—safe and happy."

"Wren, this is Chris Gregor. He's—" Chris gave him a slight warning shake of the head, and the sheriff recovered. "Believe me, I know plenty of his friends, and they're all fine men. Real fine men. The very best. You'll be safe as can be with him. He'll make sure you land on your feet somewhere. I'd trust him with my life."

"But Sheriff! I've never even met Mr. Gregor and—"

"Now, Wren, some situations you have to look at as being put into motion by the hand of the Almighty. You can't very well stay in these parts. Things just aren't workin' out. What with Mr. Hepplewhite spreading lurid tales, you'll not be safe here."

Wren flushed deeply but still managed to whisper, "I'm not a woman to follow a stranger out on the open trail."

"No one in their right mind would ever figure you and Gregor were. . .ah, misbehaving."

"But they thought Mr. Hepplewhite and I were!"

The sheriff frowned at her. "Consider the caliber of man you're dealing with, Wren."

"I'm not able to! I've never met him before."

"He's good friends with several of my buddies. That's the best recommendation you'll ever get."

Wren looked at Chris's face. She stared with great intensity, a fact that surprised him since she'd been so timid until now. Uncertainty painted her unremarkable features.

Chris no more than decided the woman was being rude when he realized her eyes looked cloudy. She couldn't focus well enough to scan him for a polite instant. "Miss Wren, I'll help you get spectacles straight off. It'll make you feel better, seeing where you're headed and what's going on."

"There you are, Wren." The sheriff absently helped himself to a fistful of gumdrops. "Mr. Gregor's got things well in hand. And now you've got that buckboard. It simplifies the move."

"She ain't goin' till she pays up!"

"That's more than fair." Chris nodded sagely. "And we'll make sure she gets what you owe her, too."

"Me? I don't owe her one red cent. She owes me rent!"

"Rent?" The sheriff reared back. "She cooks for you in return for her space here. I was here when you came to that agreement."

"I told you thangs change. She ain't all that good a cook."

The sheriff studied a red gumdrop. "Church socials and such—I've eaten what she made. Only woman around who can hold a candle to her is my wife. Wren, did you get paid for the weeks you minded the store when pleurisy laid up Mr. Hepplewhite? Or all the times he's busy and tells you to help customers?"

She shook her head.

He popped the gumdrop into his mouth and frowned at a black

gumdrop. "What about all the dustin' and sweepin' and window washin' you do? You get paid for that?"

"No," she said in a shaky tone. She took a deep breath. "He's demanded one-third of my commissions, too."

Chris kept silent.

"Well, Wren, that seems fair enough to me. After all, he's got a stake in the project—it bein' his fabric and all." The sheriff flicked aside the black gumdrop and popped a half dozen other gumdrops into his mouth.

"I have to pay him for everything I use at the outset."

While the sheriff choked on the gumdrops, Chris took a menacing step toward Hepplewhite. "It's plain to see the woman owes you nothing. Sheriff, you're the law around here. What do you estimate this *gentleman* owes the lady?"

"Plenty. Cabin next to Wren's belonged to Pickersly. He kicked the bucket last week. Buckboard's a sorry sight, but it'll make one last trip. Go hitch it up, and I'll make sure Wren gets what she needs to start a new life. Wren, run along home and pack your belongings."

"She needs spectacles first." Chris scanned the mercantile.

"Ain't got none." Hepplewhite glowered.

Chris threaded her hand into the crook of his arm. "I'll escort you home. We'll get you glasses as soon as possible."

"Thank you," she murmured.

When he stopped at the door to the place she lived in, Chris felt a spurt of gratitude that she couldn't see his grimace. The place was no more than a shack. When she opened the door, he fought the urge to slam the door shut and set a match to the place. The only furniture was a single chair by the window. She slept on a pallet on the floor.

"I won't take long, Mr. Gregor."

There's an understatement. "I'll hitch the wagon and load things up." In the few minutes he used to hitch the wagon, Wren bundled her meager possessions into a blanket. Chris silently placed it in the buckboard and drove up to the front of the mercantile.

"You're robbin' me blind!" Hepplewhite whined at the sheriff as they entered.

The sheriff slammed down the lid of a trunk. He kicked Hepplewhite's leg out of his path and sneered, "Servants get room and board and wages for their work. Clerks earn a salary, and renters don't have to give back anything more than a percentage. To my way of thinking—legal-like, you know—you owe that gal a whole year's wages for two jobs. Thin as she's gotten, you ain't fed her much, neither. Count yourself lucky all I'm doing is taking it out in goods and not takin' it outta your sorry hide."

Chris helped him heft the trunk and load it into the buckboard. "What's in this?"

"Kitchen stuff—silverware, coffeepot, skillet, and such. Spices, towels. . . Oh, I put in some soap and a washboard, too."

It would take three days to get home. "She's going to need a warm blanket or two."

"Reckoned as much. We'll use them around the sewing machine to protect it."

The heavy machine would weigh them down. Chris shook his head. "Hepplewhite's cheated and mistreated her, but sewing machines are costly."

"I own the machine."

No wonder she doesn't have much else to her name. "Then we'll take it."

The sheriff motioned to a pair of young men. They came over, and he ordered them to load up the machine. He grinned at Chris. "The thing weighs a ton."

Chris watched as Wren tucked shears, a pincushion, and sundry other sewing notions into a small box. She'd need fabric or money to start up shop somewhere. He'd rather it be money. "Sheriff, how much do you estimate Hepplewhite still owes?"

"I kept tally of what I packed. Including the trunk, the total's just shy of twelve bucks."

"While I was in Chicago, I heard some of the lasses from a factory talking. Until May, they earned almost seven dollars a week. Since Black Friday and the market's drop, it's been cut to just under three." Chris yanked a strip of brown paper from the wrapping roll and started scribbling. "How long have you worked here, Miss Wren?"

"Since May of last year."

Chris worked out the arithmetic. "Twelve months at seven bucks, and three more at three comes to ninety-three dollars."

"I been feeding her and giving her space!"

"Which is why she cooked for you." Chris stared at Hepplewhite. In a matter of seconds, the man started squirming and blustering. "You took advantage by taking part of her commissions and exacting all sorts of labor. I willna allow her to take what she didna earn, but she's leaving here fairly compensated. Subtracting the twelve dollars' worth of goods already out in the wagon, you need to give the lass eighty-one dollars."

"I don't have that kind of money!"

In the end, Wren had fifty-three dollars in her reticule and a wagonload of fabric, lace, and every sewing folderol ever invented. She went to the back room and returned with her arms heavily laden.

Mr. Hepplewhite erupted from his chair and tried to grab the clothing she carried. "Oh no! You can't take those! I'm selling them!"

Chris tensed, ready to spring into action, but Wren surprised him. She held tight to the clothes. "You wouldn't allow me to take deposits at all, and none of these garments was paid for. They're rightfully mine. I'll need samples of my work when I begin anew elsewhere."

"Git outta here and don't come in for one more thing!"

"I'll be back in just a sneeze. I still have several garments back there."

Chris smoothly unburdened her and shoved them into the sheriff's arms. "I'll help you go get the other clothes, Miss Wren."

"Thank you, Mr. Gregor." She gave him a nervous smile and sidled closer.

Wren carefully selected a shirt before stepping back to allow the men to tie the clothing beneath one of her quilts in the buckboard.

Since she was out of earshot, Chris murmured, "The poor thing's scared of her own shadow!"

"She's got a nervous constitution. Sorta shy, too, but she's helped out here and there when one of the ladies had a young'un or someone took sick."

"Why didn't anyone help her out? It's plain to see he's mistreated her."

"Hepplewhite's richer than just 'bout anyone else in the county. Most everyone's had a bad time, what with the depression and drought. They all owe him big money on their accounts. Wren never complained. I tried to get her to talk a few times, but she'd just go real quiet."

"Was he just boasting, or do you think he's. . .hurt her?"

"Not a chance. Get a few beers in Hepplewhite and he lies about everything."

The lady tied on a sunbonnet and handed the sheriff a shirt she'd kept aside. "Thank you."

"Farewell, Wren."

Chris wrapped his hand about her waist and lifted her onto the seat. He climbed aboard and flicked the reins. As soon as they'd drawn away from the town, Wren broke their silence. "I'll be happy to purchase a horse if you give me some advice. Soon as I do, you'll be free of your obligation."

"Where would you go?"

She shrugged. "Wherever I find a town. There's one a day or so south of here."

"Dogtail? You don't dare go there. It's worse than Sodom and Gomorrah. Don't you have any relatives at all?"

"I have no one upon whom I can depend." She inched a bit farther away. "Mr. Gregor, we've not even been properly introduced, but I must tell you I'm not a. . ." She blushed vividly. "That is to say, Mr. Hepplewhite made inferences, and I want you to know I won't. . . If you think I'll—"

He squinted at the horizon and added matter-of-factly, "We're traveling companions—nothing more—so you can stop fretting and fussing."

For all of her acute chagrin, she still manufactured a grateful flash of a smile, but she sat as far away from him as she could and wouldn't look him directly in the eye. Chris didn't mind the silence, but her tension grew palpable with each passing minute. "What you said was right, Miss Wren. We weren't properly introduced. I'm Chris Gregor. I had some business in Chicago and am on my way home. How about you?"

"Forgive my curiosity, but will there be a wife, children, a few dogs, and a crop waiting?"

He chuckled softly. "No, ma'am. My work involves a fair bit of traveling. I built a house in town, and my brothers live across the street from one another. I thought to take you to Rob and his wife. He's a doctor."

"Oh, I couldn't possibly impose on them!"

"Mercy'd be tickled pink to have you there. She's got a wee little daughter and another on the way. Now suppose you tell me about yourself, starting with your full name."

"I'm truly not of any interest, Mr. Gregor. My name is Kathryn Regent. I'm a very drab spinster."

He thought it interesting she chose the adjective *drab*, since that was the very one he'd mentally assigned to her. Nevertheless, it would be terribly rude to confirm her assertion. Instead, he moved his boot half an inch as he wondered aloud, "How'd you ever get stuck getting called Wren?"

"It's from my school days. I've always been plain as can be with unremarkable brown hair. I'm not very big, either. Given the last syllable of my given name and likeness, the name was inevitable."

He cocked his head to the side. "Wrens might be wee little birds, but they sing a grand song. Do you?"

Wrapping her arms about her ribs, she curled forward a bit and shrugged. Her bonnet shaded her face entirely, so he couldn't read her expression. In a dull tone, she whispered, "I haven't had call to sing in a long while."

He fought the wild urge to pull her close and soothe her. He simply reached over and hitched her shawl up a bit toward her nape. "Dinna worry anymore, little Songbird. I'm taking you to a bonny new nest."

A short while later, Kathryn stretched a little and looked down at her brooch. The tin heart nestled a small timepiece in its center. She squinted and sighed. "Excuse me, Mr. Gregor, but I can't quite manage to tell the time. Do you have an estimate?"

He glanced down at the shadows. "Close to half past three."

"I don't mean to tell you your business, but shouldn't we be going due south?"

"Not a chance."

A frisson of fear danced up her spine. After steadying herself with a deep breath, Kathryn pulled her shawl more closely about herself.

"You getting cold, Miss Regent?"

"No."

"You're shivering."

She heaved a sigh. "Frankly, Mr. Gregor, I'm concerned. I'm not particularly good at remembering directions, but the nearest towns were almost due south of us as we set out."

"Aye, that they were."

Her hand fisted in her lap. "Without my glasses, I can't see well at all, but the shadows make me think we're traveling southeast."

"Aye."

His casual tone alarmed her even more. "What must you be thinking? We could have sought the relative safety of a town and spent the night under proper circumstances."

"I told you Dogtail was like Sodom and Gomorrah, all rolled into one." His tone made it clear he considered his outrageous plan to be perfectly reasonable. " 'Twas the first town, and I'd be a fool to take you there. You'll have to take my word that neither safety nor proper circumstances are to be found there."

Shawl edges fisted in her hands and pressed to her breastbone. She croaked, "Do you mean to tell me you planned for us to remain unchaperoned for the night?"

Chapter 3

Th
"hat's about the size of it."

"Oh, dear Gussy!"

"There's nothing sweeter than bedrolling under the night sky, Miss Regent. It feels like angels are peeping at you from behind each and every star."

"Sweet Almighty, might You please arrange for one of them to be my guardian angel?" Wren hadn't realized she'd spoken her prayer aloud until she heard Mr. Gregor's chuckle. Scorching heat rushed from her bodice clear up to her sunbonnet.

"Dinna be mortified, lass," he said once his laughter died down. "I canna blame you for being a shade man-shy. Here's what we'll do: I'll keep to one side of the campfire, and you can have the other. Does that ease your mind a bit?"

"No." She turned toward him. "You know I have that money. Since we'd stop at my request, I'll gladly pay for two hotel rooms."

"We're nowhere near a hotel, and we'll be even farther from one by the time we stop tonight. You'll have to put up with things as they are."

Her heart thundered, and she could taste the salt of her own blood from having bitten the inside of her cheek.

"I appreciate a fine tune now and then, Miss Regent. Why don't you promise me you'll sing a bit as soon as I manage to bring down our supper?"

The way he switched subjects took her off guard. "Are you

suggesting I sing for my supper, sir?"

His voice lilted with humor. "Could be."

"I'll sing whatever you request as soon as we reach the hotel."

He made an exasperated sound. "Nagging willna change what canna be changed."

"Had I known you intended not to have proper evening arrangements, I'd never have come with you."

"You can trust me."

Kathryn shook her head. "I have yet to meet a trustworthy man."

His head swiveled toward her. He dipped close so she could see his piercing gray-blue eyes. "You have now."

She gasped and held that breath for so long, her lungs started to burn. *Should I apologize? No, I'm not. I won't. Thanks to him, I lost my job. Now he's compromising my reputation. Why should I think he's—*

"I'm not perfect." His Scottish burr sounded far more pronounced. "Nae, I'm no'. But ne'er once hae I harmed a woman. And ere ye ask, I'll confess I've tangled wi' a few men—and then, only because they'd broken the law or hurt someone."

I knew it. He's a bounty hunter.

"I'm accountable to the Lord for all I do. Rest assured, I'll not hae to stand afore the Almighty on Reckoning Day and say I e'er took advantage of a lass. You're perfectly safe wi' me." He nodded for emphasis. "Aye, you are. And I'll e'en give ye my Bowie knife to clutch during the night. 'Tis wicked sharp."

His offer didn't amount to enough to allay her fears, but she'd have a means to fend him off if necessary.

"I'd give it to you now, but I might hae need of it to see to supper."

Kathryn still didn't trust him. He could talk until the Second Coming, but they were just words.

Mr. Gregor heaved a prolonged sigh. She knew it was for her benefit. He leaned closer, and she fought the nearly overwhelming urge to slap him and scream. Just as quickly, he straightened back up. He'd removed his knife from his belt sheath and placed it in her lap. "Here. I've used it on occasion to shave and near cut my throat. I hold a healthy respect for that blade. Now will you calm down a mite?"

Curling her fingers around the bone shaft sent waves of relief through her. Nonetheless, Kathryn didn't want to discuss her fears. She thought it over and promised herself not to repeat the mistakes she'd made in town. By being meek, she'd given men an opportunity to push her into a bad situation. With no alternative, she'd made the best of it. *No more. I'm not going to do that again. I've learned my lesson.*

Kathryn chose to redirect the conversation herself. "Mr. Gregor, I'd best tell you I'm not a woman to touch a snake. Should you kill one, you'll need to prepare and eat it on your own."

His brows went skyward. "You plan to cook our supper?"

"I presumed that to be the plan. If you hunt it, I think it only just that I prepare the meal."

"Do you even know how to cook over an open fire?"

"As long as it's not raining, I can give a fair accounting of myself."

Chris smacked his thigh. "Grand! A lass from the city who can do more than scorch coffee and burn meat over a fire."

Just how many women has he had cook for him under the stars? She worried afresh for her safety.

The buckboard jounced along the rutted road, and even at their slow pace, the horses kicked up a fair amount of dust and grit. Chris produced a canteen and offered it to her. She took a dainty sip before handing it back. "Thank you."

"Drink as much as you'd like, Miss Regent. I packed two kegs of water, and we've a jug of apple cider, too."

She took another drink, then reached for the reins so he could have his share.

"I've got it." He tilted his head and drank deeply. After capping the canteen, he set it aside. "You didna eat this noon."

"It doesn't matter." The way he stared at her made her want to writhe.

"You're starting to wilt in the sun, Songbird. A short rest in the shade and a bite to eat'll perk you right up. When folks travel, they have to be careful, and they have to be up front about things. You're starting to feel poorly, and I was hoping you'd tell me yourself instead of me having to bring it up."

"I may not be at my best, but I'm scarcely ill."

"You're splitting hairs. I'll not scold you for this, but I'll get riled if you pull such a stunt again." He halted the wagon, leapt off, and reached up to help her down.

As his hands cupped around her middle, Kathryn tried to hide her surprise. For the past year, she'd not left town. The simple contact of a man spanning her waist hit her with stunning force. His fingers moved to give him a better grip, then clamped more tightly. She lightly rested her hands on his shoulders to help balance herself. Mr. Gregor gently lifted, pivoted sideways, and lowered her. For a brief second, they were eye to eye. She saw kindness in his eyes, then a flash of anger. She found herself suffering the embarrassing position of being held several inches above the dirt.

"You're nothing more than skin and bones!"

"Sir, you forget yourself! You've no call to be so appallingly personal."

Instead of setting her down as she fully expected him to, Chris Gregor swung her up and took better hold of her by sliding an arm beneath her knees. "You're not walking until I get you fed. If I put you down, you'd fall flat on your face!"

"You're exaggera—"

"I told you I dinna split hairs. If you believe you've got room to talk me out of my observation, you'd best think again." He set her down in the shade of a shrubby-looking hackberry. "Best for you to have something straight off. We'll cook at suppertime. For now, jerked beef and some apples might do, along with some bread. Stay put."

Kathryn watched him stalk off to the buckboard. He knew what he was doing, because he quickly located the desired food and brought it back. Everything about Chris Gregor struck her as self-assured and capable. He got a little too domineering with her, so she'd have to stand her ground. To his credit, he'd gotten her away from Mr. Hepplewhite, but would he settle her anyplace better? Only time would reveal an answer to her thorny questions.

After she ate enough to satisfy him, they were under way again. Mr. Gregor leaned toward her and asked in a conversational tone, "Just how well can you see without your spectacles?"

"I'm blind as a badger."

He chuckled. "That was alliterative but not informative in the least. Suppose you wax a bit less poetic and a heap more practical. What distance do you see well, and when do you lose your focus?"

She held out her arm three-quarters of the way. "I can see well this far. The horse is hazy, and I can only see a blur of brown and green beyond him."

"And you offered to take the reins?"

She heard the disbelief in his voice. "I supposed I couldn't do much damage for a few seconds."

"Until we rustle up some spectacles for you, dinna e'en think to be holding the reins or touching a rifle!"

Pressing a hand to her bosom, Kathryn gave him a shocked look. "Mr. Gregor, I would never even think to touch one! Papa was quite firm about ladies staying clear of men's weapons. Mama told me men didn't pick up crochet hooks or knitting needles, so women shouldn't pick up men's firearms."

He snorted.

"And just what is unreasonable about that?"

"Only those well prepared weather life's roughest storms. As soon as we get you settled in, you're going to learn to shoot a rifle. As a single woman, you have to be able to defend yourself."

"I hadn't given that much consideration." She sat quietly, and after a lengthy pause, she half whispered, "Mr. Gregor, I thought you said you were taking me someplace safe. Why would I need any protection?"

"Consider it an ounce of prevention, Miss Regent." His hand smoothed over her fists. "You were neither safe nor happy back there. This change is for the better."

She nodded mutely. *Lord, please let that be true.*

"You'll fall in love with my sisters-in-law. Carmen's forever busy with some project to help one of the locals—making a dress for some widower's daughter, going with the parson on his sick calls, and such. She's got quite a garden, too. She and Duncan live across the street. Duncan's a cobbler.

"Rob's a doctor. He's the youngest—smartest, too. Mercy's his wife. Wee Elspeth is a year old now, and Mercy'll be having another bairn in the next month or so. She's just as busy as Carmen—wi' the bairns and because she's taken to assisting Rob whene'er he needs help."

"They sound like wonderful helpmeets."

"Aye, you've the right of it, there." A second later, he shoved the reins into her hands and grabbed his rifle. Kathryn couldn't help but let out a sharp scream as he fired it. Afterward, she gave him an apologetic look.

"Dinna go lookin' so sheepish, lass. I surprised you is all. Looks like we got us some supper, though." He grinned at her a few minutes later as he carried a jackrabbit back to the wagon. "I hope you remember a fast tune or two."

She flashed back a self-conscious grin. "I know all fifteen verses of 'I Come, O Savior, to Thy Table.' Will that suffice?"

"All fifteen? By the time you finish singing, I'll have this old jack skinned, spitted, roasted, and eaten."

"I take it you don't care for that hymn."

"Maybe Mr. Perronet's 'All Hail the Power of Jesus' Name' or Wesley's 'Love Divine' if you're of the hymn-singing persuasion. They're a bit more upbeat."

"I believe I could manage that." *So he's a churchgoing man. He's told me about his family but nothing about himself.*

"You're pondering something. Mind sharing what it is?"

Figuring he'd opened the door wide for questions, Kathryn decided to take advantage. "You told me of your family but nothing about yourself."

"I'm a Scot. Was a miner back home. Since I've been here, I've done a wee bit of everything—farming, mining, construction." He shrugged.

He's being evasive. "What do you do now?"

"I work for the grand state of Texas, going around and solving problems."

"Oh." When he didn't say anything further, Wren fell silent. *He expects me to trust him when he's keeping a secret. It serves me right, though. I'm keeping a secret of my own.*

Chapter 4

Chris stopped just before sunset. "Wind'll kick up tonight, so we'll bedroll here."

They were so far away from everything, from everyone. Wren shuddered.

"Here, Miss Regent. Sit on this rock whilst I fetch your shawl. The shadow of the boulders might seem a wee bit sinister, but you'll soon note it serves as a windbreak and will bounce heat from the fire back at us. Aye, and better still, there's a wee little spring on the other side of the rocks."

"Then why don't we set up camp over there?"

He slid her shawl around her shoulders with enough solicitude to be mannerly but not so much as to hover or seem fawning. "Wind's blowing in the wrong direction. You'd be too cold."

"If it would make things easier, I could wear my other dress over this one."

"Nae, lass. 'Tisna worth fussing o'er. I'll go water Nero."

The thought of him being close frightened her, but the thought of him leaving her scared her witless. "Do you think coyotes might come around?"

"It's always a possibility. The campfire will keep all but the most brazen creatures at bay. My gun will scare those off." He rested his hands on his hips. "I'll give you the Bowie knife again for the night, but I'm needing it now so I can go dress the rabbit."

After supper Chris shoved another stick into the fire. "I dinna think I've ever tasted better rabbit, Miss Regent. You did a fine job cookin'."

"It didn't take more than a few quick turns over the fire."

"Must've been the way you basted the rabbit with your songs. You surely can sing. It was a pure pleasure sitting and listening to you."

"Thank you, Mr. Gregor."

"You look bone weary, lass. Sleep. I'll have one last cup of coffee and hit my bedroll, too."

Kathryn nodded and sidled over to her bedroll. While he'd been busy dressing the rabbit, she'd laid out their bedrolls—one on either side of the fire. Now she sat down and tentatively lifted her arms, removed all of the hairpins, and let her hair uncoil. She dragged the brush through the heavy tresses, then swiftly wove them into a single, fat braid to keep her hair from tangling during the night. That done, she opened her quilt, laid down, and flipped half of it back over herself. She didn't know if she could ever fall asleep. *At least I have his Bowie knife.*

∞

It took Kathryn a long while to coast off. Chris angled his stance so he could see her. Working in the mines taught him a man had to prepare for the unexpected. That being the case, he made a habit of carrying a knife up his left sleeve. Duncan had created a clever sheath that lay hidden there. Wren remained blissfully ignorant about it, so she'd finally fallen asleep. Even in her sleep, she clutched his knife. *Puir wee lass.*

He looked closer and scowled. Shivers wracked her frame. He got a second blanket from the buckboard and carefully sneaked over to her.

The softest, sweetest smile he'd ever seen tilted her lips when the extra weight descended. Chris fought the urge to hunker down and run the backs of his fingers down her cheek. He wanted to touch her hair, too. When she'd taken it down, he'd almost choked on his coffee. All twisted up in that stingy schoolmarm bun, it wasn't worth a second look; but hanging loose and free, it took a man's breath away. Abundant tresses flowed in luscious waves clear down to her hips, and the firelight brought out golden highlights. She had no notion how stunning her hair was. If she did, she'd have worn it in a softer, more inviting style—one that tempted a man to steal a quick touch but still prim enough that he'd have to concoct an excuse like a piece of fuzz or a speck of dust. She'd smile her thanks, and he'd melt.

Then Chris reconsidered. Maybe Wren knew how beautiful her hair was and hid it away, just as she dressed in a homely mud-brown dress to downplay her appeal. With a man like Hepplewhite bothering her, she might have hoped looking drab would discourage any attention.

In his line of work, he'd seen all sorts of people assume disguises. It took a lot to throw him off, but she'd succeeded. Beyond her ugly dress and hairstyle, beneath the dark circles under her eyes and timid ways, Kathryn Regent possessed a natural beauty. Without the thick spectacles, her eyes were an incredible color—one that drew a man closer and enticed him to examine their depths. Yes, the little wren was far more than her plumage promised.

As he did when on the trail, Chris dozed very lightly. Whenever he lifted his head to check on her, she was in the very same place. The poor thing was so exhausted, she didn't have the strength to toss and turn. He'd tell Mercy and Carmen to make sure to feed her well and make her take naps.

Moving quietly, Chris broke camp as the sun rose. Letting Miss

Regent have an extra bit of sleep wouldn't hurt anything. Hazy beams peeped over the rock, filtered down, and kissed her awake. The wisps of her hair that broke free during the night coiled in a nimbus, and the golden light turned them into a buttery halo. Sleepy eyed, she looked up at him, then scrambled to her feet.

"Good morning, Miss Regent. We've a long day's travel ahead of us."

"Good morning." A fetching blush filled her cheeks as she bent, shook out her blankets, and folded them.

Her bashful nature gave her a certain maidenly appeal. *What am I thinking? I dinna care how sweet and innocent the lass is, I'm not about to be tied down.*

"I'll refill the canteens."

"I've already seen to that and watered Nero. Here. Eat up." He pushed a wedge of cheese and a chunk of bread into her hands.

"Thank you, but I'm not hungry."

"You'll eat, regardless." He glowered at her.

Wren gave him a disgruntled look. "You're going to hound me until I eat this, aren't you? Of course you are. Why did I bother to ask?"

"The better question is—why don't you take better care of yourself?"

"I can't very well talk and eat at the same time." She took a bite.

Chris threw back his head and chortled. "I never imagined beneath your prim and proper ways you had a feisty streak."

After swallowing, she started to lift the cheese to her mouth. "In Scotland, don't they quote the maxim of not judging a book by its cover?" Straight, white teeth sank into the cheese.

If a little witty repartee would make her eat, Chris was more than willing. He crooked a brow. Just in case she couldn't see him well enough, he teased, "Whoever made up that saying never saw those dime novels. The cover is just as absurd as the contents."

"Mmm." The corners of her mouth tilted upward. "You have to have read some of them to be able to speak with such authority."

"If this were a court of law, I'd have to plead guilty to the charge." He folded his arms across his chest. "And you, Miss Regent? Have you indulged in frittering away time reading them?"

"No." She ate another bite.

Something about her tone made him suspect she hadn't told the truth. "Now how did you manage to step outside the courtroom?"

"You were in that pretend courtroom. I wasn't."

"Feeling sassy, are you? Well, well." He smirked. "I've attended some trials. If people don't want to appear but they're forced to be witnesses, they're called hostile witnesses. I'm now dragging you into my courtroom, Miss Regent."

"That's not very gentlemanly of you."

"Do you swear to tell the truth, the whole—"

"I beg your pardon!" She didn't look in the least bit upset. Instead, her eyes sparkled and her smile grew. "I'm a lady. Ladies do not swear."

He refrained from mentioning that ladies didn't speak with their mouths full of breakfast. After all, the whole notion of him standing here, goading her, was so he'd be sure she ate—and she was. "Then promise you'll be honest."

"Sir, you wound me, implying I might be dishonest. If you wouldn't believe me in times past, how could you possibly give weight to my words now?"

"If you ever give up on being a seamstress, you might think about becoming an attorney."

"Never. I wouldn't want to have to deal with the unsavory types.

But I will confess, I've read some of the dime novels. They span from insipid to inspired."

"We—" He went silent as the sound of hooves in the distance reached him.

"Yes?" She looked at him expectantly.

"Someone's coming." Chris strode over, grabbed her by the arm, and tucked her into a small cleft in the boulder. "Stay there and dinna make a sound." He turned away and grimaced. Even if Wren obeyed his edict, the riders might still spot the buckboard. Dogtail was by far the nearest town, and from the direction the riders were coming, Chris feared that was their destination. *Lord, let me be wrong. Let these be good people, or at least let them pass by on the other side of the boulders. I brought the lass out here, and I'm responsible for her.* Just in case, he reached for his weapon.

Three men stopped on the other side of the boulders. Chris silently thanked the Lord for the wind—it had caused him to camp on this side of the rocks, had obliterated any footprints he might have left, and had long since blown away any lingering scent of food or fire.

"Let's see what we got," one of the men said.

Three of them. I have the element of surprise. But I've got the woman. If something happens, she'll be at their mercy.

"Money's easy to divvy up. The rest—well, I reckon whatever each of us took, we ought to keep."

"Listen up, kid. You get what the boss decides. Get it?"

"Sure." After a short pause, the young voice added, "I've never had a timepiece."

"You fancy this one?" another voice asked.

"Unh-huh. Wow. Thanks."

A gunshot echoed off the rocks. Wren's scream mingled with it.

Wren clapped a hand over her mouth, but she knew it was too late. She'd given away their presence. One of the men on the other side of the rocks just killed his partner in cold blood. From the voices, she thought there were three of them, but she couldn't be sure. She couldn't tell where Mr. Gregor was either.

She huddled behind the bush and prayed she'd go undetected. Just to back up her plan, she carefully slipped her fingers into the pocket of her dress and withdrew the tiny pocket derringer.

For a split second, she clutched it to her bosom. Wren couldn't help but wonder if she'd loaded it correctly. After all, she'd read the instructions countless times by the flickering light of her barely lit lantern. She'd gotten the tiny weapon from Mama after Papa died. Mama told her it was a ladies' gun, so he wouldn't have objected.

Now, though, she'd have to use it. How could she shoot another human being? How could she even manage to aim the weapon? Without her spectacles, she was virtually blind.

Curses filled the air. They came closer, too. Kathryn ducked down and pressed as far back into the cleft as she could. Gunshots fired from above her. Others came from several yards in front of her. At the same time a body tumbled from the rocks and landed mere feet from her, another man shot from around the side of the rocks. From the pause in gunfire, Wren assumed Chris was reloading his weapon. He'd stepped in to defend her. She could do no less. Her hands shook so badly, she couldn't hold the derringer. Wren threw herself down on her stomach and rested both elbows on the hard ground to steady her hand.

The man sidled around the rocks and stood close enough that she saw a star shape branded into the leather on the side of his boot. Kathryn looked upward, saw badly worn trousers, a dirty plaid shirt, and a face that was too far away to focus upon distinctly. The sound of his pistol cocking made her blood run cold, and she shuddered. The action discharged her weapon.

"Whelan!" Chris fired as he shouted.

The man shot back, but just as he did, he jerked to the side and began to fall. His loud, raw words made it clear he wasn't near death. He tumbled to the side and pulled the trigger, but the empty sound tattled he'd used all his ammunition.

"His gun's empty!" Wren cried out.

Chris shouted, "Wren, get back!"

"Wren?" Whelan scrambled away. Mere seconds later, a horse galloped off.

Chris charged toward her. He halted briefly to confirm the other man was dead, then reached Kathryn's side. He grabbed her by the arms. "Are you hurt?"

Tears slid down her cheeks.

He shook her gently. "Lass, are you all right?"

Eyes swimming with tears, she looked at him and lifted her right hand. She rotated it a bit, and he sucked in a sharp breath. Her hand started to shake, so he peeled the tiny vest-pocket derringer from her fingers and tucked it into his belt.

"So that's why he flinched and missed me."

"Dead."

"Nae, lass. You dinna kill him." He stayed close. "There's blood on the ground. I probably got him. I know you did, too. I canna say for certain 'twill keep him occupied. Whelan might double back on us. I'm getting you out of here."

Wren shook her head. Her voice quavered but still held conviction. "He won't come back."

"You canna be sure."

"His gun was empty." *Gregor's a bounty hunter.* Her shaking grew worse. "I shot him."

"Aye."

Her knees gave out on her. *I shot my brother.*

Chapter 5

Wren huddled under her shawl next to Chris on the seat of the buckboard. Two horses plodded along, tied to the back of the wagon where Wren couldn't see them. A dead body was draped over each saddle. Chris scanned the landscape. The road with virtually no good ambush points led to the nearest town: Dogtail.

Once again, Chris assessed the situation. If Miss Regent weren't so rattled, he'd gladly leave all her possessions behind. As for the thieves—dead was dead. Taking care of the living rated as the priority here. He longed to dump off one of the bodies, put her on the horse, and ride like the wind. He couldn't. The poor lass would fall right out of the saddle.

"Whelan." The name came out in a low, angry rasp. He'd been tracking the man ever since Connant was slain. If he didn't have Wren along, he'd have followed the outlaw and apprehended him. As it was, all he had were two bags of loot and a pair of dead bodies.

And a witness. Wren would be able to testify that the men had brought the loot. But could she identify Whelan? "Wren, you saw Whelan."

She shuddered. "I couldn't see his face."

"Tell me what you saw."

"The man fell." Her voice quavered. "He was dead."

"Aye." He frowned at her pallor, then patted her. "But we're alive. 'Twas either them or us. They started the shooting." His words should have given her comfort, but it would probably take some time for a delicate lady to get over the shock of seeing a dead body fall within a few feet of her.

Whelan got away, but Wren would be a neutral witness who could at least connect him to the stolen goods. Pitiful as that charge was, if he'd killed anyone to gain those possessions, the connection would prove vital in court. "The one who got away—Whelan. What else did you see?"

"I didn't have my glasses."

"I'll help you get some spectacles right away. Aye, I will. You willna feel so lost and helpless then. In the meantime, I'll help you. I need your help, too. Was there anything else you did make out?"

"Just blue jeans. And boots."

His breath caught. "Was there anything special about his boots? Plain, or any designs?"

"Plain. Only one star," she said in a vague tone.

"A star? You're positive of that, Wren?" The star on Whelan's boot was a trademark piece of evidence. Lawmen knew about it, but they didn't let common folk know. It was the sort of thing, if blabbed about, would make Whelan shed his boots. "What did it look like? How big?"

Her hand shook as she lifted it. Holding her thumb and forefinger apart about two inches, she said thickly, "This big."

Whelan's boot. Clear as could be. "Tell me anything else you saw and heard."

"I shot him." She doubled over, as if in agony, and shook her head.

He took off his bandanna, folded it, and poured water from the canteen on it. "You feeling sick?"

She moaned.

"You'll be feelin' better soon. Sure you will," he soothed as he brushed several darling little curls from her nape, then pressed the cool cloth to her soft flesh. "The day's turning hotter than the hinges of Hades. This'll help. Just keep your head down for a few minutes and breathe slow and deep. Slow and deep. There you go. Take your time. When you're ready, you can tell me more of what happened."

After taking a few shaky breaths, she said, "I don't want to talk about it. When we get to a town, I'll speak with the marshal."

"Whelan and his gang killed a dear friend of mine. I'm longing to get him."

She nodded slowly and tried to straighten up.

He continued to apply pressure to keep her head down. Judging from her extreme pallor, he was sure she'd faint dead away if he let her up too soon. "So you know it's Whelan."

"You called his name, Mr. Gregor." She turned her face toward him and opened her eyes. They'd darkened to pools of blue anguish. The bandanna slithered away, and he glided his hand down to her shoulder and drew her upright. She started to tremble again, so he nudged her into resting her cheek on his chest.

"Worse, I called your name," he confessed grimly. "Wren is, unfortunately, a unique name. He's shrewd. Once he overhears someone mention you, he'll be able to track you down. I've put you in terrible danger."

"No one will talk about me. I'm utterly forgettable."

Chris snorted at that proclamation. Less than twenty-four hours after meeting her, he'd come to realize little Wren wasn't at all what she masqueraded as. Just scratching the surface showed her to be intelligent, well-spoken, and resourceful. A good cook and a fine seamstress. Pretty, too. Some man was going to get a prize when he wed her. *If I can capture Whelan before he finds her.*

"From now on you're Katie, not Wren. Not even Kathryn. Are you understanding me?"

She nodded slowly.

"Aye, and I'll be sure you learn how to fire a rifle." His brows knit with a sudden realization. "You lied to me!"

Looking indignant, she huffed back, "I did not!"

"You said you didn't handle firearms."

Blinking at him, she tilted her head. "Mr. Gregor, I told you I didn't touch *men's* weapons. We were discussing rifles, and I assure you, I haven't touched a rifle. I've not lifted any other pistol, either. Mama specifically purchased the derringer as it was listed as a ladies' firearm."

"I imagine a derringer, however small, can still kill a man. Why draw distinctions? If it shoots bullets, it's deadly."

Katie blanched. Her eyes went wide with shock, and her lips began to quiver. "Mr. Gregor, do you think my bullet might *kill* Whelan?"

"Only if we pray real hard."

Her face twisted with revulsion. "I couldn't ever think to pray for the death of any soul!"

"I figured as much. Tell me, though—just what were you aiming at when you fired the gun at Whelan?"

She blanched.

No one in her right mind aimed a gun, fired it, and hoped the bullet wouldn't do any damage. She was plumb crazy. *No, not plumb crazy,* the voice in the back of his mind corrected, *just very tenderhearted.* He steeled himself with a gusty breath and asked in a voice he considered to be remarkably conversational and restrained, "Miss Regent, gunshots can be—and often are—fatal. What possessed you to draw a weapon if you didn't plan to inflict damage?"

"Please, don't shout at me!"

"I'm not shouting!" He caught himself raising his voice enough to make the horse skittish. Embarrassed, he stated, "I'm merely being forceful. You cannot have the derringer back unless I'm absolutely certain you understand it has the capacity to take a life."

"Oh, I'd never take deadly aim! It would be sinful! I simply. . ." She tore her gaze from his angry glower and looked at her hands as she twisted them in her lap.

"What was your intention?"

She whispered faintly, "I didn't want him to hurt you. But don't think I was brave. I was shaking so badly, the gun went off before I even aimed."

"Courage isna the lack of fear. 'Tis acting in spite of the fear. You should be proud of yourself."

She shook her head. "I'm ashamed of myself. All we've done is talk about me, and I never once inquired as to whether you were injured."

She kept taking him off guard. She shifted like a prairie wind from one direction to the next without so much as a warning. For every irritating grain of sand the changes brought, there was also the sweet scent of wildflowers or a welcome gust of refreshing coolness. It made it impossible to be mad at her.

"I'm fine. I've got the Lord to thank—and you, too. I'll not forget 'twas you who shot him."

She rewarded his words of praise by scrambling down the side of the moving buckboard and getting violently ill.

⌒

She felt hideous. Mortified, too. Mr. Gregor actually held her head as she lost her meal. It served him right. After all, he'd forced her to eat breakfast. But she couldn't bring herself to be mad at a man who'd been gentle with her. Patient, too. Never once did he say a harsh word about the spineless way she handled all of the feelings roiling inside.

"Miss Regent? Katie? We canna afford to stop and let you rest. I dinna know how bad off Whelan is, but he's meaner than a stepped-on snake, and I want us as far from here as we can get. Are you understanding me?"

She nodded.

"There's a good lass." He lifted her into his arms, and she slumped against him like a rag doll. Katie tried to at least lift her head away from his shoulder, but he used his chin to nudge it back down. "Hold still. You've been through too much. 'Tis a wonder you've not swooned yet."

She missed his warmth and strength when he put her back up on the conveyance. He went to the rear of the wagon and plowed through some of the things. She was too weary to even keep her eyes open long enough to discover what he wanted.

"Take a few small sips, lass. Go slow." He held the speckled, granite-ware cup and tilted it to her lips, even though she'd tried to hold it herself. As badly as her hands shook, she couldn't very well question his judgment. The cider made her mouth taste far better. She granted him a wobbly smile of thanks.

"You're shivering." His soft tone made it clear he'd merely made an observation, not an accusation. "You've suffered more than your share of shocks these last few days. I want you to lie down, and I willna listen to a single argument. You have to rest, else you'll slow us down."

"I—I just need a minute."

He tucked a few errant tendrils of her hair behind her ear. "I made a place for you in the back."

Wrapped in a cocoon of both his kindness and her quilt, moments later, she closed her eyes.

❧

The next thing Katie knew, she woke to a pat on her arm.

"Miss Regent, I know I told you we'd avoid Dogtail, but 'twas the closest place. We'll be coming to the edge of town in about ten minutes or so. I'm going to take us someplace decent folks don't talk about, let alone go to. Keep quiet and stay wrapped in the quilt. I'm going to pass you off as an ailing lass."

She sat up and gave him a groggy look. "But why did we come here?"

"I'll wire lawmen about Whelan, and we'll drop off the bodies." He extended his hand to help her climb onto the seat beside him.

"A temporary stop seems more than reasonable, Mr. Gregor."

"One other thing—there's someone here who will store your belongings."

The man had the gall to sound as if he considered his plan quite reasonable. She fisted her hands in her lap and gritted, "I'm not leaving my things behind. I need them to start up again in a new town."

"That sewing machine—"

"Was obscenely expensive," she interrupted. At the moment, her future survival rated far above the social convention of not interrupting someone else.

"It weighs a ton. I won't have a hunk of iron and oak slow us down."

"I need that 'hunk of iron and oak' to make a living."

He crooked a calloused finger, tucked it beneath her chin, and tilted her face to his. "You won't be around to make a living if we drag that contraption behind us. The only good it'll serve is as a headstone on your grave."

Whelan won't come after me, but I can't tell him that.

"Whelan holds no regard for life. You heard him—he shot his own partner in cold blood—and for nothing more than a greater share of the loot. Revenge on us for shooting him is a far greater motive." He dipped a little closer. "The sewing machine might be costly, but life is priceless. Dinna waste your breath. I've decided, and you'll not sway me."

"If Dogtail is such a pagan town, isn't it a poor choice for a destination?"

"I have a reliable contact. Fact is, I'm not concerned with your possessions a-tall. 'Tis your safety. No matter what happens, you're to obey my orders."

She caught herself right before making that promise. *Being agreeable about everything only got me into trouble last time. This time I'm going to take charge. There's no reason a rational woman would blindly obey a man she's just met.* "I'll be certain to listen." *But that doesn't mean I'll follow every last order spilling out of this man's mouth.*

"I'll have to ask you to take your hair down, Miss Regent. Put it into two plaits. You can pass for a schoolgirl if you do, especially with you being a wee snip of a woman."

It took little time to take down her already mussed bun. Katie finger combed the tresses, then hastily plaited lumpy-looking braids. She gave him a lopsided smile. "If they're too neat, no one will believe I'm a sleepy child."

His features tightened. Perhaps he wasn't satisfied with her appearance. "Do you suppose I ought to draw the quilt up over my shoulders?"

"Clear up to your neck. Even up higher in the back. Slump against my arm, too. It'll make you look shorter and more pitiful."

More pitiful? So that was what he thought of her. He viewed her as a pathetic spinster.

He shot her a whimsical smile that erased the sting of his thoughtless words. "Too bad you still manage to look so tidy. Kids always seem to get grubby. A streak of dirt or a runny nose would do the trick."

"Dirt?"

"Would you mind?"

"I'm sure it will wash off."

A few minutes later, he chuckled as he leaned back to view his handiwork. Half a teaspoon's worth of dirt and a drop from the canteen were his paints, and he'd mixed them with avid concentration before dabbing his finger against her cheek. With a quick, downward swipe, he smeared it. "There."

A habitually neat individual, Katie fought the urge to reach up and rub it off. He looked too pleased with himself for her to do that. They got under way, and she murmured in a rather embarrassed tone, "Mr. Gregor, you'd best call me by my given name. Children aren't addressed formally."

He nodded curtly. "Lying goes against my grain. We're both believers, so I'll be telling the truth when I say you're my little sister. You leave matters to me."

Katie sat there and thought what a clever man Chris Gregor was. She cataloged his strengths and virtues. He was compassionate, respectful, and a champion of the mistreated. He was moral and good and resourceful. But that resourcefulness and his protective nature troubled her. Those qualities would compel him either to apprehend or to kill her brother.

"Aye, you leave matters to me." Mr. Gregor's voice resounded with confidence. "Your life is bound to change now."

In more ways than you know.

"I'll help you. In fact, our town is in sore need of a seamstress. Old Mr. Rundsdorf is gnarled as mesquite, so his clothes canna come out of a catalog. And he's just the start. You'll be making a whole new life as soon as I get you home. Set your mind on that."

" 'Finally, brethren, whatsoever things are true, whatsoever things are honest, whatsoever things are just, whatsoever things are pure, whatsoever things are lovely, whatsoever things are of good report; if there be any virtue, and if there be any praise, think on these things.' "

"Ahhh, yes," Chris stretched out those two simple words in such a way that she knew he relished them. "Philippians chapter four and verse eight."

Self-conscious, she confessed, "I can't ever seem to recall where verses are in the Bible. I've memorized countless verses, but I jumble up the books and chapters and verses."

"Da and Ma worked on that with me and my brothers. They knew 'twas important to drum things into our impressionable minds during those tender years."

"You were blessed to have good parents." *How would my brother have turned out if his father had been a good man instead?*

"Aye, I was blessed. But hear me well, *Katie*." He stressed what he called her and paused until she looked directly at him. "Regardless of how rough things might become, you're to think on the good that lies ahead. You'll have a safe and happy future. I'll see to it. Aye, I will."

"Thank you, Mr. Gregor."

"Chris," he corrected.

"Thank you, Chris." Burrowed in the blanket, she lapsed into silence. If it weren't for her worries over her stepbrother's gunshot wounds and the guilt that she'd inflicted one of them, life would be incredibly sweet. As it was, things couldn't become more complicated. Even so, Chris Gregor's good-hearted ways impressed her and made her feel safe and secure.

Chris told her Dogtail was Sodom and Gomorrah all rolled into one, and the short drive through town more than confirmed his estimation. She scooted closer to him on the buckboard bench. He even took the liberty of wrapping his arm around her shoulders. Under normal circumstances, she'd never allow a gentleman to behave so boldly, but this was as far from normal as she could imagine. Chris promised to make sure she was fine, and she knew he'd keep his word. . .until he pulled her buckboard to a stop before the last in a string of tawdry-looking buildings.

Katie squinted in an attempt to see where they were. Even without her glasses, the sign was clearly legible. Huge, garish red hearts had been painted before and after the lettering on the place's false front: LUCILLE'S.

Chapter 6

*T*he man's a rascal! He probably chats with Lucifer on the banks of the River Styx each week. Earlier, he said it was as hot as the hinges of Hades. He ought to know.

Katie clutched the quilt around herself more closely and shrank into its folds. Dear merciful heavens, he'd driven up brazen as a bottle-stealing sot and sat there in broad daylight so everyone could see who he was and what kind of business he wished to transact. She closed her eyes and moaned.

"Well, well!" a deep, oily voice schmoozed from beside her. Someone touched the blanket right over her knee. Her eyes shot open. She stared in horror at the bristle-faced, rheumy-eyed man. "New kitten comin' to the cathouse? I'll have to visit and listen to you purr."

Chris drew his Bowie knife. "I'll thank you to leave my sister alone."

"Hey!" The man jerked back his hand.

Another man elbowed the first. "Stop gawkin' at the woman and take a look at who's on them horses!"

"Who cares? They're dead."

Chris leaned forward. "You know who they are?"

"Not one. T'other's Skip Freelon. Wanted dead or alive."

"Well, he's dead, and I don't regret it." Chris turned the knife so the blade glittered in the hot Texas sun. "I'll slice the neck or plug a hole in anyone who tries to hurt my sis."

"She ain't really your sis, is she?"

Chris pulled some of the quilt off of her head to give the folks in the general vicinity a quick peek at her dirty face and tiny shoulders before flipping it back up. "Aye, sister. She's been sick."

"Don't look none too sick to me. Mite pale, but that's all."

"Best you think to step back. She lost her breakfast this mornin'."

The man warily shuffled back.

The other stranger scowled. "How come you got black hair and your sis gots blond?"

"Different mothers. Same Father." Chris thrust his face close to hers. "He gave us both blue eyes. See?"

She tilted her head toward Chris's. At the moment, he seemed the lesser of the evils. He hadn't told a lie, but he sure did manage to twist the truth to suit his needs.

"She's weak, my wee sister. Couldna take another day on the trail. Seein' as I didna see a hotel here in your town, I thought to ask the only place with beds to rent us a room for the night."

She made a sound of distress. He couldn't possibly expect her to set foot in that place—let alone spend a night!

"You don't happen to know any church ladies who'd come watch my sister for me for a short while, do you?"

"Dogtail don't have a church, and shady ladies is all we got. That there kid's looking right puny."

"Betwixt her ailin' and me needing to drop off the vermin who tried to jump us, I was glad to spy your town. I need to get her set."

As soon as the men ambled away, Chris gave Wren a quick squeeze. "Sorry, little one. We have to make do. You're playing along just fine. I'll dash inside for a minute and then come back out after you. If you think to cough every so often, it'd be a good idea."

She dug her fingers into his arm and hissed, "You don't mean to have us go inside there! You're just doing this to confuse Whelan, right?"

He raised his voice, "No, Katie, honey. Father would understand that I'm just trying to take good care of you. We'll stay just till you're feeling a wee bit better." He wrapped the reins around the brake lever and jumped down.

Appalled at his plan, she decided this might be her only opportunity to get away. She reached for the reins.

Chris reached for her. He was faster.

             ∽

"Katie, lass, are you runnin' a fever again? Your cheeks are all red. Come here." He deftly kept the quilt wrapped about her as he hauled her into his arms. She couldn't possibly extricate herself from the bundle. "We'll go inside. You gotta lay down and have somethin' to drink."

"Please, I beg of you," she whispered thickly against his neck, "don't take me in there!"

He patted her and said in a normal tone, "Everything'll work out." When he'd joined the rangers, he'd been given contacts where he'd find help. Though he'd never been here—or any other house of ill repute—Chris knew another ranger had saved this woman back when she'd just opened her establishment. Out of gratitude, she had an open door policy for every Texas Ranger. They were welcome at any time, for any reason. Reportedly, she provided an excellent cover for them, and she'd been good about sending telegrams and passing notes when necessary. All any ranger had to do was ask for Rahab—the biblical prostitute who helped the Israelites.

"Stop your wiggling. Trust me."

"No. Not if you plan to take me into one of those places!"

"Dinna go jumping to conclusions." Chris tightened his hold of her. The sight of her trembling lips cut straight through him. "Appearances can be deceiving."

"You said we were coming here to drop off those men and store my goods."

"And we will."

"Turn loose of me, you scoundrel." She twisted and smacked at him.

"That's some wildcat you got yourself."

Chris clamped still tighter around Katie and turned toward the sound of the entertained voice. A buxom redhead in a garish red-and-black dress lounged against the brothel's door.

Irritated by the fact that he hadn't been able to give chase to Whelan, that he was stuck with a woman who suddenly summoned gumption she should have displayed years ago so he wouldn't have had to rescue her, and that his presence provided entertainment for the residents of Dogtail, Chris wanted to snarl a response. He tamped down the urge and said in the blandest tone he could, "I'm looking for Rahab."

The woman's eyes widened very slightly, and she straightened up. "You've found her." She tilted her head toward her door. "C'mon in."

"If you try to take me in there, you'll be sorry." Katie resorted to pinching him because she couldn't do much else.

He glanced down. "Behave yourself."

"You behave yourself!" She stopped pinching him. For an instant, Chris thought she'd finally realized he didn't have any scandalous plans, but she slapped her hand onto the center of his shirt, scrunched in her fingers, and yanked the hair on his chest. "Listen to me," she ground out.

"No, you listen to me." He pried free and tossed her over his shoulder. "We're doing things my way."

Chris walked into the red brocade parlor of Lucille's and scanned the place. No telling who might be here. Even with Katie over his shoulder, he kept one hand on his pistol. The madam's cloyingly sweet perfume made his nose twitch.

"Rahab" led him into a private parlor, shut the door, and motioned for him to dump Katie into a chair. He shook his head.

An amused look crossed the redhead's face.

Before she opened her mouth and revealed he was a ranger, Chris said, "Miss Rahab, Katie's not been feeling much like herself—"

"You try hanging upside down and feeling decent!" Katie pummeled his back. "And speaking of decent—"

Chris went on speaking as if she hadn't said a thing. "She needs to rest and have something to drink."

"Follow me upstairs. I have a room available."

Katie began to thrash more desperately. "No! Please, no! You can't sell me to her!"

Chris half dumped Katie onto a nearby settee and growled, "How dare you think I'd betray you!"

She struggled to break free of the quilt and stand up. "First, you cost me my job. Then, you compromised my reputation by dragging me out overnight. Then, you killed a man. After that, you brought me to a. . .a. . .house of ill repute." She stammered, but with every accusation, her voice rose. "Now you have the nerve to order me to trust you?"

He stepped closer and towered over her. "I've dealt with thick-headed, stubborn mine mules that would look docile compared to you."

To his utter astonishment, she inched closer, stood on tiptoe, and prodded him in the center of his chest. "Don't you forget that. I'm stubborn, and I'm getting my way. I'm going to make you miserable until you listen to me and get me out of here!"

"It's not going to work." He reached down and brushed her finger away from his chest. "You made me miserable a minute after we first met. It hasn't made me follow any of your ridiculous instructions yet."

She clutched his hand. "I confessed I was stubborn. I'm not going to give up."

"If you're so intent on getting out of here, why are you hanging on to me for dear life?"

"Because I'm my brother's keeper. I can't leave you in a den of iniquity. It's fallen to me to drag you out of here and put you back on the straight and narrow."

She tugged. He twisted his wrist at that same moment. He broke free from her, and she stumbled backward to fall in a heap on the settee.

"You are a perfectly dreadful man. I can hardly wait to get away from you." She turned toward the soiled dove. "Miss Rahab, you are worthy of far more than any of this. The Lord Almighty sent His Son to redeem us all. I'm marching out the door. You're welcome to join me." The crazy woman started smoothing her skirts as if she were preparing for a Sunday stroll. "I'll help you establish a respectable new life."

"Katie," he growled.

"Everyone deserves a second chance," she snapped back. "God's forgiven me, and I have faith He'll do the same for Miss Rahab. Don't you interfere, Christopher Gregor. I want her to have this opportunity. I'm breaking free of this place, and she can, too."

"You couldn't find the door. How do you propose to escape?"

She heaved a huge sigh. "Honestly, Chris. You promised you'd help me get spectacles right away. Instead, you've dragged me across Texas and stuck me in the middle of a gunfight. Miss Rahab, do you see me wearing any spectacles?"

"No."

Katie folded her arms across her chest. "There you have it, Christopher. You have to take me out of here this instant and fulfill your promise. Miss Rahab, you're still welcome to come along."

"You need glasses?" Rahab laughed. "Go no further. I have a box full of them."

"There *you* have it, Katie." Chris relished turning her phrase back at her. "You can get your spectacles while I tend to other matters."

"Is there a doctor in town?"

He frowned and looked at her more carefully. "Why?"

"If you try to leave me here, you're going to need his services. It'll be your fault. You're provoking me."

"If that was supposed to scare me, it failed. I still have your derringer."

"It's past time that you return it. I need to dig through the wagon so I can get what I need to reload it."

"They're called bullets." Chris didn't bother to hide the wry tone in his voice.

"I know they're bullets." She sounded exasperated. "What I need are the instructions on how to load them. Never you mind. Miss Rahab, could you possibly assist me with that task?"

"No, she won't. I'm not giving that firearm back to you."

"Rahab" laughed. "Miss Katie, he'd be a fool to arm you in your present state. On the other hand, Mr. Gregor, a woman has the right to own and carry a firearm. Once she settles down, you should give it back to her."

Katie huffed. "You should listen to her. She's the voice of reason. Miss Rahab, I'm sure you can see how calm I am now. Why, I'm utterly serene. Just look at me." She stuck out her hand, palm up. "I'll take that weapon now, Mr. Gregor."

"It'll get in the way while you try on spectacles. Rahab, Miss Katie's possessions are slowing us down. Whelan's on the loose nearby, and we shot two holes in him. He'll seek revenge. Can you temporarily store the wagon's contents?"

She thought for a moment, then nodded. "Darlene left. We'll put the stuff in her room. Was that a sewing machine under the blankets?"

"Yes." Katie's voice shook.

"I thought so. I have one myself."

"You do?" Chris blurted out the words.

"What's wrong with that?" Katie bristled. "Many women enjoy sewing. Like any other person, Miss Rahab needs clothes." Just after delivering her staunch defense, Katie turned three shades of red and said in a tiny voice, "Isn't that true, miss?"

"She really can't see." "Rahab's" brow puckered. "I'll have her things unloaded while she sorts through the box of glasses and you dispose of those bodies."

"You can't leave me here!"

He thought he'd calmed her down, but the panicky edge to Katie's outraged words triggered his anger. "Much as I'm tempted, I won't."

"You tend to things," "Rahab" said. "I'll have Miss Katie sit in the kitchen and give her the box of glasses."

"Fine." Chris started toward the door. "Don't take long, Katie. I want us out of here as soon as possible."

"You're the one who hauled me in here to begin with."

"She needs a disguise." He looked at Katie, then at "Rahab," and back to Katie. "See what you can do. She's scrawny. Turn her into a boy."

"Whelan isn't going to have to track you down." Katie glowered at him.

"Because you're going to kill me yourself?"

"Of course I wouldn't. I'm a lady. But your charming ways must have earned you dozens of enemies by now."

He smothered a laugh. For as much of a bother as she'd been thus far, at least the woman was finding her backbone. That might make the difference between life and death. Instead, Chris locked eyes with "Rahab." "Do whatever you need to. We'll leave in half an hour."

Chapter 7

Katie sat at the kitchen table, blinked, and tried to read the label on the coffee tin. Though the lettering grew bigger, it also started to blur. "No," she muttered to herself. She pulled off the spectacles and winced as the right arm of the pair caught in a wisp of hair. "Ouch."

"Find a pair yet?" "Rahab" asked from the doorway.

"No." Katie sighed. "But at this rate, you won't have to put me in a disguise. I'll be bald."

The cook plunked a plate down on the table. "Things'll look a lot better once you eat."

"Thank you. I hope so." Katie's stomach lurched as she glanced at the plate. "Things couldn't look any worse."

"Spaghetti today, Lucille," the cook proclaimed proudly.

"Wonderful!"

Katie stared at the plate. It looked like a mess of bloody worms. But it did smell good. Unable to summon the courage to pick up her fork, she opted for another pair of glasses. *I'm an ungrateful coward. That's what I am. What kind of Christian witness am I being? These women need the Lord in their lives. Dogtail doesn't have a church. It's up to me to be a beacon of love and hope.*

"Well?" the cook said.

"I want to say a prayer and ask God to bless the hands that prepared the food."

"It's a waste of time. Dogtail is a godforsaken town," the cook declared. "But it's awful nice of you to wanna ask Him to think of me."

"He doesn't just think of you. He wants you to be His daughter."

The cook shuffled away. "One father was more than enough."

Katie shoved on the spectacles. Everything wavered before her, but through the ripples, she saw "Rahab" shake her head and press a finger to her lips, then tilt her head toward the cook. Without another word, she left.

Katie took off the glasses, bowed her head, and prayed. When she lifted her head, she resolutely picked up the fork. By the time she lifted the fork to her mouth, nothing remained on it. *Proof that God is protecting me.*

The cook laughed. "Wind the fork round and round in the noodles."

By following the instructions, Katie managed to take a bite. "Ohhh, this is delicious!"

"Katie, do any of the garments in your wagon fit you?"

Katie nodded in "Rahab's" direction. "My clothes are in a pink flowered sack."

"Those are all the same brown as what you're wearing. We're going to disguise you by hiding you in plain sight. What about the gorgeous blue riding outfit?"

"I don't know." Katie smiled. "I'll try it. Anything's better than his plan to make me wear britches."

She'd copied the ensemble from a sketch Belinda's grandmama brought from Paris years ago when she'd been a bride. As far as fashions went, it didn't follow the current trends, but the resulting ensemble couldn't be any lovelier. Belinda failed to show up for the past two fittings, and before then, she'd sniped about how her Parisian wedding gown was of far better quality than anything

Katie could possibly sew.

The broadcloth skirt was split, and ecru-colored ruffles spilled from the hem in a blatant show of femininity. A paletot style jacket featured long, bell-shaped sleeves, and Katie had stitched a soft, ecru batiste blouse to wear beneath it.

While eating and trying on another pair of glasses, Katie started to think of the garments she'd brought. *I'm starting anew. I could wear something pretty instead of drab now.* The thought cheered her immensely. Swallowing a bite, she slipped on the last pair of spectacles.

"I can see!" She grabbed the coffee can and read the words painted on it, then hopped out of the chair and skipped over toward the shelves. "Borden's milk. Tabasco sauce. Quaker oats. Campbell's beefsteak tomato in a can. Wheatena. Oh! Dr Pepper! I can read far better now than I could with my own glasses."

"Excellent." "Rahab" entered with the beautiful blue outfit. "Now let's see to your transformation."

ॐ

Chris paced back and forth along the hallway. His boots made a measured sound that wasn't dissimilar to the steady beat of a metronome. He pulled out Da's gold pocket watch and gritted his teeth. He'd given them half an hour. It had been fifty-eight minutes now. Snapping the case closed, he barreled toward the kitchen.

His plan had been to ride hard and get to the next railroad town. If they could hop the train, get off, backtrack, and zigzag, he could tuck her in with his family and be back out after Whelan.

But so far, nothing had gone according to his plans. As a result, he'd put together saddlebags for them. Small bags of jerked beef, dried fruit, and nuts would do. He didn't waste space with beans, rice, or coffee—those would require a cook fire. That would give

Whelan a beacon. Still, Chris carefully wax-dipped the heads of several matches and stored some in each pack, along with a knife wrapped in a towel and a bit of soap. Most important, he supplied them each with two canteens of water. The second outlaw's horse was sound, so Chris loaded an extra blanket and water on him. That way, if one of the horses went lame, they'd not have to slow down.

"We're leaving. Now." He plowed through the kitchen door and stopped short. "What happened to your hair?"

☙

Katie reached up and tugged one of the spiraling tendrils at her temple. "You wanted me to look different."

"You could have stuffed it up under a hat. You didn't have to go changing the color!"

"It's very attractive." "Rahab's" voice took on an edge. "It puts me in mind of cinnamon. You said you wanted to disguise her, and henna was an excellent solution. The reddish tinge is becoming, don't you think?"

He grabbed a hat from the table and shoved it toward Katie. "You look different. That's what's important. Lucille, thanks for all of your help. Katie, let's mount up."

"But I was going to see the marshal."

"I already dropped in on him." Chris took her elbow and hauled her to her feet.

"Thank you so much, Miss. . .Lucille." Katie turned to the cook. "And thank you for that wonderful spaghetti, too. Once I get settled, I'll be sure to send you my address so you can mail me your recipe."

"Lucille, I appreciate all you've done. One of the men I brought in had a bounty on his head. The sheriff will see that you receive it."

He took Katie over to the mare hitched beside his gelding.

Katie turned back toward the cathouse. "We have an extra mount, Lucille. Why don't you come along?"

"I'll stay and guard your sewing machine."

"I'd rather have you with us than own a sewing machine."

His anger at her dawdling evaporated. She prized her sewing machine, depended on it for her living, yet she'd not given a moment's thought about sacrificing it.

"You darling girl." The madam smiled. "Off with you now."

Katie squeezed his arm and said softly, "Maybe she's afraid you don't want her along. Invite her."

"Dinna hound the woman, lass. She can walk away from there anytime she pleases. Just be grateful she was there to help us out today."

Katie cleared her throat. "Mr. Gregor—"

"No more." He scowled so she'd understand he wouldn't put up with any further delays. "We've lost precious travel time already."

"Fine." She glowered back at him. "But I ought to warn you, I've never ridden a horse."

"You'd best learn fast." He locked his hands around Katie's waist and hefted her into the saddle. "Stay close and stay quiet."

Chris wanted to make up time. He'd never planned to waste so much of it trying to stuff Katie into a disguise. Why Lucille chose this one was beyond him. With her hair up in a loose, soft swirl and dressed in that get-up, Katie looked like a princess. The way the waist on the riding outfit nipped in showed off her tiny middle. Even the spectacles looked nice. Instead of the stingy little round lenses she'd worn when he first spied her, this pair looked like jewelry and let him appreciate the fine sight of her blue, blue eyes. *Well, Whelan won't recognize her now.*

She seemed fairly stable in the saddle, but Chris forced himself to keep to a reasonable speed. She needed to get her bearings. When she sighed, he steeled himself for the inevitable complaints.

"She's beautiful. It's a pity we don't know her name."

"I dinna care what she's called, so long as she's swift and sure."

"She is quite swift."

Chris shook his head. "We've barely set a pace. I want you to feel steady in the saddle, so we've started out slow. I'll be speeding us up. It'll be gradual so you can adjust to each change. You'll have to be able to ride at a full-on, dead run if Whelan comes close."

"I thought we were managing a remarkable pace."

He decided to give her a few pointers. "I'm not going to mince words or be delicate. If you don't want to get sore, I have to be blunt."

She hesitated a moment, then nodded.

"Always keep your thighs and upper calves right up against the mare. It'll help keep you balanced and tell her what you want her to do." Chris thought he'd heard her gasp when he mentioned the intimate parts of her "limbs," but he ignored her reaction. Instead, he went on, "Keep your knees and ankles bent so they absorb some of the jarring motion so you dinna slap against the cantle."

An icy voice inquired from behind her fancy hat's veil, "Is there anything else?"

"Aye. Dinna tiptoe. Heels down, toes up. When I get us to a fast trot, you'll see me actually stand slightly in the stirrups and rest my hand on the saddle horn. Bend at the hips and keep your elbows in."

He rode alongside her for a while, but her rigid posture and frosty silence let him know he'd offended her sensibilities. They went from a walk to a slow trot. Unwilling to put up with her snit, Chris pulled ahead. He knew the territory well. At one point, he stopped and ordered, "Have a swig from your canteen."

She nodded, loosened her veil, and obeyed. Up close, Chris

could see through the veil fairly well. She seemed to be holding up satisfactorily. After she screwed the lid back on the canteen, he pulled a small, smooth stone from his pocket. "Suck on this for the remainder of the day. It keeps your mouth moist so you don't get so thirsty."

"Thank you."

"Miss Regent, this is a rough land. We're in a tough situation. I'm not trying to offend you by being straightforward in my speech. You canna get huffy because I'm a plainspoken man. If it means I have to remark on specific portions of your person to teach you how to do things, I'm not going to mince my words."

"I wouldn't expect otherwise, Mr. Gregor."

He took off his hat and wiped the sweat from his brow. "Then why are you so mad?"

She daintily arranged ruffles on the cuff of her blouse. In a tiny voice, she admitted, "I'm not angry, sir. I'm embarrassed."

He laughed in relief, then demanded, "Stop being goosey."

∞

Katie stopped outside the rail station, dampened her handkerchief, and blotted Christopher's forehead. He jumped, but she held him still. "Shhh," she murmured. "The sun's been too much for you."

"What gave you that cockeyed notion?"

She sighed. He'd just indulged in an embarrassing shouting match when he bought the tickets, claiming that the price was far too high when they'd be getting off only two stops away. "You bought tickets on the train."

"I know I did."

Her worries mounted. He'd already given vent to his ire, and she didn't want to set him off again. What would he do when she pointed out his error? She moistened her lips, then gave him a pitying look. "The tickets you bought are on the train going back the way we came."

A slow smile creased his tanned face. "I know." He took hold of her arm and led her down the boardwalk.

Her eyes widened. "You did it on purpose."

Minutes later, dressed in widow's weeds and a heavily veiled hat Chris had just bought her, Katie bought tickets for the train. He'd sent her to do it while he turned in their third horse to the local sheriff.

A short time later on the train, Katie fought the urge to sleep. The rocking motion and her exhaustion tempted her to close her eyes. She hid a yawn behind her hand.

"Sleep, lass."

She gave him a guilty look.

"You've earned a good, long rest. Go on."

The next thing she knew, something was missing. Motion. Sound. She opened her eyes and let out a gasp. In the dead of night, she'd used Mr. Gregor's upper arm as a pillow. Mortified, she sat ramrod straight and wouldn't look at him.

"This is our stop." He rose.

She disembarked and waited as he claimed their horses from the livestock car. The very thought of sitting in the saddle made her want to wail like a pinched baby.

In the early dawn light, Chris beckoned her. She pretended not to see him. "Katie, come, lass."

"You didn't have to bellow at me," she muttered as she gathered her skirts and joined him.

The man had the nerve to laugh.

"You're demented, Chris Gregor. And you're out of your mind if you think you're going to talk me into riding all day again."

"We willna ride all day."

She shot him a sideways glance. "I'm not going to ride even half of the day."

He cupped her elbow. "You've got a sassy streak, woman."

"It's your fault. Until you barged into my life, I was sedate and ladylike. Where are you taking me now?"

"You'll see."

One of the horses exhaled loudly, his loose lips causing a scoffing sound. Katie looked over her shoulder. "I couldn't agree more emphatically." A few minutes later, she heaved a loud sigh. "Had I known you planned a procession down the center of the street, I might have woven flower garlands for the horses so people would think we were a small parade. As it is, anyone spying us will be certain we've taken leave of our senses."

He tossed the horses' reins around a hitching post and dragged her around the building.

"What a darling little cottage!"

He let out a rude snort. "It's Duncan's cobbler shop." He tugged her to make her turn to the side.

Katie stopped so suddenly, he nearly pulled her over. She'd spent her life in rough cabins, squalid rooms, and shacks—but it never stopped her from dreaming that one day she'd live in a big white house with airy-looking lacework and a veranda. The home of her dreams stood before her.

He slipped his arm around her waist. "You're almost there. Just a few more steps now."

Anticipation gave her a little spurt of energy. *I get to see this place.* As they walked up the steps to a wondrous-looking home, the sound of a baby's cries met them.

She balked. *I was an idiot to think this was his home and he was done dragging me all the way across Texas. A bachelor wouldn't live in such a grand place. Well, maybe I'll get to rest or freshen up.* The baby let out an ear-piercing cry. *I won't rest. That's for sure.*

"Whose house is this?"

"Mine." Pride rang in his voice. "I built it."

"It's magnificent."

" 'Tis who's on the inside that counts, not what's on the outside." Anticipation colored his words as he opened the door.

A woman in the rocking chair beamed. "You're home!"

"Aye, that I am." Pleasure saturated those simple words. He slipped past Katie, kissed the fussy baby on the head, and then brushed a kiss on the woman's cheek. "Ooch, now, what's amiss with our wee little lassie?"

He told me he wasn't married.

"She's cutting another tooth." The woman patted her baby and smiled at Katie. "Hello, I'm Mercy."

Mercy is his sister-in-law. Recalling that fact made relief wash over Katie. *He could have told me they all lived together.*

"This is Katie Regent. I thought you could use a little help, and Katie is needing a safe place to stay awhile."

"You're more than welcome to stay as long as you'd like. Now that Duncan's married and moved across the street, his room is empty."

"Thank you."

A man came down the stairs. "Who are you talking—Chris!" He strode over and smacked his brother on the back with a force that would have felled an ordinary man.

"Rob!" Chris gave him a powerful embrace.

Clearly, they were brothers. Both had black hair and were tall and broad shouldered. Chris's profile was craggier, his voice deeper.

He rested a hand lightly on Katie's shoulder. "Katie's come to stay awhile. Rob, I'm needing to speak with you a moment."

The men stepped outside. Katie cleared her throat. "Your daughter is beautiful."

"Thank you. Ordinarily, she's better tempered than this. She's calming down. As soon as she's asleep again, I'll get you settled in. You look exhausted."

"I'd be a liar if I pretended I wasn't."

Mercy laughed. "Between Rob and Chris having to come and go as they do and me with the baby, we all agreed long ago that sleep is a precious commodity. No one will think anything of you sleeping the whole day away."

The door opened and the men entered. "Oh, Chris." Mercy's smile melted. "I know that look. Don't tell me you have to leave right away."

"I'll be going after breakfast."

Katie let out a dismayed gasp.

"It's the wisest course of action." Chris nodded curtly. "Whelan's at a disadvantage. I've got to get him."

"I don't care how much of a bounty he has on his head." Katie fought the tingling sensation behind her eyes. She refused to shed tears. "A cornered animal is the most dangerous. Let someone else assume the duty of getting him."

"It's a matter of honor and duty."

"You'll not sway him," another man said from the front door. Katie about jumped out of her skin at the unexpected intrusion until she saw the man's size and coloring. Clearly, he was the other brother. Face grim, Duncan said to her, "Texas Rangers always get their man."

It took a second for what he said to filter through the haze of exhaustion. The meaning hit her like someone had just doused her with a bucket of icy water. Katie shook so badly, she could scarcely even breathe. Slowly, she turned toward Chris. "Don't tell me you're a Texas Ranger!"

Chapter 8

Fury made Katie's voice shake. Aye, and 'twas fury, all right. Baffled by her reaction, Chris attributed it to her exhaustion. " 'Tis true."

"Where's your badge?"

He let out an exasperated sound. "Rangers dinna wear badges."

"I've seen a ranger's badge!"

"I'm sure Katie isn't questioning your honor, Chris." Mercy stood and slipped Elspeth into Katie's arms. That show of trust let him know he'd better choose his words carefully. "Katie, it wasn't until Chris joined that I learned most rangers don't wear badges. They carry special warrants of authority."

Katie clasped the baby to herself and moved from side to side. Chris wondered if she was rocking the babe or trying to soothe herself. The dark circles beneath her eyes told the truth. She was reeling from exhaustion.

Katie looked down and rubbed her cheek against Elspeth's soft, blond baby curls. Her shoulders slumped, and she passed the baby back to Mercy. "It was nice of you to offer to let me stay, but I can't."

"What?" Chris roared.

Katie straightened her shoulders. "You've harped at me about how Whelan is bound to track me down. I've come to my good senses and realized staying here endangers everyone else—especially the baby."

"The only place you're going," Chris said through clenched

332

teeth, "is to bed."

She stood toe-to-toe with him and tilted her head back to glare at him. "You're sinfully bossy, and I don't have to put up with it. I can come and go as I please."

"Nae, you canna." He waited a second as the air crackled with tension. "You're an important witness. If you dinna pledge to remain here of your own free will, I'll put you in protective custody."

"I believe I'll start breakfast," Mercy murmured.

"I'll help." Katie turned away from him, grasping at the opportunity to get away from him.

Chris grabbed her arm and spun her back around. "You'll not do a thing until you give me your word."

"You've got my money and my derringer."

"Nice try, Miss Regent. You didna distract me, though."

She shoved back an errant curl. "You have the winning ways of a rabid skunk, Chris Gregor. And nerve! You have the nerve to demand a promise when all this time you've been lying to me."

"I never once lied." He glowered at her. "My personal information was none of your business. Now are you going to be reasonable, or am I going to haul you off to the jailhouse and lock you up?"

"Personal information. None of my business," she muttered. "Fine. If that's how you want it, that's how you'll get it. I'll stay here."

"Until I give you permission to leave," he added.

A cry of outrage curled in her throat. Chris silently admired her cunning. He'd have done the same thing—plotted a way to keep his word and still get his way. Each time he looked about the house and spied a piece of the gingerbread embellishment, it reminded him of how a prompt agreement could come back to haunt someone. Instead of rashly agreeing to anything, he now took time to consider every angle someone might use to get the better part of a pact.

"Fine. I'll stay until you get so sick of me, you'll push me out the door. There. Are you happy now?" Before he could respond, she turned to Mercy. "I'm usually not like this. Even a saint would be liable to lose his composure around your brother-in-law. Well, I can't blame him for all of it. I did let him goad me into this. It's my fault, too. I apologize for bringing strife into your beautiful home. Truly, I do."

Mercy reached over and took her hand. "The Gregor men take getting used to. They're hardheaded, but when you get past that, you'll recognize that their motives are pure. Chris loves the Lord and is seeking justice. He's doing his duty."

"Besides," he tacked on, "you willna have to put up with me much. My responsibilities keep me busy."

Katie sighed wearily. "If that was supposed to make me feel better, you failed."

∞

Chris ignored the kink in his back and watered his horse before setting out his bedroll. Frustration filled him. Almost two months earlier, he'd dumped Katie into his family's care and resumed his search for Whelan. Every other week or so, he'd drop by home. Each time he did reassured him that Katie was happy there.

Only something didn't feel quite right. He couldn't put his finger on it. Well, tomorrow he'd drift by on his way to Dallas. Maybe spend two days this time. With that thought, he bedded down for the night.

I'm making a fool of myself. It's probably just that I haven't managed to get Katie's belongings shipped to her. I'll do that soon. Real soon. And 'twill be good to see the lass again. She's won the hearts of my family, and Mercy canna sing her praises enough. And singing—aye, the little Songbird is humming or singing a fair portion of the time. She's found contentment e'en without her possessions, but 'tis her worries that hold her back from being completely happy. That truth is undeniable.

Katie Regent is a bonny lass, and as soon as I've got Whelan behind bars, she can stop fretting. Certainly, there must be men calling on her. Instead of dreading Whelan, she can turn her mind toward marriage. A man couldna court and wed a sweeter lass.

⌒

Hot, dusty, and hungry, Chris strode up the steps at home the next day. To his keen disappointment, no one was there. Then he heard Katie's voice coming from the garden. Chris headed that direction.

The sight that met him ought to have been captured in a painting. He stood for a moment and stared. The henna Lucille had tinted Katie's hair with had finally rinsed away, so her hair was back to being the exact same soft shade as a newborn fawn. She'd lost her frail look and glowed with health. Aye, bringing her here had been a grand plan.

Katie held Elspeth's tiny hand and steadied her as she took a few halting steps along a stone pathway. "Aren't you a big girl! So big!"

"Bee-ah! Bee-ah!" Elspeth declared.

Chris chuckled as he headed toward them. "Is my niece asking for beer?"

Katie laughed. "She's saying she's a big girl. And you are, aren't you, precious?" She swept Elspeth into her arms. The sight of Katie cuddling a baby seemed so natural, so right. Every time he came home, Chris marveled at how easily she fit in. He cleared his throat. "Where is everybody?"

"Duncan's in his workshop. Carmen went to Otto's to help her sister serve the field hands. Mercy is assisting Rob over in his clinic. He's removing tonsils today."

"I see. I've arranged to have your things delivered. They ought to be here any day now."

"You did?" Her eyes sparkled. "Thank you!" Just as quickly, her smile melted away. "Does the livery here store goods?"

"I suppose they might. Why?"

She hitched her right shoulder. "After Mercy's had her baby and is recovered, it would be wise for me to move."

" 'Tis nonsense you just spoke. Utterly foolish. Just because Whelan hasna discovered your whereabouts isna license for you to venture far."

"He must be far busier trying to evade you than searching for me."

"I always said the man was a fool." *What got into me? Why did I say that?* Chris shifted from one foot to the other.

"I planned to go to the mercantile today. The reservoir on the stove is full. If you'd like, you can empty it into the tub and have a good, long soak."

"I confess I'm taking a shine to that notion."

She pretended to nibble on the fingers of Elspeth's bitty little hands. "Mmm. Mmmm. Mmmm!"

Elspeth giggled with glee.

The way Katie sometimes peeped over the tops of her spectacles made a man feel as if she were flirting. In fact, she used those glasses better than most Southern belles used a fan. Best of all, coyness had nothing to do with it. Her natural charm and the effect of her blue, blue eyes in their shy appraisals made his heart beat faster. So was the habit she had of slightly pursing her lips as she considered her words before speaking. Made a man want to pull her close and share a kiss before the opportunity was lost.

Whoa. What am I thinking?

"I'm serious, Chris. Mercy is due any day now, and I'll help her as she recovers. But after that, it's time for me to move on."

"You gave me your word that you'd stay until I released you."

"So, release me."

He shook his head. "You'd be helpless."

"You once told me you'd see to it that I learned how to fire a gun. Teach me, and then I won't be helpless."

"That would only lend you a false sense of security. It would take considerable time and practice before you'd achieve any accuracy." He could see his words didn't satisfy her. Chris decided to use the truth to scare her into behaving.

"The loot we recovered that day from Whelan and the men? It's been identified. Part of it is from another bank robbery. The watch belonged to the bank president. He was killed. The rest came from a ranch they hit."

The color drained from her face.

He gently eased Elspeth from her arms and used his other hand to tilt Katie's face to his. "Dinna think you'll be safe from him, lass. His soul is black as pitch, and he'll stop at nothing to get what he wants. You must stay here."

Tears welled up in her eyes. Her attempt to blink them back failed.

"I'm sorry to scare you, but running off will get you killed."

She pulled away from him and brushed away her tears. More trailed down her pale cheeks. "You have to let me go, Chris. You have to. For your family's sake. What if he finds me here?"

"If Whelan wanted revenge on my family, he'd have done so long ago. 'Tis no secret where we live."

"You don't understand." She'd taken to wringing her hands. The distress in her voice tore at him.

Cupping Elspeth to his chest, he used his mildest tone. "Are you not happy here?"

"I've never been so happy. But that doesn't matter."

"Of course it matters. I want you to be happy and safe."

"But I'm miserable!"

She wasn't making any sense. Chris stared at her. Maybe Duncan or Rob could explain this to him. As married men, maybe they would be able to clarify what feminine irrationality applied to the situation.

"I can't take it anymore. I have to go!"

"You're not going anywhere," he half roared.

Elspeth chimed in. "No, no, no, no, no, no, no."

"But Whelan—"

"Leave Whelan to me, Katie."

Anguish clearly twisted her features. "But. . .he's my brother."

Chapter 9

Your brother."

She couldn't see his face clearly through her tears, but his voice was calm. Katie bit her lip, started to nod, and then blurted out, "Stepbrother."

"Stepbrother." His voice grew deeper as he echoed her words.

Katie reached over and patted Elspeth's back. "I have to go now. You take good care of her."

His left hand shot up and manacled her wrist. "You're not going anywhere." He hauled her in his wake over toward the workshop, bellowing, "Duncan!"

Duncan shot out of his workshop. "Aye?"

"Take Elspeth." Chris gently transferred her and pressed a kiss on her cheek as she babbled a stream of sounds. His tenderness made Katie cry all the harder.

"What's amiss?" Duncan held the baby protectively.

"Miss Regent."

"Katie?" Duncan gave her a baffled look.

"You'll never guess what she's been hiding." Chris didn't even pause. "Whelan's her brother."

"Brother?" Duncan's brows shot upward.

"Stepbrother," she corrected tearfully.

"What other lies have you told us?" Chris demanded.

"I never once lied." Anger shot through her. "The night you brought me here and I discovered what you are, I begged you to

339

let me go. You'd hidden the truth, and when I confronted you, you proclaimed you'd never once lied to me and that your personal information was none of my business."

"It wasn't."

"You can't have it both ways, Christopher Gregor. You can't fault me when you did the selfsame thing!"

" 'Tis not the same thing a-tall! My business is to bring that criminal to justice."

He marched her down the street, kicked open the jail door, and shoved her into a cell. The keys jangled loudly as he locked her in.

"What are you doing? You can't lock me up. I've done nothing wrong."

"Accessory after the fact," he said curtly. "You have knowledge concerning a criminal and did nothing to bring him to justice. Any blood he's shed since the day of our shootout—that blood is on your hands, Miss Regent."

"That's outrageous!" She clenched her fingers around the bars and rattled the gate. It made a horrible clatter but didn't yield. "How could I possibly know what he was doing when you were with me?"

"Criminals have hideaways. Where's your brother's?"

"I told you I didn't know where my brother was. I told you the day we met!"

"I scarcely believe you'd announce to all and sundry that your brother's face was on a WANTED poster and you knew his where-abouts."

"I haven't seen him in five years. Not until that day."

"That makes for a touching story, but I don't buy it. Not for one second. He's been all around Texas, wreaking havoc. You think I'm so thickheaded, I would think his stumbling into you in the wide open spaces of Texas was just a coincidence?"

Slowly, she uncurled her fingers and let loose of the bars. Sinking onto the narrow wooden plank bed, she held her shaking hands tightly together. "Believe whatever you want to. I haven't done anything wrong."

Chris sat down at the desk and pulled a sheet of paper from the drawer. The only sound in the jail was the scratch of his pen's nib on the paper.

I've been such a fool. I knew this day would come and he'd be furious. I knew it. So why did I always look forward to him coming home? And why am I so hurt that he's acting just as I knew he would?

Minutes passed. Finally, she said, "The clock's not wound."

He kept his back to her and gave a maddening shrug.

"Just how long are you planning on leaving me in here?"

"As long as it takes." He swiveled the oak chair around. The smile on his face chilled her to the core. "The game has changed, Wren. I'm no longer chasing the rat. I'm setting a trap with irresistible bait: you."

It didn't escape her notice that he'd reverted to calling her "Wren" or "Miss Regent." The way he'd pronounce "Katie" accentuated his Scottish burr, and it always made her feel as if a tiny measure of affection or protection came with the name change. But that was gone now.

"Aye, Wren. He'll come to get you."

"You're wasting your time. He left me behind when Mama died. If he wouldn't take care of me when I was only fifteen, what makes you think he'll suddenly turn into a dutiful brother? Not everyone is blessed to have fine brothers like you do."

"Your story is touching, but it's hogwash, and we both know it. A lass out on her own at such a tender age wouldna be able to afford a fancy sewing machine. I dinna ken why I didna wonder about that earlier. But that alone condemns you."

"I scrimped and saved and sacrificed for that machine!"

He gave her a mocking smile and applauded. "I believe you missed your calling in life, Wren. You should have become an actress. 'Tis rare to find such talent."

Stinging from his insult, she backed away and sat on the board. "You don't want justice; you want revenge. You're mistaken, though. You loved your friend. My stepbrother doesn't value me."

"We'll see about that."

∽

"I'd like an envelope, please."

Chris held his hand out by the bars. "Pass me the letter."

"The United States mail is private!"

"Your letter isn't in the mail yet, and it's standard practice to review all communications entering and leaving a jailhouse." He stared at her.

"Oh, all right." She huffed, yet she carefully turned her hand sideways so the pages wouldn't become wrinkled.

An intelligent woman, Kathryn Regent might well have a code of some kind. Chris moved to a sunny spot and looked down at the paper. *Dear Lucille. . .*

Chris snorted. He'd not underestimate her. The woman was as wily as could be. He shoved the letter onto his desk. "You don't really expect me to send that."

"I do. Even the Romans permitted Paul to send letters from jail."

Duncan came in, and Chris spoke to his brother, "Stay here for a few minutes while I send off a few telegrams and do another errand."

"Have you taken leave of your senses?" Duncan gawked at him. "Open that cell and free that lass this verra minute!"

"I don't tell you how to make shoes and saddles. Don't tell me how to do my job." He kept possession of the keys and stalked out of the jail.

By the time he'd sent the necessary telegrams and arranged for an article to run on the front page of the *Gazette*, Chris dared to hope he'd finally bring down Whelan. He'd need to deputize several men in town and was making a mental list of likely prospects when he walked back into the jailhouse.

"What," he roared, "is going on here?"

Mercy was pushing a quilt through the bars of Wren's cell. Carmen finished making up the bunk in the adjacent cell. A canning jar with flowers sat on his desk. Rob tromped in with a fresh bucket of water and a dipper, and Elspeth slept contentedly in a wicker basket in the middle of the activity.

"You put the lass in our care," Duncan asserted. "Aye, you did. So we're caring for her."

"I remembered you saying something about protective custody when you brought Katie home to us." Mercy straightened out and rubbed her lower back. "So Carmen and I decided she needed help making this dreary place more comfortable. We'll each take turns staying with her. It's not proper for her to be alone with you."

"She's locked inside the cell."

"And a sad state of affairs that is." Robert gave Chris a baleful glare. "I'll not hold with blaming an innocent for the wrongs someone else has done."

"Does it occur to any of you that Whelan has managed to avoid capture even with two bullet holes in him? That she might be tipping him off?"

"And how would I be doing that?"

"Any number of ways. Telegrams—"

"Carmen and I would know if she's sent any." Mercy shook her head. "She hasn't."

"Letters. She wrote one today."

"To Lucille?" Carmen smiled. "I hope you told her cook how much we love that recipe for the spaghetti."

"See? She's been sending letters." Chris spied something and stomped across the floor. He opened the small, glass-fronted door on the clock and stopped the pendulum. After closing it, he opened the face and reset the hands. "No one touches that. No one."

"It's just a clock." Mercy gave him a baffled look.

"Connant's clock." Chris stared at them. "The hands mark the time of his passing, and there they'll stay until Whelan's brought to justice."

"Time waits for no man," Rob said.

"Time might not, but I do. God's put the means in my hands to capture Connant's murderer. I'll sit and wait. The rest of you, out of here. I'll not have you in danger."

"Oh, we're safer if we're all together." Carmen smiled. "Don't you think so, Mercy?"

"Absolutely. Why, if you are at your house and I'm at mine, and Duncan's in his shop and Rob is in the clinic, Whelan might sneak up on any or all of us. There's strength in numbers."

"You have a point." Chris paused a moment. He knew he had their attention. "Carmen, you and Mercy can go stay at her grandda's or with your sister. Rob, you can go along. Duncan, I'm deputizing you."

"But—"

"This isna a voting matter. I'm the law, and you'll obey my edict. Rob, Duncan—your first duty is to your wives and the bairns. You ken 'tis a dangerous trap I've set."

"If it's dangerous, you can't put Katie in the middle," Mercy protested.

"I am in the middle of it." Katie's admission surprised him. "Whelan is wicked. From the beginning, I've feared for your safety. Please, please go. I can't bear the thought of you being in danger because of me."

"Let's all have a word of prayer before you go," Duncan said quietly.

They started to join hands, and Rob slid his hands between the bars. "You, too, Katie."

"It's kind of you, Rob, but I don't belong."

Carmen opened her mouth to protest, but Duncan shook his head.

Chris joined them, but it felt wrong. He felt like an outsider in his own family, and they'd wanted to include his enemy's sister.

Chapter 10

Having slept on hard pallets most of her life, Wren decided sleep would be a refuge. She curled up with her back to Christopher and huddled beneath the summer-weight quilt Carmen brought her. All evening long, men came and left. They'd spoken in low murmurs and cast odd looks at her.

Lord, I don't know what to do. Everything is so mixed up. Only You can untie all of these tangled threads. Please, Father, keep each of my new friends safe. Don't allow harm to come to any of them. Set Your angels about them for protection.

My attitude was wrong. Deep in my heart, I knew I should have told Chris the truth a long time ago. He was kinder to me than anyone has ever been, but fear and pride led me to keep my secret. Through it all, I haven't had faith that You would work things out. I confess that shameful fact and beg Your forgiveness. Be my refuge and strength, Father, I pray. Amen.

"Katie, lass," Duncan called softly. "Dinna weep."

She hadn't realized she'd been crying. She took a few choppy breaths. "I'm sorry. I'm okay."

"Aye, you're fine. Chris, I'm rememberin' that prayer Ma taught us. 'Now I lay me—'"

Chris's deep voice joined in, " '—down to sleep. I pray the Lord my soul to keep.'"

" 'If I should die before I wake, I pray the Lord my soul to take.'" Wren said softly, "When I was a little girl, a friend at school taught me that."

"Ma didna like that last part," Chris said.

"Nae, she didna. I'm trying to remember. Something about say and day."

Chris cleared his throat. " 'In everything I do or say, I'll serve my God both night and day.' "

"That's so very dear." Wren snuggled into the pillow. "You were blessed to have such wonderful parents."

"Aye, we were." The brothers spoke the same words at the same time.

The unity they displayed stunned her. *What would it be like to have grown up in a home where the parents were godly and love flowed so freely? What would it have been like to have a brother who loved me?*

The next morning, the rail station manager showed up with Katie's belongings. Chris was off somewhere doing something secretive. Leonard from the mercantile had been deputized and left in charge. Uncertain of what to do, he allowed Wren to have her sewing machine in her cell so she wouldn't be bored.

Old Mr. Rundsdorf came in to pay a call on her. He sat outside her cell and sanded one of his mesquite wood bowls to a smooth finish. "When you get out of there, you can open up a shop and keep treats in the bowl, just as Duncan does."

"Thank you." She smiled at the dear old man. His show of support touched her.

"When you open that shop, I'll be your first customer, too. This shirt you made me—I've never had one fit this well."

After Mr. Rundsdorf left, Leonard allowed her scissors and a bolt of fabric, so she used the bench-like bunk as a cutting table. Desperate to have something to occupy her mind, she determined to make several baby gowns for Mercy.

"Miss Regent, I have some lunch here for you."

She looked up. "Oh. Thank you."

Leonard's ears were bright red. "I'll have to ask you to go sit on the bunk whilst I open the cell door."

"Of course." As he brought in the sandwich and apple, she let out a small laugh. "Somehow, I had the notion that the only meals served in jail consisted of bread and water."

"We'll make sure you don't go hungry."

Late in the afternoon, Leonard stretched. "You sure have been stitching up a storm. That foot treadle makes for quick seams. Puts the hand-turned wheel models to shame."

"The stitches are strong and even, too."

"Never paid much mind to how much work goes into itty-bitty baby gowns. Mercy Gregor's going to be tickled pink to get those."

"She's been a dear friend." Wren finished one last row of pin-tucking. "I'd like to hide them until the baby comes. Is there some-place you could put them?"

"I reckon one of the desk drawers will do. Since we don't have a sheriff, nothing's in them."

She handed him the gowns, and Leonard chuckled. "Lookie there. You fancified these everyday ones by stitching colored lines on 'em. The buttons match. You gonna sew like this once you open that shop Mr. Rundsdorf was talking about?"

"I'll have to see how God works things out."

"Plenty of folks 'round here are bendin' God's ear, telling Him what they think He ought to do."

"I've done my share of that, too." Wren started cleaning up. "It was foolish of me. I should have done a lot more listening and a lot less talking."

"Funny," Christopher said from the doorway. "I've been thinking you didn't do nearly enough talking."

"Mr. Gregor! Mr. Gregor!" Nestor scrambled through the door.

"Nestor, what's amiss?"

"José got my shooter and won't give it back."

"Hmmm." Chris turned around and squatted to be at eye level with the boy. Wren watched how he acted as if the boy's concern were the most important thing in the world. " 'Tis a pity. A sorrowful pity. Could you be telling me just how José took possession of such a fine treasure?"

"We were shooting marbles. It landed on the line. I say that means I keep it. José says he does."

"Now that surely does give me pause to think. I'm sure there's a rule about it, but it's been a good, long while since I played marbles."

Nestor nodded. "Yeah. You're really old."

To his credit, Chris didn't laugh or scold. He nodded his head. "Aye. And years of experience have taught me that 'tis important to play by the rules. Mr. Rundsdorf does considerable reading. I'm betting he has a book that has the rules for all sorts of games."

"You think so?"

"Aye, I do. You and José are good friends. 'Twould be a crying shame to ruin everything o'er a marble—e'en if it is a prized shooter. Why dinna the pair of you agree to follow the rule, then seek out what the rule book has to say?"

"That's fair."

"Off with you." Chris rose and sauntered into the jailhouse.

"To my recollection," Leonard mused, "anything on the line is out."

"I dinna rightly recall, but they can look up the answer together instead of squabbling. A fight is rarely worth the cost. Best the boys learn it early on."

He'll be a spectacular father someday. She sighed. *If we'd had the same upbringing, maybe Whelan would have turned out better. Well, it's too late now.*

By the third morning of waiting for Whelan to take the bait, Chris sat down at Connant's old desk. The rhythmic clatter of Wren's sewing machine barely even registered any longer. She'd been keeping busy, and that suited him fine. Otherwise, she sang or hummed hymns a good portion of the time. Granted, she had the voice of a songbird, but her selections were intentional—and she hadn't sung other than when specifically asked when they'd been on the road. Now she sang and hummed constantly. Just about the time she'd finished yet another hymn and he felt certain she was using those sacred tunes just to bolster her proclamations of being a Christian, she fretted that the sleeves on the shirt she was making were a tad long. Then she shifted like the Texas wind and launched into a rendition of a silly ditty he'd overheard children sing, "Do Your Ears Hang Low?"

When night fell and she couldn't see well enough to sew any longer, the woman would strike up a conversation with whoever happened to be on guard. He'd had to grit his molars at some of the things that came out of her mouth.

At first he thought she was weaving tales to get sympathy. Fanciful tales. Like the one where she'd walk the length of a hitching post while singing to earn a free supper from a diner. With a nickname like Wren, that tale took little imagination to concoct.

When Stu Key's sleeve popped a button, she stitched it right back in place while Stu kept on his shirt. She offered, saying she had the needle and thread handy. Besides, she'd done that same task a few times when her stepfather couldn't be bothered to leave the poker table.

Her stepfather might have been a gambler and her brother was a murdering robber, but she was undoubtedly the smoothest manipulator he'd ever seen in action. He'd almost get sucked into believing her tales but at the last moment would remind himself that she'd been able to live a lie for weeks on end without any trouble.

Mrs. Kunstler bustled into the jailhouse. Chris shot to his feet. *"Guten Tag, Frau Kunstler."* After greeting her in German, he continued to tell her very politely that because of the safety risk, he wasn't permitting women in the jail.

"Unser Katie—Sie ist eine Freulein."

"Yes, I ken Miss Regent is a lass. But she's also a prisoner." He fought the urge to sniff the air. The aromas coming from the covered basket Mrs. Kunstler held made his mouth water. No matter— she'd been baking him treats ever since he transported a baby to her cousin's cousin. Cinnamon. This time, whatever it was, it had cinnamon.

"Katie," Mrs. Kunstler called. "I baked cinnamon rolls for you."

What?

"How kind of you! Thank you." Wren left her sewing machine and approached the bars. "How is Ismelda?"

"Fat." Mrs. Kunstler laughed. "My grandson should come any day now. The quilt you made for the cradle—she loves it so much, we are piecing one to match for their own bed."

"Have you seen Mercy? I'm worried she'll work too much and tire herself out."

Mrs. Kunstler looked ready to settle in for a nice, long visit. Chris cleared his throat. *"Frau Kunstler, mussen Sie gehen."*

She waggled her finger at him and answered in English. "Don't you tell me I must go. It is bad how you have her in here like a lonely chick in a big coop. My Otto—he is a good man, *ja?*"

Chris nodded.

"But did you know I had another son? No, you didn't. I do not speak of him. He shamed us all by coming to town and drinking the beer and whiskey. One day, with a broken bottle, he fought another man. They killed one another. No one talks of this. It was bad, shameful. But does anyone blame Otto? No, because he was not responsible.

"The pastor—when Otto was blaming himself for not being there to stop his brother—the pastor, he came and talked to him. He said in the Bible, you did not see the brother go seek the prodigal son. The bad son—he had to decide by himself to come back. The good boy—it was his job to stay home and be good. It is better that I have one good son than that I lost two bad ones."

Frau Kunstler mopped her face with a crumpled hankie. "What our Katie's brother has done—it is sinful. But it is not her fault." The woman thumped on her ample bosom. "In here, it hurts to know you cannot stop someone you love from doing wrong. Is that not enough? Why do you punish her?"

"Mrs. Kunstler, here." Wren extended a hankie she'd tatted around the night before. "I'm so sorry about your other son. I'm glad you have Otto. He's a fine man, and he's a good husband to Ismelda."

"Ja." Mrs. Kunstler accepted the hankie and straightened her shoulders. "I should be cheering you up, but I came and cried."

"You shared your heart with me. Even though it was a sad memory, you trusted me with it. That means everything to me."

"Ach!" Mrs. Kunstler kissed her own hand, slid it through the bars, and patted Wren's cheek. "It is a shame I did not have one more son. I would have him marry you so you could be my daughter."

As Mrs. Kunstler left, she called over her shoulder, "If soon you are not free, I will bake you a cake with a file in it!"

Chris picked up the basket and headed toward the cell. "Here."

"Please help yourself."

"I'm not hungry."

∞

"Watching that won't make it do anything."

Wren's head jerked up at the sound of Rob's voice, and she almost dropped her cinnamon roll. "The basket is full. Help yourself."

"I don't know that I want one out of the basket. That one seems mighty interesting to you."

She nodded. "It's special."

"It's a roll—just like the others," Chris muttered.

"Yes, it is," she agreed.

Chris swiveled around and glowered at her. "Make up your mind. Either it's special, or it's like all the others."

"They're all special. Mrs. Kunstler made them"—Wren's voice cracked—"for me."

Rob regarded her solemnly. "Aye, Katie. She went to the trouble just for you, and 'tis because she cares for you."

Tears welled up as she nodded.

"Chris, this has gone on long enough. Look at the lass. She's miserable, locked away in there."

"I'm not miserable." Wren sniffled. "Saint Paul was content in prison, and I understand why now. He took the time to ponder the things that matter most."

"Then why—" Chris started out gruffly.

"—are you crying?" Rob finished.

Wren took an unsteady breath. "Be–cause Duncan pr–prays

with me. And—and Mr. Rundsdorf wa–wants to be my first customer. And"—she took a big gulp of air—"Mrs. Kunstler. . .another son. . .marry!" To her embarrassment, she dissolved into a sobbing wreck.

Chris clipped out, "Frau Kunstler came by and said she wished she had another son so he could marry Wren."

"Ahhhh." Rob stretched out the sound. "Now wasn't that a grand thing for you to hear? Folks here love you. Aye, they do. You're just now figuring that out, are you?"

She nodded as her tears dissolved into hiccups.

"Oh, for cryin' in a bucket. You'd think no people ever said they loved her."

Wren's gaze dropped to the cinnamon roll she still held, and she whispered, "They haven't."

∽

Chris had to get out of there. Wren had everyone wrapped around her little finger. Her pity-me tales already set his teeth on edge, but this one—it defied any scrap of truth. "Stay here," he ordered Rob. "I'm getting some air."

Sitting around waiting for something to happen was driving Chris daft. After Da lost his arm, Chris knew he had to provide for the family. He hated going down to the mine—the walls always closed in on him—but he'd forced himself to. Rob pestered him about the few occasions when he'd gone to Thurber to give some advice on the mining conditions, but he could have saved his breath. Braver men than he would have to pry bounty from the depths of the earth.

Just sitting in the jailhouse left him restless. Cooped up, playing nursemaid to that woman. *Everyone's mollycoddling her. Have they forgotten Connant? Or the three other men her brother wounded?*

I canna fault them. I was taken in by her at first. I e'en brought her here. The most I can do is keep them away.

He scanned the street. A strange horse was hitched outside the mercantile. Actually, two. He started striding that direction.

"Ja, Leonard. I'll tell her you said so." Mr. Stein came through the door. He unhitched one of those two horses and swung up into the saddle. He rode toward Chris and halted. "Chris Gregor!"

"That's a fine-looking horse you have."

"I bought him last week. Perhaps it is foolish for an old man to buy a new horse, but I've told myself that when my grandson is a little older, he will need a solid workhorse."

"Peter will be a lucky man when you hand over the reins." From the corner of his eye, Chris saw a flash. He pulled his pistol as he slapped the horse. "Hee-yaww!" The horse bolted, carrying Mr. Stein to safety.

Two men sauntered down the boardwalk. In the scorching summer weather, they both wore coats. At midday.

Mercy's grandda halted his horse at the far end of the street. "José! Nestor!" he called. "Come here. I have something to tell you!"

The boys dashed past Chris to relative safety.

One more man rode by.

Four. Four of them. Whelan's not here yet. Chris scanned the street as he took ground-eating strides cutting across the road diagonally toward the jail.

Jakob Wahl stepped out onto his veranda and shouted, "Everyone! God gave us a little girl!" Jakob and his brother lived in that home. They were both bachelors. They'd come up with that warning call, saying it was the truth. God had sent Katie to them.

The momentary distraction allowed Chris and two other men to close the net. They waylaid one of the men wearing a coat. Chris had yet to spot Whelan, but he knew one man was in the jail, and another just stepped into the doorway, as well. Chris kept his gaze trained on the remaining one in the coat.

Suddenly from somewhere behind him, Chris heard a shotgun blast. Gunfire started, but Chris spent only one bullet. The man pulled a rifle from his coat. Chris yelled, "Drop it!"

The man fired at him, but Chris dove behind a water trough. Whether it was his shot or someone else's he didn't know, but that man fell. Chris didn't pause. He saw the muzzle of a pistol from the jail's doorway and fired a mere breath later. The man dropped his weapon while cursing profusely.

Chris rolled to his feet and sprinted to the jail. That man was trying to shove the door shut. Chris kicked it open. It caught his assailant in the chest and knocked him across the room. His head hit the wall with a loud thud, and he collapsed into a heap. Chris didn't want Whelan sneaking in behind him, so he slammed the door shut and shoved the bolt into place.

The last man backed up to Wren's cell.

He had his gun to Rob's neck.

Chapter 11

D rop your gun, or I'll kill him!"

"He's the one! He's the ranger!" Wren, still in her cell, stood directly behind the gunman. From his angle, Chris couldn't really see her, but he knew exactly where she was. She kept yanking on the man, goading him.

His brother's life depended on the smallest twitch of a trigger finger. Chris had already resigned himself to the fact that she'd betrayed his trust—but it took all of his discipline not to roar at her. "Turn loose of him, Wren. He's got a gun on Rob."

"No one's gotten hurt in here yet." Rob's voice sounded slow and steady—it carried the same tone as when he handled medical emergencies. "If Whelan wants his sister back, I'm not going to argue."

"He's the one!" Wren's voice grew more urgent. "He's got the keys."

Sweat rolled down the man's temples. He rasped, "Drop your gun!"

"Easy now." Chris tilted his head toward the desk. "I'll set it on there. It's got a hair trigger, and I don't want it to go off." He slowly edged toward the desk. If he got the right angle. . . *Lord, please safeguard my brother. Help me. Give me guidance and perfect my aim.*

"Where's my brother?" Wren continued to pester the man. "Is he outside?"

"Shut your trap!" the man roared. "Whelan ain't payin' me half enough to put up with your mouth."

"He's here, isn't he?" Wren persisted. "Tell me he's here."

The man let out a dirty bark of a laugh. "That's far enough, mister. Set down your gun, and put the keys on the desk, too."

Chris gave his pistol a longing look as he set it down on the edge of the desk closest to himself. He took the keys and started to put them in the center of the desk.

"Don't let his brother go get the keys." Wren stood on tiptoe and peered over his shoulder. "He could snatch the gun, too."

"You think I don't know that? I'm not stupid!" He waved his gun at Chris. "Just you step back until you hit the wall. Then toss the keys to me."

Chris intentionally threw the keys so they'd land short.

"Now keep your hands up where I can see them."

Chris raised his hands, threaded them together, and held them behind his head.

"Careful-like," the gunman rasped to Rob, "you stoop over and fetch me that ring of keys."

Rob waited a moment after he'd been turned loose, then inched forward. As his brother moved, Chris pulled the knife out of his sleeve. The moment Rob squatted down, Chris threw the knife.

The gunman reacted as soon as Chris's hand came into view, firing twice. The knife pierced the man's chest. Having not been struck, Chris assumed the worst: Rob had been shot. Chris let out a roar as he charged the assailant.

The man thrashed but didn't move far.

"Hurry," Wren pled. "I can't hold—"

Chris could see how she'd seized the gunman's sleeve in two places and fought to restrain him. Taking the gun proved quite easy. Chris grabbed for it, and when he met resistance, he dug the knife deeper into the gunman's shoulder. Curses and blood flowed as Chris took possession of the gun.

"Rob!" Wren finally stepped into view.

Chris couldn't turn and look yet, but the devastated look on Wren's face made him want to howl.

"I'm fine. Just knocked my hard head on the corner of that desk."

The air rushed from Chris's lungs. "Rob, get the handcuffs. Top drawer." He motioned with the gun. "You. Down flat on the floor. Facedown."

A twist and a few curses later, the man spat, "I can't."

"Dinna tell me what you canna do. Down. Now."

"He can't." Wren grinned. "I tied him to the bars."

"You what?"

"His suspenders. He thought I was just yanking on his shirt, but that was a distraction. I slid material through and knotted—oh, just come look."

Why had she—? Chris couldn't distract himself with any questions just now. He shoved the confusing fact aside and kept the gun trained on the men until Rob had them both handcuffed. He also satisfied himself that the one who'd crashed into the wall was waking and suffered no real damage. Winding a temporary bandage over the knife wound, Rob declared, "When things settle down, I'll have to suture this."

Gunshots still resounded outside. Swiftly shoving bullets into the empty chambers in his own weapon as well as the gunman's, Chris ordered, "I'm going out there to finish this. Rob, get over here and bolt the door once I'm out. Dinna open it unless Duncan or I tell you to. Whilst I'm gone, lock them into the second cell."

"Be careful," Wren called to him just before he opened the door. Desperation and sincerity colored her voice.

He no more than looked out the door than something struck the boardwalk and rolled past. Chris scanned the area. The gunfire grew sparser, but something hit again. A marble. Chris cranked his head to the side. Mercy's grandda motioned to him, then disappeared between two buildings.

Chris reached him seconds later. "What is it?"

"The bank. There are men in the bank."

The bank was located on the opposite side of the street, on the other side of the churchyard. Chris knew at once Whelan used the jailbreak as a distraction so he could hit the bank again.

"How many?"

"Just two. I found their horses. Those bad men—they might come out, but they will not go far."

"Fast thinking."

"Rundsdorf, he said there are two men still on the street."

Chris nodded. He'd listened to the gunfire and had a good notion where each of those men were. "Do you know who's in the bank?"

"Mr. Meisterson was in the diner. I think Horst was alone in the bank."

Chris nodded curtly. Chris looped behind several buildings and sneaked toward the bank. Suddenly, the bank's door flew open. One man exited. He spied Chris and fired. Chris was faster.

"Surrender, Whelan!"

"I've got a hostage!" Whelan shouted back.

Bang! Thud.

Horst yelled from inside the bank, "He's wrong. The hostage has him! I got his gun and knocked him out."

Chris took a single step toward the bank. His leg didn't want to move. He glanced down and noticed red blossoming from just above his left knee.

⌒

"Kathryn Regent, I'm placing you under house arrest."

"House arrest!" Wren stared at Chris in utter disbelief. She'd stayed in the clinic with Duncan, waiting and praying as Rob removed the bullet from Chris's leg. The last thing she expected was for him to hobble out under his own steam. Well, the second to last. "Rob, check his head. He must have gotten another injury. It's the only reason he'd say anything so—"

"Dinna be kickin' up a fuss," Duncan warned, "else he'll put you back in the jailhouse."

"You're a material witness to several crimes." Chris stared at her.

"And I'm enduring another here and now. You're stealing my freedom and peace of mind, Chris Gregor."

"You'll survive," he responded in a dry tone. He folded his arms across his chest. "I wonder how 'tis you say I'm taking your peace of mind. You've got it twisted backward, woman. 'Tis you who's givin' me a piece of your mind every time I turn around."

"That's just another reason why I shouldn't be trapped under house arrest."

Carmen and Mercy rushed in. "Chris—is he—"

"Right as rain. No need to make a fuss."

"He's putting up a fine show, but he needs rest." Rob motioned to Duncan. "We'll take him o'er to the house. I dinna want him walking for a few days."

Chris glowered. "I'll walk."

"Mercy, you and I had better have daughters." Carmen gestured toward the men. "The Gregor men are all stubborn as mules."

"Aye. And dinna forget it." Chris took one hobbling step and halted. His eyes narrowed. "Duncan, you didna tell us!"

"Tell you what?" Duncan yanked Chris's right arm about his shoulder and supported him.

Chris shook his head. "Rob and I got all the brains, Carmen. Duncan, your wife just told us all she's carryin' a bairn."

Duncan turned so fast, he almost knocked Chris over. Instead of helping his brother to the house, Duncan insisted on carrying his wife there.

Wren lagged back. This might be a good opportunity to break free.

Chris must have read her mind. He ordered, "Mercy, I've put Wren on house arrest. Dinna let her out of your sight."

It seemed impossibly rude to fight with Mercy since she was carrying Elspeth and was due to birth her baby any day now. Wren made an exasperated sound. She swiped Elspeth and declared, "I'm only staying because I choose to. I promised to help Mercy until her baby comes."

Once they reached the house, she looked about herself. The house was sizable, but it had never seemed smaller to her. Chris Gregor nearly sucked the air out of a room, so commanding was his presence and so large his build.

Chris eased into a chair. "You'll stay as long as I say, Wren."

Wren gave him a dirty look. He'd locked her up and made it clear he thought she was in league with criminals, and now he displayed the unmitigated gall to think he could order her around? "One Gregor man isn't just stubborn, he's demented," she said to little Elspeth.

Elspeth's little hand came up and patted Wren repeatedly at the base of her throat. "Ya, ya, ya, ya, ya."

"Mercy, your daughter is very bright. She agrees with me."

"No matter when Mercy has the babe, you still are a material witness. You'll have to appear in court for the trials of all those men."

"I'll be an old woman before that's done," she moaned.

"No." Chris accepted a glass of water from Mercy. "We've already sent off for the judge. Those men will all get a speedy trial, just as the Sixth Amendment allows."

Her eyes widened. "You remember the amendments to the American constitution?"

"Aye, and why wouldn't I? 'Tis my new home, this fine nation. And I respect the laws of the land. 'Tis my responsibility and duty to see to it laws are upheld. So stay you will." He scowled. "Did you think I wouldn't notice, Mercy? There's laudanum in this."

"Doctor's orders," Rob clipped. "Drink it."

Chris set aside the glass and got to his feet. "The devil will be ice skating the day I need laudanum for a wee scratch."

Rob helped him up the stairs. A second later, Chris bellowed, "Did you think I wouldn't notice, Duncan?"

Duncan chuckled. "He's going to be fine." After a few seconds, he roared with laughter. "Katie, I have something I want to share with you. Seein' as how you'll be stuck here awhile."

"What is it?"

"Gingerbread."

Chapter 12

Chris gritted his teeth and sat in the desk chair at the jail. He refused to lie about all day. One day of convalescence at home drove him to distraction.

Whelan snickered. "Another day and that leg'll fester."

Chris ignored him.

"Yep. You'll get the gangrene and die."

"Don't you ever shuddup, Whelan?" One of the other men groaned.

"You ain't gonna fare any better." Whelan smirked. "Another day or so, and that hole he carved in you's gonna plant you six feet under."

"If it wasn't for your sister—"

Whelan cursed. "I told you, all she was was a distraction."

Chris kept his back to them and opened a drawer to get paper. He'd copy down what they said and use it in court. Only one sheet remained in that drawer, so he took it and opened the next. Instead of paper, tiny, frilly white baby gowns rested there. Irritated, Chris shoved them to the side and grabbed for paper below them. The only paper he located was the letter he was to send to Lucille from Wren.

The whole while, Whelan argued with the men in the other cell. "I told you you'd get a share as long as you took care of the diversion. Didn't matter whether you sprung her free or not..."

Whelan's heated words took Chris off guard. *"He left me behind when Mama died. If he wouldn't take care of me when I was only fifteen, what makes you think he'll suddenly turn into a dutiful brother? . . . My stepbrother doesn't value me."* Wren's words flooded back.

He'd judged and condemned her, yet she'd sat there in his cell sewing clothes for Mercy's baby. And the letter. He scanned it.

Wren asked Lucille to thank the cook for the recipe for spaghetti. Little Elspeth especially loved it and made a comical mess of herself. Lucille was right in her last letter—the henna finally did completely rinse away. The flower, herb, and vegetable gardens at both Gregor residences were flourishing, but only because of conscientious watering. The church had just installed a lovely stained-glass window, and Wren would love to have her come visit to see it. Three pages of woman talk. Newsy, breezy chatter. Woven among all those tidbits were gentle references to God or the Bible or something about a dear old soul in the congregation who'd done some small kindness. In the most unlikeliest turn of events, Wren had forged a friendship with, and was showing God's love to, a soiled dove.

She was right, Lord. I wasn't seeking justice. I sought revenge. It blinded me to the truth. I have to make this right.

∞

"Wren, I'm needing to talk to you."

"Later." She continued to knead dough. Little bursts of flour swirled over her hands. "Carmen's not feeling her best. She and Mercy are both napping upstairs. After I'm done here, I need someone to take me to the mercantile so I can get her some Trenton crackers. Rob says they'll help."

"Trenton crackers?"

"The soda in them settles a sour stomach." She formed a smooth ball of dough, dropped it back into the yellow-striped earthenware bowl, and covered it. "Can you walk me there, or is your wound too sore?"

"You can go after we talk."

Washing her hands, she mentioned, "Rob's at the Kunstles'. Ismelda's in labor."

"Don't tell Mercy!"

Wren started to dry her hands. "She already knows. She wanted to go help, but Rob insisted she stay here with Carmen. Mrs. Kunstler has helped him with other births. We all prayed for Ismelda before he left."

Chris groaned and flopped into the nearest chair. "This is bad."

"Your leg?"

"No. Mercy knowing about Ismelda. The night she had Elspeth, Stu Key's wife had a baby. Mercy might think it's catching. Until Rob got back home, he oughtn't have told her."

Wren realized he was serious. She laughed.

"It was terrifying. I'm not going through a labor again—at least, not without him present."

"You didn't endure it; Mercy did."

Chris shook his head. "She'd like to have killed us. Baked cookies by the dozen, then put sugar in the mashed potatoes. Shouted her throat raw, too. And did she have the good sense to birth the bairn in that fine clinic? No, I tell you." He propped his elbows on the table and buried his head in his hands.

"Don't jump to conclusions."

Slowly, he lifted his head. "Your advice is too late."

"Yes, well—"

"Not about the laboring. About me jumping to conclusions. That's why I'm needing to talk to you, Wren."

Wren. She heaved a sigh. She'd come to loathe that nickname.

He'd not used it until he slapped her in jail.

"Sit down."

She shook her head. "The crackers—remember?"

"This is more important."

"At the moment, my friend is more important—"

"Than you? Nae, lass. 'Tisna so. You're hurtin' on the inside, and it's well past time for that to cease."

"I'm hale as a draft horse."

Chris shook his head. "I'm talking about your heart. You were right. Whelan didna care whether you were set free. He used your presence in the jail just to cause a diversion."

Wren shrugged. She'd not expected anything different.

"Mrs. Kunstler was right, too. As soon as I knew Whelan was your brother, I jumped to conclusions and judged you according to his sins. All this time, you've worked your fingers to the bone to scrape by. Then you came here and tended to my family."

"You have a wonderful family." *You cannot begin to imagine how blessed you are.*

"Lass, I'm asking your forgiveness. I wronged you."

Wren stared at him. "You don't have to do this, Chris. Awful as it will be, I'll still swear to tell the truth in court. What you say to me won't change what I must do that day."

He jolted. "I'm not talking about that. Nae, I'm not. I'm trying to tell you I might have a hard head, but the truth matters to me. Aye, it does. I canna have you thinking I'm proud of what I did. I canna let you go on believing I think ill of you."

"Okay. Thank you. Can we go get the crackers now?"

"Are you listening to me, Wren?"

"All of Texas must be listening. You don't have to shout. And once and for all, will you decide what you're going to call me?" As soon as she said that, Wren clamped her mouth shut.

"The ruse is o'er. There's no need for you to have to go by Katie any longer." His brows furrowed. "Dinna you like sharing your name with a songbird?"

She shrugged.

"Dinna feign 'tis of no consequence. You wouldn't have said anything otherwise. What's wrong with 'Wren'?"

"Wrens are small and drab and common. Everyone who called me that shooed me off like a nuisance. Katie—" her voice caught. "Never mind."

"Oh, I'm minding. I'm minding a lot. Everyone here calls you Katie. Aye, and they cherish you. You even said so yourself."

She started shaking. "The crackers—"

"Will be there an hour from now."

An hour? She didn't want to talk to him for even one more minute. She felt vulnerable, raw.

"Katie—"

"Don't call me that." The words flew from her mouth before she even thought them through.

" 'Tis a pretty name for a lovely lass. But I'll respect your wish. Aye, I will. By your leave, I'll be calling you Kathryn until I've earned the right to call you Katie."

"You've better things to do with your time. Once Mercy's had the baby and the trial is over, I'll leave."

"You'll stay right where you are. I promised I'd see to it that you were settled in a happy location."

"I have been happy here—but it's time for me to move."

"Why? Because of me?"

She bit her lip and thought through her answer. "It's not just you. Other places, once someone learned Whelan was my stepbrother, the people figured I was cut from the same cloth." She shrugged self-consciously. "I'm accustomed to pulling up stakes."

"You willna do that this time. Nae, you willna." He nodded his head. "I was in the wrong of it, judging you by his measure. You canna forfeit your happiness because you judge everyone else here by my reaction. Think on it: I had to chase folks away. Aye, I did."

Wren shook her head.

"Lass, folks here learned a lesson several times o'er in the past two years. I dinna want to offend, but I'll speak the truth, because 'tis wondrous in the end. Elspeth is the child of a vile attack."

Wren's jaw dropped open. "But Rob—"

"Loves Elspeth wi' all his heart. Folks here didna know how to deal with Mercy's predicament, so they ignored her. It nigh unto broke her heart. Carmen—bless her—was a stalwart friend, and Rob discovered his feelings ran deep for Mercy. He wed her and named Elspeth after our own Ma."

Tears filled her eyes. "Oh, you're right. That is wondrous."

"Aye, 'tis. And so is how folks learned to look past the situation and care for Mercy. But the story doesna end there. You've met Jenny."

"Isn't she a dear? And she sews so beautifully!"

"Aye, that's how we all think of her—now. Has she ever mentioned her past?"

"But that's in the past! She found Christ."

"Aye, and we all celebrated her salvation and wanted her to find happiness. Folks here gave her a second chance. And then there's Carmen."

"Carmen?"

"She's a fine woman—inside and out. Men hereabouts looked at her limp and decided she wouldna be a good wife. 'Twas foolishness. Aye, and now Duncan and she are besotted wi' one another and anticipating a wee little blessing."

Joy lilted in his deep voice. Christopher made for a complete bundle of paradoxes. He'd spoken of indelicate matters very delicately. He could be gruff and abrupt, yet he'd been careful to get down to a little boy's level and treat his concern over a marble as if it were vitally important. He sat here, telling her about how other women found happiness regardless of the past issues in their lives, yet he'd jailed her. Trying to clear her thoughts, Wren shook her head.

"Attend to me, Kathryn." His calloused hand slid over hers. "Dinna dismiss what I've said. Everyone else for miles around— they learned what God intended. Instead of allowing human nature to take o'er and making snap judgments, they're striving to see others through God's eyes. Me? I'm as thickheaded and stubborn hearted as a cantankerous old mule. Rob—he's the smart brother. Duncan? He's the one whose heart is attuned to the nudging of the Holy Spirit. Me? I'm the one who didna learn from my brothers' examples or pay heed to the message all our friends and neighbors learned from God."

She steeled herself with a deep breath and slid her hand away. The loss of warmth and shelter struck her hard. Nonetheless, she folded her hands in her lap. "Openhearted as they are, the people around here would be easy game for a wolf in sheep's clothing. God sets a hedge about His people for protection. You're prickly."

A prolonged sigh rumbled out of him. "I've thorns aplenty."

"Maybe it's for God's purpose. The Lord might have created that quality in your soul because He needed you to be a warrior and not a lamb."

"There's a bonny thought, but I canna agree fully. His sheep shouldna become ensnarled in the hedge He sets about them for their own good. I yanked you away from the flock and wounded you. Aye, I did. 'Tis a sorrowful thing I've done, and I'll do my best to make it up to you, little Wr—Kathryn."

The remorse in his eyes and voice tore at her. Carmen needed the crackers, but Chris needed her forgiveness far more. "There's nothing to make up, Christopher. Nothing. I admit, when you first imprisoned me, I was outraged. But I came to realize how my attitude revolved around my feelings, and I hadn't stopped for even a moment to seek God's will. I asked Him to reveal to me what He would have me know." Her voice started to tremble, and she blinked back tears.

"Ooch, lass," Chris moaned.

"Remember me crying when Mrs. Kunstler brought the cinnamon rolls? She labored and made a special trip and bared the ache of her heart just to comfort me. And Mr. Rundsdorf? Carmen and I have made him several shirts—but he wants to be my first customer. Regardless of how it pains him to sit up for a long time, he came and visited me each day. I wouldn't have ever learned God's lesson for me if you hadn't locked me up."

"What lesson was that?"

"That I'm not just a burden—a mouth to be fed or a pallet to be tripped over. Most people will see me as Wren, but there are a handful to whom I'm Katie." Suddenly feeling raw and vulnerable, she shot to her feet. "I really must go get those Trenton crackers for Carmen."

He rose. "I'll go along."

And that says it all. He'll never trust me. I have to leave as soon as Mercy doesn't need me. This is his home. By staying here, I'm pushing him away from his own family.

Chapter 13

I—"Wren stared down at her clenched hands. Their town didn't have a courtroom, and it didn't seem right to use a church as a site for a trial. The only other large building was the saloon. The Gregor men spent time this morning draping blankets over pictures that decent folk shouldn't see. Even so, Kathryn didn't want to look around. She swallowed and testified, "I didn't see his face."

The attorney scowled. "Your Honor, I'd like permission to treat Miss Regent as a hostile witness. She's the accused's sister."

"Miss Regent is *not* hostile, and she's his *step*sister," Chris proclaimed. "The accused abandoned her when she was only fifteen, and she'd not seen him again until the day in question."

While the judge admonished Chris that he'd accept no further outbursts, Kathryn marveled that Chris defended her. Having already testified, he was permitted to sit on the front bench and stay as an observer. He sat straight as could be and stared at her. He even flashed an encouraging smile and nodded.

The attorney peppered her with multiple questions. She bore witness to what she'd originally heard and how she'd seen the star on Whelan's boot. As she started walking away from the witness chair, Whelan sneered at her. "Don't bother comin' by the jailhouse anymore to churchify me."

Chris rose and interposed himself between her and her stepbrother.

Whelan kept talking. "I only pretended I was interested so you'd show family loyalty today."

Chris squeezed her arm. "I'll take you home."

"You need to stay here."

The gavel came down again. "It's noon. We'll recess for lunch and start back up at one o'clock sharp."

"Chris," Mr. Stucky said, "I'll take the prisoner to the jailhouse."

"No, I will." Jorge from the livery came over. "Chris, you take that pretty little filly on home. She's had a hard day."

"Katie is not a horse." Mr. Rundsdorf shouldered his way between the men. "But she needs to go rest. Chris, I'll watch the prisoner."

Otto Kunstler curled his hand around Whelan's upper arm and pulled him to his feet. "Gregor, you take care of who's important. I'll mind this one."

No less than four more men volunteered. Chris gave the jailhouse keys to Otto. "Much obliged, men."

Chris threaded her hand through the crook of his arm. "Come, Kathryn." As he escorted her down the street, Chris grinned. "You've many a champion here. Did you see how all those men fought to have the honor of keeping Whelan locked away from you?"

"Even dear Mr. Rundsdorf." She managed a fleeting smile. "Never in a million years would I have imagined he could look so fierce."

"The old gent was quite a sight," Chris agreed. He stopped and trailed his rough fingertips down her cheek.

She fought the nearly overwhelming need to lean into his touch. Confusion made her mind whirl. The day he'd rescued her from Hepplewhite's Emporium, he'd told her she could trust him. Somehow, he'd overcome her defenses and actually earned her respect—only to obliterate it all when he towed her off to jail and believed the worst of her. *But he confessed he was wrong and championed me. Do I trust him again? Dare I risk that?*

"You're a rare woman, Kathryn Regent. Aye, that you are." Chris gave her a steady look. "A man would gladly put on the armor of God and battle a legion of demons just to protect you."

∽

Her pupils dilated wildly. Chris could see he'd taken her by surprise. "I canna help thinking your brother's biggest regret must be having left you behind. He went off seeking riches and never saw the treasure he already had."

Tears filled her remarkable eyes. "I'm no treasure, and I'll not delude myself. His greatest regret is having been captured and knowing the evidence against him is irrefutable. Robbery and murder—he's done several of both. When the jury finds him guilty, he'll be sentenced—"

"Aye," Chris cut in, trying to spare her from having to speak the truth. In the days ahead, she'd come to accept the inevitable, but in the meantime, he decided to distract her. "He'll be sentenced. But for now, I'll get you home. Duncan and Rob both hold the opinion that their wives are overdoing. If you'd talk sense into them, I'm sure my brothers would be grateful."

"I'll do my best."

"Good. Good." He started walking again.

"Chris, you're trying to be kind by diverting me from thinking about what lies ahead. It won't work. Something truly dreadful lies ahead."

"Aye." He looked down at her. "Many a town would have held a kangaroo court and lynched him. We've bent over backward to give him a fair trial. Justice will prevail. With several murders and robberies against him, he'll receive the harshest sentence." He paused a moment. "You'd best prepare yourself for the worst."

She bit her lip and nodded.

His brow furrowed. "Do you hold feelings for him?"

Slowly, she nodded.

Surprise and a flash of jealousy shot through him.

"He's done wicked things, evil deeds—yet he'll always be my brother. I prayed that he'd be like the one thief on the cross and repent."

"So you've been praying for him."

"Yes." She shrugged—a tiny, tense movement. "You can be proud of Duncan and Rob. They're fine men, and they return your love in full measure." Pain flickered across her features. "Whelan's awful, but he's still my brother."

"Kathryn Regent, 'twas an understatement when I said you're a rare woman."

"Crackers," she rasped. "Carmen needs more of them."

"Did the ones we got that other time help settle her stomach?"

Kathryn nodded. "She's run out."

Though Carmen had his sympathy, Kathryn deserved his support. She'd been through so much already. If accomplishing this task gave her even a moment's respite, he'd gladly accompany her on a whole string of errands. "Then let's get them."

Once they reached the mercantile, he opened the door for her and walked beside her to the cracker barrel. Leonard hastened over. "Katie, Chris, I'm surprised to see you here—after this morning." He caught the look Chris gave him. "Thought you'd be eating lunch like the rest of us. What can I do to help you today?"

Gently wiggling the scoop so she wouldn't break the crackers, Wren said, "We just dropped in to buy a few crackers."

Chris gave the meager supply she gathered a dubious look.

"That's only a quarter scoop."

She added just a few more of the tiny oyster-shaped crackers. "How's that?"

Chris curled his fingers around hers. "You dinna ration your comfort or your friendship, Kathryn. God doesna hoard His love, either. He gives abundantly above all we can e'er ask or think." Chris guided her hand, dipped the scoop, and lifted out a heaping mountain of crackers. Several fluttered down into the barrel again. "Are you watching, lass?"

She stared at the scoop. "That's so many, you're dropping some!"

"Leonard, go fetch us something to carry these in." Chris waited until the storekeeper was out of earshot. "Kathryn, canna ye see, lass? You're looking at the wee little crackers that fall. Leonard sees the ones in the scoop. God? Well, I'm thinkin' God sees not only those and the ones filling the whole barrel, but also all the ones that will e'er be made. You've lived on the fallen scraps far too long. Dinna tally your worth by who your stepbrother is. Your heavenly Father counts you as priceless."

Leonard arrived with a pasteboard box. "This ought to do."

Kathryn bit her lip and nodded. She didn't say another word the whole way home.

◌

"To be hanged by the neck until dead." The sentence rang in Chris's head. The trial had progressed swiftly, and the evidence made for a compelling case—so compelling, the jury took only fifteen minutes to deliberate.

Whelan snorted. "Didn't expect nothin' different."

Chris rose. "Your Honor, folks here love Miss Regent, and we don't want to see her suffer any more than she already has. If it's all the same to you, I'd request Whelan's sentence be commuted to life in prison."

"I'd druther be hanged!" Whelan shouted.

The judge pounded the gavel. "Order. Order. Whelan, you'll get what you want. Hanging's what the law dictates, and that's what you deserve."

The sheriff from the town whose banker had been murdered announced, "Plenty of folks in my town already picked out a hangin' tree. We'd be happy to oblige the court."

Chris left and went back to the empty jailhouse. He felt no satisfaction in having apprehended his friend's killer. He'd seen the job through to the end—as a Texas Ranger, he'd gotten his man. In doing so, he'd probably spared several more people from theft and murder. Slowly, he wound the clock, reset the hands according to his prized pocket watch, and started the pendulum with a faint tap.

Time is a gift. Don't waste it.

At that moment, he knew what he had to do.

⌒

"Kathryn, I'm needing to talk to you." Duncan stood by the front door and half shouted the words.

"I'm a little busy just now."

"This willna wait."

She swung around and gave Duncan an incredulous look. "Do you think Mercy's baby will wait?"

Chris stood beside Duncan. Both seemed to have lost their deep tans and gone an odd shade of green. Chris rasped, "We only want a minute."

"Go on. Hurry up." Carmen gave Katie a push.

Mercy sat on the steps and glared at her brothers-in-law. "Don't you dare try to convince my friend to drag me over to that clinic."

"They willna as long as you don't make any cookies or mashed potatoes today," Rob said as he rubbed her back.

Kathryn scurried out to the veranda. Duncan yanked the door shut, and Chris tilted her face upward. "Tell Duncan you dinna mind me having as much gingerbread as I want."

"You're hungry?"

Duncan patted her shoulder. "The wooden frills, lass."

Flummoxed, Kathryn shook her head. "I don't know why you're asking me."

"Dinna you recall me sayin' I'd share it all wi' you, lass?" Duncan nodded. "I gave my word, and I'll not go back on it."

"Chris is your brother. You Gregors all bought the gingerbread. I couldn't care less what happens to it—all I care about right now are Mercy and the baby!"

"I told you so." Chris slapped Duncan on the back and strode off.

Mercy moaned from inside the house.

A stricken look swept over Duncan's face. "Chris! You'll be needin' my help!"

Kathryn headed back into the house. Soon she was busy bathing Rob and Mercy's newborn baby. As dawn broke, footsteps sounded on the veranda. The door barely opened, and Chris stuck his head into the house. "How's she doing?"

"Fine," Kathryn whispered as she sat in the rocking chair coaxing Elspeth back to sleep.

"I didna mean Elspeth."

"Mercy's doing beautifully." Kathryn smiled wearily. "You'll have to go on upstairs. The news is Rob's to tell."

Relief flooded Christopher's face, and he swiftly entered the house. "So she's had the wee bairn?"

Yawning, Kathryn nodded.

"Go on to bed, lass. I'll tuck wee Elspeth in." He stole Elspeth from her and headed up the stairs. A moment later, delighted male chuckles echoed down the stairs.

The sound rolled over her, and Kathryn's eyes sank shut. *I should have known better. Chris wouldn't care that it's another girl. The Gregors all love one another. Lillith is such a fortunate little girl to be born into such a family.*

Chapter 14

Carmen laughed as she hung diapers out to dry. "I'm trying to figure out how many diapers to make for my baby. I never paid much mind to that, and suddenly it's important."

"A dozen a day," Mercy said as she nursed Lillith in a shady spot. "But I wish I'd made more than three dozen when I expected Elspeth."

"I'll get more cloth and hem up more on my machine. It'll take no time at all."

"Would you?" Mercy beamed. "I can't thank you enough, Katie. Chris? Katie's going to the mercantile. Didn't you say you had to get something?"

"Sure," he called back. He followed Katie out the door.

As they walked along the boardwalk, he suddenly stopped.

Kathryn halted, too. She didn't want to embarrass him, but concern caused her to ask, "Is it your wound? Do you need to sit down?"

Chris stared over her shoulder. "Rob did his best on my leg, and I've recovered well, but he claims I canna ride days on end as I once did."

"After riding a horse just that one day, I cannot imagine how anyone is able to ride for a prolonged period."

"The governor willna allow a ranger to remain in active service if he's impaired. Though I canna serve as a ranger, the town's asked me to become the sheriff."

She studied him closely, but it was hard to determine what he was thinking. "I can't tell whether you are resigned or upset."

"That all depends on you, Katie."

She blinked. He'd called her Katie—not Kathryn or Miss Regent. He turned her to face the opposite side of the street. Her breath caught.

The small storefront beside the mercantile had been freshly whitewashed. Pale green and forest green gingerbread adorned the eaves and windows. A sign out front read, KATIE'S.

Tears filled her eyes.

"None of that, now." He escorted her across the street and threw open the door. "Take a peek."

Her sewing machine rested in one corner. A deep green velvet settee lined part of a wall, and walnut-stained gingerbread hung from the ceiling to form clever arches. Lighter green curtains hung from them to form a dressing room. Shelves with little gingerbread flourishes in the corners completed the wall, and her measuring tape draped around the neck of a brand-new dress form.

Tears slipped down her cheeks. "But I'm s–supposed to l–leave."

"Why would you be doing that when this is where you belong? Everyone here loves you." Chris took her hand in his. He squeezed it. "Aye, they do—but not the way I do. I love you, Katie. Truly, I do."

"You do?"

"Ooch, Katie, I did you a grave injustice the day I let vengeance rule my head and heart. Nothing shames me more than knowing I hurt you."

"I told you that was forgiven," she said softly.

"You forgave, but I couldna forget. But Da told me time is a gift and isna to be wasted. I'm tired of wasting time on regrets. I'd rather spend my days knowing the joy of being your husband." He lifted her hand and kissed it. "I love ye, lass. With all my heart, I do. I'm askin' you, Kathryn Regent, if you'll do me the honor of being my wife."

"When I saw this"—she gestured—"I could scarcely believe my eyes. This is a gift far beyond my dreams—a place of my own, a place to stay. But it's nothing at all compared to what you've offered." Kathryn paused so she'd not spoil the moment by weeping. "You've offered me your heart, Christopher. No one has ever loved me. Not until now. I love the Lord with all my soul—but you . . .I love you with all my heart. Nothing would make me happier than to be your bride."

⚭

The Gregor men wore their kilts proudly and stood at the altar. Lillith took a mind to squall like a heathen the whole time the pastor prayed a blessing for her. Once that was over, the pianist started to play the "Wedding March." Mr. Rundsdorf proudly escorted Katie down the aisle. He refused to sit down until he got to kiss the bride.

Chris proudly wore his father's golden watch draped across the waist of his plaid. He pulled Katie close and spoke his vows in a booming voice. She said hers in one that quivered with emotion. Mercy and Carmen both wore lengths of the Gregor tartan over their shoulders, but they never told her why. She'd asked, but the two of them refused to answer her.

Once the vows were said, Chris pulled a length of the lovely plaid from a leather thong at his waist and draped it over her. "We've a tradition, Katie-mine. I've wed ye and given ye my name, and 'tis the Gregor plaid I'm placing o'er your shoulder to remind you always of a love that will warm and protect you and a family that claims you. There's another tradition, too. A man says this poem only once in his life. Hear me now, for 'tis from the depths of my heart these words come:

"As fair art thou, my bonnie lass,
So deep in luve am I,
And I will luve thee still, my dear,
Till a' the seas gang dry.
Till a' the seas gang dry, my dear,
And the rocks melt wi' the sun!
And I will luve thee still, my dear
While the sands o' life shall run."

Five years later

I an, don't you dare pick that. It's a carrot, not a weed." Mercy swept up her son and tickled him. "Remember? Mama said you aren't to pick anything until she says so."

Carmen pried a small sprig of green from little Micah's grubby hand. "I'm afraid my son set a bad example."

"At this rate, we're going to have to have Great-grandpa Stein and Jenny let us put a garden up over at the farm." Katie brushed back a wisp of hair. "If we had to survive on what we grow here, we'd all starve."

"There's no risk of us starving." Rahab smiled. Since leaving the bordello after Wren's continued urgings through her letters, Lucille had changed her life drastically, including a permanent name change, which, according to her, reflected the change God made in her heart. "God provides. But as much fun as it is to visit the farm, I'd love to have an excuse to go there more often."

Mercy waggled her brows. "I think you're looking for an excuse to be near Grossvater's new field hand. You have to admit, Barry is strong and handsome."

Rahab shrugged. "In a manner of speaking, that's true enough. But I'm not interested in marrying. Helping Katie run the dress shop is enough to keep me happy. Going out to the farm," she paused as a smile crept across her face, "well, I think Jenny and

Barry fancy one another, and I enjoy watching them. Last Sunday I told him he ought to ask Mr. Stein's permission to court Jenny."

"How wonderful!" Katie gave Rahab a hug.

Duncan wandered over with his daughter. "Carmen, Anne's up from her nap." He laughed at Ian. "How did you get so grubby?"

"Weeds!"

Rob and Chris rode over. Each held one of Katie's twin boys. "Songbird," Chris said, "we've a problem. They climbed out of the crib."

Katie laughed and went over to take one of the boys. "That actually solves a problem, dear."

"Oh?"

She nodded. "We'll be needing the crib again in about seven months."

Leather creaked a bit as he dismounted. She'd never before paid attention to that masculine sound of a large body easing from a saddle and hitting the ground. Wren felt him close the space between them with a few leggy strides and heard the grit scrape softly under the soles of his boots. His hands rested on her shoulders as he brushed her lips with a kiss of abiding love.

Coming Soon from
Barbour Publishing

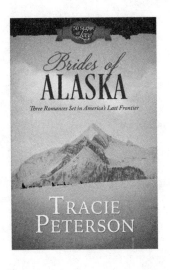

The bleak wilderness of America's 49th state
challenges three generations of women in the
Erikson family in different ways, but overcoming
the odds through faith will lead each to lasting love.

Available wherever Christian books are sold